Little Gangster

To Anita Cino, my loving wife.

Little Gangster

VICTOR JOSEPH CINO

iUniverse®

LITTLE GANGSTER

iUniverse books may be ordered through booksellers or by contacting:

iUniverse
1663 Liberty Drive
Bloomington, IN 47403
www.iuniverse.com
1-800-Authors (1-800-288-4677)

ISBN: 978-1-4917-7139-6 (sc)
ISBN: 978-1-4917-7137-2 (hc)
ISBN: 978-1-4917-7138-9 (e)

Library of Congress Control Number: 2015911523

Print information available on the last page.

iUniverse rev. date: 02/25/2016

Contents

1 Little Gangster

I knew something was up when Johnny Marino grabbed me after seventh-grade English class and told me in a serious tone of voice not to fall asleep right away after I went to bed. We were in the hallway of PS 60, our public school in the East Village, when he told me that.

"Because at ten tonight, Pepi wants to see both of us, especially you!" He glanced around and walked away, leaving me stranded in the hallway wondering why Pepi wanted to see us so late at night. I knew one thing: if Pepi wanted to see me, I was going to be there. Nobody messed with Pepi Savino, and in 1952, all the mobsters on the Lower East Side knew it.

My parents went to bed around nine thirty. At ten o'clock, I was still awake waiting for Johnny. After a few minutes, I heard a *tap-tap-tap* on the window facing First Street. I lived on the third floor of our tenement building with my parents. I got up and stood quietly by the bed for a few seconds because I didn't want to wake them. I went into the back living room facing First Street. There was Johnny on the fire escape, waving at me to open the window. I put my finger to my lips, pushed aside the drapes, and opened the window very slowly.

"Johnny," I whispered, "does Pepi really have to see us so late at night? It's past ten o'clock!"

He looked down at the street to see if anyone was watching him. "I told you I was coming!" he whispered. "Listen. You have to come to the park with me. Pepi is having an argument with Nicky Bonanti, and he wants us there. Don't let him down!"

I hesitated. I knew there was going to be trouble. "Why should I go? It's March. It's cold out there. What's it got to do with me, anyway?"

Johnny looked down nervously toward the street. "Pepi told me last night there was going to be trouble with Bonanti, and he wanted you especially to be there, so you gotta go with me. Now!"

I could argue with Johnny, but not with Pepi Savino. I turned and listened. My parents were still asleep. I told Johnny to wait for me while I got dressed.

I opened the window and followed Johnny down the fire escape. I was nervous because I knew Nick Bonanti was crazy and he was always picking a fight. I also knew that no one should be fighting with Pepi Savino. He was the mob leader who everyone paid respect to.

When we got to First Street Park on First Avenue, I saw Pepi, with his arms folded across his chest, facing Nicky, who was shouting at him. Johnny and I started walking around the park to Houston Street, where an entrance to the park was open. The marquee lights of the Sunshine Theatre across Houston Street were already out. Traffic was light on Houston.

I thought Pepi glanced toward us. We walked quietly over to a bench and knelt behind it. Nicky was still shouting at him, his arms in the air, and jabbing his finger in Pepi's face. He inched closer to Pepi, who just stood quietly, unmoved by his shouting. He was wearing a navy-blue sport jacket, white shirt, and dark blue tie. His gray flannel pants were neatly pressed even at this late hour. His blond hair was still neatly combed even at ten at night. He pushed his jacket back and placed his hands on his hips as he listened to Bonanti shouting louder and louder. Pepi finally stepped back.

"I can't talk to you, Nicky," he said calmly. "You get too excited. I asked you before to calm down, and you get louder and louder. Look at you. You're crazy! I'm leaving."

Pepi turned and began to walk away. Just then, Nicky reached into his pocket and pulled something out. He looked at it and smiled. My heart began to pound. Johnny grabbed my arm and squeezed hard. I heard a click and saw the blade of a stiletto pop out of its handle. Pepi was still walking away slowly when Nicky started moving quickly toward him.

"Pepi, look out!" I shouted. "He's got a knife!"

Pepi turned and twisted sideways just as Bonanti lunged at him. The knife missed its mark. Bonanti tumbled forward and fell to the ground, and the knife slipped out of his hand. When he tried to reach for it, Pepi just kicked it away and pulled a gun out from behind his jacket. I could see it had a short barrel. Pepi smiled and aimed the gun at Nicky.

He tried to get up. He made it just to one knee when Pepi fired. The gunshot echoed through the park like a dynamite explosion. I felt as if I were in a scene out of a gangster movie. I stood frozen at the bench. I had never heard a gunshot before except in a movie.

Nicky fell backward to the ground and lay spread-eagled on the pavement, stunned. Pepi stood over him with that hard look I had seen before—the gun in his hand, his mouth closed, his wavy hair still neatly combed, not a hair out of place. He kept shooting. I heard five or six shots. It happened so fast. It was like sticks of dynamite going off one after the other. When the gun was empty, Pepi kept squeezing the trigger. I could hear the *click, click* of the hammer.

When he was finished, Pepi just stood there quietly and motionless, his gun still pointing at Nicky. I'm sure it was only seconds. He was so still I felt as if I were looking at a photograph. I realized then that Johnny had wrapped both his arms around my arm. He was shaking.

On First Street, people were opening their windows and

looking at the park. Tenement lights started turning on in every building. Within seconds, I heard the faint sound of a police car siren heading toward us.

Pepi looked over at First Avenue. He lowered the gun, glanced at Bonanti, and then turned to me and Johnny. He did not look surprised to see us. He walked over to us slowly and casually. I was so scared—I didn't know how he could be so calm.

He stood in front of us, took a handkerchief from his back pocket, and wiped the gun clean. He looked at us and then handed me the gun! It was heavy. I had never held a gun before. There it was in the palm of my hand. The barrel was warm. I looked up at Pepi and wondered why he gave the gun to me and not to Johnny. The squad car siren grew louder. We all turned toward the sound of the siren getting closer.

"You two gotta go," he said. "Joey, take this gun and hide it. I didn't want to shoot him, but he gave me no choice, the crazy bastard. Now look at him!"

He turned to Nicky, who was lying on his back. I could see blood all over the pavement. Pepi looked straight at me and put his hand on my shoulder.

"Put that gun in your jacket, zip it up, and walk outta here with Johnny, very slowly. Take the back entrance to Houston Street, where you came in from. You understand?"

I stood up and put the gun in my inside jacket pocket. It felt warm against my chest. Johnny and I began to walk away. I turned back to see Pepi standing over Nicky, who was still lying on his back with his arms outstretched. After a few seconds, I turned to look again. Pepi was standing there calmly with his arms folded across his chest, looking down at Nicky.

A squad car pulled up, and two New York City cops got out. Johnny headed toward First Avenue, and I turned toward Second. I walked as naturally as possible. A few seconds later, I glanced behind me to see one of the cops walking fast toward me. I started walking faster. The cop began to run. I broke into a sprint and ran as fast as I could. I was very scared. I pressed one hand against my pocket where the gun sat against my chest. I kept on running faster past the back park and across Second Avenue. I wondered whether the cop had seen my face.

I turned around at the Bowery, Third Avenue. Above me, the elevated train, the El, roared by. I saw that the cop had stopped on Second Avenue and began walking the other way.

My heart was pounding. I walked up to Second Street along the Bowery, nervous because of the gun in my pocket. Drunks staggered along the avenue, some lying on the sidewalk talking to themselves. They could be dangerous, and now it was very dark and late.

As I walked on, I patted my chest where the gun sat in my pocket. Even though I was on the Bowery, I felt protected because of it. I knew it was empty, but if I pulled it out, no one would challenge me. Knowing I could do that gave me a sense of security. It calmed me down. Now I knew why gangsters carried these guns. They gave me a sense of strength knowing no one could ever hurt you because you had the gun, and you could defend yourself easily.

I waited about twenty minutes before I walked back to First Street. I wondered if my parents had heard anything. My heart started thumping hard. I prayed to God they were asleep. When I got to my building, I looked up at the third floor. There were no lights on.

I was okay. From my stoop, I jumped onto the ladder of the fire escape and made my way up to our tenement. Luckily, I had thought to leave the window open. The drapes were flapping from the open window, and as soon as I got into the house, I closed it without making a sound. I listened. The house was quiet.

I put the gun under my pillow, changed, and got into bed. It gave me a great feeling of protection, lying there in the darkness. I was beginning to feel like a gangster because I had that gun. Not many people carried a gun, and I knew now why the gangsters on First Street felt so confident and strong.

I was just beginning to relax when I realized I had a serious problem. What was I going to do with the gun? I could get into big trouble if the cops found it. I had to figure out what to do. I knew when I saw Johnny on the fire escape he was going to get me into trouble. Why didn't Pepi give Johnny the gun? Why me? Maybe he figured the cops would check out Johnny's house first or that I could figure out better where to hide it. It didn't matter. I began to sweat. I closed my eyes, thinking hard about what to do with it. I was exhausted, so it didn't take long for me to fall asleep.

A little while later, I woke up with a start. I thought for a few seconds the whole thing with Pepi and Nicky didn't happen, until I felt the lump under my pillow. I slid my hand underneath and felt the cold steel of the gun. I took a deep breath, trying to calm myself down. I tried hard to figure out what to do. Hours later, dozing in and out, I came up with an idea.

I pulled a box of toys out of my closet. In it, there were cap pistols still in their holsters, very heavy and very real-looking. These were pistols from four or five years back. I had bats and balls, baseball gloves too small for me now, Lincoln Logs, and wooden puzzles. I took one of the cap pistols out of its holster and replaced it with Pepi's gun, surprised it fit so neatly in the holster. Then I took one of the gloves and pounded it to let the dust settle on the gun.

I inspected it. The gun looked as if it had been in the holster for years. My parents would never find it there. I went back to bed, totally relaxed, and fell right to sleep.

I didn't see Johnny until homeroom the next morning. He just nodded to me.

Harold Tapper was sitting next to me, drawing cartoon characters. His red hair was curly and not combed. His freckles in the morning sun were more visible to me. His cheeks were puffed out, but he was a skinny kid. Next to Johnny, he was my best friend even though I was Sicilian and he was Jewish. We understood each other. He held the pencil with two fingers and his thumb pressed down hard, but his strokes were smooth and light across the paper. His characters had come alive. He noticed me watching him and smiled. He had drawn with one of his colored pencils a beautiful woman with dark hair, blue eyes, and a sloping nose. She smiled back at us.

"I'm good at this drawing, don't you think? That's my mother when she was still alive. I think I want to be a cartoonist when I grow up and work for a big newspaper like the *Daily News*."

Johnny came over. Harold looked at him suspiciously and folded his notebook. He brushed back his red hair a few times and started to read. Johnny just shook his head.

"What's with him?" he said. Then he whispered so quietly I could barely hear him. "Lucky you took it. They picked up Pepi, and he's in jail right now. Nicky Bonanti is at Bellevue Hospital. He's not dead! Imagine! Six shots, and he's not dead! That's what I heard from one of the guys at Pepi's club." He leaned closer to me. "What did you do with it?"

I looked straight at our teacher, Mrs. Greene. I whispered to him, "It's hidden in my house, safe. How did you get out of the park without getting caught?"

Johnny smiled a horse-face grin. "It was easy. Two cops got out of the squad car. One of them started following you, and the other one grabbed Pepi. Nobody even noticed me. They handcuffed Pepi and threw him in the car. I'm not worried. His attorney will get him out in a few days."

I whispered, "You know, somebody is going hear you. I don't think you should be talking to me right now, especially about the gun. Wait until later."

Johnny leaned closer to me. "If Bonanti dies, the gun is the only thing they have against Pepi. Scappy knows you have the gun. He wants to make sure it's safe and hidden where no one will find it. Don't let anybody find it! If this works out, Pepi's gonna take care of us. You watch!"

I started to wonder if I had hidden the gun in the right place. I thought I was so smart putting it in my toy box. What if the cops searched my house? How would I explain to my parents that I had Pepi's gun? If that happened, for sure I would be going to reform school. I panicked.

Then I assured myself that the toy box was a good hiding place. I felt good thinking about how good it really was.

Then, as Johnny went back to his chair, two men walked into

our homeroom. Cops! It was easy to tell from their ruddy skin color and rumpled suits. Anybody Italian from the neighborhood would know they were Irish cops. My confidence in my hiding place vanished.

They wore fedoras that needed a cleaning. Their gray suits were worn and wrinkled. Ties were loose at the collars of their brown shirts that did not match their suits. Both had red cheeks and thin lips. They were Irish cops, all right, and Irish cops liked to pick on Italian kids.

They looked around the classroom. Johnny lowered his head, trying not to show his face. I kept my head up and looked straight at them. I didn't want them to think I was hiding anything. They spoke to Mrs. Greene in whispers. A few minutes later, she clapped her hands. There was no need for her to do that. The class was already quiet.

"Class, these gentlemen are from the Ninth Precinct. Would all the boys please stand up so they can take a good look at you?"

Harold looked over at me and shook his head.

I glanced at Johnny. His face had turned pale. He stood up slowly and brushed back his long, black hair, which hung over the collar of his shirt. He needed a haircut.

What a strange thing to notice! I took a deep breath and stood up. I was as nervous as he was, but I wasn't going to give it away. I looked over at Rachel. Small freckles dotted her white skin. Her thick chestnut hair hung down behind small ears. Her dark eyes sometimes glanced my way. I turned to Maria—my girl, Maria Bucaro. Her long dark hair and beautiful brown eyes distracted me enough not to be worried about the cops. I fixed my eyes on her to avoid their suspicious looks.

They walked around the room studying us. I thought sure one of them would recognize me. I expected any second to be grabbed, pulled out of the classroom, and taken down to the precinct house. I took another deep breath. Maria and Rachel were not enough to control my fear, and so I imagined I was playing handball with Tommy Schwartz, the handball champ of all Manhattan.

We met in the park, and he watched me play one day. "You have talent, kid," he said, "but I could teach you how to play better." I remembered that first day, and I focused on what he was teaching me. He came down to the park same time as I did, around four in the afternoon. I focused on volleying with him, thinking where I should hit the ball to beat him. He was fast and moved around the court like a cat. I thought about those moves as the cops walked around the room.

One of the cops walked toward me. I turned and looked straight at him. He stopped in front of me and looked up. I stared at his dull blue eyes, a watery light blue. The whites of them were bloodshot as if he had been drinking the night before or perhaps had slept either too much or too little.

His face was covered with red stubble. His cheeks were lined with thin, red veins. His thick, matted hair, which he obviously could not control, stuck out all over his head. If he thought I was the one he was looking for, his eyes didn't show it.

He studied me for a few seconds before he moved on to Harold, who was fidgeting and looking down at the floor. Why was he nervous? Harold looked Jewish, and just as I thought, the cop walked right by him. He was looking for an Italian kid. He stopped in front of Johnny, who still had his head down. The cop lifted his chin. I thought he was going to cave, but after staring at him a few seconds, he went right by.

After the cops finished walking around the room, they talked quietly to Mrs. Greene. She checked her book of students, flipped some pages, and wrote something down. I thought sure they were going to come right to my desk and take me out of the room, right down to the police station and grill me. My heart started pumping away really fast.

They tipped their hats to Mrs. Greene and walked out of the classroom. I was safe. It was a miracle. The cop from the night before had not recognized me. I took a deep sigh of relief. I looked over at Johnny. He was smiling. He gave me a thumbs-up. Harold saw him, turned to me, and shook his head in disgust. He knew something was up. He was no dope.

On the way home after school, Harold was not his usual talky self. His school bag hanging over his shoulder was full of books. I said a few words about school, but Harold wouldn't answer. I knew he knew something was wrong, so I kept my mouth shut and acted as if everything was all right.

When we got to First and Ninth Street, he finally spoke. "All right. I know you did something wrong. What was it? Why do you hang out with Johnny so much? Someday, he is going to get you into big trouble."

"Why don't you mind your own business? If I want to hang out with him, why not?"

Harold just stared at me. Any other kid would have punched me right then and there, but Harold was logical. He would beat you up with his brain. He was shaking his head.

"You're a jerk! I just told you he's trouble, and you're gonna be in trouble. Do you want to be a gangster when you grow up?" He paused and stared at me. "Right now, as far as I'm concerned, you are a gangster! You're a little gangster. I know you've been doing little jobs for Pepi, carrying small bags for him here and there. You and Johnny always have money for stickball games. How come? It's because you work for him, and he pays you for it. How else?"

I didn't answer. I just let him talk.

"You can't tell me those cops were in there for nothing! You and Johnny most definitely had something to do with it. I could see it on your faces. You don't fool me. I'm telling you, Joey, you have to get away from that little creep. So tell me what happened last night. I'm your friend."

Harold really was my best friend. We got along pretty well because it seemed our minds thought alike. And since he was Jewish, the guys from the neighborhood never bothered with him. That meant that Harold was not influenced by neighborhood gangsters, and I liked that because I knew I could trust him. He always told me what he thought, and he was honest. I would have to break his arm to get him to do something wrong.

We headed down First Avenue toward First Street, and when we were far enough away from school, I told him what had happened. I explained how Pepi shot Nicky Bonanti and handed me the gun to hide. Harold turned pale. On Fifth Street, he stopped dead and stared hard at me.

"Joey, you are in deep, deep trouble! Don't you realize that? I knew this was going to happen. I mean, you're just a kid! How could he do this to you? This guy Pepi is gonna ruin your life! Now what are you going to do?"

I took a deep breath. I had no answer for him.

Then he asked me the big question. "Joey, for Christ's sake, where is the gun?"

I told him. He dropped his bag of books and sat down on the sidewalk with his feet hanging over the curb.

"Man, what a mess, Joey! You really think that's a good hiding place? I mean, it's not even hidden!"

"When I thought about it last night and figured my parents would be the only ones in the house, I thought it was a good idea, but after the cops came to school, I'm not so sure now. I think I need to find another hiding place."

Harold got up, and we started walking again. "Well, you better hope they don't come to your house. And if they search for the gun, pray they don't find it." He paused and shook his head. "I can see you going to reform school for at least a year, maybe more."

A chill ran down my back. He was right. I was in deep trouble.

We got to First Street Park. Tommy was practicing handball shots in front of First Street where there were the four handball courts on one side and four on the opposite side using the same concrete wall. He was slamming the black ball with force. When I saw him, I was ready to play him hard. I had to calm my nerves. Harold saw that I wanted to play handball with Tommy.

"Look, Joey, I'm your friend. I know I should help you, but Jesus, if I do and get caught, what do I do? How can I tell my father? I would really feel bad to hurt him. He's got nobody. If I went away, he would be alone. I want to help you out, but I don't know if I can. I'll see you later, maybe. You have to think of something to get out of this mess. You're hot right now!"

He gave me a quick wave and disappeared into his building. I thought how easy it was for Italian kids to get into trouble, especially with the gangsters in our neighborhood stealing and gambling and shooting each other. Now I had to figure out a way of getting out of trouble. Harold never seemed to have that problem. He was lucky. I didn't know any Jewish gangsters.

I walked into the park and went up to Tommy. I was going to play two games of handball with him, and since he was the champ and I was just twelve, he always kept one hand behind his back when he played me.

"Did you come to play, or did you come to sit on your tail?" he asked.

I smiled, took the ball, and pounded it against the wall. For the moment, I could forget Pepi, the gun, the shooting, all of that. I played him hard and tough. After two games, I won four points against him. I was sweating hard but felt better.

"Good games," Tommy said.

I respected him. Here I was playing with the best handball player in Manhattan, and that for me was very impressive. He was so modest, never talking once about the fact he was the champ. I was glad to know he lived on our block. I also felt good that he was a good guy to train me to be a better handball player. He kept lifting his glasses up above his nose, especially when he sweated. He tightened the bandanna around his head, wiped his face, and kept on playing.

As I climbed the stoop of my building, I noticed a man across the street leaning against a lamppost. He was wearing a dark fedora and smoking a cigarette. He glanced at me and turned away and looked down the block toward Second Avenue. I ran up the steps to our tenement. My heart began to pound. I was nervous enough thinking my parents may have found the gun.

My pop was already eating. His huge shoulders were hunched over. From the light on the ceiling, I noticed lines on his cheeks that I had not noticed before. His dark hair now had streaks of white just above his ears. Through his T-shirt, I noticed how massive his chest was.

My mother was at the stove putting the steaming pasta in a dish for me. I looked at her almost for the first time really hard. Her eyes seemed to change from green to brown and back again. Her high cheekbones gave her face a natural look of beauty. There were no lines on her face. When she smiled, she showed a set of strong white teeth, and when she looked at me, as she did tonight, she seemed to cut right into my soul. Had they found the gun? Was this the reason she stared straight at me, or did she always look at me that way?

The sweet, heavy scent of red sauce filled the air. I waited for one of them to say something, but they didn't. My mother looked up at the clock. My father took a drink from his wineglass. They had not found the gun.

"Joey, you come home so late, and look at you, sweating like a pig. Hurry up and get cleaned up."

I went into the bathroom and washed. I avoided going into my room. I was too nervous.

I sat down. My pop paid no attention to me. Instead, he kept on eating while listening to music on the radio from the opera *Cavalleria Rusticana*. My pop loved that opera because it was a Sicilian opera written by Mascagni, and the hero's name was his name: Salvatore.

My father told me the opera story of how Salvatore returns from war to find his love married to an old man. He challenges the old man to a duel and is killed. That was the tragedy of it. She shouldn't have married the old man. He nodded his head and took a sip of wine.

I was hungry. I stabbed three pieces of ziti with my fork and stuffed them in my mouth. I barely got through half my pasta when there was a knock on the door. My parents looked surprised. When my mother opened the door, I shivered. There stood the two detectives who were at school that morning!

2

My Old Toy Box

I froze with a mouthful of ziti. My pop looked at me hard and stood up. My mother folded her arms and glared at me. The detectives wore the same sour faces they had at school.

"What kind of trouble did you get into, Joey?" my mom asked. "I want to know!"

I looked straight at my mom. "Nothing, Ma. They showed up at school this morning. I don't know what they want."

Harold was right, as usual. Why didn't I hide the gun in a better spot? I could feel goose bumps on my arms and the hairs on my back stand up on end. I tried not to shake.

Both cops took off their hats. The cop with the red hair spoke first.

"Mrs. D'Angelo, don't worry. I'm Detective Brian Kelly. This is just a routine visit. We're checking all the boys in the neighborhood from First Street. There was a shooting in the park last night around ten o'clock, and we're looking for some evidence. That's all. We're not here to arrest anybody, are we, Dave?"

The other cop looked at me and smiled. He shook his head. "No. Of course not."

Yeah, right! I thought. *If they find that gun, I will be at the Ninth Precinct getting grilled in no time flat!*

My mom looked at my pop. He looked at me, and I looked at him. Just at that moment, music from the opera got really dramatic. It was the moment a village woman screams horribly when she finds out that Salvatore has been killed by the husband, the old man.

"Sure, why not?" my father said. "Go ahead. Look around. We have nothing to hide in this family, do we, Joey?"

I thought my life as I knew it was about to come to an end. My father gave me a severe look, which told me I would be in serious trouble if they did find something.

My heart was jumping out of my chest. I started thinking about Rachel and Maria. I thought about how gorgeous they both looked at school. Imagining Rachel's magnetic eyes and Maria's dark Italian looks did not totally work at school, and it did not work here. Sweat was already dripping down my neck.

The cops wasted no time. First, they went into the bathroom. One of them took off his jacket, rolled up his sleeves, stood on top of the toilet, and stuck his arm into the water tank. There was nothing there. When he got down, he dried off and started searching through the bathroom closet. It was filled with all kinds of junk my pop kept there—like batteries and flashlights that didn't work and some of my mother's pots and pans, brooms, and dustpans.

Detective Kelly spent a lot of time looking in that closet. I knew they were leaving my room for last. It was killing me. I felt my muscles tighten all over my body. He came out of the closet coughing and shook his head.

They headed to my room, my parents following behind me. I wiped the sweat from the back of my neck. They searched through my dresser, checked inside my shoes and sneakers, and looked under my bed. There they spotted the toy box! They looked at each other. Detective Kelly pulled it out. I thought it was over for me.

He started rummaging through it. I could see right away what would happen to me. The cops would handcuff me right there in my room.

I would be taken downtown. They would question me for hours. Would I be strong enough to keep my mouth shut? That was the question I asked myself. Kelly unloaded my toy box onto the floor, and as I stared at the mess, I realized the dusty holsters and Pepi's gun were missing!

There were a few moments of silence. He put the toys back into the box and stood up. Kelly looked around one more time and shook his head again. He put on his jacket and went to the front door. They stood there looking at me and shaking their heads. Kelly thanked my mom and pop and walked out. How could this be? Where had the gun and holsters gone? It was painful, but I worked my way through dinner, slowing down when I realized I was nervous and eating too fast. I finished eating, washed, and then walked slowly into my room as if nothing was wrong.

I went into my room and pulled out the toy box. It was only about half full from the night before. I could not understand what had happened. I searched the box. There were no cap pistols in it. Some wooden soldiers were also missing, and gone were the holsters and gun. I was relieved and surprised. I looked up to heaven, put my hands together, and made the sign of the cross. Could my mother have gone through the toy box without telling me and thrown out old toys?

I went back into the kitchen. That's when I noticed two brown paper bags full of old toys under the sink. The holster with the gun had to be in one of those bags. A bag of garbage stood beside them. My mom must have taken the holsters and the other toys and filled the bags to throw them out! She had saved me without knowing it! I couldn't believe my luck.

Did she know somewhere in her head police officers would show up at the house? Had she seen the gun? I began to eat. My father stared at me for a few seconds with his steel-blue eyes. I could tell he also knew something was up, but he didn't say a word. He took his wine and drank.

My mom, however, put her hands on her hips. "Joey, answer me. Are you in trouble? Did you do anything wrong? I want to know."

My father stopped eating and looked at me. I shook my head. He got up and turned off the radio.

"No, Ma. I haven't done anything wrong. I was sleeping last night."

My father spoke. "Lilly, leave Joey alone. He's a good boy. The police found nothing here. What could he have done last night? Like he said, he was asleep by ten o'clock."

My mother looked at my father suspiciously, her arms folded across her chest. She knew he was protecting me.

"Oh yes. He was sleeping!" She shook her head. "Joey after you finish eating, take the garbage out and throw away those bags of toys. You're a big boy now. You don't need them."

I finished my ziti quickly and was just about to take the bags out of the house when there was another knock on the door. My mom opened it, and there was Scappy, Pepi's right-hand man, the man who took care of matters for him. His short, stocky body barely fit through the door. His arms were so large he could have twisted me like a pretzel. I began to sweat.

"Hello, Mrs. D'Angelo, Mr. D'Angelo. How are you? Can I sit down?" He turned to me and smiled. "Hello, Joey." He pulled out a handkerchief and wiped his brow. "Oh my God, three flights is getting very tough for me. Mrs. D'Angelo, could I have a glass of water?"

My mom got him a glass of water.

"Thank you. You know, Lillian, I can't take these steps anymore. They're gonna kill me. I need some help, some young legs." He turned to me. "So, Joey? Pepi says hello."

My pop glared at me and then at Scappy. "Your boss says hello to my son? That is something! My son must be very close to Pepi that he should say hello to him!" He took his wine, drank it down, and slammed his glass down on the table.

Scappy smiled. "Everyone knows your boy, Sal, even Pepi. He's a good boy, a good boy."

My father stared at him. My mother went inside and returned with her numbers written on a small slip of paper. She showed him the numbers and handed him some money. Scappy looked at them, repeated them, and then crushed the paper in his hands. He smiled.

"Okay, 337, 347, and 437. Very easy numbers to remember."

He drank the water my mother had given him and got up. He pointed to his head. "I have fifty numbers in my head right now, but that is my limit. I need another brain to help me out. That's for sure. Young legs and a new brain! Thank you, Mrs. D'Angelo!" He walked out the door.

I took a deep breath and ate a peach. I went right to the sink. I took one bag of garbage in one hand and the two bags full of toys in the other.

I could see Pepi's gun in one holster and a cap pistol in the other. My mom opened the door for me, and I was so relieved I raced down the steps.

I went behind the staircase where the garbage cans were kept and threw out the garbage bag and one of the bags of toys. I went into the backyard. The night was lit by a half moon. I stepped into the yard and opened the cellar doors. It was so dark I kept one arm in front of me until I found the string hanging from the ceiling, which turned on the light. I pulled it. The bulb flickered. My heart skipped. A few seconds later, the bulb lit up. The cellar was a dungeon filled with junk, dark and dusty. I could see some old wooden chairs, rusted shovels, and planks of wood on the floor. Junk.

I thought I heard the rustling of a rat near the stall where my father had three barrels of homemade wine. That really scared me. I went to the back of the cellar. There, I shoved the bag against the stone wall and put a shovel and a bag of concrete in front of it. I rushed back outside, shut the cellar doors, and ran upstairs.

I went to my room and sat on my bed for a few minutes trying to read Classic Comics *Tale of Two Cities*. It kept my mind off the gun, Pepi Savino, and Nick Bonanti. For a few minutes, I didn't think about anything but the story I was reading. How could anyone give up his life for someone else as Sydney Carton did? It was a sacrifice I could not understand.

I knew why Scappy had come. My mother's numbers were an excuse. He let me know that Pepi was out of jail and wanted to see me. For sure he wanted to know about the gun. I told my parents I was going out for a little while. I was ready to tell Pepi about the gun, but the thought of seeing him now made me very nervous. I saw him shoot Nick Bonanti. I saw how he walked away so casually and wiped down his gun, and when he handed it to me, he spoke to me so calmly and with no emotion. That's why I was nervous. He was cold.

I ran down to my stoop and looked around. I saw the same man wearing the same dark hat and smoking, only this time, he was standing on the corner of Second Avenue. He was looking down the block toward me, but I didn't panic. I skipped down the stoop and darted for Pepi's social club. I glanced behind me. He was running toward me.

I got to the club. It was a storefront club. Inside was a bar on the left, and in the back small coffee tables for espresso and Italian cookies. I hurried in and Scappy grabbed me with his huge arms. I felt like I was in a vise. I thought he was strong enough to pick me up and throw me clear across the street.

"Stop running, kid," he said. "No one is gonna hurt you now. Pepi is inside. He's out on bail, and he's going to be very happy to see you." He put his arm around my shoulders and took me inside.

Pepi was at a table with three men, having espresso and Italian cookies. When he saw me, he got up and smiled.

"Boys, boys. Shut up already! Look who's here. It's Joey. This kid saved my life last night!"

The guys at the table applauded. Pepi came over to me and gave me a big hug.

"All right, all right," he said to his crew. "Have your espresso later. Leave us alone for a few minutes."

He didn't have to say it twice. Everyone at the table got up and walked out of the room. Scappy stayed. Pepi sat back down again and asked me to sit down. He looked straight at me with clear blue eyes. There was no smile on his face now.

"So, Joey, what happened to the gun? What did you do with it?" He lifted his finger. "But before you answer, I want you to know that Nick Bonanti is alive. He's not dead, that miserable bastard! Now, Joey, I know that Bonanti is not a rat. If his mother's life depended on it, he would not rat on me. You know why, Joey? He took the oath, the oath all friends of the family take.

"And you know how important that gun is? If the cops find it, they will know that it is my gun because they know I only use a .32-caliber. I like that gun. It's not heavy. I can keep it behind my back on my belt in a short holster because it has a short barrel. You know my prints could still be on that gun, Joey, even though I wiped it down. I told the cops Nicky and I were just talking and some guys came up and popped him!"

It was hard to be afraid of Pepi. He was very good looking. His blond hair was always combed back neatly. His blue eyes looked right at you when he talked. He had a soft voice, so soft he forced you to listen carefully to what he said. In his presence, I felt safe, but I was still tense and nervous, especially now when he talked about his gun. That's when he made me really scared.

"You have the gun. You hid the gun. I know the cops came up to see you, and they came up empty. So, tell me, Joey, where is the gun?"

I cleared my throat and spoke. "When I got home, I tried to figure out where to hide the gun. The only thing I could think of was my old toy box. I had old holsters with two cap pistols still inside, took one of the pistols out, and put your gun into the empty holster."

Pepi looked at me, nodding his head, thinking. He looked over at Scappy and smiled. Scappy leaned back and started laughing.

"Scappy, do you beat this kid? He hides my gun in his toy box!" He smiled.

I told him how the cops who searched my house found nothing because my mother had thrown the gun out with the garbage. I took the gun out with the garbage and hid it in the cellar. "The bag is still there," I said, "hidden in the cellar. Nobody is going to find it there."

Pepi stared at me. "That was very good, Joey. Now, very important! You have to get rid of the gun for good! And tonight, Joey. You have to because those cops are all over you. The cop who chased you is back watching your building right now. So what I need for you to do is to figure out a way to get rid of it permanently. I mean *permanently*. I don't know how you're going to do that, but I trust you. I think you're going to figure it out." He pointed at me. "Because you're a smart kid, Joey. And what's more, if you get rid of it, I have a surprise waiting for you. Now get going!"

Pepi made me feel I was part of the mob because he trusted me, but he left me with a major problem.

3 The Plan

I stood there in front of the club, thinking. I decided I needed some help. Would Harold help me? He told me already he would not. He thought I was crazy working with Pepi, but I had no choice. I had to ask him. If I asked him in a nice way, he might help me out. I decided to go up to his house. I got my answer right away. To make sure his father would not hear us, he shut the door of his tenement to talk to me in the hallway, and we began to talk in whispers.

"Are you out of your mind? Why do you think I would help you? Jesus, Joey! Don't you know you committed a crime by hiding that gun from the cops? What's the matter with you?"

"Harold, I know, but is it my fault that Pepi Savino dropped the gun in my hands? What was I gonna do? The cops were in the park, and one of them started chasing me."

Harold glared at me. "Joey, if you were not running errands for him, he would not have called you, would not have given you the gun, and you and I would not be talking about hiding his gun. I mean, Joey, you're holding evidence of a crime! C'mon,

Joey, admit it. You got yourself into this mess, and now you can get yourself out of it without me!"

Harold was right. I knew what I was doing and had kept on doing it. Only this time, I got involved without really wanting to get involved in something much more serious. He went to his door to go inside. He reached for the doorknob but hesitated.

"Okay, Harold, forget I asked you. I'll see ya later. I have to get rid of the gun tonight." I started walking down the steps, leaving him standing silently by the door. It was so quiet I could hear my footsteps.

Then he called out to me. He ran down the steps and caught up to me at the landing.

"Hey, Joey, you jerk, you know you're putting me in some spot!" He paused. "I knew someday you would get me into trouble, and I sure hope this is not the day. All right, I will help you. How do we get rid of this damn gun? Do you have a plan?"

We sat together on the landing thinking for about twenty minutes. We usually sat in hallways trading comic books, and now we were thinking about getting rid of a gangster's gun.

Harold came up with a great idea. He would be a decoy. He would follow me home and come with me into my building. Around nine o'clock, he would go downstairs wearing my jacket.

We would go down to the cellar and get the gun. Harold would leave the building and start running. The cop would start chasing him. While Harold was being chased, I would walk out of the building very slowly as if nothing were wrong and head toward Second Avenue.

Harold liked the plan because it was simple. He could tell the cop he was just visiting me and that he'd borrowed the jacket because it was cold outside. What could the cop say once he frisked him and found nothing? He would have to let him go. Harold would go home scot-free. I liked the plan because Harold wouldn't get into trouble, and the gun would be out of my building. I was feeling good until Harold came up with another difficult question.

"Joey, but what are you going to do with it once you get out of the building?"

That was a tough one. I was so concerned about getting the gun out of the cellar, I hadn't even thought about what I was going to do with it. We sat there for a long time thinking. Harold was stumped. Usually, he was very good at coming up with answers, but not this time.

I was stumped also. I felt as if my brain was stuck in a jail cell, and it couldn't get out. That made me think about reform school. That thought scared the hell out of me. I didn't want to lose my freedom.

I thought about playing handball and stickball. I would not be able to play those games if I were sent away. I got a chill down my spine. I felt most free when I played in the park. I looked at Harold. We were stuck.

"Joey, I have to get a drink. I'm so thirsty. Be right back."

He went back upstairs, and I sat there thinking. I realized I was also thirsty … and that was it!

During the summer when it was so hot, the kids from First Street would cross the walkway over the East River Drive with just our underwear on and jump into the river. The water was cold and not so clean, but anything was better than the sweltering heat of the city.

When Harold came back down, I had a big smile on my face.

"Oh, so boy genius finally figured it out."

"Yes!" I exclaimed. "I'm going to throw the gun into the East River. I know it's far from here, a lot of long blocks, but that's good because the cops will never think of the river. Nobody will ever find it at the bottom. What do you think about that idea?"

Harold sat down on the last step of the landing. "I like it, but Joey, it's a long way from here to the river, and where do I meet you after the cop stops me? And if a cop stops us on the way there, what do we do then? I'm getting scared."

"Did I say you were going with me, Harold? 'Cause you're not. Once you go downstairs with my jacket on, that's it. I'm not getting you into any trouble. After the cop stops you, you go straight home. If there's another cop, I'll just start running. He'll never catch me!"

Harold told his father later he was going to look at my comic books. It worked. My parents weren't suspicious either. They trusted Harold. We were in my hallway for about a half hour, just for the privacy of it, and we actually did start looking at comic books, but the gun was serious business, and comic books were not.

Around nine o'clock, Harold got up to leave. I handed him my dark-green jacket. He put it on and then stuffed a half dozen comic books against his chest and zippered it up. I looked at the bulge. It was perfect. I hid a flashlight in my jacket and told my parents I would be back by ten o'clock, and out the door we went.

Harold went down to the cellar with me. The moon was hidden behind clouds, and the flashlight gave off very little light, so the steps leading to the cellar were almost in complete darkness. Harold grabbed my arm as we moved slowly into the center of the cellar. I pulled on the string to turn on the light once more, but the bulb flickered again before staying on.

We crept slowly toward the back where the bag was. I pushed away the concrete bag and the shovel, and I pointed the flashlight toward the holsters. I lifted the gun out and again was surprised at the weight of it in my hand. I felt strange holding that gun. This one made me feel very powerful, but it also made me very nervous. I flashed the light at Harold. His eyes were transfixed on the gun in my hand.

It struck me how it was that Pepi could shoot Nicky Bonanti and laugh about it. I could never shoot anybody. I realized how dangerous a man Pepi was.

Harold helped me close the cellar doors. We went back into the hallway and hid behind the steps. Harold wanted to hold the gun, so I pulled it out and handed it to him. He held it with both hands. He shook all over.

"Careful!" I said. "Don't drop it, and stop shaking! It's not loaded."

"Wow!" he whispered. "It's heavy! God, Joey, this gun is very scary. You have to get rid of it right away. It's trouble! Take it back."

I took the gun from him and stuffed it back into my jacket.

"This is some mess you got yourself into—and now me too!"

"All right!" I said. "Let's go. Wish us luck! We're gonna need it!" Off we went.

I looked outside and saw a cop standing in the shadows a short distance from the lamppost, light streaming down to the sidewalk. Harold opened the door while I crouched down out of sight. As soon as he walked outside and started down the stoop, I saw the cop take a quick puff of his cigarette and throw it to the ground. He began to walk toward Harold, who had cleared the stoop and was heading fast toward his building.

The cop took the bait. He yelled at Harold to stop. As soon as Harold heard the cop, he took off. The cop took chase. He ran faster than I had ever seen him run, but another cop dashed out of the park and grabbed him.

That was my signal. I walked out of my building and started to walk in the opposite direction toward Second Avenue. Once there, I turned south and headed toward Houston Street and then east toward First Avenue and the long walk to the East River.

I walked slowly at first, staying clear of the bright lights of the lampposts. Somehow I stayed calm. First Avenue was behind me, and I headed toward Avenue A. I had a long way to go. When I saw someone, I put my hand to my jacket, where the gun sat heavily in my pocket, and patted it. I felt the same feeling of power I'd had before.

My biggest fear was seeing a squad car or a cop on the beat. I walked forever, it seemed. Then I saw a cop on the north side of Houston Street leaning against a lamppost. My heart pounded. I wanted to run, but I realized I had to keep my wits, and so I slowed down. He glanced at me for a few seconds and then looked the other way. I started to hurry, hoping that by moving faster, the time would go faster. It didn't. Every second was like a minute.

Finally, I reached the East River Drive and the ramp leading over the drive to the river. As I climbed the ramp, strong wind hit my face and whipped my jacket against my chest, but it felt good.

When I saw the river in front of me, I smiled. I was not safe yet, but I was getting closer.

I went down the ramp, walked over to the railing, and stared out at the dark river moving fast below me. I remembered how good it felt to dive into the water and feel its strength. I felt free when I was in the water, and as I stood there before it, I knew I would have another sense of freedom, freedom from the gun as soon as I tossed it to the river's bottom.

I looked down at the dark water moving rapidly toward New York Harbor. Soon all that water would flow out to the ocean. I looked around. A couple was sitting a good distance away, holding each other and kissing. They were paying no attention to me. I leaned over the railing.

Long dark barges floated by on the East River. Across the river in Brooklyn, I could see huge lighted billboards flashing. Domino Sugar was the largest. In the river, a tugboat went by, churning up water behind it. I felt the weight of the gun in my pocket and knew I would need to throw it out there as far as I could. I lifted it from my jacket and held it in my hand.

I had to throw it past the wall of the river, but I wanted it to go way past that. I felt my arm. Thank God I played handball with Tommy Schwartz! My arms were strong for a kid my age. When no one was watching, I gripped the gun by the barrel and tossed it as far as I could. It spun in the air, flying out a long way, much farther than I thought it would go. It landed with a splash and disappeared beneath the surface of the water. It was gone, and I was safe.

I took a deep breath and suddenly realized I was shivering. I took another look around. No one had seen me toss the gun. Pepi would be okay with what I did, and that meant I was okay. I ran home as fast as I could. I was so relieved that my nightmare of a problem was over.

When I got to Houston Street, I stopped to make sure no cop was around. Then I walked up First Street as if nothing had happened. There was no cop under the lamppost. When I opened the door to our tenement, my mother was waiting for me at the kitchen table, knitting. My father was fast asleep, snoring.

"Joey," she said. "Look at the time. It's past ten o'clock! You have school tomorrow. Where have you been?"

I never wanted to lie to my mother, but again, I had no choice. I told her I went over to see Harold, and we were reading his comic books. She stared at me as if she didn't believe me.

When I got into bed, I thought about the gun at the bottom of the river. As I started to fall asleep, I wondered what Pepi meant when he said he had something for me. That thought made me feel pretty good. I punched my pillow, closed my eyes, and fell asleep, exhausted but totally relaxed for the first time since the shooting. I realized then I had been more worried about Pepi than the cops, and so I slept a deep sleep.

The next day at school, I told Johnny about throwing the gun in the river. He must have told Pepi right away. When I went to the club the next night, I saw Scappy standing outside. He nodded to me to go in. Pepi saw me and got up. His men, all tough, mean guys, did the same. No one said a word. The light fixture on the ceiling gave off little light. Pepi and his men took me into the back of the club. It was darker than the front room. Now I was nervous and scared.

It was so hot I felt as if I were suffocating. I noticed a small window clouded with dust facing the back of the building. It was closed. I could barely see through it. I tried to figure out how I would get out of that room if there was a fire. For a moment, I nearly panicked, thinking I could be trapped. It didn't help that I was just a kid, and all Pepi's guys were standing so close to me. I felt trapped. Pepi came up to me. It was very quiet.

"Joey, you know why you're here? To take the oath of silence. That doesn't mean you're one of us; it just means you promise never to rat on anyone in this room. You understand me?"

I was scared, but I had no choice. I took the oath of silence. Harold was right. By taking that oath, was I now a little gangster? What had I gotten myself into? I didn't want to be there. I could have been with Harold trading comic books. Pepi grabbed me by the shoulders.

"That was a great idea throwing that gun in the East River,

Joey. I'm gonna remember that. If you ever get into trouble, I want you to know I'm here for you."

Pepi smiled, patted me on the back, and put his arm around my shoulder. He looked at his crew.

"So whatta ya think of this kid? Is he somethin' or what?"

They all smiled and one by one came over and patted me on the back. Some shook my hand. Then they filed out of the back room. I went outside with Pepi and felt the cool air in my lungs. All I could think of was that I was happy he was on my side. God forbid I ever crossed him. I didn't want to wind up like Nicky.

"Joey, I want you and Johnny to work for me running numbers. I hear you have a good head for numbers. With me, you're gonna make a lot of money. Believe me. Besides, Scappy needs help. He's getting tired and a little too heavy for this job."

It was that way with Pepi. One day he could be so scary, and the next day, he could be like a big brother taking care of me. That's the way I felt about him. I saw the good and the bad in him.

When I got home, I didn't say a word to my parents about what happened. In my heart, I knew what I had done was not a good thing. I knew Johnny and I had a job with Pepi, and I wasn't sure that was a good thing either. I went to bed that night thinking I wasn't at all sure I was doing the right thing, but one way or the other, I was going to find out, sure enough.

4
My Father's Second Job

It was not long after when, instead of going to bed at ten o'clock, I had to go out again, this time for my father and not Pepi. My mother and father had an argument earlier that night while we were having supper because she did not want him to go to a second job he had taken all the way over on the West Side.

We lived on the Lower East Side on First Street, just off Second Avenue. Construction was slow, and he told my mother we could use the extra money for now. It would not be for long, he told her, because his union told him he would be back to work in two weeks.

I knew one thing: Pepi Savino would not be working a late-night job to make extra money. He didn't need it. He and his mob friends at the First Street Club always had rolls of money in their pockets. They slept late, were well dressed in suits and ties, hung around all day at the club, and never worked.

My father shook me at ten just as I was about to fall asleep. My mother insisted I go with him. I had no idea what she was thinking. What help could I be? I found out later that night why he would need me. She was psychic. I had just two hours of sleep, and I was exhausted. Lucky for me, it was Friday night. I could sleep late on Saturday morning and be fresh for the stickball game on Saturday afternoon. It was 1952, I was twelve, and I loved to play stickball.

I washed, slipped on my pants, a heavy, plaid cotton shirt, and a plaid woolen jacket. In late March, the air in New York City was cold and damp. My mother gave me a soft kaiser roll and a glass of milk, which I gulped down because my father was already out the door holding a duffel bag. I did not know what was inside the bag. I could see it was heavy, but not for him. He was five foot ten and had large shoulders and huge arms from working construction. He had the dark skin of many Sicilians, long, thick brown hair, and blue eyes.

"This job is on the West Side, Joey. Are you warm enough?"

I nodded.

Living on the Lower East Side, I never had any reason to go to the West Side. Johnny and I usually got as far as Washington Square Park. My father and I passed Third Avenue, the Bowery. I saw a partial view of the Empire State Building mostly blocked by the elevated train, the El, above Third Avenue. We walked down Eighth Street heading west and approached Washington Square Park at the foot of Fifth Avenue. On each end of a huge white archway stood a statue of Washington in brilliant light. People sat around the circle in the middle of the park listening to a man playing guitar. Smoke rose in the air like the club smoke in *Casablanca*. Many huge maple and oak trees were in the park. The air was clean and had the faint hint of leaves and mint. Four-story townhouses lined the north side of the park.

As we headed uptown on Fifth Avenue, tall buildings appeared on both sides of the avenue. Doormen stood in full dress uniform of gray or blue with hats on like the one Douglas MacArthur wore. As we passed by those elegant, well-lit doormen buildings, I thought of the tenement buildings on First Street with broken-down stoops and locked front doors. We turned on Thirteenth Street and headed west. The farther we went, the darker the streets became. Some of them were deserted. Not a soul in sight.

My father walked a good, strong walk, and sometimes I had

to take an extra step to catch up to him. It was late, and I was tired. We reached Hudson Street. I could see just a bar open, one person hunched over the counter being wiped down by the bartender. Hudson Street had lots of small two- and four-story houses. I began to smell something bad. The only light came from dim street lamps.

We passed Hudson and entered a large square. The stench of dead meat hung in the air and filled my nostrils. I took a handkerchief to my nose. I saw the reflection of a dim moon on greasy, slippery cobblestones. We walked carefully. Small, old buildings bolted shut had run-down metal overhangs, and in front of them were platforms four foot high that looked as if they had not been cleaned in years. My father looked around, saw what he was looking for, and headed toward the center of the square. I was ready to throw up.

He came to a large sewer with me right behind. He pulled a large flashlight out from his duffel bag and then a chisel and pried loose the manhole cover. I stood there shivering from a cold wind ripping through the square from the Hudson River. It helped to drive the stench away. The square was dark and deserted. He lifted from his bag a portable shovel and an iron pipe about two feet long. I heard the swishing of water below in the sewer. I had no idea what he was about to do.

"Now, listen to me, Joey. I am going down into the sewer to clean out the garbage from the drain, but I don't want you to look down. Understand me? Don't look down! Now stay back, and remember what I said!" He took the shovel in one hand and the iron pipe in the other and began to descend a ladder of metal bars attached to the wall of the sewer.

As he lowered himself into the hole, I heard him banging the bars of the ladder with the iron pipe. Suddenly, I realized I was alone in the square. My pop had disappeared from sight. I looked around with just the faint light of the moon. The beat-up meat buildings looked as if they were about to collapse from the strong wind. My pants flapped. I had no cap, and my long black hair blew across my face.

My short woolen jacket gave me little warmth. I stood there as the wind gained strength across the square and nearly blew me down. I tried hard just to stand there on the slippery cobblestones. I was scared.

After a few more hits of the iron pipe against the ladder, I heard not a sound. I went closer to the sewer but did not look down. I heard the swishing of water and a shovel scooping what I figured then must be trash blocking the sewer hole itself beneath the water. I could hear my pop's iron pipe banging the ladder again. The noise echoed across the square. I could not see him. I was alone above ground. Despite his warnings, I could not resist looking down into the hole. I leaned forward and saw the light of the flashlight jumping.

There was my father banging at gray long-tailed rats climbing up and down the ladder and trying to get away from the blows of the iron pipe. I heard the scream of a rat after the pipe hit it, a thud first, its scream and nothing more.

"Oh my God, Pa, get out of there! One of them is going to bite you!"

My father looked up at me and continued to strike blows at the rats, their long tails swishing away, bulging stomachs and sharp teeth white as snow against their gray skin in the light of the flashlight.

"Be quiet!" he shouted at me. "I told you not to look down, and you looked down! Now get away from the sewer! Now!"

I backed away. My pop had stopped hitting the ladder. I figured he was knee deep in the water. I could hear him shoveling away until finally I heard water draining and his shovel scraping stone. Against his wishes, I looked down again. He was shoveling away the last bits of garbage. The last few inches of water were draining out of the sewer. He had finished and began to climb the ladder out of the hole.

Suddenly, a large rat came scurrying behind me and between my legs. Before I could shout, he jumped onto my father's back and bit the back of my father's neck. My father screamed, grabbed the rat with his bare hand, and threw him against the wall of the sewer. He took his iron pipe and tried to hit him, but it was too late. The rat had disappeared into the swirling water draining into the cleared sewer.

"Damn it! Damn it! I was done already, and now this!" He reached for the back of his neck. Blood was pouring over his fingers. He pulled out a handkerchief and held his neck while he climbed slowly up the ladder.

I leaned forward and grabbed his arm and helped pull him up and out. He stood up clutching his neck. With one hand he placed the manhole back over the sewer.

"Well, I finished, anyway. That's good. Next time, you listen to me! Now let's go!"

We rushed back, his handkerchief he held tight against the bite wound. All the while, he said nothing. There was no hint of pain from him. I was amazed. I would have been screaming my head off. As we crossed Third Avenue, he stumbled. I reached for his arm and placed it over my shoulders. He leaned against me. He was heavy, but we kept going.

We got home, and my father sat down while I woke my mother. When she saw him, she screamed, *"O Jesu Cristo,* Sal! What did you do to yourself?" She took out a clean towel and drenched it in hot water and then slowly pulled away his handkerchief.

She screamed again, loudly enough for the entire building to wake up. She slowly padded the hot, wet towel on my father's cut. For the first time, I could see he was in pain. He winced.

"Jesus, Lilly, quiet down, and take it easy. I'm not made of stone!"

"You crazy fool! How did this happen? Tell me. I want to know." She turned to me. "Joey, tell me. Now!"

I looked at my father. He decided to answer for himself.

"I was cleaning garbage in a sewer in the Meatpacking District, and soon as I finished, a rat jumped on my back and bit me. I don't think he liked that I was in his territory because he took a really big bite and held on until I slapped him off."

"Sal, you are so crazy. Why did you take this job? I know we could use the extra money, but this job? My God, you are crazy.

Are we so hungry that you need to work in the middle of the night and put your life in your hands? Joey, get the alcohol and the iodine from the bathroom cabinet. Hurry!"

My father groaned. "Oh no! Alcohol and iodine? Iodine burns like hell!"

"Oh, be quiet, you damn fool! You got bitten by a rat! You want to die of some horrible disease? You are never going back to that job! I'd rather see you sell potatoes on the street than do that work ever again!"

I handed her the alcohol. First she squeezed as much blood out of his wound as she could, and then she poured alcohol over the bite. She dried his neck and then took the iodine and smeared it across the deep red marks. My pop screamed this time, and my mom smiled.

I made up my mind that night when I went to bed that I would do whatever I needed to do not to be poor. I could see now why Pepi and his friends decided not to work and to make easy money. It was easy money for me and Johnny also to work for him!

My pop later agreed to quit the job. My mother shouted at him that he almost killed himself to help feed the families of his sisters whose husbands were out of work. "Dumb!" she shouted at him. "Never again!" A few weeks later, we took a train from Grand Central Station into Westfield. My father and I carried two brown paper bags each loaded with food for his sisters. That was his reason for his second job.

Early Saturday morning, the horse-drawn fruit wagon coming down First Street woke me up. The old, bald driver smoking his pipe would interrupt his smoking by shouting, "Hey, peaches!" He woke up every woman on the block, but my mother and her friend Josephine were already down there, both smiling because they were picking from the wagon the sweetest, freshest peaches, cantaloupe, bananas, oranges, and apples. It was a little early for fruit, but he was there anyway. It was a sign that spring was coming. After a hot bowl of Quaker oatmeal, I played handball in First Street park.

In the afternoon of our stickball game, a bright sun warmed

the air. The back park where we played stretched along two traffic lanes of Houston Street. In the park behind the infield was a fence with a cutaway entrance to the outfield where I played, and the back of the outfield was a fence along Second Avenue.

The other guys—Alan Dino and his brother, Eugene, and Anthony Diaz—played infield in front of me. From center field, on my left, I could see the backyards of the tenement buildings on First Street, including my own, my window on the third floor with my shirts, pants, and underwear flapping in the wind, hanging to dry from a clothesline. Even in cold March air, my clothes came out soft and fluffy.

Spring was almost on us. Small pods, which popped out of large, oak, maple and elm trees, crunched under my feet. It meant to me that tree branches would soon be thick with fresh, green leaves that blew in a soft wind and not cold, moist air that cut through my woolen coat and make me shiver. That Saturday afternoon, we played our stickball game against the guys from Third Street. Before each game, the referee came over and collected our bets, fifty cents for each game. That was a lot of money, and every time I handed that money over to him, I was happy that Johnny and I were working for Pepi. We beat them badly.

I would be playing a lot of stickball as long as Pepi Savino gave Johnny Marino and me money to run those simple errands. All I had to do was carry a small paper bag over to Italian blocks like Elizabeth, Mott, and Mulberry Streets to other social clubs where guys from that neighborhood would take the bags and go inside the back room. It was very secret. Johnny and I never thought about what was in those bags. I didn't care. It kept me from working at six in the morning at the grocery store across the street from my building. That was painful. And if my parents knew about my working for Pepi, I would be in trouble for sure.

With the extra money we won playing stickball, on Sunday afternoon, Johnny, Harold Tapper, and I went to the movies, and sometimes I just took Maria. It was the Orpheum or St. Marks Theatre on Eighth Street and Second Avenue or the Jefferson on Twelfth Street. That day, Maria and I went to see *White Heat* with

James Cagney, Edmond O'Brien, and Virginia Mayo, a rerun from 1949. The movie was black and white with fast action. Cagney played a psychopathic killer who listened to his strange mother who urged him on to a life of crime. Whenever James Cagney was about to shoot somebody, Maria would get closer to me and grab my arm, sometimes biting her nails. I liked that.

I kept thinking how good my mom was. I could never imagine a mother like that! I liked to sit way up in the balcony, especially when Maria was with me. Two movies played with a cartoon in between the movies.

The second feature this afternoon was also a rerun, *D.O.A.* with Edmond O'Brien. My favorite actors were Gregory Peck and Burt Lancaster. The actress I loved the most was Hedy Lamarr. She was just drop-dead beautiful. We all loved her. Ava Gardner was a close second on my list of beautiful women in the movies. I didn't like blondes.

I will never forget the end of one movie, *Duel in the Sun.* Jennifer Jones and Gregory Peck shoot each other in the end, even though they loved each other, and die in the hot desert sun. I guessed it was the love that was too great in them that killed them. I wondered if I could love Maria like that. I held her close to me.

The following Sunday, Johnny, Harold, and I took the subway from Second Avenue up to Yankee Stadium. We didn't have enough money for the main tickets, so we sat in the bleachers, way out there from home plate. The year before, in 1951, right after the season ended, Joe DiMaggio retired. It was a shock to us, and so we decided to go to Yankee Stadium to see the new center fielder.

We sat in the bleachers. In front of us was center field. There we waited for this big new kid who was taking DiMaggio's place. Who could take the place of Joe DiMaggio? The bleachers were fifty cents and out there—far, far away from home plate. I couldn't imagine anybody hitting a home run here, but I had heard that the new outfielder from Oklahoma was very strong, a real farm boy. His name was Mickey Mantle.

He didn't have a great year his rookie year in 1951. We were curious about him anyway. The beginning of a Yankee baseball game was always exciting. The music played, the Yankees ran out onto the field, and everybody stood up and cheered!

Then we saw this monster of a player come trotting out from the dugout to center field just in front of us. We all wondered if the Yankees had made the right choice to go with this new player, Mickey Mantle.

He looked very strong, and he trotted almost right up to us. He was huge! His blond hair was flapping in the wind. I think he was nineteen years old. He looked like a giant. His shoulders spread out and sloped from his neck like Lou Gehrig's. He looked up at us, and we all smiled at him. Johnny, Harold, and I waved to him, and he waved back and smiled. I thought that was great.

Johnny, always a troublemaker, cupped his hands to his mouth and shouted at him, "Hey, Mantle!"

Mickey Mantle turned around and stared at Johnny.

Johnny shouted again, "You'd better hit some home runs! You look like you could hit them, but I'll tell ya right now, you got big shoes to fill, and it ain't gonna be easy. That's all I got to say!" Johnny laughed and sat down and pounded me on the shoulder. *What a jerk!* I thought.

There was no protection from the hot sun in the bleachers. Harold's white skin was getting red, and his freckles were becoming almost invisible. His reddish hair was getting bleached. He punched Johnny in the arm.

"Hey, what's the matter with you?" Harold said. "He just started out! Leave him alone."

I agreed with Harold. I tapped Johnny hard on the back of his head.

Mantle looked up at Johnny with a straight face and for a few seconds didn't say a word. Instead, he just pounded his glove harder and harder. Then he shouted back at him, "Don't worry, y'all! I'm gonna hit a few of them right here where you kids are sittin'. You wait and see."

Then he turned around just in time to see a practice fly ball hit about forty yards to his right, almost into left field. Mantle raced to the ball, stuck his glove out, and caught it on the run. We were stunned at how fast he ran to the ball.

"Holy crap!" Johnny said. "Did you see that? This guy is fast!"

We sat down, amazed at the speed of this new outfielder for the Yankees. I thought after that catch he would for sure hit a lot of home runs over center field during the year, he was so quick and strong. He didn't disappoint us that day. He hit a home run in the third inning. It sailed over left field and hit the seats for a shot that went at least four hundred feet. He swung so easily, and then, as the ball sailed into the seats, he trotted around the bases as if he owned Yankee Stadium. I felt better about not ever being able to see Joe DiMaggio play baseball again after Mantle hit that homer. That shot won the game for the Yankees.

That night, I was pretty tired. It was exhausting being out in that sun. We had a game to play on Saturday the following weekend, and I couldn't wait. I was glad to see Mantle play, since I played center field in our stickball games, and now I wanted to be as fast as he was.

Some nights we played basketball at the Boys' Club. It was great. We played all the other teams from the neighborhood, and later we took hot showers, swam in an Olympic-size pool, and played around by whipping towels on one another's asses.

I never expected what would happen to me there at the Boys' Club a few weeks later. It was not only a surprise but a real shocker to me, and it basically turned my life upside down.

5
The Scholarship

It was a Saturday afternoon in April, and I realized how important Pepi and his gang had become in my life when I needed them. Our stickball team was on the field in the back park on Houston Street. We were playing the team from Third Street. It was the seventh inning, and we were winning 4–2. The air was cool and fresh to taste.

I stood as center fielder in the back park behind a fence that separated me from the front of the back park and what was the infield during the game. Leaves on oak and maple trees had turned lush green just above me. My problem was the concrete benches in the outfield, which often cut my hands.

When Spalding balls were hit over the fence, I needed to hold on to the backs of them while I maneuvered to get under the fly balls. It was tough enough for me to fight trees whose leaves were now thick on strong, bending branches and moved easily to any soft breeze. I would cut my hands easily.

The game was almost over. The next batter was taking his time getting ready to hit. My mother had hung out my wash on a clothesline, and the spring breeze was blowing them dry and fluffy—my T-shirts, underpants, and shirts and a clean pair of dungarees blowing free. Trouble was about to start.

Across Houston Street, I could see the marquee of the Sunshine Theatre. A second run of *The Third Man* was playing with Orson Welles and Joseph Cotten. I could never understand how that woman could love a killer. Next to the Sunshine was Yonah Shimmel's potato knish store, the best knishes in New York City. I was getting hungry and hoped the game would be over soon. Their batter had just taken a swing at the ball. It went up high and left, landing on the sidewalk on Houston Street.

Some kids who looked like college kids were watching our game. There were about five of them. They were not from the neighborhood. They wore khaki pants and crewneck sweaters, green and red and blue. They all had short blond hair, except for one of them. They stood there, fingers holding on to the fence, watching the game when the ball hit over the fence landed in front of one of them. He picked up the ball, smiled, waved the ball at us, and put it in his pocket. They were all laughing and started to walk toward Second Avenue.

Johnny Marino ran over to the fence and shouted at them, "Hey, give us our ball back! We don't want any trouble. Just give us the ball back."

These kids were about eighteen and tall. They looked bigger than usual for kids that age. I thought they might have been football players. They kept on walking and laughing until the kid who took the ball shouted back, "Look, you little guinea slimeball, if you want your ball back, come and get it!"

Johnny ran outside the park and tried to get the ball from the kid. His friends just laughed. Before I knew it, they were punching and kicking him. Our team ran outside and tried to help him, but they were too big. I ran over to Johnny, who was already on the ground and flat on his back. One of them punched me from behind. It happened so quickly.

Johnny was bleeding from his mouth. His right cheek was scraped up as if someone had run a cheese grater over it. I thought the best thing to do was get some help because our guys were getting clobbered. Quickly, the college kids walked across Second Avenue to the subway on the west side of Houston Street and disappeared down the steps.

I ran across Second Avenue to the Second Street Bar next to Provenzano Funeral Home. Pepi and his boys usually hung out there having a beer on a Saturday afternoon. I got lucky. They were all at the bar watching a Yankee game on a small television screen just above the bartender. Pepi's boys were laughing and shouting at the television, beers in their hands. Pepi just sat there quietly at a small table having a cup of espresso, watching the game with Scappy sitting next to him, also with an espresso.

I ran into the bar and screamed that these kids were beating up our guys. The mob guys turned to me and stood there silently.

Pepi got up first and said, "Let's go. What are you guys waiting for?"

I ran outside first and headed into the subway entrance. The college kids were already on the subway platform waiting for a train to pull into the station. The kid who had taken our ball was juggling it in his hands.

Pepi ran down the subway with his men behind him. Each guy had a billy club in his hand, and each grabbed a college kid and began to beat him. It was strange to watch. The college kids were big, and the Italian mob guys were short but stocky. They were beating the kids with no mercy. These tall college kids had no idea what was happening. Blood splattered all over the platform. The train pulled into the station, and the doors opened. Passengers getting off were stunned and tried hard to circle the fight. The crowd allowed the college kids to get loose and get onto the train. Some of them were pushed and punched onto the train floor, while a few of them raced to another car to get away. One by one, they managed to get on the train.

One last boy was getting hit by Scappy, who was pounding him with no mercy. The doors began to close. He saw that and panicked. He put his arm between the doors while his friends opened the doors to let him in. Finally, the train pulled out. Some of the sweaters of the college kids were full of blood and torn from their bodies, some of them in shreds. Cuts and blood were all over their faces. It was a terrible sight to see those kids beaten up that badly.

One of the mob guys kept banging on the window of the doors. The train finally pulled away. I saw the college kids wiping their mouths and heads, blood pouring out of them. They were all in shock. I could see that in their faces.

Pepi walked over to me and put his arm around me. "Smart, Joey, that you went to get us. Those kids deserved to get beat up. I was ready to kill the one with the ball. Kill him! Nobody messes with the kids from our neighborhood. Nobody!" That was Pepi.

With his arm on my shoulder, we walked up the steps and out of the subway. Pepi's guys were laughing. Scappy was wiping blood off the heavy side of his club. They were talking and laughing while Pepi and I crossed Second Avenue together. Johnny was at the water fountain cleaning his head with his handkerchief. We finished the last inning and won the game.

"Come and see me next week," Pepi said to me and Johnny. "I have another job for you to do. This time, you're gonna make some good money."

Even after the fight, his curly blond hair was neatly in place. Johnny and I walked away smiling. I felt good that Pepi was going to put us to work again, but I was getting nervous.

After we ate knishes at Yonah Shimmel's, we went to the Boys' Club on Tenth Street near Avenue A to play basketball. Some of the Third Street guys also came down and played against us. Naturally, Johnny got into a fight with the biggest kid on their team.

Tom Mansfield, our basketball coach, broke up the fight. He gave Johnny a good shake, but Johnny just pulled free and walked away. Tom just shook his head.

"Johnny is getting wilder every day. You be careful! Joey, when you have a chance, can you come up to see me and my wife? Come on up after you shower. We want to talk to you. Okay?"

I just shrugged.

I told Johnny, and he sneered. "What does he want with you? What? All of a sudden you're so special? He probably wants you to do some volunteer work for nuthin'."

I went downstairs and showered. Harold had already finished. He had a towel and was rubbing dry his red hair. I noticed how skinny he was. He was never a good athlete, but he was on all our teams. I liked him because he was smart, and we were both good at math. We understood each other. I told Harold that Tom wanted to see me and asked him what he thought.

"Joey, whatever it is, it's gotta be good. Go see him. What's the big deal?"

Johnny sneered. "Who knows what these guys at the Boys' Club know?" he said.

"For all I know, they're all working together, the cops and the Boys' Club, watching us in case we get into trouble!" Harold laughed.

"Just shut up, you idiot! You're just jealous. You don't trust anybody, do you?" Johnny laughed. "All right, Joey," Johnny said, "we'll wait for you outside. Enjoy your little meeting with the coach and his pretty wife!"

I went up to the third floor. Tom met me at the front door, smiling. He shook my hand and went into his tiny apartment. On the left, there was a large bookcase packed mostly with paperbacks. Against the back wall under a window was the bed. On the right was a small kitchen built against the wall. In the middle of the room on the left was a deep-blue beat-up sofa, and there were two maroon chairs on the right with a coffee table in front of them. An oriental rug covered the middle of the room's wood floor.

I said hello to Sue, but she just nodded her head and said not a word. I was uncomfortable to begin with, but that made me more uncomfortable.

"So, Joey, sit down. How about a Coke?"

I nodded and sat down.

He put some ice in a glass, poured out the Coke, and placed it in front of me. I was thirsty. It was cold, and the sugar gave me a boost. It was quiet for a few seconds. I looked over at Sue. She sat on the chair with her legs folded, wearing shorts and a Boys' Club T-shirt. Her dark hair hung straight down over her ears. Her eyes were dark brown. She fixed her eyes on me but said not a word.

What's with her? I thought.

Tom started right away.

"Joey, I want you to know that Sue and I think you are a bright kid. We think you have a great future, and we want to make sure you do the right thing moving forward in your life. We have not yet spoken to you about being considered for a scholarship to prep school. Peter Capra and his Yale buddy, Dwight Davis Jr., son of the tennis star, had an idea about a scholarship for underprivileged kids. It was begun to honor their friend Joe Brooks, who died in a duck hunting accident a couple of years ago, just fifty years old. They were devastated by his untimely death.

"So they hit on the idea of starting a scholarship here on the Lower East Side. Well, to tell the truth, it hasn't worked out very well. The first three boys Mr. Capra picked went to school and did not make it. Frankly, you were never considered because of your connection with Pepi and his mob friends. I'm not telling you what you don't know. All the boys sent to boarding school came back after two months. They quit. Then I talked to Mr. Capra about you. He was very reluctant to select you—believe me—because he knows of Pepi. In fact, everyone knows that, Joey, but then he told me there were few choices left, so he reluctantly asked me to ask you if you were interested. I am being as honest as I can be."

There was a long pause. "What exactly do you mean by prep school?"

Tom smiled, but his wife still was not smiling. "Prep school is short for preparatory school, a school which prepares its students for college. I know it will give you an opportunity to get away from Pepi's influence and make something of yourself instead of becoming a gangster and wasting your life. Once out of this neighborhood and away from him, I know you will make an excellent candidate. My wife, Sue, however, honestly, had reservations about you from the beginning, to be quite blunt about it. But I'll let her tell you what she is thinking."

I sat there and turned to Sue, knowing now what she had against me. She was studying me carefully. For a few seconds, she made me uncomfortable; I didn't like how she looked at me, but I wasn't going to let that bother me. I thought I would let her know that.

"Prep school sounds a little like reform school to me, except for the college part." I smiled.

"Not exactly, Joey," she replied softly. "It is not reform school. Quite the contrary! It is an elite school, an educational institution for the privileged in this country, and Mr. Capra thinks the privileged should be joined by kids who are not so privileged. He means to level the playing field a little bit. You understand?"

I understood, and I didn't like the way she was talking to me.

"For you, it will mean taking grammar and reading lessons from me and Tom. Your math grades are excellent, but your English grades are not good enough. It will mean hard work, sacrifice, and commitment on your part. If you ever get there, you will need to take an admission test, and if you pass that test, your life will change forever. If you fail, however, you can go back to your little games with Mr. Pepi Savino." She paused and sighed and shifted her position on the couch. Her legs folded easily underneath her body. She put her hand through her dark hair and placed her arm on the sofa top.

"Joey, I want to be honest with you," she said, still staring at me. "We think you have a good head on your shoulders, and we both think you can be a pretty good student at prep school. I know how well you do at school here. There is no getting around that, but I have serious concerns. Naturally, you need a lot more training in English grammar, as I mentioned. Your diction is terrible, and your command of the language is atrocious. It's not your fault. Your parents are immigrants, as are most of the families here on the Lower East Side, but this problem can be solved. The biggest problem I have with you is that you hang around with boys in the neighborhood who spend too much time with the young gangsters on First Street."

I looked at Tom. I felt my cheeks heat up. Jesus! If Sue and Tom had known I was the one who threw Pepi's gun in the East River, she would have had a heart attack right then and there. I relaxed.

I stared at her and didn't say a word. I noticed how her eyelids slanted sleepily over her eyes. She folded her arms on her lap. Her straight black hair hung down over the sides of her face just below her chin and barely moved. She tilted her head when she looked at me and brushed her hair back often. Now that I saw her for the first time up close, I realized she was very good looking.

But I felt very angry. No one ever criticized me about who I hung out with, and I felt insulted by what she said and how she said it. I folded my arms and stared at her. Tom looked a little upset.

"I don't think we ought to be going into that right now, Sue."

She ignored him. "Also, Joey, Pepi is Johnny Marino's cousin, your good friend! Now, mind you, I have nothing against Johnny Marino, but the fact is he is here in the Boys' Club because Peter Capra thinks we can help him before it is too late. Johnny is a problem for me, Joey, because you hang out with him, and you are too close to Pepi."

I could see Tom was getting really angry, but she kept on talking.

"How can I recommend you for this scholarship program knowing what I do about you? It's not only about brains, Joey; it's about character. Your friends are a problem for me."

I felt caught. Were they going to recommend me or not? I was really angry now. Tom put a banana split in front of me, and she was taking it away. At first, I wasn't even sure I wanted to be in this program, but she got me so angry, it suddenly became a challenge to me. I wanted to show her I could do it. I wanted to show her and myself that I could do it in spite of all the obstacles she talked about. Deep down, I knew in my heart she was right about that. Pepi and Johnny were going to be problems for me.

"Joey, Sue is very outspoken. All she means is that you have choices ahead of you. Which direction you take is up to you. You are twelve years old. It's time for you to start thinking about those choices."

Sue said, "How you conduct yourself over the next few months will determine how convinced we are as to whether you fit in this program, and if you do fit, it will make an exciting and positive change in your life."

I turned to Sue. I wanted to make one point. "Sue, I have a lot of friends who are good kids. Harold Tapper is one of my best friends, and he is a very good kid. He is Jewish. He lives with his father. And Johnny is not all that bad a kid! He is my friend, and I like him."

"Well, Joey, you know how I am thinking. It is all up to you! You have a long way to go. Think about it."

My mind was racing as she spoke. I wasn't sure how I felt about the idea of prep school. It meant going away from the neighborhood, my friends, my parents, and Maria. Jesus! I wasn't sure if I could. I understood why the first boys they sent away did not make it. It must have been weird for them to leave New York City and go to a strange place.

I thought about the neighborhood, stickball games, and handball with Tommy Schwartz. I had to think about that. Tom and Sue were challenging me. I thought, *I am just twelve! How could I even think about leaving everything?*

Tom spoke. "Joey, I want you to ask your parents if I could come by for dinner to explain the program to them. Would you do that?"

I told him I would. I got up and shook his hand. I nodded to Sue and left. I walked out of the apartment and took a deep breath before going downstairs. I was thinking that I had dodged a bullet. I went downstairs, and outside the club, Harold and Johnny were waiting for me. How would I explain to them what had just happened?

6
Topsy-Turvy

How could I have known that this scholarship idea was going to cause so much turmoil in my life, with my friends, my parents, Maria, and Pepi?

"Did they mention the gun?" Johnny asked.

"No!" I said. We headed home, Johnny on my left, Harold on my right.

Harold smiled. "See? What did I tell ya, Johnny!" he said. "You were worried about nuthin'!"

"So what did they talk about?" Johnny asked.

I wasn't sure how to answer that question; I didn't know how they would react. I just came out with it.

"Tom thinks I could get a Boys' Club scholarship to go away to prep school. It's a high school, only they call it prep school because it prepares kids for college, but Sue doesn't like me, because she thinks Pepi is a bad influence on me." I paused. "It means I would go away to a boarding school."

Johnny stopped dead in his tracks and started laughing. Harold and I stood looking at him.

"Oh boy! You faggot! Wait until my cousin Pepi hears about this! So you would leave the neighborhood to go away to school? Are you kidding me? This is a joke, right?"

"What's so funny about that?" Harold said. "This is a good thing for Joey. What do you want him to do? Go to reform school, grow up, and become a gangster and waste his life? You make me laugh. You're just jealous! You think they would ever pick you? You're a little crook!"

Before I knew it, Johnny started throwing punches at Harold. Johnny was bigger than Harold, but Harold fought back. Johnny knocked Harold to the sidewalk, but Harold got up and started punching back. Harold didn't look tough, but he was. I grabbed Johnny by the back of his shirt and pulled him away.

"Johnny, what the hell is the matter with you? Are you crazy?"

"Well, he shouldn't be calling me a crook!" Johnny yelled.

Harold shot back, "You work with your cousin, don't you? And you got Joey here involved, didn't you? C'mon!"

"All right, cut it out, both of you. I'm not going anywhere," I said, "so let's drop the subject."

We headed home. Maybe Johnny was right. It was a joke. No one spoke. Already, I felt different. The scholarship had caused my two friends to fight, and I wondered how my parents would react to the idea of my going away to school. And Maria! My God! How would I explain going away to her? I realized if I won the scholarship I would most likely lose Maria. How could I leave my home and the neighborhood? It was a sacrifice I was not at the moment prepared to make.

When we got to First Street, we all went home. I didn't say a word to my parents about the scholarship until my mother had finished the dishes. I sank my teeth into a peach.

"Mom, Tom wants to come over for supper one night. He wants to talk to you and Pop about prep school."

"Prep school?" she asked.

My father finished his wine and tilted his head. I explained what it was all about. It meant going away to school for four years. It meant not seeing them all year long except on holidays.

My mother stopped what she was doing and stared at me. "Where do these people get such ideas? What is he crazy?"

My father smiled and poured himself a glass of wine. "What is so bad about that? Tom is proposing that Joey get a better education than public school. I like the idea. Yes! I like this idea of prep school. Joey will have a better education. Tell Tom he is invited."

"What? I don't have a say in all this? How do you expect Joey to go away from us and live in someplace he knows nothing about? I am against it! He is not going anywhere. He stays home. Joey, tell Tom to forget about it!"

My father shook his head. "Lilly, at least we should listen to what he has to say! Why deny him the right to tell us what he can do for Joey?"

He paused. My mother shook her head and folded her arms. My father kept on.

"Lillian, think of Joey. In the short run, we sacrifice, but in the long run, it will be very good for him. Think about that."

She was not happy. She finished the dishes and silently poured out a cup of espresso for my pop. She looked at me with sad eyes. I thought she was going to cry. I was upset over the turmoil I had caused between them.

"Okay. Invite Tom over this Friday," my mother said. "I will make him a shrimp sauce with penne."

My father would not look up at my mom. She stared angrily at him. I told my mother he had mentioned how great her sauce was. He was impressed. That made her feel much better. For the moment, there was peace.

My father greeted Tom with a tall glass of homemade wine he had fermented all winter long in three huge barrels down in the cellar. My mother was stirring her fish sauce with an old wooden spoon. It had been cooking for four hours. She invited Tom to sit down. My father lifted the gallon jug he kept by the foot of his chair, poured a glass of wine for Tom, and then refilled his own. Tom commented on the sweet scent of shrimp, which my mother had just thrown into the red sauce.

The table was set with a dish of black olives, a basket of fresh, sliced Italian bread, a small bottle of olive oil, and a bowl of freshly cut lettuce mixed with beets and beans. Tom looked at the food and smiled broadly. I knew Sue didn't cook for him the way my mother cooked for us.

My mother filled his dish first with steaming pasta, shrimp and red sauce. Tom already had a fork in his hand. My father laughed. The sweet scent of sauce filled the room with steam rising high above the table. My mother filled my father's plate and then mine. We began to eat.

When Tom was finished, he patted his belly and smiled. My father poured him another glass of wine, which he refused, but my father insisted.

"Mrs. D'Angelo, I have never tasted in all my life such delicious sauce! Will you let me have the recipe? I would like to have Sue make it for me."

My parents laughed. I smiled.

"Tom," my father said, "do you think your wife can make a red sauce to taste like my wife's, a recipe that has been in her family for seventy-five, maybe one hundred years, just by writing down the recipe for you?" He laughed. "Drink your wine, my friend. You are not Sicilian. Where are you from, anyway? New Hampshire? Forget about making a sauce that you will never be able to make. Tell me instead how you intend to make my son a professor in a university. That is what I would like to hear from you tonight."

Tom smiled. "You are right, Mr. D'Angelo. I could never make a red sauce like your wife, and my wife couldn't either, but I can help your son become a professor in a university if that is his ambition. That I can do, but it is up to you and Mrs. D'Angelo—and Joey, of course. He will have to go away to boarding school, a prep school away from home that prepares young men for college. This is an opportunity Joey should not miss! Oh, I understand your sacrifice of having Joey leave home, but it is a sacrifice well worth it for Joey to have such an education. And then college. And maybe then a university professor!"

My father smiled and tapped me on the shoulder. "I like the idea. Joey is smart. He will be a good student."

My mother had cleared the table of dishes and quickly replaced them with bowls of peaches and grapes. She did not look happy. Alongside the peaches, she placed a green bowl of pecans, while the scent of espresso already brewing on the stove filled the room.

She was about to place on the table a bowl of cherries when she glared at Tom. "You want to take Joey away from his mother? Out of the question! You will have to find another way to get him to college because he is not going to a boarding school if I have anything to say about it!"

My father laughed and called me over and hugged me. "Momma, he is my son too, and he is very bright, and Tom here knows how bright our boy is. Joey will need training, and Tom and his wife will give it to him. He will become a professor because he has it in him to do that. In fact, he can do whatever he puts his mind to! Think of the opportunity! Is it not what this country is all about? Is it not why we came here from Sicily, a land of rocks, hard soil, and dust? We need to give our son this opportunity! We must! And to get him out of this neighborhood!"

My mother poured out two cups of espresso. "He is also my son, and don't you forget that! We will have to talk more about this school away from home where you two wish to send my son. For me, it is out of the question! It will be harder for you both to change my mind than to move Mount Etna! Now have some fruit and pastry and drink your coffee! Enough talk."

I wasn't even sure now I wanted the scholarship. Already, it started trouble between Johnny and Harold, and now between my mother and father. Then Tom casually mentioned the subject Sue had brought up.

"Of course, Joey will have to stay out of trouble. My wife was very tough about that. You understand."

My father looked at my mother for a few moments in silence. I thought I would die.

"I understand exactly what you mean, Tom. You have nothing

to worry about. Joey will stay out of trouble. I am sure of that. Isn't that right, Joey?"

He looked straight at me. I blushed and nodded agreement.

A few moments of silence passed while my pop and Tom sipped their coffee. My mother poured herself a cup, dropped a thin slice of lemon into the cup, and drank quietly without a word. I did not realize my father had such dreams for me or that my mother was so possessive of me, so I said nothing. I took a biscotto from the pastry dish and kept my mouth shut. It was settled. My father had won the argument. I would go for the scholarship. I left them still talking and went downstairs to play handball.

Johnny was waiting for me. "I told my cousin Pepi that Tom was coming over to see your parents. He wanted to know what that was all about. I told him I didn't know for sure why he came over. I think he's a little suspicious, so he wants to talk to you face-to-face." He had a smirk on his face.

I was so angry I felt like punching him. "Why did you have to go see Pepi? Why? You're always getting me into trouble! I told you it was about the Boys' Club scholarship and not the gun. I'm going to tell him the same thing I just told you." I stared at him. "I don't know why I'm friends with you. Trouble is your name!"

He put his arm around my shoulders. "Joey, we've been friends since we're babies. I'm like the brother you never had. Okay, so tell your story to Pepi. You have nuthin' to hide, so what's the problem? C'mon, he's waiting for us. Stop worrying. He's not gonna shoot ya. You won't be smiling if he tells us not to work for him!" I thought about that and the scholarship. It dawned on me that Harold was so right. Was I going to grow up becoming a gangster, sleeping until noon and hanging around all day long in an Italian silk suit?

"You know, Joey, if Tom ever found about you, me, and Pepi, he would dump you so fast!"

"Stop talkin', will ya? I'm trying to think about what I'm gonna say to Pepi."

"All I gotta say is that it had better be good, Joey!"

When we got to the club, Scappy was there, as usual, standing at the door and smiling.

"Glad you're with us, kid," he said. He put his big, beefy arms around my shoulder.

Pepi had two husky guys sitting at the table with him. They were sipping espresso slowly. Pepi was whispering to them. I never could figure out why in the club, with no one around except his crew, he would whisper. When he saw me, he smiled, but I sensed a difference now. I was nervous.

"My two boys! Look at these kids. Tough as nails. I can't wait for them to grow up!" Pepi said.

I thought I knew what to expect from him, but today, I felt he could get angry at me in seconds. I stood there this time thinking he was going to get crazy. I braced myself. I didn't say a word.

"All right, fellas," Pepi said, "beat it! I want to talk to my boys!"

The beefy men at the table pushed their chairs back. I could see guns in short holsters inside their jackets. They made no attempt to hide them. As they left, they gave Johnny and me pats on the back. The biggest guy patted me so hard I nearly fell down. As soon as they left, Pepi came right to the point.

"All right, Joey, what's this all about? Johnny tells me the guy from the Boys' Club came over. I just want to know if he mentioned anything about shooting Nicky Bonanti? Did he?"

Pepi just leaned back in his chair, quietly staring at me with a straight face and waiting for me to speak. He wasn't smiling now.

I cleared my throat and shook my head. "No, Pepi," I said, "he never said a word about the shooting or the gun or anything about that. He just came to talk to my parents about a scholarship I might be able to get, and that was it."

Pepi got up. He straightened his jacket and stood next to me and then turned to Johnny. "Okay, Johnny, beat it. I want to talk to Joey privately."

Johnny left.

I looked around the room and saw a column of smoke rising from the corner at a table where a man sat in shadow. I could see his shoes but nothing more. I could hear a cup tap the dish. From the dark corner, he was barely visible to me.

"Don't look at the corner, Joey; look at me," Pepi said, tapping his chest with his finger. "Joey, you're sure about the gun? He never said a word about it? You're sure he just talked to you and your parents about this scholarship?"

I nodded.

Pepi stood right next to me. He looked at the table in the corner, but the man kept silent. I didn't know what to expect from him. He was getting me very scared.

"Okay, Joey, so he wants you to work at getting a scholarship, but what does that mean? Does that mean you don't work for me anymore, even for small jobs? Now that's gonna hurt you, Joey. You know that. Maybe you should not be working for me. Maybe you can work in the grocery store on First Street, packing milk in the refrigerator at six in the morning! Is that what you want to do to keep change in your pocket and for betting on stickball games? Tell me, Joey, what do you want to do?"

I hesitated before answering him. He looked very agitated. He glared to me as if he were going to explode. He took a sip of espresso, waiting. I had to think quickly for an answer that would satisfy him. He was not acting like a big brother to me now. I felt so much pressure he left me no choice. I thought maybe he was really concerned about the gun, and so I went to that.

"Pepi, nobody knows about the gun, honest. Tom just wanted to meet my parents and tell them about a scholarship from the Boys' Club to go away to prep school. That's a boarding school. It prepares you for college!"

"College? Tom wants you to go to college? Well, isn't that something? Joey, let me tell you something. Did you see those kids who took your stickball last Saturday? Do you want to wind up like them—arrogant, nasty, bullying other people? Is that what you want?"

"No. I don't want to wind up like them, but maybe someday I could be somebody."

Pepi stared at me. He sipped his coffee. There was a long silence in the room. Pepi smiled.

"College is a long way off, Joey. In the meantime, I have some small jobs for you and Johnny to do. Are you quitting on me? Do

I get someone else to take your place? You want to leave Johnny on his own? Just let me know, and I'll get someone else."

"No, Pepi, I don't want to walk out on you, and I don't want to leave Johnny alone. He could get into big trouble. He takes too many chances. I keep telling him that. I'll stay."

Pepi smiled. He sipped his espresso. He was happy.

"Okay, Joey, good boy. I knew you would stick with me. I have some work for you as I promised. I'll let you know. Now beat it before I go nuts. And remember, the gun is our secret. Keep your mouth shut!"

As soon as I left the club, Pepi's guys piled back inside. I never saw the man sitting at the table, and I wondered why he sat there in the dark. I left thinking Pepi did not totally believe me. I figured I blew it with him.

"Well, how did it go?" Johnny asked. "Are we gonna be okay?"

I nodded. "I'll tell ya, I'm very happy I'm outta there."

He gave me a nasty look. "Jesus, don't tell me you screwed up!"

"No, I didn't screw up. I told him Tom never mentioned the gun. He was happy about that. He said he had more work for us. So I guess that makes you happy!"

"Joey, if we lose this job, we have no money for stickball. Thank God you didn't blow it."

I heard a voice calling me from the park. It was Maria, and she was waving. Then she put her fingers to her lips and whistled. I heard that, all right. I smiled and waved back. What a relief it was to see her!

"Johnny, I hope you didn't say anything to her about the scholarship. I mean, how much trouble could you cause me in one day?"

He smiled at me and elbowed me in the chest. "Quit worrying. She cares about you, for Christ's sake! Go. I'll see ya tomorrow! It's getting late already. You did the right thing, Joey. Trust me!"

He walked away. How could I trust him? He always did what he wanted.

I walked into the park, went right over to Maria, smiling, and hugged her. She glared at me. Then she pushed me away and slapped me hard. It stung.

I put my hand to my face. "What did you do that for?" I asked.

She put her hands on her hips and just stared at me, her dark eyes fixed on mine. She wore a zippered black leather jacket that fit tightly around her thin frame.

"How could you leave me and go away to school? I thought you cared about me?"

Johnny did tell her!

She brushed her dark hair from her face, her eyes sizzling with anger. Her nose sloped down in perfect symmetry, straight and slender. She bit her lower lip, which forced me to look at her lips—soft, full, and moist. I wanted to kiss them badly, especially because she was angry with me. She told me one day she wanted to be a model. I could see that easily. Her sharp, straight nose, dark eyes, high cheekbones. She would be a perfect model.

She punched me on the arm. "You bastard! You don't care about me!"

She backed away, folded her arms, and stared at me coldly. She was beautiful, no doubt about that. And when she punched me, it hurt. She was thin and slender but full of muscles. She loved to dance and kept herself in good shape. I loved that about her.

"Wait a minute! I don't know what Johnny told you, but I'm not going anywhere!"

"Liar!" she said, and she started walking away at a fast pace toward Mott Street. I caught up with her as we crossed Second Avenue.

"What's the matter with you? Why do you believe that guy? I'm not going to any boarding school! Stop already! Will you please?" I grabbed her by the arm. She stopped, pulled her arm from my grip, and put her hands on her hips. If she had a gun, she would have shot me right there on the spot.

"Well, Johnny told me the Boys' Club gave you a scholarship, and you're going away for good. I'm never gonna see you again!"

She stared at me and then began to cry. I took her and held her. I never saw her cry. She was the tough one, sticking up for her friends and always ready to fight back in case any of her friends were picked on. That's what I loved about her. She had a sense of caring for the underdog.

She put her head on my shoulder. I pulled out my handkerchief and handed it to her. Cars on Houston were honking their horns so loudly I could barely hear her crying. She wiped her eyes.

"Listen to me, Maria. I'm not going away to school. One of the counselors from the club came and asked my parents to think about a scholarship for me. That's all! Nothing else happened. My parents argued about it, and he left. That was it!"

She turned to me, still wiping tears from her eyes. She calmed down. I felt terrible that I had hurt her. After a few minutes, I rubbed her back softly. She stopped crying and blew her nose with my handkerchief. I took her gently by the arms and pulled her toward me. I didn't want her to cry. I wrapped my arms around her. She put her head on my shoulder again and put her arms around me. I was so relieved she did. That calmed me down.

We stood there holding each other for a few minutes more, and then we walked slowly to Mott Street. At her front door, I kissed her softly. She opened the door of her building and went inside, turned, and smiled at me.

"I gotta go," she said. "I'm too upset. We can talk tomorrow." She disappeared up the steps.

I walked back home very upset. The scholarship was killing me.

The next day after school, I played handball with Tommy Schwartz. After three games, I left him and went over to drink from the park fountain. It was close to four o'clock. I looked up and saw a 1951 Buick pull up to the social club. A stocky guy in a dark suit got out of the car and stood there with the back door open. Scappy nodded to him, went inside, and came out with Pepi.

Just then, I saw my father walking down the street toward Pepi. They were no more than thirty yards away from each other. My father's jacket and baggy pants were covered with white powder from poured concrete. His brown work shoes were also covered with the same powder. His body tilted to his left slightly from carrying his heavy duffel bag. He looked tired. Pepi looked fresh and alert, his navy-blue jacket wrapped neatly around his body. His dark-gray pants were creased sharply down to his black wing-tipped shoes, and he stood straight up as he walked.

When my father saw Pepi, he stopped and stared at him. He was angry. His face turned to stone. Was he jealous of him, or did he know that Pepi took care of me with money? Pepi suddenly turned in his direction and returned the stare. For a few moments, I could see they were focused on each other and nothing else.

My father suddenly put down his bag and headed toward Pepi. I stiffened. My pop would win that fight. Scappy stood nearby watching them. Instead of confronting my father, Pepi turned away and walked slowly toward the waiting Buick. Scappy saw my father and intercepted him just as Pepi took one last look at my father and disappeared into the backseat of the car. His driver slammed the door shut, and the car sped off. I was very relieved.

Scappy put his arm on my pop's shoulder and smiled. He shook my father's hand. He said some words to him I could not hear.

I watched as Scappy, still with his arm around my father's shoulders, walked with him back to his bag, picked it up, and handed it to him. He patted my father on the back and walked back to the club. My father stood there for a moment staring at Scappy, who was still smiling as if nothing had happened.

It was then I yelled to my father and ran across the street to him. He hugged me and brushed my hair back. We walked past the club together. I felt very safe with him. He put his hand on my shoulder. We walked home without a word. He was tired. I could see that. I felt him lean on me as we climbed the stoop of our building, the way he did when the rat bit him on the neck. This time, I was able to let him lean on me easily. I felt stronger.

Pepi said he was putting Johnny and me to work. If he did, I was not going to say no to him. I never thought an opportunity for a scholarship would cause so much trouble in my life. I think Johnny was right. It was all a whole lot of nuthin'.

7 The Runner

Pepi promised he would give us more work, and he did—running numbers. We took numbers from neighborhood people who bet on the last three numbers of the income earned at one of the racetracks in New York City. It was rigged. No doubt about that. Usually they bet a dollar and sometimes two dollars, but never more than that. Johnny and I were climbing up and down tenement steps way up to the fourth and fifth floors of the buildings on Second and Third Street. Pepi gave us just two buildings to do on First Street because he didn't want my parents to find out we were collecting numbers.

One person he insisted we do was the old widow Tscacalusa. She was playing numbers for years, and he knew she waited for Scappy every Saturday morning. She didn't have to wait long for me. I ran up the steps.

The old widow was shrouded in black, as usual, a black hood over her head, black shawl over her shoulders, and black dress that hung down to her ankles, with soft black boots that were often left unlaced because she could not reach down to lace them.

As I ran the steps to her fifth-floor tenement, I recalled how she would call me from her window years earlier and throw down coins in a bag to buy her milk and bread.

The door was open. I went inside and saw her sitting at the window. When she turned and saw me, she smiled. I went over to her and knelt down. Her shoelaces, as always, were untied. She patted me on my head with wrinkled, bony fingers. I tied her laces tight, hoping a neighbor would come in later that night and untie them.

"Ah, my little Joey who is now so big!" she said to me in a gravelly, old voice that came from deep in her throat. "Scappy told me you were coming."

Her dark eyes were buried deep inside their sockets, so small they were hard to see. Deep wrinkles lined her pale gray face from lack of sun. She had no teeth, but she had a pleasant smile. I thought she must be ninety years old by now. She got up slowly after I finished with her laces, and with shoulders bent, she shuffled across the room to her bedroom, her black dress swishing across the dusty floor behind her. I looked around. The walls were dark.

She returned clutching a black purse, which she opened with shaking fingers and pulled out a wrinkled dollar bill. Her bony fingers slowly unfolded it. She placed the dollar in the palm of my hand and closed my fingers. She gripped my hand tightly with both her hands, looked up at me, and smiled.

"353!" she said.

I never knew why that number was so important to her, but Scappy told me she played it every Saturday. Then, as I was about to leave, she called me back and pulled out a dime from her purse. Holding my wrist, she placed it in the open palm of my hand and smiled again.

"Maybe I will win today. Joey, you will bring me good luck!"

I left, wishing she would win, because in all the years she played, she had never won. I think Pepi wanted her to win. I closed the door behind me and heard her shuffle back to the window.

I knew collecting numbers was gambling, and it was illegal, but the thought of getting caught just never occurred to me. I didn't think there was anything bad about it either. I would knock on the door, and an old man or woman would answer. I would be handed a number written in pencil on a piece of paper. I made certain I matched number with name, memorized both, and left, leaving the paper behind. I felt safe. I had no paper in my pockets, but it was the money in my pockets that made me worry just a little.

Johnny's pockets were full of money and small notes with names and numbers. I thought that was crazy, and I told him if he were ever caught with all that money and those little pieces of paper, he would be arrested. The cops would have evidence against him. I worried also that it was Pepi's money, and if I ever lost it, I would be in deep trouble.

It wasn't as if a cop could pick my brain for evidence. On top of that, in the worst case, I knew I could run as fast as anyone on my stickball team. I knew that from racing the guys before games. I was very fast, so I knew I could run faster than any cop in the precinct house. I proved that when I ran from the park with Pepi's gun.

I also did not have to pack milk at the grocery store and had money for stickball games. The scholarship idea was completely out of my mind.

I trotted down the stoop of Tscacalusa's building, happy that I had taken care of her, but the smile on my face turned sour really quickly. From the stoop, I saw cops getting out of a black car. Any kid on the Lower East Side could recognize a cop. They wore rumpled suits and were very white. No one ever thought they were smart. Most of the neighborhood thought they were pretty stupid. Now I had a serious problem.

From the stoop, I jumped to the sidewalk. Johnny still had not seen the cops, so I shouted at him to duck back inside or start running. I skipped down the stoop and headed toward Second Avenue. I saw another black car at the end of the block. No doubt about it. I was going to be caught!

Before the cops could get out, I walked across the street and headed fast toward First Avenue. I glanced behind me to see two cops holding Johnny. One of them was reaching into his pockets grabbing dollar bills and his notes. I kept walking and headed toward First Street Park.

Suddenly, I heard one of the cops shout, "Hey, kid! Stop right there! Don't move!" Was he kidding? I took off as if a gang of Puerto Ricans was after me. I ran fast between cars to get into the park. It was then I saw Maria sitting on a bench.

She looked beautiful, with her thick brunette hair, piercing dark eyes, pointed ears holding back her hair, and high cheekbones. She looked like a young Ava Gardner. She was leaning against the bench, her arms hanging over the green, wooden backstop, tapping her fingers on it and looking around.

God was with me, but I could see she was angry. I dashed over to her, pulled out every bill I had, breathing heavily, and dropped them on her lap. Her dark eyes tore right through me.

"I gotta go. They grabbed Johnny. Take the money and hide it! Whatta you doing here?"

"You jerk!" she shouted. "You were supposed to meet me at twelve o'clock."

I admit sometimes I was absentminded, but this was not the time to explain anything, since escape from the cops was the only thing on my mind.

I checked my pockets to make sure I had no more dollar bills, and, looking at her angry eyes, I said, "Well, I'm here, aren't I?" Then I ran as fast as I could down Houston Street past the Sunshine Theatre and into the back park.

"Jerk!" she shouted.

I stood frozen on the spot in the park where second base would have been if we had been playing stickball. It was no use.

I could see squad cars pulling up on Houston Street. Heavy, squat detectives got out of their cars, leaving doors open and lights flashing. Traffic stopped. Outside the park along the fence, people stood like statues watching the action. I didn't have a chance. They had me.

I was surrounded. I looked up at my building. I prayed to God neither my mother nor father was at the window of our tenement. It was open, and I was lucky. I could see curtains in the window and clothes on the clothesline flapping away, but no one was there. I avoided disaster for the moment.

Two cops in plainclothes grabbed me and started frisking me.

"All right, kid, where are the numbers? Where did you hide them? And the money? Where is the money? C'mon, we know you were running numbers!"

The other big cop stood me up and shook me like a rag doll. He held my arm and slapped me across the face.

"C'mon, don't be a wise guy. You're not a wise guy! You're in trouble, kid. Tell us what you did with the numbers. We got your friend Johnny with numbers and the money, so tell us what you did with your money!"

I kept silent. No doubt they would have pocketed the money if I had it on me.

They pushed me into the back of their squad car. I prayed to God my mother stayed away from the kitchen window. I was also praying my father was not heading for the bocce court in the front park. He would have run over to find out what was going on. I sighed.

I saw Maria watching me. She had guts standing there on the sidewalk with her purse full of Pepi's money. I forced myself not to look at her and promised myself that I would either strangle her if she got caught standing there or give her a giant kiss if no one caught her. She was tough.

They took me to the Ninth Precinct on Fifth Street. It was full of cops walking around holding papers in their hands, casually wearing .38s in their holsters. Johnny was already sitting at a desk in front of a detective, lined in a row with other desks where other detectives sat typing away, cigarettes dangling from the corners of their mouths.

The place needed a cleaning really badly. Paint was peeling off the ceiling. Walls were stained yellow and brown and filthy. I could see balls of dust on the floor. Another cop pulled up a chair.

Johnny sat at the desk directly in front of me. This was it. We were caught, and we would be sent away. I began to sweat. Was I safe because I had no money or numbers? At that moment, I thought that. Was it going be every man for himself?

I remembered Pepi's demand for our oath of silence. If you ever get caught, don't talk! I decided I was going to stick to it. I would never rat on Johnny, and he would not rat on me. It was about loyalty and courage. It was about standing with your buddy when he was in trouble.

I focused on the Irish cop in front of me—an unshaven red face wrinkled beyond its years, thinning hair, and dull, brown eyes—wincing as he wrote, trying to see through his own cigarette smoke as it trailed up to the ceiling. He threw his pen down on a desk cluttered with piles of paper, crushed his cigarette into a filthy ashtray filled with burned-out butts, and smiled as if he were about to kill a bug. He was ready to grill me.

I had to make sure I never said a word about Maria. She was cool sitting there as the cops chased me down, waiting at the fence for them to clear out of the park, holding tightly to her purse. The cop in front of me, his shirtsleeves sloppily folded up, stared at me. As the last flame of his butt smoldered in the tray, he sneered at me, his large teeth spaced and stained yellow.

"So, c'mon, let's have it! It's Saturday. It's spring. I work only half a day, and it's already past twelve. I am not happy! Understand? I want to get home to my wife and kids, water my lawn, have a beer, and watch the Yankees. We already have Johnny's numbers. I want to know what you did with your numbers and the money. Where is the money?" I knew then why I didn't like cops. He talked to me as if I were a gangster. Did he know Johnny and I had a connection to Pepi?

As I sat there trying to be cool, I knew one thing: being arrested on Saturday afternoon made me think really hard about becoming a gangster! Was reform school now worth expensive shirts and silk suits and worse, losing the scholarship opportunity? I wanted no part of reform school!

"Officer," I said softly, "I never got any numbers from anybody.

I don't have any money on me, and I never worked for anybody running numbers. I'm not a runner. I'm just a kid who likes to play handball and stickball. That's all! I just wanna go home now. I never did anything wrong. My mother is probably waiting for me for lunch."

Johnny was listening. He looked at me and started to laugh. He had a slightly protruding jaw, and when he laughed, he leaned back and opened his mouth like a donkey showing his big mouth and large teeth.

This cop, however, was in no mood for smart-ass talk. He jumped out of his chair and slapped me hard across the face. It stunned me, but I acted as if it didn't hurt. I felt like getting up and punching him, but I stayed calm and just stared hard at him. I could feel my cheek heat up.

He pointed his finger at me. "Shut up, you little shit! And you, Johnny, keep on laughing and I'll throw you down below. Your father won't find you for a week. You want that?"

We just sat there quietly.

Another detective came over, tall and good-looking. His thick black hair was combed neatly back with a part on the left side like Tyrone Power. He was dressed neatly. His shirt was a crispy light-blue, his maroon tie knotted neatly, his charcoal-gray pants sharply creased under a navy-blue sport jacket. He dressed like Pepi. He stood there for a few seconds staring at me and turned to the detective handling me.

"Charlie, we're going let Joey go, but hold on to Johnny Boy." He turned to me. "C'mon, kid, let's go!"

He took me by the arm gently and lifted me from the chair. I was stunned. I looked over at Johnny, who was no longer smiling. His face was turning pale as he watched me walk out.

I stood there for a moment, relieved that I was being let go but upset because Johnny would still be there. It was not looking good for Johnny. He sat there, his eyes pleading to go with me, but there was nothing I could do. I felt helpless. The tall detective led me outside the precinct house, let my arm go, and pointed his finger at me.

"Keep your nose clean!" he said, and he went back inside.

I never thought that the course of my life would be changed because I memorized a set of numbers, but it saved me that day. I turned to see if I could see Johnny. I could not. I thought about Johnny's mother, who died in a warehouse fire along with 150 other garment workers. I thought that if his mother had survived that fire, Johnny would have been a different kid.

After she died, Johnny went a little wild, stealing and hanging out with the gangsters and running errands for them. He got me into it for the money.

Now he was inside, and I was outside. I felt alone. I missed Johnny already, and I was scared for him. I ran home and avoided the social club and Pepi. I was anxious to see if my mom or pop had seen me. I turned around at my stoop to see if anyone had followed me. No one had.

I ran up the steps. My mom already had on the table a ham and cheese sandwich and a Coke. I was very thirsty. My mom was very good about feeding me, but I wasn't hungry. I told her that.

"Eat," she said. "If you don't eat, you do not grow."

I sat down and began to eat. I must have been eating very slowly, because she asked me what was wrong with the sandwich.

"Nothing, Ma. I'm just a little tired—that's all." That was the truth. I was very tired, but I was also deep in depression thinking about what would happen to Johnny. I also realized that I had to eat fast, since Pepi was waiting for his money, and Maria was waiting for me. Now I had more to worry about. Was Maria still holding on to Pepi's money?

I ate quickly, wondering if cops were still in the back park. I looked out the window of our kitchen. There was no sign of a squad car or cops. The afternoon sun was high in the sky. Light streamed into the kitchen and spread across the table where my mother had placed fresh peaches she had bought in the morning from the old fruit vendor. I finished eating my sandwich and drinking my Coke, washed up, and ran downstairs.

Scappy was already waiting for me, standing at my stoop. He grabbed me by the arm.

"Pepi knows they got Johnny. He also knows they let you go because you had no money or nuthin' on your person. He wants me to tell you to get the money wherever you hid it and get it to him right away. Understand?"

I understood.

"Good," he said, and he walked across the street to the club.

I ran fast down to Mott Street and raced up the steps of Maria's building. When I knocked on the door, her mother came out. A gray cardigan sweater was draped over her drooping shoulders. She was no more than forty, but her hair was already gray and hung down the side of her face. Her eyelids looked heavy over dull, lifeless eyes. Bags of wrinkled skin were already under them, and her mouth bent at its corners.

"Oh, it's you, Joey," she said.

She called for Maria. Leaving the door ajar, she walked back inside. In her eyes, I could see the eyes of Maria. I prayed to God that Maria would not look like that at age forty, that she would grow strong and healthy, that she would have a good life, and we could be together. I prayed all that. Maria came to the door.

"C'mon inside," she said.

I walked into her bedroom.

She put her finger to her lips and whispered, "You are really crazy! I know why you gave me that money! You were doing numbers for Pepi, and you got arrested!"

"No!" I whispered. "I didn't get arrested, but they got Johnny. He had all the money on him, including the numbers written on pieces of paper. He is in big trouble! Is the money safe?"

She looked at me with her hands on her hips. "You think I'm a jerk. Of course it's safe. You're the stupid one for getting yourself into this mess! Did you make sure no one was following you?"

I told her I ran all the way, and no one was following me. She looked out her window and then went to her closet. She pulled out a pair of green socks bulging with the money. I looked inside the socks, and it looked as if it was all there. I gave her a big hug.

"I love you, baby! You saved me!"

"Here! You take the money and get it over to Pepi right away before the cops find you with it. I don't want you or me to get into trouble, but you already are in trouble."

I wanted to, but I couldn't take the money then.

"Don't worry—calm down," I said. "How could they connect you with Pepi's money even if they found you with it? Look, I have to go. I have the stickball game, remember? We're playing just one game today. I'm glad, since Johnny won't be playing. I can meet you back here in an hour or so."

She gritted her teeth and shook her head, thinking about whether she should go along with me. She glared at me. She was very angry. She looked down and shook her head. For a few moments, she was silent. I looked at her and then kissed her on the cheek. I felt terrible.

"I'm really sorry I got you in this mess, but I had no choice. You saved me, Maria! If they had caught me with this money, I would have been arrested. Just hold on to the money for a little while longer until after the game."

She gritted her teeth and then punched me hard on my shoulder. "I don't want to, but I'll do it. You'd better not get me into trouble, Joey!"

I leaned over, kissed her, and ran out the door before she changed her mind.

I thought it was important to act like everything was normal. I did not want the cops to think I was hiding, so I decided it was a good idea to play stickball and act as if nothing had happened. That was my strategy.

It seemed I was always running. I ran to the back park. The guys were already there practicing. I picked up a bat and start hitting balls, first into the infield and then to the outfield, as if nothing had happened. Harold was out there.

I hit some high fly balls to him. He missed most of them. I went over to Anthony and told him he had to play second base because Johnny was sick. I gave him a dollar, and he ran over to Patsy, who was counting out the money for our team with the other captain.

When the referee had all the betting money, our team all ran out into the field. I ran out to the outfield. The money I bet didn't matter anymore. I was thinking of Johnny sitting in the precinct house and Pepi waiting for his money. It was strange to see Anthony at second base. I tried to focus on the game, but it was very hard to do that. The game started. Maria casually walked into the park and sat down. She looked totally relaxed. She was so smart and so cool about everything. Nothing seemed to bother her except when she found out about the offer of a scholarship.

I played pretty well through the third inning, dodging trees and park benches. I worked my way over to Spalding balls sailing through the air, over the fence, and into the back of the park, center field.

Huge leaves hid balls sailing toward me but slowed them down. That allowed me a few seconds more to catch them. The best hitter on their team came up and whacked the ball high in the air, sailing it well into center field. I danced around benches and trees checking out the ball's flight and then stood calmly where I knew it would land. I cupped my hands to catch it. Suddenly, I heard Pepi's voice.

"Hey, Joey! When you're done with your game, I wanna see you! You hear me?"

I turned to him, briefly taking my eye off the ball. I looked back at the ball and saw it bounce off a branch. I cupped my hands and waited for it to land gently into them. Instead, it bounced in and out and to the ground. I listened to the thumping of my heartbeat. I picked up the ball and threw it to second base. It was too late. The runner had made it to second.

I turned to Pepi. He looked sharp in a white short-sleeved shirt and pressed dark slacks. He looked at me seriously.

"Too bad, kid," he said. "Make sure you come see me right after the game." He slowly walked away.

We lost the game, but it didn't matter to me. I noticed Maria was no longer sitting on the bench, and I figured she most likely went home. I had to see her to get Pepi's money.

I was nervous seeing Pepi because I felt a little threatened, even though I knew Maria had the money in those socks, safe and sound.

I didn't have time to waste.

I ran to Mott Street. She was standing in front of her building with Jimmy, a kid from her block. She was talking to him and smiling. He was leaning too close to her. I got really angry. I walked quickly over to Maria and, ignoring Jimmy, asked her what she thought she was doing. Jimmy took a step and worked his way between me and Maria, pushing me back a little.

"None of your business," Jimmy said.

He was bigger than I was by a few inches. I went crazy. I pushed him hard. He fell backward, banging his head with a thud on the sidewalk. He got up and came after me, and we started throwing punches. Maria was screaming at us to stop.

I landed a solid punch on the side of Jimmy's head, and he fell backward again. He sat there on the sidewalk, sitting with his hands down flat and shaking his head. I stood over him with my fists still clenched but bleeding from my lip. He didn't look so big lying there on the ground. Maria was upset.

"Are you crazy?" she shouted. "We were just talking!" She pushed me back and then helped Jimmy get up. "Now stop, both of you. Just stop!"

I felt my lip. Blood was running down into my mouth. Maria came over and dabbed it with her handkerchief.

"Jimmy, go home and get cleaned up. Look at your shirt! It's filthy, and one of the buttons is ripped off. Your mother is gonna kill you if she sees you like that. Just get home!"

He looked at me as if he were ready to kill me, but he just stood there and rubbed his head and then walked away. Maria glared at me and pulled at my sleeve. I don't know what got over me.

"C'mon, let's go upstairs, you jerk! I have the money under the bed."

We walked up to her tenement. Her mother was in the kitchen stirring a pot of red sauce. I could smell the garlic and tomatoes. She turned to look at us for a moment and then went back to her sauce. I said my hello and followed Maria to her bedroom. *That woman,* I thought, *is really disturbed.*

Maria pulled out the money from under her bed. We sat down.

She leaned over to see if her mother was still in the kitchen and then began to count it. As she counted, her hair dangled in front of her face, bobbing her head while she counted.

"Yeah!" she said when she finished. "It is exactly $101. Man, you must have picked up a lot of numbers."

I smiled. "Scappy had a lot of people betting numbers. I still have their numbers in my head."

Maria took a brown bag and placed the socks into the bag. She sighed and dropped back down on her bed. I could not resist. I reached down and kissed her full on the lips. It was a full, wet kiss. She wrapped her arms around me and pulled me down to her. Sweet mother of Jesus! I took a deep breath and came up for air, sweating.

She stared at me, turned around toward the kitchen, and whispered in my ear, "We have to stop! My mother is in there, remember, genius?"

I leaned over and kissed her on the cheek. She went to the kitchen to see if her mother was listening and then came back. We started stuffing the money in the bag. With a rope at the neck of it, I tightened it. We got up and went downstairs. In the hallway, I gave her a gentle soft kiss and stood there for a moment looking at her wet, dark eyes, relieved that I had the money and that she was not angry with me anymore.

"Thanks," I said softly. "I'll see ya later." I pulled her closer to me gently and hugged her for a little while. It really felt good. I could feel her heart pounding against my chest. I let her go, leaving her there next to her building, watching me as I headed back to Pepi.

I walked quickly down the street toward Houston. I crossed Second Avenue and turned onto First Street. I held the bag tight to my body.

I looked back and thought I saw Tom Mansfield. What would he have thought if he knew I was carrying Pepi's money? Hell, what would my parents have done to me if they had found out? All these thoughts began to swirl in my head. I started to feel guilty.

I wondered if Johnny was still at the Ninth Precinct. It was my fault because I listened to him. I should have been telling him to listen to me. I had to start thinking what to do next as soon as I returned Pepi's money. As I rushed to the social club, I worried more about him. It drove me a little crazy knowing he was still there. What was going to happen to him?

I walked into the social club, still thinking about Johnny. I saw Pepi and put the bag on the table where he was sitting with his bodyguards.

He took the bag, lifted it, and looked at me. "What's the matter, kid?" he asked.

He didn't seem too concerned about Johnny. I was surprised. I shrugged and rattled off to Scappy the names and numbers of the people who gave me the money.

After Scappy finished counting the money, he smiled. Pepi placed the money into a small, brown leather bag and zippered it up. I turned to look at the corner where the man I saw earlier sat. He was not there. Pepi took a sip of his espresso and smiled at me. His pals also smiled.

"I never doubted you, kid," he said, and then he took out of his pocket a large roll of bills, flipped it open, and neatly peeled off a five-dollar bill. He handed me the money. "Take it. You deserve it. Go ahead. You'd better go. I heard your mother was looking for you."

I put the bill in my pocket. "What about Johnny?" I asked. "Are you going to be able to help him out?"

Pepi was silent. He poured more anisette into his espresso. "I don't know, Joey. He had money and the numbers on him. How do I beat that evidence? You tell me. I have connections, but I don't think I can do anything for him."

He sipped the espresso. My heart sank.

8
Reform School

It would be reform school for Johnny. I turned and walked out the door without looking back. When I got outside, I took a deep breath. Pepi must have helped me get out of the precinct house. How else did he know I had gotten out? He must have connections with the cops, no doubt about that, but for Johnny, even Pepi was helpless.

I walked across the street to my stoop and sat down. I was relieved I no longer had the money, but I was depressed over Johnny. What could I do? I felt alone for the first time in a long time. Johnny was right about that. He was like a brother to me.

I decided to play handball.

Tommy was not at the courts, so I volleyed on my own, slamming the black ball against the wall until my hands inside my gloves swelled. I kept on volleying, building up a sweat, thinking that it was not true that Johnny was in jail. I was drenched in sweat and exhausted. I finished and slowly walked home.

The sun was setting. My mother took out veal cutlets she had stored in the icebox and heated them up while I went over to the kitchen sink and stuck my head under cold water.

"Joey, how did you get so sweaty? Look at you! Go in the bathroom and clean up the right way and sit down. I have corn to go with the veal cutlets. After you eat, you should do your homework."

"Ma, you know it's Saturday. No school on Saturday!"

I was exhausted. I ate. I went into my room and put my head down on the pillow, still thinking about Johnny. Was he still in the precinct house? Maybe they had let him go. I closed my eyes and fell asleep.

When I awoke, darkness had fallen. I was tempted to run over to his building to see if he was home, but I thought it would be better to stay away. If the cops had let him go, I would see him tomorrow or maybe on Monday at school. My father was already at the table eating. After he ate, he cut a juicy peach into his wine and drank.

Later, I leaned out the window in the living room facing First Street. Across the way, people were also looking out their windows, some of them sitting on their fire escapes with sweaters over their hunched shoulders. A cool breeze was blowing in from the East River. Usually Johnny came out about this time, but this night, he didn't. I was alone. I was not used to being alone. I felt terrible. I thought of going to see Harold, but it was Saturday, and he spent time with his father, who honored the Jewish Sabbath on Saturdays.

I did not see Johnny on Sunday, and he did not come to school Monday morning. I was really depressed and worried about him. Harold came to me in homeroom and patted me on the back. The whole neighborhood had found out that Johnny was picked up.

Maria and I went to the park after school. We sat on the same park bench where I had dropped the money into her lap. It seemed so long ago. We talked about Johnny not being around. She thought he might go away for a while.

"I really don't want to talk about it," I said. I fell silent.

She leaned over and kissed me. "Everything will be okay," she said. "Stop worrying."

I began to worry also that Tom had found out about Johnny's arrest and had agreed with his wife to take me off the scholarship list. I realized I may have lost an opportunity.

The following week, I found out at school that Johnny was going to reform school. I never saw him before he left.

Johnny had never been away. I thought of him every day. It killed me to know that he was gone. Could I have done something about it? Worse, I could have been up there with him. I kept wondering why that detective let me go. What was that all about? Did he see that I was just an innocent kid who had gotten himself into trouble, or was it Pepi who got me out? Basically, I figured that maybe not all cops were bad, and some were just doing their job—and a terrible job it was, putting their lives in danger every single day they went to work.

I made up my mind I would never become a gangster. Never! That detective must not have wanted me to become a gangster either, so he let me go. That is what I thought. Reform school had a way of making gangsters out of kids. I knew it could happen to Johnny. I was determined it would not happen to me.

It was Saturday night, and I had just finished dinner. Johnny was gone. Harold was with his father, and Maria told me her mother was sick. I was alone. After I ate, I decided to run down to the East River and hang out near the Brooklyn Bridge where we went swimming on hot summer days. The long walk kept me busy. I went to the pier where the jump in from the iron bars against the dock was about ten feet. It was getting dark. Lights were already lit on the Brooklyn side.

I stared at the East River flowing swiftly downstream and heading out toward New York Harbor. Under the bridge, it seemed to move faster. The wind blew strongly. There were very few lights on the Brooklyn shore, but I could see the huge Domino Sugar sign lit up. I stood there and peeled off my shirt. Then I unbuckled my belt and dropped my pants. I knew it was a stupid thing to do, because I was alone and the water was freezing, but I had to do it. From the railing, I jumped in with just my shorts on.

I felt the rush of cold, dark water shiver my body. Kicking

hard, I lifted myself to the surface and swam to the pier columns that had iron rungs hammered into them. I climbed back onto the dock, shaking. That was the idea—suffer physical pain and forget—but no amount of cold water could make me forget that Johnny was gone.

I stood up, still shivering. I jumped back in. After three jumps, with my shirt, I dried myself off as best I could and got dressed. Still soaking wet, I stood there watching flat barge boats go by. A few minutes later, more boats cruised by slowly, their engines humming softly in the calm water. I had never felt so alone. I heard a foghorn in the distance. It was growing dark, and when no horn blew, there was a stillness in the air. Even though it was a clear night, the horn blew over and over again. I felt good hearing that horn. Somebody was keeping watch out there, and that thought calmed me down.

Later, when I got home, my parents were waiting for me. I rushed into my room before they saw me drenched to the skin.

I began to take off my wet clothes, but before I could, my mother came in and screamed, "My God, Joey, you are soaked! How did you get so wet? Is it raining?" I told her I went swimming in the East River.

She took me into the kitchen and looked out the window while she pulled my shirt off. Then she reached for my buckle, but I jumped back. My father laughed. My mother came over and dried me down with a soft towel. I went into my room and put on a clean, blue cotton polo shirt and went back into the kitchen. My mother had made me a hot cocoa drink.

"So he went swimming in the river. Big deal!" my father said. "Leave him alone." He saw that I was down. "Come here, Joey. Come over here."

I went over to him, and he opened his huge arms and gave me a bear hug. I started to cry.

"Johnny went away, Pa." I cried with no shame.

My father patted me on the back.

"I'm afraid for him. Who knows what's gonna happen to him up there?"

"He'll be all right. It's just a month. What could happen to him? Joey, sit down and have the cocoa. You'll feel better." If my pop knew, the whole neighborhood must already have known about Johnny.

I began to warm up, and that made me feel better. I calmed down. My mother put some Italian cookies on the table. I grabbed a couple of reginas and dipped them in the cocoa.

Another week had passed since Johnny had gone away. It was Friday afternoon. I was coming out of the front park after playing some handball with Tommy. As I walked home, I saw a tall man coming out of the social club where Pepi hung out. A black car pulled up in front of the club, and as he took his hat off to get in, he saw me standing there and smiled. It was the detective who let me go and sent me home!

He leaned down and talked to the driver and then walked across the street to me. He was well dressed in a dark-blue suit.

"How are you, kid?" He smiled and put his hand on my shoulder gently.

"I'm okay," I said. "I'm waiting for Johnny to come home."

He nodded. "Yeah, too bad about your friend Johnny. We had too much evidence against him. There was nothing I could do. But we had nothing on you, and that really helped me get you off. But it didn't hurt, either, to get that phone call from your other friend—the big guy in there in the club, Pepi!"

I was shocked. "No. That can't be!" I said. "He told me he had nothing to do with getting me out!"

The detective smiled. "Oh, well, that's Pepi. He likes to play with words. He didn't directly get you off; *I* did that. He was the one who called to ask me to get you both off, but I could only take care of you. We had too much on your friend Johnny. Pepi and I go back a long time. We played stickball together, right in that back park where my cops picked you up, just like you play stickball with Johnny. That's how far we go back. We just went different ways. That's all.

"When he called me, I thought about what he was asking me to do. I don't want to see you kids get into trouble, and I talked to Pepi blue in the face about that, but sometimes he just won't listen. He figures he has me to get you kids out of trouble. When you kids got caught, Pepi had a change of heart.

"Pepi doesn't want his cousin to become a hoodlum either. He knows the risks. It is not a good life. Trust me on that one. Reform school for a month would teach Johnny a lesson and keep him out of the mob. That's what Pepi was thinking. At least for now he is thinking that way; but who knows? Pepi is Pepi. Who can tell what he will be thinking tomorrow."

He turned and walked back to his car and drove off. I walked over to my building and sat down on the stoop. I sat there a while digesting what he had told me. Pepi was the big surprise to me. He was sometimes very good and sometimes very, very bad. That was his way.

I spent time playing handball and stickball while Johnny was away. I worked hard at school and thought more often about the scholarship, but it was just different without Johnny. I figured it would never be the same again the way it was. I was on my own. That made a giant difference to me. I relied on him and found out soon enough the hard way how much I did.

9

Street Cats

I was sweaty and tired. From the fountain in the park after a game with Tommy, I drank gulps of water. I walked slowly out of the park, still thinking about Johnny. He had been gone a couple of weeks. I had to admit I felt tougher with him around, and when I was on my own, I didn't feel so much like that. I was very upset. I had not heard from Tom, either, about the scholarship. The idea was beginning to become more remote to me. Nothing like losing before winning.

I turned and waved to Tommy, but he did not see me. His multi-colored bandanna was drenched in sweat. I watched him crouch low and slam the black ball against the wall, as low to the base of the wall as it could possibly go without touching the ground. Nobody could return that one. It was an ace. He moved like a cat, determined to be the best, and he worked at it. I was determined to move that fast. It was a cool but sunny spring afternoon, but I was still hot.

As I walked home, I saw that the card game in front of the social club had stopped. The old men were out of their chairs.

They were standing there straining their necks and looking up. Cards and money were on the table. I saw kids also on the other side of the street looking up, their arms folded against their chests. There was no one standing on my side of the street. I couldn't see anything from where I stood, so I walked over to the other side and looked up also.

There was a boy up on the roof of 41 holding something in his hands that squirmed and twisted hard to get free. The boy had a wild crop of black hair, which hung all over his face. I looked closer. I could see he was holding a cat by the neck. Its tail was twisting and turning fiercely. Its body turned violently in the boy's hands, struggling to break free from his strong grip on its neck, but it was no use. The boy held the cat by the neck so tightly I thought the animal would choke to death. He grabbed the tail of the cat. I heard a frightening scream from the animal, and it squirmed to free itself. It was then the boy opened his wide mouth and let out a horrible, guttural sound.

A boy next to me pointed at him and shouted, "That's crazy Freddie! He has a cat in his hands, and he's gonna throw it off the roof!"

I saw Freddie swing his arm and throw the cat out into midair and off the roof. My heart began to pound hard. I was terrified for the cat. Freddie jumped up and down and screamed in delight, swinging his arms like a crazed monkey. I fixed my eyes on the falling cat. It twisted out of control as it flew down to the sidewalk. It tried to right itself before it ran out of falling space, but it fell too fast. I heard a soft thud as the cat landed not twenty feet away. I saw it writhing on the sidewalk. It made a whimpering, painful sound and began to kick its legs to get up, but it could not.

I ran over to the cat and knelt down. I put out my hands to hold it, but I was not sure what to do. It looked at me. Its legs kept on kicking while its body jerked to the kicking of its legs. I could hear Freddie up on the roof laughing. A crowd of kids had gathered quietly to stare at the cat, while its body kept on shaking in fits and starts.

Harold came over and put his hand on my shoulder. "Joey, we can't just let him die here. We have to try to save it! Pick it up!"

I was nervous. I slowly placed my hands under its body, but I could not figure out how to pick it up without hurting it. Harold threw his jacket down in front of me and spread it out on the sidewalk. I slid my hands under the cat, lifted it slowly, and placed it gently on the jacket, but the cat still let out a scream. I looked at Harold.

"Now what?" I asked.

Harold stood up and pointed toward First Avenue.

"We can take him to the drugstore on the corner to the pharmacist. He'll know what to do. Maybe we can save him!"

The thought of picking up the cat sent a chill through me. Harold and I lifted it slowly, but it let out another scream. I wrapped the jacket over it and stood up with it cradled in my arms. I felt the cat's chest heave up and down against my own heart beating hard. I could see its ribs just beneath its skin. I tried to hold its head steady, but the cat's body kept jerking back and forth in my arms. Its green eyes were glazed and watery. I was very upset.

"We have to get him to a doctor now! The cat is gonna die if we don't."

Harold walked beside me, his hand under the cat as I held him against my chest. The other kids followed. As we approached the drugstore, the cat grew still. The kids stayed outside, and Harold and I walked in with the cat.

The druggist, Mr. Johnson, stood behind the counter. As I walked slowly to him, he looked at me and then the cat.

"What have you here?" he asked.

"It's a cat. Freddie threw him off the roof," I said. "I think it's still alive. Can you take care of him?"

Mr. Johnson came out from behind the counter. His white smock matched a thick shock of white hair combed neatly back. With soft blue eyes peering just above his glasses, he looked first at the cat and then at me. He took a white cloth and placed it on the counter and then gently lifted the cat from my arms. It did not scream this time. There was no blood coming from the cat. It lay still on the white cloth. Its eyes were open.

The druggist placed his hand on the cat's chest and listened. He began to stroke the cat's head. The cat did not move. Then, as if by magic, its torso, paws, and legs slowly began to stretch out, and after that, it ceased to move.

Mr. Johnson kept on petting the cat. "I'm afraid he's dead. He's gone, son, gone."

I stood there and stared at the cat, hoping he would move to show he was still alive, but there was no motion. I moved closer to the counter and saw the eyes of the cat staring out vacantly. I placed my hand on the cat's back and wondered why there was no blood. I cried. It just came out of me. He came over and patted me on the back.

"Sorry, son. I'll take care of him," he said. "You go on home."

"He didn't have to throw him off the roof, Mr. Johnson! He didn't have to kill him!"

Mr. Johnson handed me a tissue. I wiped my eyes. I didn't want to look at Harold. My body heaved until I finally calmed down. I dried my eyes and looked at the cat one last time.

Harold and I walked out of the drugstore. The other kids were waiting for us outside.

"He's dead," I said. "The cat is dead."

We began to walk home.

Suddenly, I saw Freddie coming toward me. He looked like a wild man. He was much bigger than I was. His black hair flopped all over. His nose bent slightly to the right. There were spaces between his front teeth, and his black eyes glinted angrily. He pushed me against a parked car, grabbed me by the shirt, and pinned me against its hood. He was so strong. I could not move.

"Where's my cat? He's my cat! I saw you take him off the sidewalk. Where is he, you little bastard?"

I felt Freddie's huge hands lift me up like a doll. He slammed me against the hood again and held me down by my shirt collar. Harold ran over and grabbed Freddie by the neck, but Freddie just laughed and pushed him with one hand.

"You stay out of this!" he growled. "It's between me and him."

I thought he was going to beat the hell out of me. He had his fist pressed against my chin.

"He's in the pharmacy. He's dead," I said. "And you killed him."

Freddie gritted his teeth and smiled. "Good. They're nuthin' but filthy little animals, and they deserve to die! I'm glad I killed him. And you! Don't ever touch one of my cats again, dead or alive. You understand? Because, if I have to, I'll throw you off the roof. I will!"

He pulled me away from the car, threw me to the ground, and kicked me. Harold jumped on his back, but Freddie just stood straight up and elbowed him in his rib cage, sending Harold to the sidewalk. He gave me another kick and stood over me with fists clenched, blocking the sun with his body, and yelled, "Stay away from my cats!" He turned and headed toward First Avenue and disappeared.

I got up, took my handkerchief and pressed it against a cut over my eye.

"Are you okay?" Harold asked.

I dabbed the cut a few times. "I'll live. I cut it on the sidewalk. That crazy bastard! He is nuts!"

We headed home. Harold went inside his building. I climbed the three flights up to our tenement, feeling a little woozy. I held on to the banister and was glad I had made it all the way. I opened the door, threw off my jacket, and went right to the bathroom.

My father shouted at me from the kitchen table, "So what happened to you? How did your jacket get so dirty?"

I finished washing. I could see in the mirror that the cut had stopped bleeding. I sat down at the table.

My mother looked at me and sighed, crossing herself. "O Jesu Cristo! Joey, another fight?"

I tried to ignore her, but it was no use. My father stopped eating, and my mother sat down next to me and lifted my head to look at the cut over my eye. She went for the iodine and poured it over my cut before placing a large bandage over it. It burned.

"All right, now tell us what happened," she said.

I had no chance to take a bite of my roast beef sandwich.

"Okay, I will tell you. It's that new kid on the block, Freddie Foulduty. He lives with his mother and his stepfather across from First Street Park. He's crazy. He lights fires in the park, empties garbage cans in the street, and he's always pushing kids around at school until they give him money. This afternoon, the whole block saw him throw a street cat off the roof of 41. Harold and I took the cat to the druggist, but the cat died. Freddie went after me and beat me up because I carried the cat over there. The cat was in my arms when he died in the drugstore."

My mother sighed.

My father shook his head and emptied a glass of red wine in front of him. He slammed down his glass when he finished.

"You stay away from him," my mother warned. "I don't want you to fight with him. You hear me? When you see him, go to the other side of the street!" My mother began to rub my back. "My Joey," she said.

"Oh, I see," my father replied. "You want your son to grow up a baby, a coward, someone who runs away from trouble."

Another argument was coming. My mother glared at him but didn't reply. Instead, she put her hand on my shoulder protectively and looked straight at me.

"Joey, listen to me. I want you to stay away from him. He can hurt you. Besides, any boy who throws a cat off a roof must be crazy! I don't want you to fight a crazy boy who has such anger in him. Look at you! Your ribs are sticking out of your chest! You are still growing. Someday, when you are big enough, then you can fight him, but not now."

My father kept insisting to my mother I must fight him no matter how big he was. I wasn't thinking of Freddie but of the dead cat. I thought of funerals I had been to. Most who had died were old and in coffins. This cat I picked up off the street was alive, and a few minutes later, it was dead. Never had death come so close to me. I was worried about Freddie. My parents were still arguing when I went to the window.

I looked out over First Street. In the west, I could not see the sun behind five-story buildings on Second Avenue, but I could see its last, peaceful rays stream down on the block and to the street. I looked down and paid attention for the first time to the cats scooting back and forth from under one car to another. They were all over the street.

On the sidewalk, I watched as a black cat darted under a car and then raced across the street. I saw it turn and look around carefully. It began to lick its paw. I saw a black-and-white cat lapping water from an open spout of the fire hydrant, also lifting his head high, turning its neck back and forth to be sure he was safe.

Their lives were hard, I thought, living in the street under cars, catching mice, and eating food from garbage pails, but they would never be hungry in this neighborhood; they were lucky that way. But now the cats had Freddie to deal with, and that was not good. I began to worry about them.

I sensed motion across the street and turned my attention to the first cat, now joined by another. This second cat brushed against the first. She rubbed against her again and again until they sat together just behind a car, watching people walking back and forth on the sidewalk. I never liked being alone, either, and so it was good that the cats were together on this cool night.

I went to bed thinking about the danger the cats were in with Freddie. Did they sense the danger? Animals had stronger instincts than human beings, and they were probably very aware that Freddie was a killer. Who knew what he would do if he got his hands on one of them? I pulled the blanket up to my chin and closed my eyes. In the darkness, I shivered. I thought of Johnny. I wished he were here and not in reform school.

And the cats? Freddie could be throwing a cat off a roof right now! Sometimes the dark stirred monsters from the movies in my mind. Freddie reminded me of Frankenstein, once dead and now alive, out of control and ready to do violence on anyone who confronted him. I wished that Johnny were home.

The first time I saw a Frankenstein monster in a movie theater, I was terrified. It was only a movie, but it scared the hell out of me.

I had never seen a monster film. I was just five. Frankenstein was very real to me. I shivered when I saw heavy rains falling at night on the gray hilltop castle, lightning flashing and thunder booming through high ceiling windows. Terrifying music signaled the approach of the monster stalking his creator.

As he approached I stared at his dull, dead eyes, eyes of the living dead. I listened to his growling when he saw Dr. Frankenstein. I shut my eyes, shaking with fear. I buried my eyes in my thin, scrawny arms, unable to look up at the screen. These fears rarely held me, but now I pulled up the covers and tried not to listen to the strange sounds in the hallway. Was it Freddie or the monster I heard? I asked God to let me sleep and wake quickly to the bright light of the morning sun. I calmed down quickly, knowing that the monster was not real, not at all.

It happened just like that. Before I knew it, the sun's bright rays came through the window. I got out of bed with a smile, happy to be awake. I got dressed, grabbed a buttered roll, drank a tall cup of hot chocolate, and went off to school. The bell rang for homeroom to be over.

I skipped down the steps with other students. Harold was just in front of me. Suddenly, a hand from behind pushed me forward, and I tumbled down the steps. I tried to roll, but my body hit the edge of every step down to the landing. My books and notepads were scattered on the steps, and there was Freddie coming at me.

Along the way, he stepped on every one of my books. He stood over me with his fist clenched. The rest of the class went rushing past, avoiding Freddie. His wild mane hung over his ears as he growled at them going by.

"Sucker! That'll teach ya to get in my way when I'm killing my cats."

He snarled, lifted me up, and punched me in the jaw. I fell back against the wall. I was dazed by the punch, and for a few seconds, I had to lean against the wall just to stay up. I felt blood on my lip. He grabbed my shirt and leaned closer to me. I could smell his bad breath and see how yellow his teeth were. I turned away from his face.

"You look at me when I talk to you, you little shit. If you ever try that crap again, I'll come at you with my knife and kill ya! I will."

Students just went by avoiding us. He ignored them and punched me again, this time in the stomach. Before I knew it, he took off down the hall and out of sight. Harold came running back to me. I felt my lip. It was bleeding, all right.

"This kid is one crazy kid! Joey, what are you going to do about him?"

I took out my handkerchief and held it to my lip. "I don't know what I'm going to do. He's so damn big, and he's crazy! He just snuck up on me, and before I knew it, he punched me, and I went flying down the steps. Even if I could, I didn't have a chance to fight back!"

"Oh no, Joey," Harold said, "you don't want to fight Freddie. He'll beat the living daylights out of you. And I heard he carries a knife in his back pocket."

"I wish Johnny were home. He would think nothing of taking a stickball bat and whacking Freddie in the head. I know you would never do that. How am I going to explain my fat lip to my parents?"

I could not explain it except to tell them it was Freddie again.

And that was the beginning. I tried to avoid him, but it was no use. Freddie would sneak up on me and start punching me. There was no escape from him. If I left school without Harold, he would attack me. To avoid him, I walked down Avenue A, where the Puerto Ricans lived. Even though Italians hated them, my fear of their beating me up was nothing compared to my fear of Freddie. He would attack me whenever he could. What could I do?

Walking home from school and thinking myself safe, I felt a thud in the back of my head. I turned and saw an open tin can on the ground. There was Freddie laughing. I felt the back of my head and saw blood on my fingers. I went home holding my handkerchief to my head and feeling dizzy.

When I sat down at the table, my mother screamed. My father knew right away.

"It's nothing, Ma," I said.

She ignored me, took me by the arm, led me to the sink, and pushed my head under cold water.

"I banged my head on the concrete playing handball. My head feels better already."

My father pressed a cold towel on my head. "Joey, this boy Freddie is big trouble for you," he said. "I am getting very angry. If you know where he lives, I will pay a visit to his father."

My mother glared at me. "Joey, you stay away from him. You hear?"

My parents exchanged angry looks. My father mumbled under his breath.

"Speak up if you have something to say!" my mother barked. "He's my boy also, you know! You want to find him on the street someday with a knife in his chest? Is that what you want?"

My father slammed down his wineglass. "I want my son to grow up like a man, not a mouse! In his life, he will meet a Freddie everywhere and every day! You know that! Now let's eat. Joey, eat. Nothing should interfere with our supper!"

The table was silent. I thought about what my father said. He made sense as I sat there in the safety of the house, but fighting back was a lot tougher when I saw how huge and vicious Freddie was. I finished eating and went to the window overlooking First Street.

I saw Pepi come out of the club and light a cigarette. He stood there calmly looking out at the street. I thought he might be able to help me with Freddie, and so I went downstairs and approached him. I told him my problem. He stood there looking at me, nodding once or twice as I spoke. Then he told me to go inside the club with him.

"Look, Joey," Pepi said. "This is a problem I cannot help you with. This problem is your problem. We all have our fighting to do. And trust me, you will deal with this situation. This boy Freddie is very bad, no doubt about it, but he's only a kid, like you, and after you get up the guts to challenge him—and you will—win or lose, you will come out in the end a winner!"

I walked to the park and played handball with Tommy. It was good to play him. I was able to focus on the game and not on Freddie. It gave my mind a rest. I was relieved. It was easy for Pepi to say not to worry about Freddie, but I still worried. I was so tired thinking of Freddie that I just wanted to forget him.

I went home and jumped into bed, exhausted. I closed my eyes and tried not to think of Freddie. I struggled. What to do with him? How could I fight him? He could knife me!

The next day, I went over to see Tom and Sue. It was Sue who sat there ready to review grammar. We went over verbs, adjectives, and pronouns. I worked hard. Sue was pleased. She never spoke about Pepi.

After her class, I went down to take a shower and then jumped into the pool and relaxed. I came out of the pool and sat there at its edge looking down at myself. I noticed my shoulders were large and strong.

Tom had just finished a swimming class. He came over and told me he had heard about Freddie bullying me. He knelt next to me.

"This boy is a challenge for you, Joey," he said, "but it won't be much different from any other challenge you're going to face if you get that scholarship. There will be new students and teachers and a different environment. You're going to have to get used to that, and that's going to take courage."

It seemed a long time that I had even thought about the scholarship.

"And you escaped Peter Capra. He doesn't know anything about you being involved with Johnny. Keep your nose clean," he warned.

Harold and I walked home, hardly talking to each other. He put his arm around my shoulder and without saying a word made me feel better. I was so angry I thought that if Freddie were there, I would have enough courage to fight him, but he wasn't there.

I left Harold at his building. He told me if he needed me to call him right away. I said I would. Cats darted back and forth across the street. Some sat quietly under cars, alert to danger. I turned to see if Freddie was around, ready to grab one of them. I wasn't sure what I would do if he had, but I was so angry I didn't think this time I would turn away.

When I came closer to my building, I was surprised to see a black-and-white cat sitting there at the top of my stoop. I walked to the foot of the stoop, moving slowly so not to frighten it, but as I stood there, the cat just looked down at me and purred.

I climbed the steps slowly, and as I did, the cat stood up and began to swish its tail. Its ears perked up, and it lifted its front right paw. I was amazed that it was so friendly and sensed no danger. I reached down and petted him gently, stroking the smooth, short hair of its back, which curved like a bow in response to my petting.

I had never petted any of the street cats. It was strange to me, but I felt good about it. Why did the cat suddenly become so friendly? We sat there at the top of the stoop, watching the action on the street. After a few minutes, it stepped down the stoop, turned to look up at me, and walked slowly away, disappearing under a car to safety.

Down the block, tired Italians were coming home from work, their construction boots covered in dust. Women with scarves around their heads carried brown bags with groceries. Their children tagged behind. I decided to get a Coke at the grocery store.

Just then in front of 41, a brown paper bag fell from above and hit the sidewalk softly. I looked up. It was the old widow Tscacalusa at her fifth-floor window, smiling down at me. She motioned me to go across the street. From the street, I could see she was smiling that toothless smile of hers. Over her head, she wore her black scarf.

"Milk!" she cried.

I picked up the bag.

Johnny's uncle, his white, stained apron still wrapped around his large frame, leaned over a broom in front of his grocery store. He saw the bag drop. He placed his broom against the front window of his store and went inside. I ran across the street and followed him in. Her bottle of milk was already on the counter. I opened the bag and from it pulled out a dollar bill. He gave me change, and I went up to her tenement.

When I was younger, I was terrified of her. She stood there now in darkness except for the light of dimly lit candles. At that time, I thought she might have been a witch. Now, beneath her shroud, her small, dark eyes smiled at me. When I first saw her, she grabbed my hand and held it tightly. I thought then she was going to kill me and make human stew out of me. These thoughts I had when I was seven, taking milk to her for the first time, but now, I thought only about helping her.

The wind was cool as twilight approached, and I shivered crossing the street. I knocked on the door. In her gravelly voice, she called me to come inside. On the table in her dark, musty room, candles flickered. I walked in, placed the cold milk bottle on her kitchen table, and tied her shoelaces. She got up and hobbled to the table and put the milk away. She was weak and frail.

Her black dress hung down to her ankles, and her black shawl was still wrapped around her humped shoulders. She reached out and grabbed my hand and smiled. I put the change in her shaking hands. "Ah, Joey, you are growing so big!" she said. "I remember you, your mother's little baby."

I looked at the shadows on the wall cast by the candles. She picked up her purse and struggled to open it. I turned to the door to go.

"Don't leave yet," she said.

She reached down to the bottom of the purse, and while she did, she looked up at me and grinned. I stared at her wrinkled face and her long, crooked fingers rummaging through the debris in her black purse. Then she smiled and pulled out, as I expected, a dime.

"Oh yes!" she said. She had found another and gave it to me.

She took my hand as always and turned it palm up, placed the dime there, and squeezed it closed. Then she turned to the wall behind her where her shadow and mine danced from the flames of the candles.

"See, up there, Joey. It is only your shadow and mine. You are no longer afraid of them. You used to be. They are just shadows. I carried you in my arms when you were a baby and held you as if you were my own. It hurt me to think that, years later, you were afraid of me. You don't remember that. You are not afraid of me now. I can see that. You have grown up. Yes, you have. I can see you care about me now. Go, Joey; your mother is waiting for you to eat. And don't be afraid of anything!"

She closed the door behind me gently. I stood there for a moment at the landing, listening to her shuffle back to the window, wondering how she knew my heart so well, my fear of her now barely a faint memory. She made me think. I flew down the steps and back home where food was already on the table. My father emptied his glass of wine and turned to me. He picked up his empty gallon jug as if he were thinking of a serious subject.

10

The Cat on the Fence

"Good. You are here, Joey. Take this bottle and fill it in the cellar from the first barrel of wine. Hurry, before you have trouble finding the string for the light hanging there. Take this flashlight!"

The last thing I wanted to do was go down into the cellar.

My father gave me the empty gallon bottle and the flashlight. The pale, amber sky I had seen at Tscacalusa's had already faded. The sun lay buried beneath the horizon. It would be dark in the cellar. I went downstairs to the backyard. My father's fig and peach trees were black shadows of themselves. I opened the cellar door and started down the steps into the darkness. I pressed the flashlight switch, but it did not go on.

I shook it, but the light flickered on and off. I heard the wind behind me whistle through dark, shaking leaves. I kept shaking the flashlight to keep it on so I could find the string in the ceiling. I heard mice and rats scurrying on the cement floor just in front of me. I wanted to get to that string. It didn't bother me to go down there before, when I had hid Pepi's gun, but it did now.

Was it possible Freddie had followed me home and was now in the backyard waiting for me to climb out of the cellar? The flashlight turned on. I moved the light left and right and found the string and turned on the light.

I kept walking deeper into the cellar, shuddering. I turned to make certain the cellar doors were still open. I saw mice racing back and forth on the cement floor. Some climbed the walls and disappeared through thin cracks. My mouth grew dry from the dust in the air.

As I walked deeper into the cellar, I began to panic. The flashlight started to flicker on and off. I had to calm myself down. I took a deep breath.

To the right, I could see the wine stalls. Inside were the wine barrels. I quickly opened the door of the first stall, pulled out my father's empty gallon bottle, and opened the spigot. The dark red wine sputtered at first and then poured out in a slow flow. I watched its progress with anxiety. As I crouched in the stall, holding the bottle in one hand and the spigot in the other, it seemed it took forever to fill. A sound behind me caused me to turn. I saw nothing but darkness. Droplets of sweat poured over my forehead. As the bottle finally filled to overflow, I wondered how I could ever overcome my fear of the cellar.

The flashlight I held under my arm finally stayed on, lighting the grimy foundation wall behind the wine barrels and revealing to me odd-shaped shadows I imagined to be strange, unknown beasts large enough to grab me and tear me to pieces. Or perhaps coming in from the darkness behind me was Frankenstein!

I placed the cork in the bottle, slammed shut the stall door, and pulled the ceiling string, turning off the light. I fled to the safety of the backyard, slamming down with great relief the wooden doors of the wine cellar and enclosing for a time the imaginary monsters I had feared would get me had I stayed in the cellar one more minute. I hurried up the steps with great relief, gave the gallon jug to my father, finished my pasta, and wolfed down the chicken. I slumped back in my chair thinking of Freddie.

"That was good, Mom," I said. "I'm full now."

My father glared at me. "So if your belly is full, why do you look so sad?"

I was quiet. I wiped my mouth clean.

"It's that boy, Freddie? He is still giving you a lot of trouble. Am I right?"

I put my head down. I didn't want to talk about it, but my father *kept* going.

"Well, I'm waiting to hear what he has done to you."

My mother stared angrily at my father. She got up and put her hands on her hips. "Go ahead, Joey, tell him what Freddie has done to you."

"I know already. He beats you up for trying to save the cat, he pushes you down the steps at school, and then he throws a can at you and cuts your head open! Well, isn't it time to face him? You cannot get away from him, and so you have to deal with him!"

"But, Pa, he's bigger than I am and stronger, and he carries a knife in his back pocket!"

My father nodded thoughtfully. My mother took the steaming little pot filled with espresso and filled his cup. She took sambuca and poured just a bit into the cup, adding a small slice of lemon. He stirred the coffee slowly and then sipped it. He nodded.

"Joey is right, Sal. He could hurt our boy who is not that big."

"Yes, yes. I know he is dangerous, and, yes, he may even carry a knife. You don't think I had to deal with knives and bullies in my life? You are a young boy, soon to be thirteen. When you get to be a grown man, do you think it will be any different? These boys, if they are not stopped, will become more violent, and when they become men, they will do more terrible things than beating up younger boys smaller than they are. No, Joey, you must deal with this boy now! I know it will be difficult, but there is no choice for you, unless you want to grow up always being afraid of cruel boys who later become vicious men, and then, as a man, you will have these men to deal with!"

My father sighed and took a sip from his espresso. I felt the soft hands of my mother on my shoulders. I sensed that she was worried.

"Sal, I don't want to argue with you. Are you giving him good advice? Joey could be hurt very badly. Do you think it wise to tell him to face this boy? I think he should avoid him and perhaps wait until he gets a little older. He will be bigger and stronger next year, and maybe he could fight him then, but not now. He could get hurt! Do you want something bad to happen to your son?"

"Lilly, this boy is our boy. We are both strong, and so he is strong! I am confident he will take care of himself in this situation. Besides, I do not want him to be afraid of this bully any longer! It is time. You understand, do you not, Joey? It is time to grow up! And, Lilly, I know it is difficult for you, but you know it is best for him."

My mother stared at my father. I could feel her hands rub my shoulders firmly. She kept on rubbing them for a few moments longer, choosing her words before she spoke.

"Sal, I do not agree with you. Look how these boys grow up in our neighborhood. Violence is all around them, and when they become violent, it is only a matter of time before they become gangsters. No, I want my boy to avoid violence and live to see another day. There are too many hoodlums in this neighborhood. Look at them, dressed in their silk suits and flashy ties with guns in their pockets! Who are they? Nobody! They grow up to get old and fat, if they are not killed first, and waste their lives playing cards on the sidewalk. Enough said! Have your fruit, Joey. It's good for you after pasta."

Just then, we all heard screaming from the stairs. It was a woman.

"Lillian! Lillian! Help me! Help me!"

My mother opened the door, and there a neighbor stood, a friend of my mother, bleeding from her lips, and her left eye was half closed, puffed up, and purple.

"Oh my God!" my mother shouted. "Sal, help me with Josie!"

Josephine's screaming was muffled by a table napkin my mother gave to her, which she placed across her face. Tears ran down her cheeks. She could not stop crying. Her eye swelled larger as she sat there while my mother comforted her.

"That bastard! It was Gino again, your husband! He did this to you. He did, didn't he?"

Josephine stopped crying and pressed her head against my mother's chest. She nodded her head. "Yes, but, Lillian, don't tell him I told you. He will beat me again. He came home drunk again tonight, not fifteen minutes ago. I had a nice steak already waiting for him, but he was drunk. He staggered into the house and stared at me like a lunatic. I could see he was going to beat me. I was afraid he was going to kill me, and for no reason, he shouted at me, 'It's all your fault! I have to kill you now!' I put down the frying pan I had the steak in and turned off the stove. 'Gino,' I said. 'Please, you are drunk. Don't hit me!' No sooner did I get the words out of my mouth than he punched me in the eye. I fell to the floor, and he held me by my hair and started punching me like I was a bag of straw. He punched and punched. Lucky I had my hands around my face. I fell to the ground, and the bastard kicked me right here!"

Josephine lifted her skirt and showed my mother her thigh. I leaned over and saw a huge purple lump on her leg.

"What am I going to do, Lilly? If I go home, he's going to kill me!"

My father got up and put on his jacket and headed to the door. "C'mon, you come with me. If he touches you, I will take care of him. Believe me."

My mother blocked his path. "Oh no, you stay here. Take off your jacket. I am going with Josie. I will take care of Mr. Big Shot who beats women. I will grab that frying pan and beat him myself if he so much as comes within six feet of her. And if he tries anything, I will take care of him pretty good."

My father laughed and took off his jacket. "The poor bastard. He is in for it. It would have been better if I went with her." He looked at me. "Joey, you get your coat and go with your mother. If Gino tries anything, you come and get me. You understand?"

I nodded, and we took off, Josephine, my mother, and I.

On the way to her building, 47 East First Street, Josie held on to my mother, who walked very slowly. At one point, she stopped and shook her head. She did not want to go, but my mother insisted. She held her by the arm and kept on walking.

"Don't worry, Josie. I am so angry I could kill that man this very night. I could kill him, so help me God!"

I trailed behind her wondering whether my mother could really do that. I looked at her when we began to climb the stoop of 47. I think if she had to, she would have killed him.

My mother opened the door to Josephine's tenement. There was Gino sitting in a chair at the table with a bottle of Budweiser in his hand, the steak still on the stove, untouched. He was huge. He wore just an undershirt with hair sticking out of his armpits. He had a glazed look in his eyes. His belly was so large it hung over his belt. I thought I should stay close to the frying pan because I thought I would need it. Gino growled.

"Oh, you're back—and with your protection, Lillian and little Joey. Whatta ya want, Lilly? A beating the way I gave your girlfriend here? Is that why you came for? Well, I will be glad to take care of that!" He pulled himself from his chair and stood up, wobbling back and forth.

He headed toward my mother. I wasn't sure what to do—stand and help her or run for my father. My mother answered that question. She stormed right up to him as he was about to raise his fist and shoved him backward so hard he landed right back into the chair. He was stunned.

"Now you shut up, you son of a bitch, or I will take that frying pan and knock your brains out, what little you have up there!" She leaned forward and wagged her finger at him. "You listen to me. You lay one more finger on Josie and I will personally come back and beat you to death, so help me God! I will, so help me God!" She put her face right against his, so close Gino had to lean back. "As God is my judge, I swear I will come back and kill you, and then I will let God decide if I am guilty of committing murder on a man who is nothing but a piece of gutter shit!"

I was shocked at my mother's courage. This man was at least six feet tall and two hundred pounds. He could have picked her up and thrown her out the window. For a moment, nothing happened. All was still until my mother saw the frying pan with the steak still on the stove.

She went to the stove, picked up the pan, and poured it out into the sink, the steak with its juices flowing all over. She took the pan and held it to Gino's head. "With this frying pan, I will return and kill you if you lay one more finger on my girlfriend here, my friend, who I love. You understand me, Gino? I will kill you!"

He sat there on the chair, speechless, and with eyes wide and staring at my mother, he nodded his head meekly.

"Promise me before God. Swear to God you will not touch her, you will not lay a finger on her. Swear to God!"

Gino looked terrified. Then he opened his drooling mouth and wiped it clean before he spoke. "I swear I won't hit her. I swear."

My mother placed the pan back on the stove. She stood back and faced Gino defiantly, her hands on her hips.

"Well, Gino, you're not as stupid as I thought. Josie, if he lays a hand on you, you come back to my house and tell me. I don't care if it is one o'clock in the morning! You come to my house. Now come on." She turned to Gino. "You stay put in that chair, you miserable bastard." Then she let out a shout. "I hate you, you son of a bitch!"

We went for the door. Gino was too drunk to reply. He lifted himself with difficulty out of his chair and shuffled to his bedroom. Josephine had already calmed down and was cleaning up the tablecloth of steak juices. She wrapped the steak in a brown bag and put it in the icebox. She kissed my mother. Her eye was a deep purple still, but she managed a smile.

"Remember what I said. If that bastard wakes up and hits you, you come over to my house, and he will be one very sorry son of a bitch!"

My father was waiting for us. In his hand, he held a glass of red wine.

"Did you beat the hell out of him, Lillian?" he asked, smiling.

My mother stared at him. "I think Josie will have nothing to worry about from her husband tonight!" she said. "Joey, take your jacket off and wash up. It's getting late."

I saw my mother differently now. She was tough, and she taught me a lesson. I was her son and my father's son, and I left the house feeling good about that. Yes, I thought about Freddie, but I had a sense in my mind that once I did see him again, it would be different. Most problems I could solve with my head, but the solution to this problem was a problem of guts. I needed to have guts to stand up to Freddie. I needed to stand up and fight him and probably take a pounding doing it.

I felt like church. I walked up Second Avenue to Third Street and stopped at the Church of the Nativity, climbed the marble steps, and went inside.

Soft amber light permeated the church interior, but the brighter glow of white light from the huge altar forced my eyes to the crucifix hanging on the wall directly behind the altar. To the left of the altar, a statue of Mary stood as Our Lady of Fatima, wrapped in a white robe with gold lining that went from hood to hem. Her hands were clasped in prayer as she gazed down lovingly on the three small statues of the young seers of Portugal.

I walked up to the altar of the empty church. Candles were lit in bunches on both sides. I stood there mesmerized by the crucifix. Up close, I saw the broken body of Jesus hanging limp, his forehead bloody from a crown of sharp, tangled thorns embedded there, his bloodied head hanging to one side, arms outstretched, the palms of his hands pierced, the bleeding wound from his ribs, and long black nails impaling his feet. I knelt and decided to ask him a favor.

"Lord, you gotta help me. I don't wanna be scared anymore." I prayed for some time with eyes closed and hands pressed together. Looking up at the crucifix, I listened to hear a voice and to see a sign, but there was no voice and no sign. I got up from the pew and began to walk out, turning once to look back at the altar.

It was then that a burst of heat surged through my body. A sense of calm overtook me until finally I felt a peace I had not felt since Freddie had attacked me. I left the church refreshed, took into my lungs the cool night air, and walked home slowly, encouraged by a quiet confidence that had suddenly come to me.

The next day at school, I did not see Freddie. I went to the handball court to play Tommy, and I was very relaxed. As I did my stretches before the game, I noticed I saw no cats on the sidewalk. They were all under cars turning their heads this way and that, nervously looking around and careful to stay right under the middle of the cars.

Tommy was already smacking the black ball against the wall, as always, in total control of the ball and his hands. We began to volley slowly, first to the right and then to the left. Then Tommy picked up the pace and let the ball go a little faster, making shots closer to the base of the wall and forcing me to chase them and work harder to return the black ball to the wall.

Tommy served a low shot that barely crossed the line. I slammed the ball hard to the right side of the wall. Tommy saw the ball clutch the right sideline and lunged forward to reach it, but the ball flew right past him. I had scored another point against him! Tommy smiled and threw the black ball to me.

"I think in five years you're going to give me trouble. How old are you now?"

I smiled as I caught the ball and went to the line to serve. "I'm going to be thirteen. That's my lucky number, thirteen."

Tommy took his position at the end of the court, ready for the serve. "Okay, I'll give you three years, and then you're going to challenge me."

I laughed and bounced the black ball as I always did before I served. I leaned forward, still bouncing the ball. As I was about to serve, I paused. I thought I had heard a whining noise on the other side of the wall. I stood up and listened. Tommy stood up and turned his head. The sound had come from the other side of the wall.

I heard a long, shrill scream of pain. It was the sound of a cat. I threw the ball back to Tommy and ran through the opening between the wall to the other side. My heart was pounding. There was Freddie holding a cat against the fence with strands of thick twine wrapped around its paws, spread-eagled on the fence and struggling to free itself.

It was the same black and white that sat with me at the stoop! On the ground around Freddie were spent matches. He was laughing that guttural laugh of his and about to light another match against the side of the matchbox.

He lit the match and, with the flame blazing, stuck it right into the chest of the cat, which let out a terrifying scream of pain. I went crazy.

"Freddie, you bastard!" I lunged, head down, slamming into him and sending him flying backward onto the concrete. He lay on the ground, stunned. I turned to the cat and pulled one paw and then another out from under the ropes that held it. When all its paws were loosened, I carefully lifted it from the fence. The cat leaped down and raced out of the park onto First Street.

I didn't see Freddie's punch. It landed on my jaw, and down I went. I got up quickly and rammed my body against him. I caught him in the jaw with my right hand. He couldn't believe it! He started swinging wildly at me, hitting me in the head and ribs, but I lifted my arms, covered my head, and swung at him once he gave me an opening. I caught him in the jaw, and then he went plain nuts.

I crouched and tried to cover my head, but it was no use. I hit him one more time before he caught me on the side of the head with his right, and down I went again onto the concrete. I lay on the ground and saw that he was reaching into his back pocket. And then he pulled it out.

Grinning, he showed me what he was looking for. I stood up slowly but still kept my eyes on him as he pointed a knife to the sky and pressed the black button on its white handle. It clicked, and the blade popped straight out of the handle.

Freddie smiled. He crouched with the open knife in his hand and began to circle me. Tommy started for him, and Freddie shouted at him, "You stay out of this! I'm gonna cut him wide open!"

But Tommy was too quick for Freddie. In seconds, he was on

him, grabbing his wrist and slapping his arm. The knife flipped in the air and fell to the ground.

"No knives, Freddie," Tommy warned. "If you want to fight, make it a fair fight!"

Freddie just smiled and reached down for his knife.

Suddenly, I saw a huge man grab Freddie's collar from behind. His beefy arms tugged at Freddie and pulled him to the ground. The man leaned down on one knee, raised his fist, and punched Freddie in the jaw, and then he hit him again and again until blood poured out of his mouth. The man kept screaming at the top of his lungs,

"I told your mother you were no damn good! I told her! I told her, all right!"

Tommy grabbed the man's arm just as he was about to land another blow. "That's enough!" Tommy shouted. "What are you trying to do, kill him?" Tommy stood between Freddie and the man and then gently pushed him back. "All right, calm down," Tommy said.

I couldn't help notice the same cold eyes the monster Frankenstein had. His long, dark straight hair hung in a mess to his shoulders. His wrinkled face was red from drink. He stumbled backward as Tommy kept moving toward him, keeping him away from Freddie as he struggled to get up. The man's shirt hung out over his belt, and he tried to pull it back into his pants but struggled with that. His worn leather jacket had slits across the arms and shoulders. Its brown collar was filthy. His baggy pants were rumpled and hung too long over his dusty work shoes.

"I told his mother he was no good. No good! I told her she should send him away to a home where doctors could fix his head. He's got some screws loose, and no amount of pounding is gonna do any bit of good. I tried that, all right, and it doesn't work." The man finally tucked in his shirt, turned, and shuffled slowly away. He turned around, and holding his balance with difficulty, he pointed at Freddie. "You be home in time for supper, or I will give you a beating you will never forget. You hear me, boy?" He swayed from side to side and then stumbled his way out of the park and out of sight.

Freddie felt his bloodied lip and began to cry softly. Tommy leaned over and pulled him up. Freddie kept on crying. I picked up the knife and handed it to Tommy, who stood there trying to wipe the blood from Freddie's mouth.

"Stand still," he said. "I'm trying to stop your mouth from bleeding. Don't move." Tommy reached into his gym bag and pulled out a clean towel and handed it to me. "Put some water on this towel," he said to me.

I ran over to the fountain, drenched the towel, and ran back to Tommy. He took the towel and dabbed Freddie's face and then wiped it down slowly and carefully. Freddie stopped crying and looked down at the ground, sniffling and shaking.

Tommy turned to me. "You okay, kid? You did all right. I'm proud of you. Freddie, leave the towel on your face." Tommy took the knife, closed it, and threw it into his gym bag. "I'm keeping this one," he said to Freddie. "You're just a kid! What are you trying to do, kill somebody?"

Freddie didn't reply.

"My advice is if that was your father, you stay away from him, at least for tonight."

Freddie mumbled that it was his stepfather.

"Even worse. It figures. The older ones who just got here are sometimes like animals. Now, you stay away from the cats! They never hurt anybody. That man who just left this park is one mean person, and even if you don't get out of line, he will think up a reason to beat you."

Freddie, with his head down, nodded weakly. I watched as Tommy dusted him off.

"You know, kid, just because your father is bad doesn't mean you have to be bad."

Freddie looked strangely at Tommy. He grew calm as he listened to him.

Tommy patted him softly on the back. "Take it easy, kid. You'll be okay. All right, go on home, and take my advice; stop getting into trouble!"

Freddie shook his head, turned, and without looking back, walked out of the park, still holding on to Tommy's towel. I watched Freddie walk away, turn onto First Avenue, and disappear from view. He was no longer the bully I knew.

"You feel okay, Joey?" He looked me over. "Ah, you don't look so bad. C'mon, let's finish our handball game!"

He put his arm on my shoulder, and we walked back to the court and began to play. I played hard, but I lost anyway. After the game, I walked out of the park and down First Street. But I knew after that day, I would play Tommy someday and beat him. I knew that.

Freddie was a different boy after that. He kept to himself at school and actually tried to pay attention in class. He never bullied anyone either. I noticed also he came to school with his hair combed back and neatly in place. His clothes were cleaner. He had learned his lesson.

I thought about Johnny. He had one week to go before coming home. That was a great thought to keep in my head. I knew also I didn't have to explain to my mom and pop how I got the bruises on my face. I had to admit it also felt good to land a few punches on Freddie.

I thought about the cats in the street. I felt great knowing I had helped them, and I no longer had any fear they would be hurt. I would not have to worry about seeing a cat being mauled again or thrown off a roof. That made me feel really good.

For the time he was away, I thought only about the good times with Johnny, not the bad, and I learned a little more about how to take care of myself. I also learned soon enough how quickly he could get me and the rest of the guys into trouble. It didn't take long after his return.

11

The Treasure

It was late May. It felt like summer. Anthony, Eugene, Harold, Johnny, and I went to Jerry's candy store for Cokes and egg creams after a Saturday afternoon stickball game. Johnny had finally come home. He put nickels in the jukebox, first to play "Cry" by Johnnie Ray and then "Wheel of Fortune" by Kay Starr. He was bragging about how easy reform school was, but it was not the truth. He was different, a little harder than before he went away.

Even though we had won, he looked miserable. He sat at the edge of the counter drinking a Coke, and he was sulking over something. He bought a box of Good & Plenty and started popping them into his mouth. Within minutes, he opened up.

"Reform school wasn't so bad. Hell, I could have been there another month easy. The thing that got me upset about being away was that my birthday came and went, and I never got a gift from anybody, except for one person, and that was Pepi!"

That didn't sound like Johnny to me. If he was going to complain about reform school, it wasn't that his birthday had passed. I was suspicious. I knew he had something on his mind.

"So what's the big deal? You're gonna have lots of birthdays. I'll give you some of my comic books. How's that?"

Harold also thought something was up with Johnny.

"It's not fair, that's all." Then he pulled out a ten-dollar bill and smiled. "Look! Pepi gave it to me when I got out. He was very happy I didn't squeal on him. I went over to Wanamaker's, and boy, they have some nice watches, but I'm not gonna spend all this money on a watch just to make John Wanamaker rich! Joey, come over here. I wanna say somethin' to you in private."

Harold looked at Johnny suspiciously. Johnny motioned me to lean over.

"Joey," he whispered, "I was thinking we could go to Wanamaker's before it closes at nine next Friday night. Our parents won't mind us being out late since it's Friday. We can hide under the toy cabinets, and after it closes, we can grab anything we want. It's like a treasure hunt. All we gotta do is go in there and take our treasure, and mine is a beautiful watch!"

I leaned back and shook my head. Harold heard Johnny.

"No way. Count me out!" I said. "Are you out of your mind? You just got out of reform school, and you wanna commit a crime? It's burglary. They'll put us away for a year! I want no part of it. You're on probation. Are you crazy?" I turned to the guys. "Hey, guess what? Johnny wants to burglarize Wanamaker's Department Store over on Eighth Street. If you guys are smart, you won't get involved."

Johnny just stared at me and kept popping the licorice into his mouth. "Joey, what's the matter with you? Are you going soft on me? I heard about the fight you had with crazy Freddie. That took guts! So what's the problem? Whatta you afraid of?" He stared at me and smiled.

All the guys looked at me. Harold just shook his head. He was baiting me.

"If we get caught, it's reform school. I'm not going to reform school!"

"Okay, Joey, I understand." He opened the door and turned around. "Believe me, I don't think you turned chicken. I don't!

Really! But that's not the Joey I knew before I went away. You had balls then!"

I was so damn mad I was ready to kill him. "It's got nuthin' to do with guts! It's got to do with being stupid. I know what you're doing. You're trying to make me look bad with the guys. You're challenging me. That's all. This burglary is dangerous!" I walked back to the table and drank the rest of my Coke.

"Yeah, Johnny," Harold said. "They could send you back to reform school for a long time, not just a month."

Johnny walked back to the table and sat down. "We're not gonna get caught! The plan is perfect! We hide in the toy cabinets, and after the store closes and everybody leaves, we take what we want and walk out!" He looked around. "Whoever wants to go can meet here next Friday at eight o'clock. We'll walk over there, get into the store, and that will be it." He looked at me. "I'm not gonna break anybody's arm to go!" He got up and went to the door.

"Joey, remember what I did for you! Did I rat on you? No! So now you gotta do for me! You owe me!" He walked out.

I could not argue. He was right. I slammed my Coke down on the table. He had me.

"Don't listen to him, Joey!" Harold said. "And, you guys, you don't listen to him, either. You're gonna get into big trouble."

"Harold, you never want to do anything Johnny wants to do," Anthony Diaz, half-black and half–Puerto Rican, said. "What's the big deal? We're not gonna get caught! We get in there, we take what we want, and we get out."

He and Eugene glared at me and Harold. Then they walked out.

We sat there thinking. No one else objected, and I was thinking that Johnny was right. The guys also must have thought I was chicken. He did not rat on me, and I owed him for it. He put me on the spot.

"It's no use," Harold said. "They're gonna along with Johnny. I got a feeling you're also gonna go along with him, but I'm not. My father would die if I ever got caught doing something like that. And, Joey, what about the scholarship? It would be over for you! Think about it."

We walked the short distance home.

"Don't do it, Joey!" Harold said.

If I didn't, the guys would think I was afraid. Nobody wants to be called a chicken. Johnny put a seed in their heads. I left Harold and went home.

My mother had leftover chicken. I stared at the chicken on my plate. Johnny was getting me to go in a direction I did not want to go. This time I knew he was dead wrong, but the pressure I felt from the guys was too much for me. I thought I would go along with him just this once, but I was very nervous about it. I saw how risky it was to burglarize Wanamaker's.

Now I realized what it meant to go to reform school, and I also realized how important the scholarship was becoming to me. I was caught.

I had lost my appetite. That night, I lay in bed thinking. This burglary was a bad idea. I fell asleep thinking that, for all the reasons I should not do it, I would go along with Johnny because I could not let the guys think I was afraid to go. Johnny had challenged me to go, and I owed him for keeping me out of reform school. I could not back out.

I left the house the next night, telling my parents I was going to Sixth Street to hang out. I did not feel good about lying to them. When I got downstairs, I headed right to Jerry's candy store.

Johnny gave me a big hug. The guys were all there except for Harold. I knew I was making a huge mistake, but I went along anyway, hoping we would not get caught. Wanamaker's was a huge white building that covered the entire block from Fourth Avenue to Broadway on Eighth Street. Next to the double glass doors on Fourth Avenue, an old man stood to the left behind a small table with a large jar. A sign on the table asked for money for the poor.

Johnny walked in first with me, and the other guys followed. I went over to one of the counters where shirts were laid out. I needed shirts badly. Johnny was already smiling at the girl behind the counter where the watches were laid out neatly in a row. He picked one up and tried it on. She was thinking he was going to buy it, and he was thinking how easy it would be to steal it.

"This one is going to be easy," Johnny said to me in a whisper. "Soon as they announce the store is gonna close, we wait until the counter girl leaves. When she leaves, we duck into the cabinets below the counters. Tell Eugene and Anthony to hide under the toy counter over there. I'll give the signal to come out, and make sure Anthony goes first! He's the biggest and could make a lot of noise."

At nine, Anthony slipped into a cabinet under the toys. Eugene stood in front of him, blocking him from anyone's view. The store began to empty.

When no one was looking, Eugene followed. He shut the door quietly behind him. I held my breath and turned to see Johnny smiling. Everything was going to Johnny's plan.

It was my turn. I stood behind Johnny next to the watches. The counter girl had already left. I wondered how Johnny intended to get to the watches, since they were under glass. I didn't have time to think. Johnny tapped me on the shoulder, and I slipped into the cabinet. The door shut behind me with a click.

It was dark in the cabinet. A strip of light streamed through a thin space between the doors. I didn't hear Johnny move away, but I figured he must have made his way into a cabinet across the aisle. I sat in that cramped space, barely able to breathe. The air was hot and dusty.

I thought for certain I was going to sneeze. I reached out into my back pocket for my handkerchief and held it to my nose. I couldn't hold it in. I sneezed and hoped to God no one had heard it. I was getting very nervous. I began to sweat. What a mistake! I hated the dark, especially when I could hear no sounds at all. Why didn't I listen to Harold?

And then the lights went out. I was in total darkness with my legs crossed. Dust began to fill my nostrils. I sat there with my arms folded. I moved my legs to avoid a cramp, but I knew that would not happen. I played too much handball. I felt as if I were trapped in that cabinet for hours, but I was there for only minutes. I thought for sure we would be caught.

And then I heard a tapping on the cabinet. It slowly opened. It was Johnny. He had his finger to his lips. He grabbed me by the arm and pulled me out. I stood up and stretched. It felt good to be out of the cabinet and to see from light coming in from the glass windows of the store. Anthony and Eugene were already out. We all stood in the center of the aisle between two racks, one of toys the other of watches. I could not hear a sound in the store,

"So far, so good!" Johnny whispered. "If you guys want anything, get it now. I'm staying here. I wanna get those watches. The bastards got them locked up under this glass!"

Anthony and Eugene were grabbing giant teddy bears. I stood there for a few seconds, not knowing where to go, but then I saw the shirt counter in the other aisle. I walked over quietly and picked up a blue shirt. It was a size fourteen neck, but the sleeve length was too long. I picked up three white and three blue shirts and checked the sizes by the light of the window.

They were size fourteen collar and thirty-two sleeve. They were my sizes. I quietly took off the tissue one shirt was wrapped in and felt the cloth. The cotton had a soft feel to it and felt good to touch. It was not the rough cotton I was used to, and it looked expensive. I held the shirts to my chest.

I looked out the windows. The man who was begging was gone. The square on Fourth Avenue had just a few pedestrians walking quickly and very little traffic. It was past nine thirty. There was light enough for us to see, but no one outside could see us. I began to relax.

I held my six shirts tightly and walked over to Johnny, who was still at the watch counter trying to open the glass case.

"Joey, take a look at that one. It's a Bulova. I love Bulova watches. Pepi has a Bulova, and that's the one I want. There's only one problem here. The case is locked! I had a feeling about that, the bastards! Well, I came prepared!" He looked at me, smiled, and pulled out a small hammer.

I looked all over. I saw no one except the guys. They were all anxious to leave. I was very nervous. Anyone could still be in the store.

"Johnny, I don't think that's a good idea! What if there is an alarm hooked up to the glass? You break that glass, the alarm goes off, and we are cooked! Don't do it!"

He just smiled, pulled out his handkerchief, and wrapped it around the head of the hammer. Then he tapped the glass gently, hoping it would break easily, but it didn't. I kept looking around, thinking someone was going to catch us, but I saw no one and heard nothing.

I still warned him. "No, Johnny, don't do it! It's not worth it!"

It was too late. Before I could finish the sentence, Johnny smashed the hammer against the glass, which shattered all over the watches below. I expected an alarm to go off, but nothing happened. Johnny reached into the case and pulled out the watch he wanted, stuffed it in his pocket, and smiled at me. He grabbed a few more and stuffed those in his pants pocket.

While he was busy clearing out the watches from the case, I felt Anthony's beefy hand on my arm. I looked up. He had his fingers to his lips. He was clutching a teddy bear to his chest. His eyes were wide open.

He whispered to me, "Joey, I hear something! Can you hear it? Quiet. Listen."

We all stiffened and listened. I turned my ear in the direction Anthony was pointing. I kept very quiet. We stood staring across counter after counter of shirts, pants, toys, and jewelry.

Then I heard a soft whistling from across the floor. The whistling grew louder. We crouched below the countertops and waited. Above us, I saw a light moving across the ceiling. I could hear the creaking of shoes, and the *tap-tap* of another sound, but I could not figure out what. I was dripping with sweat. My heart was pounding. Anthony's eyes were wide open. He was terrified! The steps stopped, and the light on the ceiling disappeared only to appear in the aisle.

I heard clearly the steps of a heavy man walking closer to us. They stopped at the end of the aisle where we crouched, and a light flashed toward us. I could see a large shadow of a man, and next to him, a huge dog with large, pointy ears wagged its tail, its mouth open and its tongue hanging out of its large head. It stood there staring at us.

The night watchman took a step back, surprised to see us. We all stood there not moving. I knew that he was about to let the dog go, and I got ready to run. Suddenly, Anthony let out a shout.

"Oh my God! It's a German shepherd! Look at those ears! Don't let him get me!" He dropped his teddy bear and ran toward the front doors.

"Hey, you! Stop right there!" the guard shouted. Did he think Anthony would?

He reached down and unleashed the dog. It took off in great strides and was quickly on us. We all scattered. The dog stopped and looked around. Then he saw Anthony heading toward the front glass doors. He gave chase, and Anthony, heavy and slow, began to scream even louder. The dog reached him, growled once, and bit into his rear end, ripping a huge, jagged hole in the back of his pants. Anthony screamed. The dog took another bite and ripped one leg of his pants right off and then the other. He began to tear them to pieces, growling at the same time. Anthony stood there with only shreds of pants covering his legs, too terrified to move.

The guard started to run after Johnny, but he took slow, heavy steps. I could see how large he was. There was no way he could catch Johnny. In a few minutes, the guard stopped and then began to walk, and he finally reached down to catch his breath. Johnny turned and laughed at him.

The guard stood up and then did the strangest thing. He took out a whistle and began to blow it, shouting at us to stop.

Johnny shouted at him, "Schmuck! Idiot! You think I'm gonna stop because you're blowing your whistle?"

We all raced to the front door. I tried to open the doors, but they were double-locked. There was no way out. Why didn't we think of that before? We were trapped. Johnny forgot to mention the doors could be locked. I turned to see the night watchman lumbering toward us. Johnny lifted his small hammer and took a step toward the guard, who stopped dead in his tracks.

"You come any closer, I swear I'll kill ya!" he shouted.

I shook my head. Was he going to kill him with that tiny hammer? We all stood there watching the standoff between Johnny and the night watchman, not thinking for a moment that our goal was to get out of the store—and fast!

It was then I had a desperate moment of clarity. I looked at the heavy glass doors and then at the thin storefront windows on each side of the doors. I could see them wobble slightly back and forth from the wind that blew outside. The windows rested on a brick foundation not one foot high.

I took the shirts and put them on top of my head. Thinking no more about it, I dropped my head and rammed right into the window. I jumped as high as I could over the foundation. Huge pieces of glass fell around me. Shards of glass bit into the back of my hands. Once through the window, I felt the crunch of shattered glass beneath my feet.

A rush of cold, fresh air smacked me across my face. I still held on to two shirts. The others were strewn all over the glass on the street and sidewalk, but I was free! The guys just stood there inside the store, staring at me. I looked down at my hands. They were covered in blood, but I felt no pain. There in front of me was a large gaping hole in the window.

"C'mon!" I screamed. "What are you waiting for? Get out of there!"

One by one, they leaped through the window.

I started to run, but I felt dizzy. I stopped and knelt down. I could hear the guys behind me, their feet crunching on the glass as they hit the sidewalk. I watched them pass me by. I felt a piece of glass in my leg and looked down to see blood pouring out of me just above the knee. I tore open my pants. A small piece of glass was sticking out of my leg. I slowly pulled it out as Anthony and Eugene raced past me toward home. I felt wobbly.

It was Johnny who stopped. He looked at my leg.

"C'mon," he said. "You can worry about that later." He looked fuzzy to me.

"No, Johnny, I have to get this glass out of my leg, and my hands are bleeding!"

He looked back in the store. The guard was nowhere in sight. With his handkerchief, he pulled out a good-size piece of glass from my leg. Then he leaned down and ripped my pants open to see if there were any more pieces. There were none. He picked me up, and we started walking.

"You're okay. C'mon, we have to get outta here!"

We began to run, slowly at first and then faster. Johnny kept holding on to my shirt. When we got to Third Avenue, the El train was just passing by. The streetlight was red. We waited impatiently. Drunks were staggering up and down the Bowery. The noise from the El was deafening. The sidewalk shook. Johnny looked back to see if anyone was following us.

"Don't worry, we're safe," he said. "Joey, you are one crazy bastard!"

I turned around to see if anyone was following. I saw blood behind me.

When we got to First Street, Eugene and Anthony were nowhere to be seen. I stopped at my building stoop, took out my handkerchief, and tried to clean my hands, but blood was still pouring out of the cuts. Johnny took his own handkerchief and tried to stop the bleeding, but it kept on coming. He pressed down hard, and after a few minutes, the blood flow slowed. I told him I was all right and to go home. He stayed with me a few minutes more and then started home, turning a few times to see if I was all right before disappearing into his building.

I walked up the stoop and sat down on the top step, exhausted. I sat there for ten minutes until I could see no blood coming out of my hands. Then I climbed up slowly to my tenement.

I felt weak. The front door was unlocked, and the lights were out. It was a little past ten. I thanked God it was not much past ten. My parents were asleep. I slipped quietly into the bathroom, turned on the faucet, and let cold water pour over my hands. I checked them for pieces of glass.

I was tired and could not see clearly, and so I could not be sure if I had removed all the glass. I checked my leg. I had a good-size cut just above the knee, but the bleeding had stopped, or so

I thought. I washed, brushed my teeth, took off my clothes, left them in a pile at the foot of my bed, and went to bed exhausted. I closed my eyes and thanked God again we were not caught. I could not believe how dumb I was to listen to Johnny, but I also realized he was the one who stopped and held on to me as we made our escape home. I could not have made it home without him.

My bed was so comfortable that I fell asleep quickly. I realized that I would have to explain to my parents how I cut up my hands and tore my pants. I would have to lie to them. Did I have a choice? I took my handkerchief and pressed it against my leg wound. I didn't want to lie to them anymore. I wanted to be truthful, but how could I tell them what I had done? I was in a serious dilemma. I asked God to help me out. As I fell asleep, I kept on hoping my prayers would be answered. What a mess I had gotten myself into!

12
Tarnished Treasure

I woke up to my mother shaking my arm gently. She pulled the blanket off me and looked in horror at the bloodstain on my leg. A large, dried brown stain was on the sheet. She held her hand to her mouth.

"My God, Joey, what happened to you?"

She called my father, who picked me up as if I were a baby, took me into the kitchen, and sat me down. He looked at my hands and then at my leg and told us he was going to take me to Bellevue Hospital right away.

He carried me down the hallway steps and down our stoop and walked to First Avenue. He was barely out of breath. He stood me up and hailed a cab. Bellevue Hospital was on Twenty-Sixth Street. It took less than five minutes to get there. We were in the emergency room when a young doctor came out and checked my hands and leg and then sent us into an examining room.

A nurse and doctor came in and brought in surgical equipment on a tray. The doctor began to pull tiny bits of glass out of my hands. He checked my leg after that and found no glass. After he had finished, he cleaned my wounds with iodine. It stung, and I winced every time he dabbed them. He stitched me up in minutes, wrapped my wounds in a soft cloth, and fastened it with small clips. He looked straight at me.

"Okay, son, you were lucky. Now you want to tell me how you got those pieces of glass in your leg and hands?"

I didn't answer him. I was surprised by the question. I flushed. I wasn't going to say anything to him about it. I am sure he and my father knew I had done something wrong. Both of them looked at me suspiciously. I was getting nervous. The nurse pulled the surgical tray out of the room.

My father saved me for the moment. "My son is a little shy. He doesn't like to talk too much!"

I lowered my head. He was protecting me, and he knew I would not tell the doctor where I had been.

"You did a wonderful job taking care of my son. I appreciate what you did for him. I do."

We walked out of the hospital. My father waved down a cab, and for a second time, I rode in one. When we got home, my mother made me oatmeal. I wolfed down the cereal. I felt pain in my hands and leg. There was not going to be any stickball for me this day.

"Joey, are you ready to tell us what happened last night?" my father finally asked

I stopped eating and looked down at the table. I did not want to say a word. My mother was about to say something, but my father stopped her.

"Let me handle this, Lilly, please," he said quietly. "Joey, it is important to be honest, and especially with your parents. If you got yourself into trouble, tell us so we can help you. If you stay quiet, we cannot help you. Doesn't that make sense?"

I nodded. He was right. I wanted to tell him the truth, but if I said anything about the burglary, I would have had to mention my friends. I didn't want to do that. I was caught between being honest with my parents and loyalty to my friends. My silence at the moment was the only solution I could come up with.

"Pa, I have reasons why I cannot tell you and Mom what happened; I can't right now." I realized after I said it I had made a mistake.

They looked at each other silently for a few minutes while I sat there and finished my oatmeal.

"All right, Joey," my father said. "We won't talk about it now. You think about it, but I will tell you right now, I want an answer, and I am not going to wait long for it. You understand?"

I did understand.

On Saturday, before the stickball game, Johnny came over to the bench where I was sitting to see how I was. I told him my leg was hurting and I couldn't play. No one said a word about the burglary. After the games, we went back to Jerry's store. I told them I did not tell my parents anything, but they were very suspicious.

"That's good, Joey. I know you lost all the shirts you had, but I got my watch and a few more watches that I'm gonna make some decent money on when I sell them, and when I do, I'm gonna give you guys a cut of whatever I make."

I shook my head. I was angry not only with Johnny but more so with myself. "Listen, Johnny, I don't want any part of that money. I came here to tell you guys that I don't want to talk about the burglary ever again. I'm finished with that stuff. It's stupid. You can all split the money from the watches. I want no part of it."

He looked at me suspiciously. "Are you sure you didn't say anything to your parents? Give me your word that you didn't!"

I didn't reply to him. If he couldn't take my word when I said it, I wasn't going to repeat it. I got up and walked out. Johnny was not happy, but I really didn't give a damn what he was thinking. I was really upset. It was damn stupid of me to take the risk I did, and all because I was called chicken. I went to the handball courts and watched Tommy play handball.

That night, I came home feeling good that I had taken a stand not to steal again, but not so good because I expected my father to confront me. The scent of the hot sauce had a calming effect on me, and I was home and felt secure.

But I was ready to be grilled, and now my decision to keep

quiet sounded very lame to me. What was the right or wrong thing to do? To tell the truth was right, but it was also right not to rat the guys out. I was caught in a moral dilemma, confusing and upsetting to me, because I could not figure out what was the more right thing to do. I was not going to get away with silence. The table was too quiet.

Stirring his cup of espresso, my father stared at me. "Now, Joey, tell me what happened last night."

It took a few moments for me to answer. "I can't tell you what happened, Pa. If I did, I might get my friends into trouble, and I don't want to do that." I could see terrible disappointment in my father's face.

My father spoke softly. "Joey, it is always necessary to tell the truth because it will come out anyway. Better to tell us now, don't you think? And then we can help you. But we cannot help you with this problem if we do not know what we are dealing with! I understand you want to protect your friends, but the truth is more important than the protection of your friends. Now, tell me, Joey."

He had me. I wanted so much to tell him the complete truth and clear my conscience, but then I would be a rat. I thought about the code of silence Pepi asked me to take. I remained silent, not wanting to lie and not wanting to break that code and hurt my friends. I decided I would protect them.

Before I could answer, there was a hard knock on the door. My mother looked at me. I was really nervous. She opened the door. In walked the same detectives who went through the house looking for Pepi's gun! They were not smiling this time. I felt a gush of blood pumping through my heart.

The red-haired detective spoke. "You remember me, don't you, Mr. D'Angelo? Detective Brian Kelly. Dave and I were here a while ago. Your son, Joey, may be in serious trouble this time." He came right up to me. "Mr. D'Angelo, do you mind if I check out Joey's hands?"

My mother was biting her finger and looked very worried. My father nodded quietly and kept shaking his head.

There was nothing to check out. There were still bandages on my hands. He came over and looked at them. Then he knelt down and lifted my pant leg just above the knee. He saw the wrapping on my stitches. He stood up.

"Mr. D'Angelo, Mrs. D'Angelo, there was a burglary last night. A few boys broke into Wanamaker's Department Store and stole off with some watches and toys. The watchman told us the boys were locked in until one of them rammed his head right into the plate glass with a pile of shirts on his head. It was easy to find out who it could be. My partner and I, we just went down to Bellevue over the weekend, and the only boy who came in with cuts on his hands and legs was your son, Joey!"

He stared at me. I was caught.

Detective Kelly looked hard at me. "Joey, I'll tell you what. I'm going to give you a chance to walk away from this thing. If you tell us who else was with you at Wanamaker's that night, you tell me here and now, in front of your parents, and I promise you, I won't arrest you. You have my word. It will be a lot easier for you if you tell us who you were with." He paused and stared at me. There was a long silence. "I'm waiting."

I had really made a mess of things. I was going to be arrested! I looked at my parents. I was so ashamed. I was ready to tell them everything. God, I was really tempted. I would be let go and free of this terrible burden. I would save my chances for the scholarship. All I had to do was tell them who else was with me. I realized now how important the scholarship was to me.

And yet, I still knew I could not rat on my friends. It was one thing for me to know the consequences of my wrongdoing, but how could I add to the wrongdoing by ratting? Johnny would be sent away. Maybe all of them would be sent away, and I would be left alone in the neighborhood and marked forever as a rat! I could not do it. I had to take punishment for what I had done and not rat on my friends.

"I can't tell you who was with me. I can't."

Detective Kelly knelt down and faced me directly. He must have been no more than six inches from my face. He looked straight at me.

I lowered my head and kept silent. He took my arm gently. I stood up and looked at my mother, who was wiping tears from her eyes. I was crushed not only because I was in trouble but also because, for the first time I could remember, I had caused her pain.

"Okay, let's go," he said.

My father held me and asked if he could go down to the station with us. Detective Kelly agreed, and still holding my arm, he walked me downstairs to a waiting police car and drove off to the Ninth Precinct.

The detective who had grilled Johnny sneered at me.

"You kids never learn, do you? Now look what kind of mess you're in!"

Detective Kelly began to rattle off some charges. Were they going to throw me into jail? I was really scared. I began to shake all over. I didn't know what was going to happen. Detective Kelly took us into a private room and told us to wait for him. He left. There was no guardian angel waiting for me now.

Outside, I heard him talking to a tall man. My father stared at me glumly. He hugged me.

"Don't you worry, Joey; we'll get out of this mess, and when we do, promise me you will never get into trouble again!"

I nodded and promised him, tears flowing down my cheeks.

I let my parents, Tom and Sue, and myself down all because I did not stand up to Johnny and had not listened to Harold. I had ruined my life, all because I didn't have the guts to say no because I was called chicken.

I was ready to cry. He patted me on the back.

"Joey, you made a serious mistake, and now we all must pay the price of that mistake. But, Joey, you are right—better not to stain your integrity and make matters worse. You cannot sacrifice your friends in return for freeing yourself from punishment. When you do wrong, you should expect punishment. That way, you think twice about doing wrong again." He paused. "Let's leave this problem in the hands of God."

I was, frankly, stunned by his understanding.

Detective Kelly walked back in. "Okay, no arrest. You are a

lucky kid. For now. You have an appointment with the judge this Thursday morning downtown on Centre Street at ten o'clock—family court since Joey is a minor. Don't be late, and, Mr. D'Angelo, get him an attorney!"

I walked out of the precinct house relieved not to have been arrested but still depressed. My father had his arm around my shoulders. He did not say a word to me all the way home. I wished that he had. When we walked in the door, my mother broke into tears and held me. My mother looked at me and shook her head. She was not so sure I would be all right.

It wasn't long before everyone in the neighborhood knew I had been picked up for the burglary. I saw Johnny and the other guys at school. They walked right by me. No one talked to me except Harold. It was clear I had to stay away from Johnny and the others. In class, I saw Maria. At three o'clock, she walked downstairs with me and out of the school.

"I can't talk to you, Joey. My mother said she doesn't want me hanging around with you. She doesn't want the cops to think I was with you. I love you, Joey." She kissed me quickly on the cheek, squeezed my hand, turned, and walked away. I watched her head toward First Avenue until I could not see her. That was a moment I felt alone. I was isolated from my friends, my parents, and my girl. My spirit was crushed.

When we sat down to eat that night, my parents were very quiet. I had built a wall between them and me. Should I explain to them that I did not want to burglarize Wanamaker's?

Would that have helped? I thought about it, but then my father would have said to me that I should have shown more courage. I should have stood up to Johnny. I should have been a man and stood my ground. That's what it meant to be my own man—to do the right thing and not cave in to pressure to do the wrong thing just for being called a chicken. I understood that now.

I looked at my father. He smiled at me and patted me on my shoulder.

"Finish eating, Joey. You need strength. Don't worry. Everything will be all right."

Suddenly, there was a knock on the door. I froze. In walked Pepi Savino! Behind him was a man I had never seen.

"Hello, Mr. D'Angelo!" Pepi smiled and stuck out his hand.

My father grimaced. He rose and shook his hand without smiling. He was not happy.

"Don't get me wrong. I came to help out. This man is my attorney, Angelo Perelli. I didn't mean to interrupt your dinner. Could we sit down, or would you like us to come back?"

"No, no, sit down. Lillian, fix a plate of pasta for Pepi and one for his friend."

Pepi's maroon tie hung straight down his clean, white shirt. His dark-blue suit was neatly pressed. It looked so perfect on him. He shook his head.

"No, thank you, Mrs. D'Angelo. We already finished eating. I don't eat much, and I eat quick. That's why I'm so thin!"

He unbuttoned his suit jacket and smiled. He was right. His waist was flat. He and his attorney sat down on folding chairs my mother pulled out for them.

"You're probably wondering why we're here. I want my attorney to represent Joey when he goes to court next Thursday. I know you really can't afford a good attorney, and I know you don't want your son to go to reform school."

He looked around the room and up at the ceiling. I looked at the walls also. Paint on our kitchen ceiling was peeling.

"Mr. Perelli is the best criminal attorney in New York City. He will defend your son. He will say your son cut himself with a mirror you were throwing out. It was a coincidence it happened the day after the burglary. That doesn't mean it was your son. I think he will convince a jury that Joey had nothing to do with this crime. What do you think, Mr. D'Angelo?"

My mother placed three cups of espresso on the table. My father offered them sambuca, and both men poured it into their espresso. They drank.

"Mr. D'Angelo," Pepi continued, "this is a neighborhood where we have to take care of one another. We're all Italians, aren't we? We need to protect our own. That is why we are here.

You can't afford Mr. Perelli, but I can. I want Angelo to represent your son. I want him to have the best legal mind to keep him out of reform school."

Perelli had a heavy crop of brown hair and a large jaw. His eyes were blue, and he looked very assuring when he spoke.

"Your son may be guilty in the eyes of the court," Perelli said, "but I will plead that he is innocent, that if anything, he should get probation and nothing more. It would be his first offense. I will keep him out of reform school." His large jaw tightened. "I will win! Your son stays home, keeps his nose clean for six months, and then he is off. How does that sound?"

My father sipped his espresso. He looked at my mother, who folded her arms and looked at Perelli defiantly. She stared at him. He looked smart. He was as well dressed as Pepi. He could defend me, all right! Then she turned to Pepi.

"What is your interest in my son," she asked Pepi, "that you come here to offer such great assistance? What is in it for you? I don't understand."

Pepi smiled. He finished his espresso and stood up. Perelli also stood up. They walked to the door.

"Mrs. D'Angelo, I like your son," Pepi said in a soft, smooth voice. "Everyone in the neighborhood knows he is a good, honest boy. I want to protect Joey because I think he has a bright future. He can't throw his life away because of one stupid mistake, now can he? And someday, he will make us proud. You'll see! Think about it." They got up and walked out.

"I don't trust him," my mother said. "He has other reasons for offering his attorney."

My father nodded agreement. She poured him another espresso.

"I have no doubt he is protecting his cousin Johnny," my father said. "That is what I think. And yet, he may have a soft spot for Joey, as well." Then he looked at me curiously. "You see, Joey, how easily it is to be caught in a trap? On the one hand, I want him to help us, but on the other, I am taking help from someone who is a bad influence on you. I want to protect you, but how do I protect you, Joey? How?" He shook his head and sipped his espresso to its finish.

Later that night, he went downstairs to see Pepi to tell him he would accept his offer. He told my mother and me later he did it because he wanted to protect me. He was taking a gamble, he said to us, but it was a gamble he had to take to protect his son. He sat down and took a large glass and filled it with wine.

"I'm ashamed of myself, Lilly; I just made a pact with the devil," he said.

My mother lifted her chin and folded her arms. "Don't be too sure you made a pact that will last!" she said, and then she turned to me. "It's a good thing, Joey, you go to church on Sunday, because maybe God will answer your prayers and get you out of this mess you got yourself into. Just maybe!"

13
Verdict in the Courtroom

Thursday morning arrived very quickly. My parents and I stood in the huge hallway of juvenile court waiting for Angelo Perelli. The ceilings were at least twenty feet high. White plaster walls were turning yellow. The floors were made up of large slabs of blue-gray marble. We sat down on a wooden bench just outside the courtroom, listening to the muffled echoes of conversations and watching attorneys in dark suits with black briefcases walking back and forth, neatly dressed, hair combed back, and all looking very official, but no Angelo Perelli.

A clock above the courtroom doors showed ten in the morning. My father looked down the hall, shook his head, and motioned my mother and me to go through two heavy doors into the courtroom. The courtroom was fifty feet wide and at least seventy-five feet deep; it also had twenty-foot ceilings. The judge's bench stood higher than the brown wooden benches where we sat. I was cold. I zippered my jacket and sat there shivering. I shivered also because I was scared. I felt no blood in my cheeks. I must have looked white.

The court officer who stood to the left of the judge's bench wore a holster packed with a .45. The belt hung loosely around his waist. To the right of the bench, a woman sat in front of a machine, loading it with paper. On my right, there stood a man I thought might be the prosecutor. A woman seated next to him kept handing him folders, which he examined and then placed in a pile. She looked at me a few times but turned away quickly.

Time passed slowly. My father came into the courtroom and shook his head. He sat down next to me and put his arm over my shoulder. He was also nervous, but he gave me comfort. My mother, on the other hand, kept looking straight ahead. Minutes went by, and there was still no sign of Angelo Perelli.

The court officer stood at attention. In a loud voice he shouted, "All rise!"

The judge entered. He was bald with blue eyes and fair skin, and he was tall. His black robes reached down below his ankles. He straightened out his robe, sat down, and looked at my parents. He nodded slowly and then stared at me. I looked down and blushed. He turned to the prosecutor standing there with a set of papers in his hands.

I glanced behind me one more time. The courtroom was empty except for two police officers at the front doors. I started to shift in my seat. The judge spoke.

"My name is Joseph Weinstein, the presiding judge in this case. This is juvenile court and as such is charged with the hearing of cases involving misdemeanors and felonies by juveniles.

"In this case, Mr. Joseph D'Angelo is being charged with the burglary of Wanamaker's Department Store. This is a preliminary hearing, not a trial." He paused and looked our way. "I don't see an attorney present for the defendant." He turned to the prosecutor. "Counselor, does the defendant have representation?"

"He does, sir. Mr. Angelo Perelli, but he is not present at the moment."

The judge looked at the clock. "Well, it is now ten past ten. Mr.

Walker, do you have available a court-appointed attorney who can represent Mr. D'Angelo?"

He nodded. "Yes, Your Honor, Mr. Irwin Job is available. I took that precaution."

"Good. Let's call him in. If it is all right with the parents of the defendant, I will appoint Mr. Irwin Job public defender for Mr. D'Angelo. Granted, he just received the file, but there really is nothing the court can do but move forward. The court has a very busy calendar after this case."

A heavyset man in a brown suit, with thick, graying, scruffy hair, came out from a side door of the courtroom and shuffled toward us. He looked about fifty years old and distracted. His beat-up brown suit jacket hung loosely on his shoulders. His pants had no creases. His shirt was wrinkled, and his tie hung loosely around his neck. He shook my father's hand. My father turned to my mother and shook his head. My attorney proceeded to the front table where he lazily threw down his worn-out brown leather briefcase and read the charges. He made some notes and addressed the court.

"I'm ready, Your Honor," he said.

I knew I was in deep trouble.

The prosecutor began to state the charges against me. He described the crime: how I must have hidden in the cabinets along with others unknown and, therefore, unnamed. He told how the burglars found the doors locked and, finding themselves being pursued by a guard and his watchdog, hurled themselves through the plate-glass windows of the store. He went on to tell the court that I was the only one who entered Bellevue Hospital the day after with extensive cuts on my hands and leg. Officers found a small trail of blood in front of my building.

He ended his presentation by telling the judge that when Detective Kelly from the Ninth Precinct talked to me at home and asked about the cuts, I could not explain them, and I would not admit who else was with me. My silence, the prosecutor said, was evidence of my guilt.

I was finished. I slumped down on the bench and put my

hands over my eyes. There was a stillness in the courtroom as the prosecutor prepared to make his recommendation to the judge. I could hear a brief shuffling of papers, and all was quiet.

"Your Honor," he said, "I recommend reform school for six months for this boy. It would do him good to get away from that horrible neighborhood where gangsters breed like flies." He sat down.

My mother put her arms around me. That made it worse for me. I felt deep guilt over the pain I had caused my parents. It was over for me.

I realized at that moment what I would leave behind: my parents and my friends, Harold and Johnny, Maria, school, handball and stickball, movies on Sunday afternoons. I was not only leaving my life, as poor as we were, but I had thrown away my future. I held back tears. There was nothing I could do. My situation was hopeless. Only God could save me now.

Suddenly, I heard the doors behind me open. The judge looked up, and so did the prosecutor. The court reporter stopped typing and leaned over to see who was coming into the courtroom. My parents and I turned around.

There was Tom Mansfield! Walking in front of him was an old man, bald and wearing metal-rimmed glasses, a white shirt, blue paisley tie, and a dark-blue pin-striped suit. He looked very dignified to me. They sat down directly behind us. The old man looked around the room. Then he folded his arms across his chest and looked directly at the judge and smiled.

Judge Weinstein asked my attorney to speak. He mumbled a few words in my defense, telling him that I had no prior record, this was my first offense, and I should not be sent to reform school. I had learned my lesson. The judge listened, took notes, and then looked at me grimly.

It was one of the darkest moments of my life. I started to shake all over, barely holding back tears. My mother held me tighter. She too was holding back. My father leaned forward with a face of stone, staring at the judge who held my life in his hands.

The judge was just about to tell us his decision when suddenly the old man stood up and, with a booming voice, began to speak.

"Your Honor, if it pleases the court, I would like to say a few words in defense of this young man who is one of my boys at the Boys' Club of New York. My name is Peter Capra, and I am the director of the Boys' Club. May I address the court?"

I was shocked.

Judge Weinstein leaned forward in his leather chair and looked at the prosecutor, who nodded his approval. The judge waved at Capra to come forward. "Yes, of course. I am familiar with your reputation, Mr. Capra. Please, tell us what information you can provide."

Capra moved to the center aisle and walked slowly up to the front of the bench. He stood ramrod straight and turned to acknowledge with nods of his head the prosecutor and then my attorney.

"Your Honor, I have never spoken to this young man. However, he has been at our Boys' Club a few years, and in those years, he has made a deep impression on our counselors, who have found him to be a boy of character, strong intellect, and an extraordinary memory. I have no doubt this incident was the result of young Joey being unwillingly pushed into a situation he was against from the very beginning, because his counselors tell me he is basically an honest boy who would not steal.

"There are many bad influences in our neighborhood, and too often, the bad overtake the good, and bad things happen. I suspect Joey was caught up in doing the wrong thing and now finds himself, of course, facing the penalty for his wrongdoing.

"I would ask the court to allow the Boys' Club to place him under our supervision. Don't send him away, Your Honor. This young man has learned his lesson and now sees the path to a good, moral life. We need to give him that opportunity to become a contributor to a better society.

"For this boy is a treasure, Your Honor, a treasure who will someday bear fruit for our society and perhaps for the world. But how will we know if this treasure is truly valuable if he is not given the opportunity to prove that he is something of value? Give him that chance! Thank you, Your Honor, for allowing me the time to plead for this young man's future."

He turned and slowly walked down the aisle to his seat. The courtroom was silent. The prosecutor was speechless. My attorney scratched his disheveled hair and patted me on the back. The judge stared at Capra and then turned to his court officer, who smiled and nodded.

He looked at the prosecutor, who dropped his papers and nodded agreement. Judge Weinstein looked over at his court reporter. She looked up at him, and she too nodded agreement with a smile. I was stunned. No one had ever talked about me like that before.

Weinstein asked both attorneys to approach the bench. They huddled, each talking in whispers so low I couldn't hear them. A few minutes went by. My mother held my hand and squeezed it. My father put his arm around my shoulder. When the attorneys finally left the bench, I took a deep breath. The judge spoke.

"Mr. D'Angelo, Joey, please stand."

I squeezed my mother's hand tighter and stood up.

Judge Weinstein looked straight at me. "Joey, I want you to know you did a terrible thing. You committed a crime. You caused your parents great suffering. You nearly threw your life away with one act of stupidity. However, you are a lucky young man for having a great supporter in Mr. Capra! I am going to grant you a six-month probation and place you in his care. In six months, if you do not violate your probation and if you stay out of trouble, I will end your probation and strike this hearing from the record. That means this hearing will be sealed, and you will have no public record. Court is adjourned!" He banged his gavel on the bench.

I fell back on the bench, stunned at my good luck and with tears I wiped away. My father hugged me. My mother began to cry and kept wiping tears from her cheeks. My attorney was smiling and scratching his head in disbelief.

The prosecutor walked over and shook my hand and wished me well. "Son, make sure you behave yourself. You are very fortunate to have had Judge Weinstein on the bench today. Any other judge would have sent you right to reform school!"

Tom and Mr. Capra came up to us. Tom shook my father's hand and hugged my mom.

I turned to Capra. "Thank you, Mr. Capra!" I said.

He came up to me and shook my hand firmly. He looked directly at me. He was not smiling.

"Monday of next week, right after school—you arrange it with Tom here for exact time—I would like you to come up to my office. Will you do that?"

I nodded.

"Good! And don't be late. I'm a busy man, you know." He patted me on the back. "You are a lucky young man. Let's keep it that way."

Capra and Tom left. My parents and I walked out of the courtroom. We stood there for a few minutes deciding how to get home. My father wanted a cab, my mother a bus. They argued.

Just then, a squad car pulled up. The back door opened, and out came Angelo Perelli! He turned to help a second man out of the car whose hands were cuffed behind his back. It was Pepi! His suit jacket was unbuttoned, his tie hung loose, and his hair flapped in the wind. He stood up awkwardly, trying to manage the cuffs on his wrists. A policeman took his arm and walked him toward the court steps. Perelli followed closely behind.

If either one of them saw me, they didn't show it. My parents and I watched them go up the steps of the court. We stood there quietly until they disappeared inside.

My mother shook her head. "You see, Sal, how God is there when we least expect him to be? Your pact with the devil is over!"

That day, I lost respect for Pepi. I had great respect for him because I always thought he was too smart to get caught for any crime. Now I saw him arrested and in handcuffs. I feared him, but now I understood that my respect had come out of that fear of him.

On Monday afternoon, I went to see Peter Capra. When I walked into his office, he was sitting in a large, brown leather chair, writing at a large mahogany desk. He looked up at me briefly, and with his pen, he pointed to one of the two chairs in front of him. I sat down.

On the wall, there were framed photos of him with Mayor Robert Wagner, Governor Averell Harriman, and Governor Thomas E. Dewey. In every photo, he was smiling. He was not smiling now.

Five minutes went by. I shifted a few times in the chair, feeling very uncomfortable. The room was so quiet. Light, parted by blinds, streamed in from large windows facing west. The sun's rays were strong, and I was getting hot. The room was painted light beige, and the navy-blue carpet gave it an official, dignified look. It fit Capra, who finally put down his pen, picked up the sheet of paper he was writing on, folded it, and placed it neatly into an envelope. Then he looked at me hard.

"Now you listen to me," he said in the same loud, booming voice I heard in the courtroom. "You are never to do something that stupid again! It was a criminal act! You understand? If you do, that means many years in jail, I guarantee you! A smart kid like you wasting his life like that, and for what? Do you understand me?"

I nodded.

"I will throw you out of here and recommend to Judge Weinstein he send you to reform school, and you can forget all about prep school! Don't cross me, kid! I will do it! Do we understand each other?"

I was stunned. My cheeks turned red. I sank into my chair. He got up and stood over me.

"You think life is a joke? You think you can do anything you want, like those bums who hang around in silk suits? They will get theirs. You can count on that." He pointed to the pictures on the wall. "See all those men up there with me? They are friends of the Boys' Club and my friends also, and some of the most important people in this city. You have embarrassed the Boys' Club and me! I work hard for my boys because I never want to see any of them go wrong, and that includes you.

"Without these men, the Boys' Club will no longer exist. Now if I have frightened you, that is good, because that is exactly what I am trying to do. Do you want to be a gangster, or do you want to make something of yourself? Treasure? My tail! A treasure does not behave like trash!"

I nodded meekly one more time. He sat back in his leather chair and rocked back and forth, staring at me. I was terrified.

"You have great potential, but you're no treasure as far as I am concerned, not until you straighten out that head of yours and pay attention to becoming a real man, and that means doing the right thing."

I held on to the arms of the chair and agreed with him with another nod of my head. He must have known he had really frightened me because he softened his tone of voice and rocked back in his chair for a few seconds more before talking again.

"Deep down, I know you're a good kid," he said in a softer voice, "and I know if you stay out of trouble, you will become a good man, and that is my goal. Then, my boy, I can say you are truly a treasure, and I will be proud to call you one of my boys.

"Now, some members of the board of directors are very skeptical about keeping you on their list for that scholarship. It took a lot of arm twisting, but I kept you on it even though I am not sure myself you still belong in this program; but my gut tells me you are, so you must keep your nose clean and make me show them I was right. If I can see some acts of kindness, goodness, and generosity out of you, maybe I can convince myself that I am doing the right thing in keeping you in the program.

"I would feel better if, in the coming months, you can show me a good heart instead of criminality and that you can do the right thing. I am expecting that from you. This Boys' Club has a lot riding on you. You succeed and others will follow. Now go on, get out of here, and remember what I just told you."

I got up to leave, but he stopped me, stood up, and extended his hand.

"Now come over here and shake my hand. I never let anyone out of my office without a handshake."

He grabbed my hand with a firm grip and smiled at me. He had scolded me because I deserved it, but that handshake made me realize he still had confidence in me. He wasn't giving up on me. That handshake made me feel really good.

I couldn't go against him now, because I understood he was letting me have it for good reason. He was looking out for me, but the meeting was a stern warning to me also. I understood that, all right.

I went downstairs to the lockers, put on my bathing suit, and showered. I washed away all the dirt and sweat I had piled onto my skin during the day. I felt clean after that. And then I dove into the swimming pool. The cold water made me feel refreshed. I swam to the bottom of the pool, touched its checkered marble floor, and then swam to the surface. I got out and dove in again. I felt as if a weight had been lifted from my shoulders. I had learned my lesson. Peter Capra had made it easy for me to learn that lesson.

I felt different after that swim, and I went home feeling pretty good—but not about Pepi Savino. I could see now he was really nothing but trouble for me. I learned that soon enough.

Capra laid down the law for me. He wanted to see the good side of me. He wanted to see acts of goodness, kindness, and generosity. How could I do that? I didn't know where to begin. It was a challenge to me. He left me with a job to do but with no guidelines to do it.

That was going to be tough. I had it tough at home also. My father understood me, and he felt I had been through enough, but not my mother. She realized she needed to teach me a few hard lessons of her own.

14

My Cousin Jimmy

My father forgave me for taking part in the burglary of Wanamaker's, but my mother did not. And so when our cousin Jimmy, on my mother's side, was shot and lying in Bellevue Hospital with a ruptured spine from a bullet wound, she decided to teach me a lesson.

We took a bus up to Twenty-Eighth Street and First Avenue. It disturbed me that she held my hand as we walked inside and up the elevator to intensive care. We approached the front desk and asked for Jimmy Rizzo. The woman turned her head left and pointed down the hall to two double doors. We walked through them, and it was then we heard the first scream, which startled both of us. It was Jimmy who was screaming. In between screams, I could hear him sobbing. My mother asked me to wait in the hall; she wanted to go in first. I sat on a bench in front of a nurse who was busy pushing a cart loaded with bottles of drugs, and that was the moment when Jimmy screamed again.

"Mama! Mama! Don't let them hurt me anymore! Please, Mama! Please, it hurts! Take the pain away, Mama, please!"

I was stunned. Jimmy was a tough kid being groomed by the mob.

My mother walked into Jimmy's room. I could not see her from where I was sitting, but I could hear Jimmy's mother, Angela, let out a muffled scream when she saw my mother. I got up and walked toward the room. I could not see Jimmy, who was still crying, but I could see my mother hugging her cousin Angela. I hesitated. My mother was holding her cousin, who was resting her head on my mother's shoulder and sobbing softly.

"For ten dollars," Angela said. "This man shot my Jimmy. My handsome boy, Jimmy. Look at him, Lillian," she said softly. "Look at my little boy, my little baby. He just made nineteen! Nineteen years old! What did I do in my life to deserve this tragedy?"

My mother took Angela by the hand, and they walked over to the bed. I stepped closer to the door. I didn't really want to see him, but I could not help myself. I decided to look at Jimmy.

Jimmy was lying on a mesh net just above his bed, his arms and legs stretched out and in bandages. The net was supported by wires hanging from the ceiling. He could not move. I stood there at the entrance to the room where I could see Jimmy, tears streaming down his face, screaming for a few seconds and then silently staring at the ceiling. He screamed again. He could not turn his head. When his mother approached him, he turned his eyes toward her, and his face cringed in pain. I was terrified to see him there near death.

"Mama, please don't let them kill me! I don't want to die, Mama. Please, I don't want to die! Please!" Angela turned to my mother in search of an answer, tears flowing freely.

My mother had no answer. That was all. She turned to leave the room and saw me at the door. As I moved from the door, I heard Jimmy whimper, "Mama," and I could hear him after he called her name, still crying softly. It was over, and he knew it.

We walked outside the hospital. It felt so good to be outside. I took a deep breath. I felt good to be alive. My mother grabbed my hand and stared at me as we crossed First Avenue on our way to catch the Second Avenue bus.

"Your cousin Jimmy is just nineteen, Joey, and he is going to die." She held my hand tighter. "He's going to die, and for what? A miserable ten dollars!"

She grimaced. Her jaw was taut, and she walked quickly from the hospital, holding my hand as tightly as she could. I understood the lesson she had taught me.

15

A Death at Josephine's House

It was a quiet Saturday morning, and I was having a relaxing breakfast of shredded wheat drowned in milk with bananas and blueberries my mom had just bought from the fruit wagon. I was happy to see the sun shining into the kitchen, which always let in light because it faced south.

I didn't expect the soft knocking at the door so early in the morning. It was barely eight o'clock, and I was thinking about the stickball games that afternoon. Who would be coming to our door so early in the morning? My father had already gone out to First Street Park to play bocce with his friends. That was his way of relaxing on Saturday morning. My mother would start putting together artificial flowers, which she had brought home from a small shop she worked at on Second Street. This money she would stash away somewhere in the house and not show to my father.

She put down the flower she was working on and went

to the door. It was her friend Josephine. This time, Josephine looked pretty good. Unlike the last time she came to our door, she did not have a single mark on her face. And this time, she was not hysterical. She was quiet, but I saw in her eyes that she was nervous. They shifted back and forth quickly. She kissed my mother, held her hands in a tight grip until hers became red, and finally pulled my mother to her and hugged her. Then she whispered in her ear. My mother clutched her chest and gasped.

"Can we talk in front of Joey?" Josephine asked.

"Joey? Of course! Joey is coming with us anyway. Sit down, Josephine. The coffee is up. It's fresh. I'll pour you a cup of coffee, and you can tell me what happened." My mother heated the coffee on the stove, poured a cup for her friend, and then sat down to listen to her story.

"Lillian," Josephine whispered, "I think my husband is dead, and I think I killed him." She began to cry and took out a handkerchief to wipe her nose.

My mother shook her head. "But, Josephine, this husband of yours is almost two hundred pounds! How could you, 120 pounds, kill this big, fat tub of a husband? How could you kill him? Tell me. I want to hear the whole story, and start from the beginning."

Josephine began telling my mother that her husband, Gino, had come home the night before, late and drunk. He staggered into the apartment and looked at her darkly in the way he usually did just before he beat her up. His bloodshot eyes glared at her, and she knew he meant to kill her that night. His arms hung down along his body like a gorilla, and his hands were already tightened into fists. Josephine said she'd been terrified.

"It was then I knew I had to go to the kitchen, just like you told me, Lillian, to protect myself. I went in and pulled out from the cabinet next to the stove the heavy, black frying pan you like so much, the one I use for eggs in the morning. That one! I pulled it out and held it to my chest. I was afraid he really meant it this time. He was going to kill me!" She broke into tears.

My mother looked at me, shook her head, and made the sign of the cross.

Josephine went on, "Gino followed me into the kitchen. He did not say a word until he stopped at the kitchen doorway. He leaned against it to keep his balance and told me that he decided that night, while he was drinking with his friends, that he was going to kill me! He thought of it before this night, he said, but tonight, he had decided he was not going to wait. He said he was going to kill me and dump my body into the East River with rocks around my ankles!"

Josephine began to cry. I felt very bad for her. My mother leaned over and hugged her again.

"I suffered with this man, Lillian. You know how much I suffered. He beat me so bad one time I could not straighten my back for a week! When he punched me in the face, my lips were so swollen and sore I could not eat. One night he stayed out so late I just went to bed, and next thing I knew, Gino, smelling of liquor, dragged me out of bed and beat me until I fell to the floor.

"While I was lying there, he kept punching me, but I kept my arms around my head. That saved me. He must have gotten tired of hitting me, because he suddenly stopped, staggered into bed, and fell asleep. He was afraid of you, Lilly, but not me, never me! Every night he came home drunk, I was afraid he was going to kill me!

"So last night he came home drunk again, followed me into the kitchen, told me he was going to kill me, and then lunged at me. I had the heavy black frying pan in my hand, and with one swing, I hit him right on the forehead. Right here, on the forehead! His head went back, and so did he. He stumbled backward and fell down hard on the floor, headfirst. I heard a loud thump. He lifted himself up halfway and felt the back of his head. He leaned against the kitchen door and held his hand against the doorway. He turned to me with a look like a wild animal. 'I won't kill you tonight,' he said, 'but tomorrow morning when I feel better, while you're still sleeping, I'm going to slash your throat with the large kitchen knife you use to cut up my steak, wrap you in a sheet, put you dead in a sack, and dump you in the East River!'

"He headed to the bedroom, sat down, and fell backward onto the bed with his arms hanging down and his face tilted. You know what I mean, tilted to the left. I could see his face. One eye, I could see, was open. He looked like he was dead! I put the frying pan on the stove and lay down on the sofa in the living room, my eyes opening and closing all night long for fear he would wake up. I woke up this morning, and there he was in the same position as the night before!

"Oh, Lilly, did I kill him? I was afraid to go into the bedroom, so I just left him there on the bed. What am I going to do, Lillian? What?"

My mother held her close while Josephine cried. My mother kept patting her on the back until she finally calmed down. I listened to Josephine almost in a hypnotic state. I had stopped eating my shredded wheat while Josephine kept on crying and then sobbed softly, until finally she stopped altogether. She kept on shaking.

My mother lifted her from her shoulder and looked at her firmly. "So you think you killed the son of a bitch? Well, let's go see, but good if he is dead. He deserved it! C'mon, go to the bathroom, and wash the tears from your eyes. You look like hell. I'll take you back home. Joey, you come with us in case Gino suddenly wakes from the dead and tries to hurt us. Is the frying pan still on the stove? Joey, if Gino wakes up and comes after us, you pick up the frying pan and hit him with it! You understand?"

I nodded. I was not happy with the idea of hitting a man with a frying pan to knock him out again if he should wake up—and maybe kill him for good—but I listened to my mother and went with them to Josephine's apartment. I was very nervous about seeing a dead man.

Sure enough, there was Gino lying on his back on the bed, his legs dangling and one eye wide open, but there was no life to it. My mother told Josephine to stay in the living room while she checked to see if Gino was really dead. She told me to take the frying pan and wash it down right away with a Brillo pad.

"Wash down the handle especially, and hold on to it," she said.

I went into the kitchen and picked up the black frying pan. It was so heavy I had to lift it with two hands. I almost threw up. I thought I saw small beads of blood. I put on the hot water, let the pan soak, and washed it down with the Brillo. The pan was so heavy even Gino could not take a hit with that frying pan and still be alive.

"It's done, Ma," I told her. I wondered if I had committed a crime washing that pan down. Had I gotten rid of the evidence of a murder?

"Good boy!" She went into the bedroom. She was in there a few minutes and then came out.

"You were right, Josephine. He's dead. No doubt about it, but don't worry—I checked and saw a huge gash on the back of his head. Your frying pan didn't kill him; it was the fall that opened his head up like a watermelon. I saw a lot of blood on the pillow. You didn't commit murder, Josephine, and even if you did, it would have been self-defense. The miserable bastard killed himself because he was drunk!"

I lifted the frying pan to show my mother and Josephine that it was clean. While my mother was checking out the frying pan, Josephine grabbed me by the hand and went into the bedroom to take a look at her dead husband. It was scary seeing a dead man just lying there. I began to shake all over. We came back out to the kitchen.

"Thank God I didn't kill him! I feel better now. He killed himself, the miserable bastard!" Josephine said.

The police came by later that afternoon to inspect Gino still on the bed where he died. Another man from the coroner's office inspected Gino. They knew he was a drunk and so accepted Josephine's explanation that he came home drunk and fell forward, banging his head. He got up and then fell backward trying to get to the bed.

Josephine asked my mother to sit with her at Gino's funeral at Provenzano's. Gino did not have many men friends, and so I noticed that most of Josephine's friends were at the funeral, sitting quietly in black and holding black kerchiefs, paying their respects to Josephine.

My mother sat with her at the end of the casket. I saw Josephine holding a handkerchief to her face while tears streamed down her cheeks. I could not understand that, considering Gino beat her every time he got drunk. After I paid my respects to his body, I went up to Josephine and my mother, who also had tears in her eyes.

My mother later told me that Josephine was in no mood to cry, and so my mother decided to tell her how happy she would be without Gino, and maybe she could meet someone who was not a no-good son of a bitch. She also told her jokes which first made her smile, then laugh inside her handkerchief. Josephine laughed so much she had tears in her eyes.

Later that night, my mother also told me that Gino did not have a gash in the back of his head. She made all that up to protect Josephine. She killed him sure enough with that frying pan hit to his forehead. That was my mother, Lillian.

16
Central Park

It was easy to know the lesson that Peter Capra had given me, but it was not so easy to abide by it, let alone meet the challenge he laid down to carry out acts of goodness, kindness, and generosity. It was tough enough not to be bad. Pepi's men were always thinking about how to steal. I knew that, and whenever Pepi needed me, he would call me. That was a problem for me if I was going to stay in the scholarship program. I knew that for sure.

A few weeks after I had seen Capra, I thought I would go down and play handball with Tommy. It was hot outside, and I felt tense. I think I felt that way because I had not seen Maria except in school. She was still upset with me. Handball always relieved my tension. It kept my mind clear.

After just one game, Johnny showed up. He was very excited. As I was about to hit an ace on Tommy, Johnny shouted out to me, "Hey, Joey! Stop playing for a minute! I have somethin' to tell ya!"

"What? All of a sudden you're talking to me again?"

Johnny smiled. "Oh, forget that. All that trouble is over now.

The cops are not even thinking about the burglary. They have more important things to worry about." He smiled.

I asked Tommy to give me a few minutes, and Johnny and I walked to the water fountain.

Johnny turned his head back and forth and whispered to me, "Joey, I have something hot to tell you. Pepi's guys hijacked a truckful of clothes last night." He smiled. "And the cops are looking for the truck in our neighborhood because they figured that somehow Pepi was involved even though he was supposed to go to court today. Could you imagine the nerve of that guy! He is going to court, and his guys go out and hijack a truck!"

I knew right away he was going to ask me for something. That made me tense. He was suckering me in again.

"Look, Johnny, I don't want any part of the truck, and you have to stop asking me to help Pepi with his illegal activities."

"Illegal activities!" he shot back at me. "Pepi did a lot for us and made us a lot of money!"

"Well, I can't get involved with him anymore, and you know it. We're on probation!"

I started to walk back to the handball court, but he grabbed my arm.

"Wait a minute, Joey. You don't have to do anything bad—or *real* bad. You just have to be a lookout, that's all."

"I don't want to be a lookout. It's too dangerous."

I tried to walk away, but he held on to my arm. I don't know why I just didn't walk away. Old habits, I realized, were tough to beat.

"Listen, Joey, Pepi wants you to watch the truck. He wants you to watch it tonight because the truck is hidden in the empty lot two buildings away from your building. It's a cinch."

I lived practically next door. Pepi was very clever. Johnny kept on talking. "He covered the fence so that no one could look inside. Do you believe my cousin? He goes and steals a truckful of clothes and hides it on the same block as the social club. Who would ever think the truck was on our block? Nobody! And since you live close by, Pepi figured nobody would be suspicious that you were hanging around your own building. In the meantime, if a cop shows, you throw a can at him, he gets distracted, and he starts chasing you! He'll never catch you."

We sat down on a bench. Johnny stood there smiling and talking. I barely heard what he said. I knew one more time I was getting involved and going back on my word to Peter Capra.

"Listen, Joey, it's not a big deal. The guys are watching the empty lot, but they can't do anything if a cop comes by. That's why it's a perfect plan. You can figure out how to distract him. Then the guys will move the truck out as soon as the cop is gone. It will all take a few minutes. You can taunt the cop while he's chasing you. You have to do it, Joey! It's Pepi who's asking."

I glared at Johnny. I knew that Pepi would keep on asking me for something, and the only way I could not be asked is to get away from him. Once again, it seemed to me I had no choice. It was a simple assignment. The theft had already taken place. The cops could not connect me with the truck and the stolen goods, and since I ran pretty fast, I felt confident that I would not be caught. After my talk with Peter Capra, I went against my own intuition and agreed to go along with Johnny.

And just like that, all my determination and willpower melted! I don't know what had come over me. How could I have given in to Johnny so quickly and without a fight? I realized that telling myself that I would not get into trouble anymore was not going to keep me out of trouble.

It became very clear to me that turning away from trouble was much more difficult than I had realized. No longer could I just say to myself that I would not get into trouble. I realized I had to make a great effort to find a way to keep clean, but at the moment, I had given my promise to Johnny that I would be lookout just for this one night. It was a terrible promise.

That night after I ate, I went downstairs, headed toward Second Avenue, and passed the empty lot. Against the fence inside the lot was a large canvas cloth that hid the truck from view. I walked around the block to the back park. From there, I could easily see all the backyards of the buildings on First Street. I walked over to the empty lot.

Through the trees, I could see that the fence separating the park from the back lot was also covered with a large piece of canvas. Pepi's guys had thought of everything.

I walked back hurriedly to First Street, took out a Spalding ball, and started playing stoop ball on my own at my building just to calm down. It was a good exercise because I hit the ball first to the left and then to the right and hit it back with both hands. I increased my hitting speed until finally I missed one, and the Spalding flew by me to the other side of the block. I turned to see Scappy standing in front of Pepi's club, watching me.

I retrieved my ball, went back to the stoop, and started bouncing the ball again. Suddenly, I turned to see a cop walking down the block from Second Avenue. I stopped bouncing the ball, but then I realized that would make the cop suspicious. I could not just stand there with a ball in my hand and do nothing. I started slapping the ball again against the stoop, hoping he would not notice that the fence in front of the empty lot, which held the truck, was covered.

I took a quick look at Scappy, who was leaning to see what the cop was going to do. My heart beat a little faster. I was hoping he would keep going, but he didn't. He kept looking through the holes in the fence, trying to see what was inside the lot behind the canvas cover.

Then he pulled out a flashlight and went to the side of the fence. I thought I had noticed a slight opening in the canvas when I had passed. I was very worried now he was going to see the truck. I knew I had to do something right away to distract him. I had the ball in my hand.

I moved a little closer to him while he was still attempting to find out what was behind the fence. It was then I lifted my arm and threw the ball hard. It sailed straight to him and caught him on the head. His hat fell off, and he dropped his flashlight. As soon as he turned to me, I bolted the other way. He picked up his flashlight, but it was too late for him to see me, or so I thought. I ran across the street, and as I had hoped he would do, he gave chase.

I flew down the block toward First Avenue. The cop was already chasing me. I heard him cursing as he ran. He could not catch me. I was already on the corner of First Avenue when I turned to see him stop and turn the other way. I thought I was safe, but then someone grabbed me from behind. It was another cop! I was caught. He held me by the neck for a few minutes. I was stuck and didn't know what to do.

Just then his grip loosened. I heard Scappy's voice.

"Let him go, or I'll blow your head off right here! Let him go!"

I turned around. Scappy had a gun to the cop's head. His left hand was over his eyes.

"You get going," he said. "Go on, get outta here. Beat it."

I took off as fast I could up First Avenue.

When I reached Third Street, I knew I was safe from being caught. I wondered how Scappy would be able to get away. I worried that the cop had seen my face and could identify me, but it looked as if Scappy had covered his eyes pretty well. I turned at the corner on Third Street and looked back. One of Scappy's men was blindfolding the cop. They pushed him into a waiting car. At the courthouse, I had lost faith in Pepi, but Scappy was watching me, and so I realized Pepi was protecting me all the while. That made me wonder what kind of person he really was. He could shoot a man and then watch over me. He was making it hard for me to walk away.

I ran up to Third Street and waited there about ten minutes. Then I walked to Second Avenue past the Church of the Nativity. I looked up at the white marble steps. Here I was walking past the church thinking I had one more sin to confess. I felt guilty. I had let Peter Capra down again.

I had gone back on my word. I knew then I had to do something different to give myself the strength to do the right thing and not listen to Johnny. I had to overcome my weakness of will. As I passed the church, I vowed once again to keep my word to Capra and to remember to keep that promise. This time, I was determined.

It was the next morning when I passed the lot. The canvas

cloth was gone on the fence, and the lot was empty. I breathed a sigh of relief on the one hand because I had done my job, but I felt terribly guilty about Peter Capra. I was no longer conflicted about crime. I knew if they had committed a crime, they would someday have to pay for that crime. I was done with crime.

I understood now the importance of getting away from the neighborhood, if only not to see Johnny or Pepi. I wanted no money for what I had done. I wanted the whole episode to go away. It was then I decided to see Harold. Why did I not listen to him more often?

It was early Thursday morning, hot and sunny and a teacher's day off, and so we were off. We met at Jerry's candy store. He made us egg creams, cold and sweet. I suggested to Harold we get away for the day.

"Harold, I did a stupid thing last night, and I want to get off the block and out of the neighborhood. I don't want to see anyone or be seen."

He sipped the bottom of his egg cream. "Why, I want to know, is it so difficult for you to stay out of trouble? Now what did you do?"

I told him how Johnny grabbed me while I was playing handball with Tommy, told me about the truck Pepi's guys had hijacked, and needed someone to keep watch at the empty lot where the truck was hidden. Johnny had explained it was for one night. I agreed to do it. It was wrong and stupid of me. Worse, I had no will to tell Johnny I would not do it, because I knew it was not really Johnny asking me but Pepi. Right now, though, I wanted to get away from Johnny, Pepi, and the cops, because the cop I threw the ball at may have seen what I looked like.

"What do you wanna do?" he asked. I told him I wanted to get up to Central Park. I loved the park. It was full of trees, I loved the animals at the zoo, especially the seals, which were very happy and didn't have a care in the world. It was peaceful for me, and most importantly, we would get away from the neighborhood.

"Yes, but how do we get up there?" Harold asked. "I spent my last dime on this egg cream."

"I have fifty cents," I said, "but I thought we would save that for hot dogs, a Coke, and maybe some peanuts for the monkey cage." The monkeys gave me an idea. "Harold, why don't we hitch up there by truck—you know, on the back of a truck? We can go up Third Avenue and get off at Sixty-Fourth Street and then take another truck over to Fifth Avenue. What do you say?"

He agreed. We walked over to Third Avenue. There were many trucks in traffic heading uptown. Some of them had their tailgates down. I worried only that Harold would not grab on fast enough to the chains of the tailgate or that he would not have the strength to hold on to the chain as the truck moved on a bumpy Third Avenue.

I waited for a truck whose tailgate was down to stop for a traffic light. Some trucks came by but did not have their tailgates down. It was not a long wait. There was a moving truck that stopped on Third Avenue and Third Street. The light was red. I grabbed Harold's arm, and together we jumped onto the truck's tailgate. I grabbed the chain on one side and told Harold to grab the other side quickly. He did. He looked whiter than usual. We got stares from drivers watching us sitting on the back of the truck, and fortunately, no cops saw us.

The truck moved along Third Avenue. We were smack in the middle of cars and trucks, taxis, and even horses pulling wagons with fruit on them. Horns were honking, and luckily for us, traffic was moving slowly. It was a tough ride for Harold, especially when the truck stopped short for a traffic light. It was just minutes into the free ride when the truck hit a huge pothole.

Harold screamed. He had lost his grip on the chain and began to slide off the gate. His feet were dragging along the street. I grabbed his arm and held on to him as the truck slowed and then stopped for a light. I jumped off and lifted him by the arm, and he jumped back on the gate and grabbed the chain with both hands. He was terrified. The truck kept hitting deep potholes, but we were able to hold on.

On Forty-Seventh Street, the truck took a right-hand turn, and as it stopped to make its turn, we jumped off. We stood there waiting for another truck to go by with its tailgate down. It didn't take long. As it waited for a light, we jumped onto the back and rode it all the way to Sixty-Second Street. We were lucky again. This truck took a left-hand turn, and we rode all the way to Madison Avenue. From there, we walked one short block to Fifth Avenue and then up to Sixty-Fourth Street to the zoo entrance.

As we were about to go into the park, I saw a small crowd surrounding a man with a large moustache and dressed in a dark-blue suit. I stopped and saw that he was signing autographs. When traffic stopped along Fifth, I looked again and, pointing at him, turned to Harold.

"Harold, look! I think that guy is Thomas E. Dewey! It is! Let's get his autograph!"

He looked across the avenue and nodded his head.

"I'm not sure, but let's find out!"

We ran across the street and pushed our way to the front. It was Dewey!

"Hey, you're Thomas E. Dewey," I blurted out, "and you ran for president and lost!"

After I said that, I realized my mistake. Dewey turned to me and studied me carefully.

"You know who I am! Well, how about that?" He looked us over. "You boys are not from this neighborhood, are you?"

He kept on writing his name to pads being handed to him. The adults were very polite. They were not pushing their way to the front. They waited for Dewey to finish one signature and then go to another.

I looked at him carefully. He had a large head and watery blue eyes. His moustache was large and had a slight upward twist to it. When he looked around, it seemed as if he was thinking many thoughts at once. I saw how smart he was. He seemed to take in everything around him. He continued to write signatures and talk to us at the same time. He looked very intelligent to me.

"No, we're not, but we still would like to have your autograph. My father got this union notice that told him to vote for President Truman, and he did."

Dewey stopped writing, looked at me carefully, laughed, and asked a man for a writing pad. "I probably would have won if his union had told him to vote for me, but it was not meant to be. Even though your father did not vote for me, son, do you still want my autograph?"

I didn't hesitate. "Yes!" I paused as he began to write and stared at him. For some reason, I just blurted out to him what I was thinking. "It looks like you're looking everywhere at once, and your head is so large, I think you're thinking a lot of thoughts at the same time." Again, I realized I may have said the wrong thing.

Dewey leaned his head back and laughed again.

Harold elbowed me. "Joey, quiet. You talk too much!"

Dewey was smiling. "So where are you from, if not from here?"

This time Harold answered. "We're from downtown, the Lower East Side."

"Oh, downtown. You must be Boys' Club boys! What is your name, son?" he asked me.

"Joey D'Angelo, and my friend here is Harold Tapper."

He wrote out his signature on a notepad he was carrying, tore off the page, and handed it to me. Then wrote another and handed it to Harold and then repeated my name and wrote it down. I wondered why. I thanked him and crossed Fifth Avenue and into Central Park. I was pretty excited about meeting Dewey.

When I turned around, he was still writing autographs, but then he paused for a moment and looked at me and Harold. He stood there smiling, nodded his head, and waved to us! I was impressed. I waved back.

We went into the park filled with parents and kids, past the seals playing in a large pool. From there, we walked along winding lanes, past huge trees of oak, maple, and elm. The air was clean and fresh and good to smell. We walked through the birdhouses and the monkey house and stopped to watch polar bears lounging in their lair. One of them was swimming on his back in a large pool at the base of the rock. I thought they might be very hot in the humid June air.

We saw a hot dog stand and grabbed two hot dogs and Cokes. We sat down on one of the benches near the monkey building and watched everyone walk by. It was hot, so we walked over to the lake where kids were sailing little boats. Shades from thick foliage of trees kept the sun from beating down on us. We sat there eating and just watching people go by, smiling and happy. A cool breeze blew. We were far away from our neighborhood. It was peaceful and seemed as if it were another world here. We walked over to the big clock where, on the hour, statues of animals circled round and round, banging their musical instruments. I was relaxed, and for a long time, my head was clear, and my mind was at peace.

After a few hours, we walked outside the park and down Fifth Avenue. Doormen stood in front of glass doors, letting people in and out of huge buildings. Women in high heels walked small dogs on leashes. Even though it was hot, men wore suits and ties.

Harold and I walked down the avenue not saying anything to each other. It was not a neighborhood like ours, and we both felt different. For me, it was this time away from the neighborhood where I could think in peace and not be worried about Pepi. I realized I didn't want to ruin my life, and I could see if I hung around my neighborhood growing up, I could easily do that.

I got home around six in the evening. As soon as I sat down to eat, there was a knock on the door. A chill went through me. Had anyone found out I helped Pepi looking out for the hijacked truck? Blood drained from my head.

It was a false alarm. In walked Tom Mansfield. My first thought was that he was going to give me and my parents bad news. My parents greeted him with homemade wine and pasta. He thanked my mom and sat down with a smile on his face.

"Mr. Capra, the director of the Boys' Club, wants to see Joey Saturday morning in his office. Would that be all right with you? It has to do with the scholarship."

My father shrugged. "So he wants to see Joey. I have no problem with that. Do you, Lilly?"

She shook her head. "Is he the one who is to make the decision about the school? Joey can see him, but I must tell you, Tommy,

I am not happy with all this talk of Joey going away from home. Aren't there any good schools here in New York he can go to? What is so special about boarding school?" She sat down.

"Mrs. D'Angelo, there are just too many distractions for Joey here in New York. Once he goes away from the city and the neighborhood, he will be able to focus on studies. Also, from a good boarding school, he has a better chance to go to a good college. He can go anywhere to college, but Joey should have the opportunity to go to the best college we can get him into. Mr. Capra wants to talk to him about that."

He had said enough for me. I ate my pasta without a word to anyone. A gloom fell over me. I was already nervous. Had Capra found out that I was a lookout for Pepi? Somehow, he managed to know everything that happened. He had so many sources of information, it seemed. He knew everything I did. Why would he call me in so soon after I watched the lot for Pepi? He had to know!

I walked into Capra's office on Saturday morning, and he asked me brusquely to sit down.

He did not look happy. This could be the end for me. I sat there for a few minutes looking up at the pictures on the wall behind his desk of him and other men, smiling. I leaned forward to see another photo of him and Dewey. Before I could speak, Capra put down his pen and stared at me. He shook his head. If he asked me about the truck, I vowed to tell him the truth.

"Joey, I don't know how you do it, but it seems whenever I am having second thoughts about your being in the program, you surprise me!" He leaned back in his chair. "You realize, of course, that after your court hearing, I was seriously thinking about dropping you. God knows, after three boys had already come and gone, I needed to find someone who would not let the Boys' Club down one more time." He pointed his finger at me. "That is why I need to be absolutely sure about you. You understand me, Joey?"

He leaned back and rocked in his chair a few times with his arms behind his large, bald head, staring at me through large-framed glasses. "So tell me, Joey, how did you convince Thomas Dewey to call me on your behalf?"

I was stunned by the question. I thought for certain he would ask me about the hijacking. "I don't know, sir. Harold and I decided to go up to Central Park, and I saw him signing autographs on Fifth Avenue. We ran over and asked him for his autograph, and he gave it to us. He asked us where we were from. I told him we were from the Lower East Side and that my father was a Democrat and voted against him. He asked me how I knew him, and I told him he ran for president against President Truman and lost. That was it!"

Capra smiled. "That was certainly not the most diplomatic statement to make, but he must have been surprised that a boy of your age from the Lower East Side knew that. You were just nine when he lost, so he must have been impressed."

Capra stared at me, nodding. I looked down for a few seconds but looked right up at him. I figured now he was going to hit me with the truck and my involvement. I was ready.

"Joey, I wondered these last few weeks what I was going to do with you before Dewey called me. Yes, I know him. He is one of many supporters of our Boys' Club. And there is another man who has played a role here, and his name is Dwight Davis Jr. I have asked him to talk to you. I want his impression of you, since he and I thought of the scholarship idea that bears Joe Brooks's name. We were all good friends, and his word counts very much to me."

He took his pen and began to write. "I will give you the time and date of your appointment with him. He asked me to send you to his club, the University Club, on Fifth Avenue. You will meet him for lunch next week. What he tells me after your meeting will help me in making my decision."

He handed me a note. "Joey, it is not enough to have brains. You need to want this scholarship. You need to convince me that you are serious and that once we select you, you will not disappoint us. And, Joey, I want to see some progress on your part. And stay out of trouble! Understand?"

I nodded. Capra got up, shook my hand, and walked me to the door.

"You got a boost from Mr. Dewey. Now let's see how well you do with Mr. Davis!"

I left his office and headed down First Avenue back home. I'd dodged another bullet, and he had me thinking. I looked around as I walked down toward First Street. People were outside their tenement houses just talking. It was getting hotter, but I was anxious to take some steam out of my system by playing handball.

As I approached First Street, I saw Scappy getting his shoes shined at the corner stand.

"Hey, Joey! Wait a minute!"

The shoe-shine man snapped the cloth hard on one shoe and then the other. Scappy's black shoes sparkled.

"Okay, okay! Enough!" Scappy said.

He handed the shoe-shine man a dollar, got off the stand, grabbed my arm, and smiled.

"Pepi has been looking all over for you. He wants to see you. That was a very smart move, Joey, running right past me and letting the cop chase you. Right after that, I told the guys to get the truck outta there. Very smart move, and Pepi is very happy. I don't know what you do to this guy, but he likes you like his own son, I'll tell you that. I'll tell ya one thing! That cop won't bother you anymore. He got the message when I put my gun to his head! Ha!"

I knew that Scappy, if he had to, would have pulled the trigger. I'd made a big mistake helping Pepi.

As Scappy and I walked to the social club, I saw Maria sitting on a park bench in the park with her girlfriend Connie. She turned toward me and stared at me. I waved at her, but she did not wave back. She kept on staring at me. Scappy kept walking with his arm around my shoulder. She was still upset with me. But why? Everything had cooled down. Now she was making me very upset with her attitude.

When he saw us, Pepi got up and put his arm around me.

"Joey, you saved me again. That was a smart move you made. You know, soon as you got that cop away from the lot, Scappy got the boys to take the truck to Brooklyn. We stashed it there in an old warehouse. And you know what, Joey? We sold everything in the truck. Every shirt, sweater, jacket, and slacks on that damn truck. We made a lot of money, Joey. Sit down. You want a Coke?"

I sat down. Pepi asked one of his men to get me a Coke. He sat there tapping his fingers on the table, smiling. I knew he really liked me, but sometimes, he got me very nervous. How was I going to get away from him? He was so good to me!

"Yes, Joey, we made a lot of money."

The Coke came filled with ice. I was thirsty and drank fast. It cooled me off. I sat there waiting for Pepi to say something. He waited for me to finish drinking. Then he stood up and pulled out his wallet and opened it. He pulled out a ten-dollar bill and was about to hand it to me, but then he put it back inside and took out a five-dollar bill and five singles and handed them to me. I held the money for a minute and then put it on the table.

"No, Pepi, you don't have to pay me. I did it as a favor for you. I don't want to take the money." I was thinking that if any detective asked me, I could tell him I earned no money.

He looked at me, surprised. "Are you sure, Joey? Are you sure? We made a lot of money on that truck."

"That's all right," I said. "Next time."

Pepi looked at me suspiciously. He wasn't used to anyone turning his money down. He shook his head, picked up the ten dollars, and put it back in his wallet.

"Oh, okay, Joey. I understand now. You're on probation." He sat back down and pointed to the Coke, which was half-full. "Finish your Coke, Joey."

"Yeah, if somebody asks me, I can tell them I did nothing wrong and never got paid for anything."

Pepi smiled.

I left and then ran to the park to see if Maria was still there.

She was gone. I sat down. She made me angry leaving like that. I thought she would be back. Johnny was talking to me, and it would be just a few more days before she did. I was convinced of that, but I still missed her. How would it be if I went away to school? How could I leave her? If I missed seeing her for just a few weeks, how would I get by not seeing her for months? I sighed and shook my head. I thought that I must really love her.

I turned to see if Tommy Schwartz was at the handball courts. He was not. I heard some shouting. Behind the courts, the old Italian men from First Street were standing on the bocce court walking toward the white ball and their own black balls to see which of their balls came closest to the white ball. The winners let out a shout, laughing and pushing each other.

The week went by very quickly. I decided I would meet with Dwight Davis wearing a blue shirt and a tie. I sometimes wore ties on Sunday, but never on Thursday. I took a subway up to Fifth Avenue and Fifty-Second Street. I was not too far from Central Park. I looked around. The buildings were huge. Ladies' shop windows were lit brightly with elegant women's dresses. Men's shops had expensive suits and jackets.

Tiffany's window sparkled with diamond rings and bracelets and beautiful white-as-can-be necklaces. Above the buildings along Fifth Avenue, I could see a huge expanse of blue sky and puffy clouds lazily moving east. The air was clean. People were dressed neatly and walking quickly. Everyone was in a hurry.

I looked down at my pants to make sure they were clean and neatly pressed. They were. I checked my shirt and made sure my tie was straight. After I did that, I walked two blocks up Fifth Avenue to the University Club. A large forest-green canopy covered the entrance. Huge columns stood on each end. Curved railings guided me to the front doors. I walked up the marble steps to go in, but soon as I got to the door, the doorman got in my way and held his arm to my chest.

"So where do you think you're going, kid?" he said in a tough tone of voice.

He held his hand on my chest. I looked down at his hand. Already I was angry, and I didn't want to be. I wanted to be as pleasant as possible for Dwight Davis.

"I have an appointment with Mr. Davis, Dwight Davis. Would you call him, please?"

He kept his hand on my chest and pressed harder. He shook

his head. "Look, kid. Mr. Davis is having lunch, and I'm not going to let you in here just because you happen to get his name from somebody coming into the club. You get me? So beat it!"

Then he gave me a little shove and sent me flying backward. I managed to grab the curved railing just in time, or I would have fallen down to the sidewalk.

I checked to see if I had ripped my shirt or my tie. I checked my pants. They were okay. He was a tall man. He now had his hands on his hips, smiling at me. I was angry. I went back up the steps. He stuck his arm out. I pushed it away, and then he grabbed me. I put my hand on his arm and squeezed tight.

"Look," I said, "all you have to do is call him and let him know that Joey is here. You're making me late! Call him if you don't believe me. You're making a big mistake!" I gave him a defiant look. I was not about to back off.

He hesitated but then called over another doorman. He whispered to him, and the second doorman went inside. I waited. Men in dark suits, white shirts, and striped ties came up the steps. They stared at me while the doorman blocked my way. I didn't care. I had an appointment with Mr. Davis, and I was going to make sure I saw him.

The doorman came back with a tall, thin man about fifty. He had a smile on his face. His hair was wavy brown and parted on his left side. Long, thin wrinkles lined his cheeks down to his mouth. He wore a smart dark-blue pin-striped suit. I noticed his shiny cordovan shoes. He smiled at me and then stopped smiling when he saw the doorman holding on to me.

"What is the meaning of this? Here, let him go immediately. You must be Joey, right?"

The doorman put his arm down. I nodded.

Davis glared at the doorman. "Why didn't you let him in? I have an appointment with him."

The doorman flushed and stepped back.

"Idiot!" Davis shouted. He took me by the shoulder and led me into the club. "Sorry about that, Joey. Come, I'll take you to the dining room."

I was amazed at the height of the ceilings; they were at least thirty feet high. The entrance hall was large, about one hundred feet across and just as long. On the walls were huge murals. In the dining room, maroon curtains hung on the windows that looked to be at least ten feet high. I could hear the tap of steps on the marble floor beneath us. Waiters in gold jackets and black trousers, with white napkins hanging on their arms, stood against the walls.

We sat down at a table with many pieces of silver. I felt a little uncomfortable. At home, I had a knife, a fork, and a spoon. Mostly men were seated at the tables surrounding ours.

"So, young man, you are Joey D'Angelo. I am absolutely delighted to meet you."

He shook my hand and then put his napkin on his lap, and I did the same. I figured also if I watched him use his silverware, I would pick up whatever utensil he picked up.

He asked me if I wanted a drink and called the waiter.

"Yes, Mr. Davis, the usual scotch for you, and what about your young friend?"

"I'll have a Coke with lots of ice," I said.

I looked around. Davis smiled.

"Pretty impressive, Joey, isn't it? Yale alumni started coming here years ago, and pretty soon, the club was opened to the public. Well, not exactly the public, but you know, the so-called elite of New York. And now, Joey, you're here!"

I looked at him, thinking the only club I belonged to was Pepi's club. I had a long way to go. Our drinks came. Davis took his scotch and drank. I noticed how red his cheeks were. His blue eyes looked very watery.

"I suppose, Joey, you are wondering how you came here, how this scholarship program all started. I suppose you're wondering about that."

I drank from my Coke and noticed that men at other tables were staring at us. Davis also noticed. He just smiled and waved. One of the club members came over to the table, leaned over, and shook his hand. He turned to me.

"And this, my good man, is my young friend Joey D'Angelo. He is from our Boys' Club downtown. Someday, he will be a member of this club. What do you think about that?" He smiled as the man looked at me and smiled also.

"Any friend of Dwight Davis Jr. is a friend of mine. Glad you could be here, young man!"

Then he extended his hand and shook hands with me. I was very surprised and felt much more comfortable. We ordered lunch. I ordered a ham and cheese sandwich with lots of lettuce. Davis laughed and ordered a turkey club sandwich. He took another drink of scotch and emptied the glass. The waiter returned a few minutes later with another one.

"Well, Joey, a few years ago, Peter Capra, Joe Brooks, and I went on a short trip to North Carolina, a duck-shooting trip." He paused. His face grew grim, and he looked down at the table and sighed.

"We all sat there in the early morning. It was a beautiful morning on that calm lake. It was surrounded by tall trees. Birds were chirping away. It was early dawn, the sun just coming up on the horizon, and we were all calm and quiet.

"And then it happened. A mallard, a duck with bright green coloring, flew out of the bush. Joe stood up and was about to shoot, but the boat was rocking slightly when he stood up. Joe somehow lost his balance. He slipped and fell with his shotgun spinning in the air. When it landed, it went off and hit Joe in the chest. There was blood all over. We tried to stop the bleeding, but it was no use. He was dead a few minutes later."

He cleared his throat, took another sip of scotch, and sighed, biting his lip and wiping tears away from his cheeks. He composed himself.

"Pete Capra and I decided to do something in his memory. He was our best friend at Yale. He was a great man, friendly, kind, and generous to all who needed help. And that is why we decided on a scholarship for a young, underprivileged boy who would have a chance to become someone, someone like Joe Brooks." He paused and took another sip of his drink.

"Joey, Pete Capra thinks you're that boy who will take that scholarship and run with it. Oh, I know he has his doubts, but I know, Joey, you can do it. I can see that. I like what you did out there. You have spunk, sticking around when the doorman pushed you away. I liked that."

I brushed back my dark-brown hair, which fell over my forehead. I noticed how white Davis was. I looked around and realized my dark skin set me off from the rest of the people in the room, including the waiters.

"You know, Joey, my father was a great man, a great tennis player. They named a trophy after him. It's called the Davis Cup. That cup is in honor of my father who did so much for the game of tennis. I like to think that this scholarship will do as much for the young men of your neighborhood." He paused again. "It's up to you Joey, and I'm glad your name is Joey."

Davis began to tear up. I looked down as he wiped his eyes. He lifted the scotch and drank down almost half the glass. He looked elegant in his dark-blue suit and blue paisley tie with red dots.

Our lunch came, and we began to eat. I hardly said a word. He spoke throughout lunch, but as he spoke, he made me realize what a responsibility I had to make good with the scholarship if they offered it to me. It was not only a scholarship offer; it was a commitment by Dwight Davis Jr. and Peter Capra to honor the life of their friend. I understood that now.

After lunch, he walked me outside and shook my hand. He had a smile on his face when I left.

I wondered what Davis was going to say to Pete Capra about me. I thought I had a good lunch with him, and I felt pretty good about the next meeting at the Boys' Club with Capra. I had not seen Pepi, and the hijacking of the truck was ancient history in the neighborhood. I thought it would be a good meeting, and for the first time, I was not nervous meeting with him.

I tried to see if Maria was in the park. I couldn't go to her place. By Sunday night, I was really upset with her, and I vowed I would be really tough with her when I had a chance to talk to her, but I knew deep down, when I did see her and she smiled at me, I would give in. She would wrap her arms around me, and my anger would melt away.

Capra called me that Monday afternoon. He must have spoken to Dwight Davis. I liked the man because he defended me and scolded the doorman. He was interested in protecting me, a young kid he didn't even know. He knew my feelings were hurt, and he did the right thing. That showed how good a man he was.

I sat down again in front of Capra. I was surprised to see that he did not look happy. He glared at me and then threw his pen down and folded his hands. *What did I do now,* I asked myself, *that he should be so angry with me?* I shifted in the chair.

"Joey, I'll get right to the point! Did you help in the hijacking of that truck?"

I was stunned. I thought about my answer to him. I was not really involved with the hijacking. I was just a lookout for the truck, and so I answered that I was not involved.

"Did you get any money from the hijacking?" he asked.

That was an easy question to answer.

"No, sir, I did not." I looked straight at him when I said it. That was tough.

"And, Joey, did you know it was Pepi Savino and his gang of thugs who stole that truck?"

That was another question I could answer honestly. I told him I knew only after I found out from Johnny that a truck had been hijacked and that while Pepi was in court, some friends of his stole the truck. I wasn't even sure that Pepi knew about it until he got out of court.

Capra leaned back in his chair and stared at me. I kept a straight face, but somehow, he knew something was not right. He shook his head. Fortunately for me, he had failed to ask me the right question. Was I at all involved in the hijacking? If he had asked me that question, I would have been finished because I would have told him the truth. He didn't ask that question.

"Well, all right, Joey. I'm not going to repeat myself about Pepi. You stay away from him!"

He paused again. "I talked to Dwight Davis. He liked you,

Joey. He told me you had spunk. He told me he thinks you can get up there to school and make it through. He thinks you will survive. You will last where the other boys did not, he said. Is he right, Joey? Will you last?"

I bit my lip. How could I answer his question? I could not. I wasn't even sure I wanted to go away to school, but I knew that if I had lost the opportunity, I would be very upset. I didn't want to lose—not in handball, not in stickball, and not in the hunt for this scholarship. It was in my blood to win. Even though this opportunity had fallen to me, I knew I wanted to win it because I hated to lose—I would if Capra pulled the opportunity.

But the decision—if it came to that—to accept the scholarship would mean a complete upheaval of my life. I was not ready to answer that question even for myself.

"Mr. Capra, I know that if I win that scholarship, I will have a big responsibility to you and the Boys' Club and to Mr. Davis also. He told me about Mr. Joe Brooks. How could I turn down such a chance, and yet, how can I leave everything behind? I'll know the answer to that question if I get the scholarship. That's the most honest answer I can give you right now."

Capra shook his head and then smiled. "I like that you're honest with me, Joey. I like that you laid your heart out on the table. I like that. Honesty is very important to me. You keep your nose clean, understand, and maybe you will get lucky. Maybe you will have that tough decision to make, and let's hope you make the right decision. That's all I have to say."

He extended his hand. I shook it and left. I didn't feel honest after that meeting. Should I have offered the information that I had been a lookout after the truck was hijacked? Would he have thrown me out of the program at that point?

I felt tainted for not being completely honest. I excused myself for being only human, but I had misled him by not speaking up when I should have. I vowed once again to be honest. I made it a point to try to keep that promise to myself. I vowed that given the chance, I would tell the whole truth no matter what the consequences.

I walked home alone thinking about Maria. In a month, summer would begin, and the school year would end. I would have to work with Tom and Sue. I wanted to see Maria now more than ever.

But if Maria would not see me, then what? It happened that as I thought about Maria, I saw Rachel walking up First Avenue. Even from a distance, I could see she was beautiful. She walked with confidence, her head up, and she had a good strong stride. She had a bounce to her walk. She appeared from a distance to be smiling in a quiet sort of way. Her hair was cut just below her shoulders. I would try to get with Rachel most definitely if Maria kept on ignoring me.

I wasn't sure if I was being honest with Maria at that point for thinking about Rachel; I thought that if she didn't want to see me, then I was free to do what I wanted. It was one of those questions I could not quite answer. It was just too complicated for me. Was I doing the right thing in just thinking about Rachel? I thought about it. Perhaps I was letting my anger at Maria express itself. Here I was, facing another problem. Only time would tell what I was going to do next.

17 Rachel

I thought I had passed one more hurdle in getting the scholarship after I met with Dwight Davis Jr. At the moment, though, I was actually thinking more about Maria. The only benefit to her staying away from me was that she did not know how important the scholarship opportunity was becoming to me. Any idea that I was going away and she would have dumped me.

Maria told me her mother still wanted her to stay away from me just a couple of weeks more. I could not figure that one out. Her street was full of kids getting into trouble with plenty of gangsters hanging out on her block, stealing and hijacking trucks any chance they could, so what did she have against me?

My deeper interest in Rachel came to me when Harold and I were trading comic books one night. It was also the night I had the first and last fight I ever had with Harold, and the fight was over Rachel.

I was in my room after we had eaten and saw my old comic books stacked high against my dresser. So much had happened to me over the past few months that I found myself no longer interested in them, so I asked Harold if he wanted to trade with me. I would trade two for one, just to get rid of them. It was in the well-lit hallway of 48 East First Street one night in June when the trouble started.

Harold and I each had a large stack of comic books. Just a year earlier, I had loved the heroes who could do extraordinary things, like Superman, who could move mountains and fly into space, and Batman, who had a double identity, the Batmobile, and Batplane. Harold liked Wonder Woman. I thought it was because he missed having a mother around. She died when he was a little kid. In the hallway, he picked up a comic with a picture of the long-legged Wonder Woman dressed in the red, white, and blue colors of the American flag and kissed it.

"Wow, look at her. She's gorgeous! Hey, you know who looks like her? Rachel in our class!"

I put my comics down on my lap and thought about her. I remembered how she walked with such an air about her, confident and sure about herself. She had dark-brown eyes and high cheekbones. There was no doubt she and Maria competed as the best-looking girl in our class. I was definitely attracted to Rachel, but I loved Maria, no doubt about that. I missed her.

I wanted to get to know Rachel better. For some dumb reason, I thought it would be a good time since I was not seeing Maria. I knew it could be a big mistake, but Rachel was so beautiful, I could not resist, and I didn't. I thought of her sometimes when I went to bed at night and woke up in the morning. I thought about wanting to hold her tight to me and kiss her softly. So I stupidly thought if Maria did not want to see me, Rachel would.

I remembered how Rachel was always dressed elegantly and neatly. I liked her best in her blue blouse and plaid skirt, black socks, and soft flat shoes, her dark hair sometimes pulled back tightly and held there with a maroon ribbon and sometimes just hanging loose. She was soft-spoken, and she smiled often with her mouth closed. Her dark eyes looked at me, and they also smiled at me.

In class, she looked over at me and saw that I was staring at her. She smiled back. I knew then she liked me, but I never talked to her because of Maria.

When Harold brought up her name like that, I got very upset. He handed me a Superman comic book.

I said to him, "Listen, Harold, Rachel likes me. I see how she looks at me, and I'm gonna ask her out. School will be out soon, and if I don't ask her now, I will miss my chance."

He just smiled which was more like a smirk to me, and threw down an Archie comic that was so old the paper had turned yellow and the edges of the pages had frayed. He shook his head. I could see now he was angry.

"Joey, you are making one giant mistake, for Christ's sake! She's Jewish, and you are Italian. I am Jewish; so who do you think she should be going out with?"

He waved his hand at me. "Okay, you're good looking, green or brown eyes—I can't figure out what color because they change so much—and everybody knows you hang out with the big, bad guys on our block, but still, I'll say it again: she is Jewish, and I am Jewish, and you are Italian. So that settles that! Besides, don't you know she is from a special sect of Judaism? Her father would kill you if he saw you with her. He might even kill me; but at least I have a shot. You! You got nuthin'!" With a parting shot at me, he said, "And don't you think Maria is going to get upset with you?"

It made no difference to me what kind of Jew she was or that I was Italian. I didn't even understand why he brought it up. I wanted to take her to the movies, hold her tightly, and kiss her hard. That is what I wanted.

"Okay, Harold. I'll tell ya what. Let's flip a coin. The winner asks Rachel out. How does that sound to you?"

He slammed down his comic book and shook his head. He was very upset. His argument about Jews and Italians when it came to girls was very weak, and I didn't buy it. I just didn't give a damn about religion when it came to a good-looking girl.

He fumbled in his pocket and pulled out a nickel.

"You're an idiot," he said. "You don't want to listen to me. All right, I'll flip a coin with you." I just smiled.

That was the moment trouble really started. Harold called heads and flipped the nickel. It rolled and rolled, finally resting on its side against the wall, but with the tail side facing out. I declared myself the winner of the toss. We began to argue, and in a few seconds, we started throwing punches at each other. Comic books were strewn all over the hallway floor. I caught Harold with punches on both sides of his head. Then he surprised me with a punch to my jaw. He got me pretty good.

Harold's father must have heard the commotion, because he was down the steps in seconds. He broke up the fight and shook his head.

"Friends—and look at you both! Fighting like animals!" He made us shake hands and then asked what the fight was about.

I told him. He just laughed.

"In ten years, you won't even remember this girl. If it's so important to you, I will flip the coin. I don't get it, Joey. Harold told me you had a girlfriend!"

He flipped the coin, and tails came up. I began to wonder. Was he right? Would I forget Rachel? And if I would forget Rachel, what about Maria?

"Okay, Joey, you won, but remember this: never let a girl come between you ever again! You understand me? Just make sure you both forget about it and stay good friends. Now it's getting late, Joey. Time for you to go home."

I gave Harold a hug. I really loved that kid. "Sorry, Harold, for punching you!"

He looked at my jaw. "I gave you a good shot there, didn't I?"

We laughed.

The next morning, I saw Rachel at her desk. I looked over at Harold. He was shaking his head. He came over to me.

"You have no chance," he said, motioning with his hands as if he were an umpire calling a runner safe. "And don't tell me later I didn't warn you! In fact, I don't think I have a chance either. She's Hasid, you idiot!"

I paid no attention.

Sore loser, I thought, and I smiled at Rachel. I got lucky. Maria was not at school that morning. At noontime, I went over to Rachel and told her how I liked the maroon ribbon in her hair, her white collared blouse, and the blue pleated skirt she was wearing. Her white socks were raised above her knees. I asked if she would she let me walk her home. She looked at me with an expression I could not read.

"I'll think about it," she said. "I'll let you know after school."

I went back to my desk wondering. It was just like a girl to keep a guy in suspense. Guys would tell you right away what they were thinking, but not girls.

In the afternoon, Mrs. Beanstalk, our English teacher, a tall blonde with bright blue eyes, discussed verbs and adjectives. It was getting on close to three o'clock. I liked English class, but today the lesson dragged. I was getting anxious.

When I looked over at Rachel, she didn't seem too excited about my offer. She seemed to be concentrating on her work and barely looked my way. I shrugged it off to girls acting smart and coy, especially when they wanted to hide their feelings. With Maria, I always knew where I stood, but not with Rachel.

When the clock hit three, I turned to her. She smiled at me as she packed her bagful of books. I packed my backpack and stared at her. She was keeping me in suspense until the end. Finally, she walked over to my desk.

"Well, let's go, then!" she said. "What are you waiting for?"

We walked out the door toward Eldridge Street. I was hoping none of the guys from First Street would see me because for sure they would have made catcalls at us and maybe said something about Maria.

We walked south on Forsyth Street along the park. Tall oak and maple trees shaded us from the sun, and a cool breeze made her skirt flap up and down. Kids in the park were playing stickball. My long hair blew from one side to another. We talked about school, the kids in our class, and Harold. She thought Harold was cute and liked him a little, but he was too talky and nosy even though he was smart. Boy, was I glad she didn't really like him in that sort of way.

She was just so pretty with that maroon ribbon at the back of her head, her soft white neck, dark eyes that smiled at me, white freckled face, and puckered lips that looked juicy. I wanted to kiss those lips really badly. Was it possible to love two women at the same time? I wondered about that.

She smiled a good bit and glanced at me occasionally from the corner of her eye. I told her that someday I wanted to become a lawyer or a doctor.

She liked that. I asked her what she wanted to be, and she said one thing she did not want to do is be in her father's business. It was then it happened. Just as I was about to ask her what that business was, Rachel let out a muffled cry and held her hand to her mouth.

He was about six feet tall and wore a white shirt, a long black coat down to his knees, and a large black fedora on his head. His beard was graying, thick, and full, and curls of hair hung down over his ears. He looked at me angrily and then at Rachel. I hadn't realized I was holding her hand. We both stood there frozen. I knew right away it was Rachel's father. Harold tried to warn me, and I didn't listen.

Her father grabbed my arm and pulled it away from Rachel, took her hand, and gave me a shove. I fell backward, tripped on a crack in the sidewalk, and landed on my head with a soft thud. He caught me by surprise. I was stunned and a little dizzy.

I picked myself up slowly. I felt the back of my head. It was soft and wet. I looked at my hand and saw blood on my fingers. Rachel and her father stood there briefly watching me and then began to walk away. Suddenly her father turned to me and, still holding her hand, pointed and shouted at me.

"You stay away from my daughter! She is not your kind!"

His words stuck in my head. I wondered at first what he meant by them, but then it was clear to me. He was upset because I was Italian and not Jewish, but Harold also told me he was of a different sect of Jew. Of these things, he was light-years ahead of me. I was just a street kid. Harold was more aware of being Jewish than I was of being Italian.

I felt my head again. A lump was already forming. I didn't care. I was thinking about Rachel. Things were going so well up to that moment. I took my handkerchief and put it on the back of my head. I never thought I would have a chance to date Rachel now, to talk or do anything. I became so depressed, I didn't think much about the dizziness I was feeling. I was too hurt.

I got home and washed and thought the bleeding had stopped, but when I heard my mother gasp after looking at my head, I knew I was still bleeding.

"Look, your head is bleeding like a cut pig! Your shirt is full of blood! It's ruined! Didn't I tell you never to fight? O Jesu Cristo!"

In seconds, she had me lying facedown on my bed with ice wrapped in a cloth pressed hard against my head. It felt very cold and very wet.

"Wait until your father comes home!" she warned. "You have a lot of explaining to do. You have a bad temper, just like your father, and now look at you! That's what your temper will get you in life. A bleeding head! Didn't Mr. Capra tell you to stay out of trouble?"

"Ma, stop! It was an accident! Really! I just tripped and fell on a crack in the sidewalk. I was not in a fight!"

She did not believe me. She pressed the ice firmly against my head. My father walked in the door. He looked at me and shook his head.

"Look at your son," my mother said. "And he promised he would stay out of trouble! What are we going to do with him?" She checked the back of my head and saw that the bleeding had stopped. She took the ice pack off my head.

"Joey, I know when you are not telling me the truth. I know you are hiding something from us. I just know it."

The witch in my mother was speaking. If I did not tell all the truth, somehow she knew it and would come down on me hard. My father went in to wash up and returned to the table, filled a glass of wine, glared at me, and shook his head.

"So what happened this time?" he asked.

I was stuck. How could I tell them that Rachel's father pushed me and I slammed my head on the sidewalk? My father had a temper, and I did not want any more trouble than I had already started. I thought the truth would come out in the end anyway, but I just did not want it to come out at that moment. A knock at the door bought me time.

My mother opened it, and in walked Harold. He came into my room, took one look at me, grabbed his lower lip with his teeth, and shook his head.

"Oh my God, what happened to you?"

"That is exactly what I want to know!" my mother said.

He looked at me and hesitated not a second before telling her everything he knew, for Harold had his own code of honor, and his code included telling the truth most of the time. He also had a big mouth. I got out of bed and sat down at the table.

My mother put out a plate for Harold, and he blurted out the whole story: the comic books, the fight over Rachel, the walk I took with her, and then to make things worse, he just had to mention that he warned me about Rachel's father, and he figured that Rachel and I met her father. It was a guess on his part, but when he looked at me, silent and head bowed, he nodded.

"Oh, yeah. They met her father, all right!"

I could have killed him, but I knew he never meant any harm to me. We were buddies, after all.

"Rachel and her parents are Jewish but also Hasidic! They're the most conservative Jews! Joey is Italian. I just figured that Joey met Rachel's father, and the rest I don't know."

I never thought Harold was lacking in brainpower. He was smart, all right. My mother turned to my father and then to me.

"Joey can fill in the rest," she said," but let's eat first."

I felt a small lump in the back of my head and checked my fingers to see if the blood had clotted. It had. I began to eat, still feeling a little woozy. The usually talkative Harold began to eat and kept shoveling in the pasta, quiet now that his words had stirred the pot.

My father asked Harold if his father knew he was at our house. Harold nodded and lowered his head. My father filled his glass again from the gallon jug he kept at the foot of his chair, scooped up with a slice of Italian bread the last bit of red sauce sitting at the bottom of his plate, empty now of ziti, and ate it with great satisfaction. Then he turned from Harold to me.

"Now it's your turn. You can start where Harold left off, and don't leave anything out!"

I took a deep breath and told them the truth of what had happened. "He looked at me and then his daughter, and I could see he was really upset. Then he pulled my hand away and gave me a little shove, which caught me by surprise, and it was then I fell backward and hit my head."

I could see my father's massive chest heaving up and down. He folded his arms across his body and glared at me.

"So he pushed you, and that is how you fell down. Is that right?"

I nodded.

He took a deep breath, emptied his glass of red wine, and slammed it down on the table. Harold and I nearly jumped out of our chairs.

"We will have to have a little talk with this Jewish man who sees fit to push around little Italian boys. No offense to you, Harold."

I wondered why, even though Jewish and Italian families were very much alike, my father thought it important to remind us that Rachel's father was Jewish. Why would he say that? I looked over at Harold. He just shrugged. It made no difference to him or me. Harold was my best friend. I didn't care what religion he was.

I knew my father had a temper, and I realized that I was very much like my father. I had gone crazy with Harold almost without cause. I was angry with him, but was that enough to start a fight and punch him around?

I should have just punched him on the shoulder to make him hurt a little but not go wild and hit him as if I wanted to kill him. My father leaned over the table and pointed at me.

"And Harold is right about Rachel. You stay away from her.

What do you think, Joey, there are no Italian girls for you out there? What happened to Maria?"

I stared at him. I never told them I was not seeing her. I kept quiet.

My mother put down her fork, folded her arms across her chest, and glared at him. "And who are you to tell Joey who to see and not to see? I can't believe you said that! You are no better than Rachel's father! If Joey likes this girl, he should see her, and that is that." She had fire in her eyes. "If you want to argue with me later, I will, but not now!"

My mother was always ready for a fight.

18 The Confrontation

I did not sleep well that night. The next morning at class, Rachel barely looked at me. What could she say? Her father shoved me. That was not a good thing to do. My father was right about that, and now he intended to right the wrong. The trouble was I did not know what he was planning to do to right the wrong. Maria was in class and barely looked at me. I had to do something about that, but at the moment, I was concerned about Rachel and me.

What was my father up to? Right after school that day, I found out. Harold and I were waiting outside because I was determined to talk to Rachel. When she came out and saw us, she looked pale and nervous and passed right by us.

I found out why quickly. There was her father standing on the sidewalk. He took her hand and began to walk toward First Avenue.

Just then, I heard my father calling me. I turned, and there he was. As I walked down the steps with Harold, my father took me by the shoulders and, pointing to Rachel's father, asked quietly,

"Is that the man who pushed you? Tell me the truth!" He was the only Hasidic man around. I nodded.

Rachel and her father were walking quickly. My father walked faster to catch up to them, and when he came within shouting distance of them, he called out to them. Rachel's father stopped and turned around. Rachel stood next to him silently. Then she grasped his hand with both hands. I could see fear in her eyes.

I felt terrible for her. I got her into this mess.

I thought what was going to happen now would end forever whatever chance I had of getting to know her. I wanted to be with her so badly now, more than ever, because it looked as if I would never be able to see her again if my father and her father began to fight.

My father walked straight up to them and pointed a finger at him. He was slightly shorter than Rachel's father, but because he had a huge chest and muscular arms, he looked much bigger.

The large hat on Rachel's father looked much higher than I remembered. Curls hung down over his ears, and his black coat seemed too large for him. I could see he was not in good shape. In fact, he looked heavy to me in contrast to my father, whose shoulders for his big frame were huge, stretching out beyond his torso, very much like the shoulders of my baseball hero, Lou Gehrig. My father began poking him in the chest again and again.

"Don't you ever dare touch my boy again! You hear me? Ever! Who gives you the right? He cut his head open when he fell! Do you realize that you hurt my son?"

Rachel's father shook his head. Rachel stood next to her father, still holding his hand. Her head was down, her face flushed.

He backed away slightly during my father's outburst, and then he replied in a soft tone, "I am sorry if I hurt your son. I did not mean to. And I have no intention of ever laying a hand on him. It was, I thought, an accident, which I did not mean to cause." Then he glanced at me where I stood about thirty yards away and pointed his finger at me. "Just tell your son to stay away from my daughter! He is not to speak to her, ask her to walk home, nothing! That is all I have to say." He paused. "Well, enough said. We understand each other, then, you and I, do we not?"

My father took a step back and saw how Rachel was quivering behind her father. His tone grew softer.

"You bet! That is all right with me. I will tell my son to stay away from her for good. But, of course, what they do in school is another thing. I have no control over that, and you do not either." My father began to walk away. "And if I never see you again, I am just fine with that also!" he shouted.

These words were knives in my heart. I stood there with Harold, who did not look happy either. He was pale and looked at me very sadly. I wondered what he was thinking. I didn't know what he was upset about, because he would now be the one who could ask Rachel out. To his credit, he was not thinking of his good fortune but rather of my bad luck.

He would be able to take Rachel home after school, take her to the movies and to the ice cream parlor for cold, delicious egg creams, and just talk about nothing. He would even be able to hold her and kiss her. That thought got me really upset. Harold put his arm around my shoulder. Rachel and her father turned and walked away.

My father came back to where we were standing, turned, and looked at Rachel and her father. I kept looking at Rachel. All hope for us to be together was lost. She suddenly turned to look at me over her shoulder. She was still looking when they turned the corner and disappeared. She was gone and out of sight. I was crushed. My heart sank. My father looked at me angrily.

"Joey, I want you to listen to me. You stay away from her. I gave that man my promise, and when I give my word, I stick to it. You understand?" He turned to Harold. "Sometimes I think you have a better head on your shoulders than my own son. At least you listen!" He stormed away.

Harold looked at me very seriously. "Joey, I want you to know I'm not going to go behind your back with Rachel. In fact, I made up my mind not even to think about dating her. I know how you feel about her." He paused. "You shouldn't have asked her home.

You were a big jerk to do that, and I would be a bigger jerk if I asked her out. I'm your friend, you know?"

I gave Harold a big hug. He made me feel a lot better.

We started to walk home. At the park entrance, he tapped me gently on the chin with a closed fist, ran across the street to his building, and went inside. I stepped into the park and sat down on one of the benches near the entrance. I looked up to see Tommy Schwartz hitting a black ball against the wall harder and harder. I wasn't interested in playing handball.

I must have looked upset, because he came over to me and asked me what the problem was, since usually I would run right over, get my handball gloves, and start warming up. This day, I sat on the bench with my head down. He stood in front of me, flipping the ball in the air.

"There's this Jewish girl in my class. Her name is Rachel. Maria is playing hardball with me; she keeps avoiding me. So I decided to ask Rachel out. She said I could take her home, and when we started walking home, we met her father. He is a Hasid. What did I know about that? Nothing!" I told him the rest.

"Look, kid, forget it. If she likes you, she will give you another shot. Mark my word. Now let's play some handball. You need to focus and concentrate, and that means mental discipline! You know what I mean by discipline? It means you block everything out and pay attention only to the game. So you have girl problems. Big deal. Get over it for now and let's play!" He saw I was still not interested.

"Look at you, twelve years old, and girl problems! I could see it coming: a good-looking Italian boy like you, black, curly hair, that natural tan skin, those brown-green eyes. In your life, you will have plenty of girls. Trust me! You think you're the only one with girl problems? We all have girl problems! C'mon, let's play some handball! I want to see that speed of yours. I want you to get some points off me."

I took a deep breath and looked up at him. He kept patting the ball in the air, smiling.

"Okay, let's go," I said, and we started to play. It must have been the anger inside of me that caused me to play as hard as I did. He was right about concentrating. In the first game, he beat me 21–3, but then in the second game, he beat me 21–6. I actually got six points off him! Rachel was far from my mind.

I was very proud of myself. After the second game, I took off my gloves and went over to the fountain for a drink of water. I was exhausted. Tommy was still hitting the ball in the park. He worked hard to be perfect. I headed home.

Then I thought of Rachel. I was down again. I wanted things to be the way they were. *How in the world,* I thought, *will that ever happen?* That night at dinner, my father told my mother what had happened. She was furious.

"Now what kind of stupid thing was that to do?" she barked. "I did not marry an animal. I married a good, decent, hardworking man, and this is how you behave in front of your son, his friend, the girl he likes, and her father! My God! What shame you have brought to this house! Shame on you, Salvatore! You must go to her father and apologize!"

My father just stared at her, for a moment, speechless while I scooped up my spaghetti.

"Apologize? I will not! Why should I? He started this trouble, not me. He proved it by apologizing to me!" My father glared at me. "Remember what I said, Joey! There are plenty of Italian girls out there. Remember that!"

My mother pounded her fist on the table. I stopped eating. Here was another argument coming!

"Not again! You tell him he should only meet Italian girls! Who cares what her nationality is as long as she is a nice girl? Besides, Joey is too young to be thinking about girls! He should be thinking about school! Joey, listen to me. You take your time with girls. Don't be in such a rush. When you get older, you think about them, and I don't care if they are Jewish, Italian, or Greek!" She folded her arms across her chest, stuck her chin out, and stared at my father defiantly.

I kept very quiet. I could see where my obsession over Rachel had gotten me. My parents were arguing again. I had to do something about this problem. I just could not stop thinking of her, and somehow I could not believe I would never be able to talk to her again outside of school. For me, that was out of the question. I was determined to see her, but how?

When I was stuck with a problem, I figured it was a good thing to go to church and pray for a solution. I resolved that I would pray to God and his mother, Mary, to help me out, even though I knew everyone else asked God for help. It seemed selfish of me to ask him to help with so small a problem.

On Sunday morning, my mother laid out a beautiful white shirt she had bought me the year before, but its sleeves were too short for me, and it also fit too tightly around my chest. My mother also noticed the tight fit.

"Joey, no movies for you today. We have to go to Orchard Street and get some new shirts. You ruined one already, and this one does not fit. You have grown, Joey! All right, get to church, and say some prayers for me. God knows I need them, living with your father and his temper. Pray also you don't inherit his temper! Hurry, you're going to be late. It's almost nine o'clock!"

I was surprised she didn't realize I had already inherited his temper. In fact, it seemed to me that my parents hardly knew me. My mom knew I was growing physically, but my parents were not so much aware that I was growing mentally as well.

I ran out of the building, made it to Church of the Nativity in about two minutes, skipped up the white marble steps, and walked inside. I took holy water and made the sign of the cross. The church was filled with old Italian women, some with black kerchiefs on their heads, others with brightly colored ones. Hardly any men were in the church. I felt my heart pounding as I walked in. Above me in the balcony, a woman choir singer was singing "Ave Maria."

I sat in a crowded pew close to the front of the church and stared at the statue of Saint Joseph to the right of the altar. He was blessing the congregation. On the left was a statue of Mary, the Mother of God, dressed in a white gown as Our Lady of Fatima, her face glowing with stunning beauty from a brilliant light streaming in from stained glass windows all around the church. In that light, She came to life for me. I could not help thinking she was caring and loving me, but I realized also she was caring and loving all of us.

I asked her for help. "Dear Mother of God, I haven't asked much lately, and I don't expect a miracle, but I could use just a little help with this problem I have with Rachel. I just want things to get back to normal, that's all!" I made the prayer simple. God knows she had many prayers to deal with!

My mother asked me every week to pray for her. I could not remember when I had ever asked God for anything, although I knew I had before. I felt humbled by the great cathedral. I meekly said an Our Father and a Hail Mary and begged Mary to forgive my sins and get me out of the mess I had caused, not only to get Rachel back to normal—whatever that was—but also to undo the damage I had done.

Around one o'clock, my mother and I walked down Houston to Orchard Street. It was hot, and the block was already crowded with shoppers, mostly mothers with their kids in strollers trying to make their way through pedestrians walking along narrow sidewalks on both sides of the street. Each store had an open stand sitting on the sidewalk filled with shirts, pants, and sweaters laid out in rows. Hasid men were watching their goods. Above us, men and women were looking out of tenement windows, the men in undershirts and smoking.

My mother had one store in mind, the one with no name except for a large, worn-out sign that said, "Sale!" It was in the middle of the block. She passed a number of stands. Owners stood in front of their stores, watching their merchandise closely. None of them had on their overcoats. It was too hot for that, even though it was nearing the end of the school year. Some wore black vests, while others had on just had plain white shirts. All had either skullcaps or fedoras. There were so many people it was almost impossible to get close to a stand to see what they were selling.

We got to the store my mother knew that had cotton shirts that fit me and were of good quality. There, laid out on a stand on the sidewalk, were boys' shirts of all colors. The owner came out of the store. I could see from stains on his shirt collar he had been sweating heavily. Curls hung limply over his ears. I looked more closely at him. My heart took an extra beat. It was Rachel's father!

I turned the other way so he could not see me while my mother checked out the shirts. I was glad she knew what she wanted. I was hoping she could finish quickly, and he would not have time to recognize me. I kept turning away while glancing back to see if it was really her father. It was! *Dear Mother of God, is this how you help me?* I kept my back to him.

My mother, meanwhile, picked out three shirts she liked, checked the collars to see if they were cotton, and then checked the prices on the sleeves. She looked at Rachel's father and frowned. She threw the shirts back down onto the stand and shouted at him. I knew she would. "Too much money! Much too much money!" She started to walk away.

Rachel's father called to her in a loud voice. "Lady, come back here. I can make a deal for you." He picked up one of the shirts. "See this shirt? It is regularly $3.99, but for you, I make it on sale for $3.50." He picked up two more shirts. "You can have all three for ten dollars!"

My mother stopped, turned, walked back to the stand, picked up the shirt again, and shook her head. Rachel's father kept his eyes on her.

My mother sneered. "What do you think? I was born yesterday? You probably paid $1.00 for these shirts, and you want to make $2.50 on me? I will take three shirts for $2.50 each. You make a nice profit on me, and you don't have to cheat me with these high prices of yours! Look at these shirts. The cotton is poor quality. Next fall, I will have to come back again, because by then, they will be worn out!"

She paused, picked up a shirt, and pressed it against my chest for size. It was then that Rachel's father looked at me more closely. He cocked his head and took a step toward me. I was not sure he had recognized me. I lowered my head. Then my mother drew his attention.

"Okay, I buy the shirts for $2.50. Wrap them up, and I pay you right now." She reached into her purse and took out seven dollars and then pulled fifty cents from her purse and extended her hand with the cash to pay him. Rachel's father was concentrating so much on the sale of the shirts that he never looked back at me. He waved his hands at my mother, who still was checking out one of the shirts.

"No, lady, I cannot do that. Please, the shirts are good quality. Anyone can see that!"

My mother folded her arms across her chest and shook her head. He sighed.

"How can I give these shirts away for that price? I cannot. I cannot. I will let you have them for $3.00 each, and that is it. I cannot go any lower. You will steal them from me at $2.50. Take it or leave it! Three dollars."

My mother shook her head, threw down the shirt, and began to walk away. Rachel's father turned and headed back into the store, glancing one more time at my mother. I thought that if they had both compromised to $2.75 per shirt, the sale would have been made, but it would not be made. I was safe.

It was then that it happened. As we were walking away and Rachel's father had disappeared back into his store, a boy about seventeen came in front of me. His eyes were fixed on the shirts. He shoved me aside, grabbed a pile of them from the stand, and ran right past me and my mother, the shirts held closely to his chest. It was an instinctive act.

I shouted at him, "Hey, you crook! Bring those shirts back!"

He was taller and bigger than I was, and had he stopped, he could have pounded the hell out of me. I don't know why, but I ran after him anyway. I saw him run into the street, which was less crowded than the sidewalk. I did the same and still managed to keep an eye on him. I was running pretty fast, dodging people, and still able to keep up with him. But I noticed he began to slow down. So did I.

I heard my mother above the crowd calling my name, screaming at me to come back. I stopped for a moment and turned around. Rachel's father was in the street and behind me, but bent over, with his hands on his hips. He was huffing and puffing, totally out of breath. My mother ran up to him, grabbed his arm, and pointed to me and the thief.

"My son! My son! He's going to kill my son! Joey, come back here! Forget the shirts!"

At that moment, I turned back toward the thief, who caught me by surprise. He had stopped and turned to me, not more than twenty yards away, and smiled. One by one, he threw down four shirts onto the sidewalk. I stopped dead in my tracks. Clutching the other shirts, he ran off, laughing. I watched him disappear into the crowd. I walked over to the shirts and picked them up, wiped them down, and walked back to my mother and Rachel's father.

I handed him the shirts. He began to count them.

"Four shirts you saved me. Thank you, my boy. That was so good of you!"

He looked at me, strangely at first, straight in the eye, and then he pointed at me with a surprised look on his face.

"It is you! You are the boy who was with my daughter, Rachel! Are you the boy?"

Did I have a choice? I lowered my head slightly and told him I was.

My mother paid no attention to what he said. Instead, she checked to see if I had any cuts or bruises on my body. She checked my shirt to see if I had torn it and then turned to Rachel's father.

"My boy is a good boy! Look, he saved all those shirts for you!"

If she had known that he had recognized me, she didn't show it.

He dusted off the dirt from the shirts' tissues and looked at me. Then he placed his hand on my shoulder and nodded with satisfaction.

"Your mother is right! You are a good boy. Come, let's go back to the store. I want to sell those shirts to your mother, the ones she liked so much, for $2.00 each!"

We went back to the shirt stand. He picked out the ones my mother wanted and handed them to her.

"Six dollars! That is enough! It's my gift to you and your son!"

My mother nodded and then smiled. She took out her purse and pulled out six dollars and handed it to him. He handed her a bag with the shirts inside.

"You see, Joey? It pays to be good. Look what this nice man did for us today. He rewarded you for your courage and for doing the right thing." Then she turned to Rachel's father. "I know you are grateful for what my boy has done. I think you should give us the shirts for what you paid for them, a dollar each!"

They both laughed. I smiled.

"Next time he saves me from another thief, I will do just that." He turned to me. "I am sorry, Joey," he said.

My mother looked at him curiously, and we left.

We walked back home, and I turned around to see him still looking at us with his hands at his side. I thought I saw a faint smile on his face. He pulled out a handkerchief from his back pocket and wiped his brow, looked up at the sun, and disappeared back into his shop.

Next day at school, I saw Rachel in homeroom. When she looked up at me, she saw I was looking at her, and she turned away. I was upset. Her father had not spoken to her. At three o'clock, she hurriedly picked up her books and walked out of homeroom. I watched her. She stopped for a moment, glanced at me quickly, and disappeared into the hallway. Harold waited for me in homeroom. Everyone had left. I was taking my time. Harold knew that I was upset.

"Look, Joey. It's not Rachel. It's her father and her family. You can't be upset with her! She has to do what her family wants her to do. That is their tradition. You understand? Her mother grew up that way, her grandmother was that way, and she will live that way. That's it! Look, take your time. I'll meet you outside. Okay? It's hot in here."

I took my time putting my books together. He knew I didn't want to talk to anyone. I stood there in the empty classroom for a few moments and then walked out into the hallway.

A few students were still leaving school. Suddenly, a closet door opened. An arm grabbed my wrist and pulled me inside. I heard a whispered "Shush." It was a girl's voice. She closed the door behind her, leaving just light coming in from the space between the door and the floor. I could smell the sweet scent of her body.

"Don't say anything!" she whispered.

It was Rachel! She helped me put my books down on the floor, took my arms, and wrapped them around her waist. She pulled me closer to her, took the back of my head with her left hand, guided my lips to hers, and kissed me softly. I was so excited my knees wobbled. She kissed me again. We said nothing. I touched her face. She was sweating. I was also sweating, but it didn't matter. She had the scent of roses. Her small bosom was pressed against my chest. She placed her head on my shoulder and kept it there for a few moments.

"I love you, Rachel," I said, and I kissed her again.

We stood there in the darkness of the closet silently holding each other. She was so warm. I felt her soft, thin body pressed against mine. I put my cheeks to hers and felt how smooth they were. I kissed her again, a warm, tender kiss. She returned another kiss. Then she took my arms away and picked up her books.

"You don't love me, Joey. You love Maria. We're just attracted to each other, and sometimes that's just how it is. I have to go now. My father is waiting for me outside. Don't tell anyone, especially Harold. He talks a lot."

She quietly opened the closet door, looked into the hallway, and left. And she was gone. I waited inside for a few minutes, thinking of what had happened, and then I left the closet and met Harold outside. He kept asking me why I was so quiet.

In the afternoon, I was full of energy. I played Tommy and managed to get six points in the first game and seven in the second. That night, my mother made a special meal for me of thin chicken cutlets, peas, carrots, and potatoes. The cutlets were stacked on a huge plate on the table, steaming. I grabbed a fork and took three of them and began eating as if I had not eaten in a week. I was thinking of Rachel and me in the closet. I began to eat and eat. And then there was a knock on the door.

My mother got up and opened it.

"May I come in?"

My mother opened the door wider, and in walked Rachel's father with Rachel! I put my fork down, wiped my mouth, and straightened up in my chair. My eyes opened wide. My father sat there astonished, and then stood up, speechless.

Rachel's father wore a fedora this time. He took it off and solemnly asked if they could sit down. At his side, he had a large shopping bag. My mother immediately pushed out two chairs. He got right to it, addressing my mother.

"My name is Isaac Rubin. I came over to tell you that you were absolutely right. It was not enough what I did for you and your son, and so I brought over one of my most expensive shirts for Joey, one size bigger because I could see he is a big boy already and growing. By next year, it will fit him. And this one you do not pay for. Not one cent!" He pointed his finger toward the ceiling. "This is a gift for you and your son!"

My mother examined the quality of the shirt and smiled. "Very nice. Very nice," she said. "Have a seat, you and your beautiful daughter. I am Lillian D'Angelo, and my husband here is Sal."

My father nodded and extended his hand to Rachel's father, still confused.

I was having trouble keeping myself from staring at Rachel.

"Sal, Joey ran after a thief who tried to steal this man's shirts. He came back to thank Joey. And this is your daughter?"

"Yes, my daughter, here, is Rachel. Say hello, Rachel, to Joey's mother and father." My father continued to look confused.

Rachel nodded her head and said very softly, "Hello."

I couldn't help smiling. Suddenly it dawned on him it was Rachel's father. and with no comment about their previous encounter, he smiled and said, "My name is Sal, short for Salvatore. Come have a glass of wine with me. It is not kosher, mind you. I made it myself in the cellar last winter. Do you mind that it is not kosher?"

Isaac shook his head. My father poured out the wine.

"Maybe, just this once, God will forgive me for not drinking kosher wine." He lifted his glass. "Rules, rules. Moses made so many rules for us sometimes they just wear me out!" He laughed and drank the wine.

My father laughed and poured him more wine.

"You should be Catholic if you think you have so many rules! *Salud*!"

He lifted his glass, Isaac lifted his, and they tapped their glasses and drank. Isaac nodded his approval and then turned to Rachel.

"Rachel, why don't you go inside and talk to Joey? It's all right."

I was shocked. Before I knew it, Rachel had taken me by the hand and guided me into the living room where we sat holding hands and stealing a kiss when we knew we were safe. She smiled nervously.

For the few moments we were silent, we overheard her father talking.

"Well, Sal, I am getting tired of this neighborhood. I make a good living on Orchard Street, and so I am taking Rachel and my wife to a new apartment across the East River to South Williamsburg. I can live in a wonderful three-bedroom apartment for next to nothing and take the train, which will leave me off on Second Avenue. From there, I walk a few blocks!"

I looked over at Rachel. She had already lowered her head. I was crushed. She would be gone from my neighborhood, gone from school, and out of my life! Rachel grabbed my hand and placed it into hers.

"Don't worry, Joey. Williamsburg is just over the Williamsburg Bridge! You can take a bicycle there in fifteen minutes!"

She leaned over and kissed me. Then she hugged me tightly. I felt I had lost her forever. My arms went limp.

"Don't think we won't see each other, Joey. We will, if we want to."

"I don't own a bicycle, Rachel."

A few minutes later, Rachel and her father left. I went into the living room and watched them go down the block toward First Avenue. Her father was holding Rachel's hand the way he was holding her hand the day he pushed me. She looked back and saw me looking down at her from my window. She smiled and waved, and then she and her father disappeared down the block. She was gone.

19

Boy with the Voice

I thought I was doing very well during my probation period. It had been a few months, and when I saw Tom Mansfield, he told me that Capra had heard about how I had run after the shirt thief. Capra was happy to hear I was stopping thieves rather than being one. He was smiling when he said that. He asked me how I was doing at school. Had I gotten into any trouble? Was I getting good grades?

I also decided to help out at the Boys' Club with the younger kids who also had a basketball team. Actually, it was fun, and I enjoyed teaching these kids how to play basketball. It also kept me from thinking about Maria. Without her, I had time to help out. Capra liked what I was doing. I also enjoyed leading these kids. It was good.

When I said I was not in any trouble and my grades were improving, he recommended that I start working with him and Sue on English grammar on Saturdays. I was not happy about that. I had stickball! I was just not ready for that kind of sacrifice.

I kept thinking about Rachel, but my thoughts were always

turning to Maria. Was it possible to love two women at once? I was conflicted all right. My thoughts were now on getting back with Maria. I had to do something about that because Rachel was going away. I had to face that hard fact, and that was a dagger to my heart.

I hoped she had not found out about Rachel, but I got my answer to that question when Johnny Marino came over to me during lunch recess and told me that Maria was in Tompkins Square Park next to the parallel bars. He had a smirk on his face.

I knew something was up, so I walked into the park with him, and I saw Maria looking up at someone on the bars doing dips. I didn't recognize him. He was pumping his arms up and down very fast. I could not believe anyone could do so many dips so fast.

"The kid on the bars," Johnny said, "who Maria is looking at is Mario LaRusso. He just got transferred from a school in the Bronx—until the end of the year, anyway. And, Joey, you got a problem! He is in our class, but that's not the problem. Maria just met him, and she likes him!"

I walked over to Maria. I stood there with my arms folded while Mario finished his dips. She turned to look at me and practically sneered. She glanced at me and then turned her attention to Mario.

When he jumped down from the parallel bars, he smiled at her, and she smiled back. I was not about to be made a fool of. I could see he had been doing more than dips. His chest and arms were very firm and well formed. He was taller than I was, older for sure, and most definitely stronger. I could tell that right away. I paid no attention to him. Instead, I turned to Maria and put my hand on her shoulder.

"Listen, Maria, I may be on probation, but that's no reason not to see me anymore. The burglary case is over. What is the point now? It's been a while, so talk to me."

She took my hand, lifted it slowly off her shoulder, and stood facing me with her hands on her hips.

What a tough lady! I thought.

She was chewing gum. Her dark hair hung behind her ears. Her eyes stared at mine. She had that hard look on her face, the look of an angry Sicilian woman. I knew that look. *God knows how tough she will be when she grows up!* It made me nervous, but I could not help loving her more. I was so close to her. She was like a magnet drawing me to her, and I could not resist.

"Joey, do you think I'm an idiot? I am not an idiot. I know what happened with you and Rachel. Do you think I'm stupid?" She pointed her finger at her chest and leaned toward me. "I am not stupid, and I am not going to let you make a fool out of me!" She took the gum out of her mouth and threw it into the bushes nearby. Then she turned to Mario. "So, Mario, you work out a lot. I can see how strong you are. You work out a lot, right? What are you, thirteen? Joey, here, is twelve, but he doesn't have arms like you do."

Mario looked at me, folded his arms, and smiled. He rolled up his sleeve and lifted his arm. Maria smiled and felt his arm. She really got to me then!

Johnny shook his head. "Whoa! Joey, you gonna take that from her?"

I looked at Johnny, and then Maria, and then at Mario. "Listen, Mario, this here is my girl, Maria. We had a little falling out, but right now, we are getting back together, so I think you ought to go back on your monkey bars and do your tricks. Maria, I'm sorry what I did with Rachel. I know I did wrong by you."

She walked over to Mario and stood next to him. I couldn't believe she did that after I had apologized.

"Well, I'm not ready to forgive and forget," she said. "C'mon, Mario, let's go back to the school. I'll show you around!"

She grabbed him by the arm, and they began to walk away.

She should not have done that. I really cared about Maria, but I wasn't going to let her make a fool of me. She was right. I made a pass at Rachel, and so she thought she could make a pass at Mario, but I was not going to let her insult me in front of this new guy.

I grabbed her arm and pulled her toward me. Before I knew it, Mario stepped in and pushed me pretty hard. I fell backward and landed on the cobblestone behind me. I looked up at him and Maria. I saw that Johnny was about to go after Mario, but I got up quickly, shook Johnny off, and then rammed into Mario. It was like banging into a wall. I didn't knock him down!

He grabbed me by the shirt and punched me in the jaw. I fell backward again. I got up again and lifted my fists. He lifted his. I bluffed hitting him with my left and caught him in the jaw with a right cross. His head popped back, but it barely fazed him. He came at me again and landed a quick right hook to my jaw, which stunned me. He kept on throwing punches at me. I stepped back to catch my balance, but it was too late. He caught me on the side of the head, and I fell down to the pavement. It happened so fast. I tried again to get up, but I could not.

Next I knew, Johnny was helping me get back up. Mario and Maria were gone. He helped me to a park bench, ran over to a water fountain, came back, and pressed a wet handkerchief against my lips. I could feel them begin to swell up. I was blinking and shaking my head to get the dizziness out of me.

"Joey, are you okay? Wow! This kid really handed it to you. Not only is he strong but he is fast! I never saw anyone throw punches as fast as he did." He looked at his bloodied handkerchief and handed it to me. "Now what are you gonna do? You can't fight this kid. He's just too strong for you. To tell the truth, he made you look very bad in front of Maria." He shook his head. "You got a problem, Joey!"

"Yeah, he hit me pretty hard. I can tell ya that! Where is Maria?"

"She grabbed Mario, and they went back to school. I don't know, Joey. How are you gonna handle this one? It looks like maybe it's over with you and Maria."

We slowly walked back to school. Johnny didn't have to tell me I had a problem. I was surprised that Maria had left me on the ground and went off with Mario. I knew I did wrong by her with Rachel, but by fighting Mario, I realized I made him look good.

How was I going to explain Rachel to Maria when she would not even talk to me? Worse, I now had very serious competition for Maria's attention! My jaw hurt, and I was stumped. I had no answer, and usually when I could not figure out what to do, I turned to Harold for advice.

Just after our last class, I saw Maria in the hall talking to Mario. He had the sleeves of his shirt pulled up and his arms folded against his chest. Maria turned and glanced at me and then turned to Mario. He was good looking. I gave him that. He had the dark skin of an Italian, thick black hair, green eyes, and high cheekbones. He looked a little like me, actually, but bigger.

Rachel followed right behind me and gave me a look over her shoulder. I glanced over to her and nodded, but my focus was Maria. As Harold and I turned to leave the building, I looked back at Maria. She was looking at me over her shoulder. She was not happy. She must have seen Rachel look at me. I was happy she did, because I knew then that she still cared, but how could I get her away from Mario?

We walked out of school and headed home. I didn't have to spend too much time explaining the problem to Harold. He knew before I said a word what my problem was.

"Joey, you didn't have to fight Mario, and when you did fight him, that is when your problem got more complicated. Mario was defending Maria! You understand what I mean? You made it easier for Maria to walk away from you because he was defending her! By the way, you look terrible!"

I shook my head. "Harold, I understand your point, but did I know Maria's mother was going to make such a big deal about my probation? And when I thought it would be okay for Maria to see me, I made the mistake of taking Rachel for a walk, a walk that got me nowhere! She is moving to Williamsburg. Did you hear? Maria has nothing to worry about. So what is her problem?"

We went to Jerry's candy store. I took out twelve cents and asked for two egg creams. We sat there at the counter quietly. I let Harold think. I tried to sip the milk and ice cream from the bottom of the glass, but my straw kept getting clogged. While I was sucking the ice cream from the end of the straw, Harold suddenly smiled at me.

"I think I know what is going to happen. I know Maria still

likes you a lot, and I think this kid Mario must not have a lot of brains in his head. He's a muscle guy! Look at him! He is more worried about his body than his brain. Maria is bound to find out he is a boob. She is smart. What talent does he have besides those muscles of his? She is going to get tired of him real fast, and then she will come back to you. Just sit tight!"

Harold had a good point.

"I hope you are right, Harold," I said. "I don't think I can stand being without Maria very long, especially with this big kid hanging all over her."

It wasn't long before Harold's theory about Mario would be tested. Wednesday was music class. Once a week, our class would gather in the auditorium. Harold, Johnny, and I sat on the left side of the auditorium facing the stage. On the other side, I could see Maria sitting next to Mario. I noticed also that most of the girls, including Rachel, were also sitting on that side. They were looking at Mario and whispering to each other. My problem was becoming more serious.

Mrs. Meriweather came on stage. She was tall and blonde, hair flowing down to her shoulders, and not exactly thin, but not heavy either. Her blue dress fit tightly around her body. As soon as she walked onto the stage, the boys started to stare at her, and the class quieted down.

"Class, we have a special treat today. We have a new boy here, Mario, but what you don't know is that he has a very good voice. It is so good that I think someday he could become a professional opera singer, which he has told me he would like to be. So would you all welcome Mario LaRusso to the stage? He is going to sing for us right now an aria from *La Bohème*."

I began to sink in my chair.

Mario jumped from his chair and bounded down to the stage with a huge smile on his face. Everyone in the class except Harold, Johnny, and me were clapping. I glared at Harold. He looked at me and shrugged.

"No talent! Is that what you told me? We'll see!"

Mario began to sing—and in Italian! It was a deep voice

as I thought it would be since his body was so muscular. His chest expanded as he lifted his head to the ceiling and sang this beautiful aria from *La Bohème,* a sad play that Mrs. Meriweather had summarized for us. It was from Puccini's *La Bohème.* The man was singing about her hands and how cold they were. It was a sad song. Mario's voice reached every seat in the auditorium. I could see as I looked around how he had grasped the attention of everyone in the room, including Maria, who sat there staring at him with her hands folded under her chin. As I sat there listening, I wondered how I could ever compete with him for Maria's attention. He had a terrific voice!

Just as he finished, there was a moment of silence, and then applause, loud and very noisy. I turned to Harold, who was clapping also. I stared at him. Harold smiled and shrugged. I was becoming depressed.

"I'm finished, Harold. And if he gets an A in math, you might as well start throwing the dirt over my body."

Harold leaned toward me and smiled. "You know, Joey, who knows how it's going to turn out? Maybe he has a tragic flaw, like a Greek hero."

He paused, looking at Mario, who was bowing as if he were already an opera star.

"You can't give up now just because he has talent, good looks, and a body full of muscles." He looked at me with a straight face. I was getting depressed.

Mario bounded off the stage. The kids were still applauding. He skipped the steps to get back to his seat and sat down next to Maria. Immediately, he planted a kiss on her cheek. Maria was surprised. She leaned back a bit and then leaned forward to see if I had seen the kiss. I shook my head in disgust. I was sinking fast and knew it.

Later, Harold and I sat in the lunchroom thinking about my problem.

"Harold," I said, "I think I have one last shot. Mario can't be smart also, and we have math class this afternoon. What do you think?"

"Joey, I have my own problem. My father wants me to go to Hebrew school! I go part time, but now he wants me to go full time! It is so boring—you have no idea! Besides, the kids over there are jerks. All they do is read and speak Hebrew and listen to the rabbis with their long beards and long black coats and talk about the Torah. I must have heard the story of Moses a hundred times. I have a real problem, and so do you, by the way.

"I think I got it wrong about Mario. He does not look like he is stupid. In fact, nobody could sing the way he does and be stupid. He has to learn his lines. He has to understand rhythm. He has to practice, and he sings in Italian! Stupid kids can't do that. Mario is a smart kid. Isn't there any other girl in the class you would like to go out with besides Rachel?" He paused. "When does Rachel move to Williamsburg?"

I glared at him. Sometimes I thought Harold was a very insensitive kid. Did he have to bring up Rachel? It had not happened yet, but I felt as if I had already lost Rachel to Williamsburg. So why did he have to bring her up now? I stared at him and shook my head.

"What? What's the matter?" he asked me.

"You know how to hurt my feelings without even trying. Let's go. We have geometry class. Let's see how our boy Mario performs there. Mr. Greene always likes to test new kids to see what they know."

We piled into class and sat down. I noticed Maria had taken a seat next to Mario. I was getting really upset, and she knew it. I looked up at the chalkboard. There were already drawn on the blackboard the triangles Mr. Greene had given us to identify for homework. He was not wasting any time.

"Class, would anyone care to tell me their names?"

A few hands went up, but Mr. Greene saw Mario sitting in the back.

"Mr. LaRusso, before I let anyone answer, would you like to share your knowledge with us first? I know you were not here; it is a bit unfair of me to ask you. Do you think you can name these triangles?"

Mario looked up at the board and studied them for a few moments. Then he looked at Mr. Greene, smiled, and nodded.

I was not only sinking, I was drowning!

I listened as he rattled off the answers. He identified all the triangles, the equilateral triangle, the isosceles, and finally the right triangle. I was impressed. I looked over at Maria. She was smiling and nodding her head. There was nothing he could do wrong. This kid was perfect, and it was driving me crazy!

Harold and I walked out of school on our way home. I did not see Maria, but I did see Mario run toward the park and disappear from view. Harold and I followed him along Tenth Street. When we got to the parallel bars, there he was doing his dips. He was moving as fast as I had seen him a day earlier. I took another look around. Maria was not in the park. I felt much better knowing she was not with him.

I thought I would go to Mott Street after I ate my supper and see if she were around. I reached her block. Lucky for me, she was standing outside with one of her girlfriends who saw me. She grabbed Maria by the arm and pointed toward me.

Maria turned and kept on talking. I thought she would dash upstairs, knowing that her mother told her to stay away from me. She knew I would go up to her apartment to get her. That she stood there was encouraging to me. When I reached her, she ignored me and kept on talking to her girlfriend. I expected that slight.

"Maria. What are you doing? Why do you have to be so difficult? I told you I was sorry about Rachel. I'm not going to do anything like that again. You have to believe me!"

Her harsh eyes cut me to the bone. She was still angry. She turned to me and folded her arms across her chest and started tapping her foot while leaning her head sideways, glaring at me with one eye.

"So all of a sudden you have competition, and it's killing you, right, Joey?" She was angry, but at least she was talking to me. She pointed at me. "Soon as I'm away, you jump all over Rachel! It shows how much you care about me!"

"Maria, of course I care about you. I wouldn't be standing here if I didn't! I was just lonely for you, and I know you don't have feelings for him the way you have for me. You just don't! I'm here because I do care about you. You know that!"

"How do you know how I feel about Mario? You made me look really stupid to my friends—and the whole school, for that matter. How could you do that to me? If you had real feelings, you would not have hurt me so bad. You hurt me, Joey. You really did."

Her girlfriend stared at me also with her arms folded across her chest. She was loving this fight. Another Sicilian woman just itching for a fight.

"C'mon, Maria, you know I love you," I said.

She looked at me coldly and turned to the door leading into her building. "Show me, Joey. Show me something. Right now, I think you're a rat. Yes, I have feelings for you, but I don't know what kind of person you are after what you did with Rachel. I need to know you got something inside of you that will make me feel good about you. Right now, I don't feel good about you. I have nothing good here, in my heart. Show me, Joey!"

Another challenge, I thought. Is this the way life would be—full of challenges?

She and her girlfriend went into her building, and I was left standing there, alone and more depressed than ever. I was so depressed I didn't even want to play handball. Usually, no matter how bad I felt, I could play, but not now.

I would let all my emotions out, my problems temporarily forgotten, and give in to physical exhaustion. Afterward, I could relax with my depression gone. This time, I went home, ate a little pasta, read a Classic Comic version of Rudyard Kipling's *Captains Courageous,* and went to bed thinking Maria and I were finished.

20
The Substitute Teacher

It was a bad few days for me. Maria spent no time with me. When she saw me, she turned away. Sometimes, she glanced in my direction, but when I tried to make contact with her by smiling and waving back, she just ignored me. I wondered if I would ever get her back.

It was at music class that week, all of us already seated, when we were surprised to see a strange woman enter the auditorium. I had expected Mrs. Meriweather, who was always smiling and happy. Instead, we found ourselves looking at this older woman of about fifty shuffling slowly across the stage with her back bent, dressed in a black dress and high black boots. Her white, straight hair reached only to the top of her neck. Her pale face was wrinkled. Her small black eyes were darting back and forth warily at the class. She was not smiling.

She repeated these sharp glances until she got to Mrs. Meriweather's desk on stage, where she proceeded to brush away papers to make room for her own black briefcase. I could see her silhouette easily from where I sat. Her nose slanted sharply down to thin lips, which she kept licking with her curled tongue. She fidgeted with music sheets, paused, and then looked up at the class with an icy stare.

"I want to introduce myself. I am Mrs. Monfree. Mrs. Meriweather is ill. She won't be back for at least two weeks, and so you will have to put up with me!"

The class groaned.

She put her hands to her hips and looked around the room. Not a sound could be heard. She sat down at Mrs. Meriweather's desk. I had a bad feeling about her. I was not alone. I could see the stone faces of my classmates. She was trouble.

"I have taught music for many years at many schools," she continued, "and often in time of emergency, such as this one."

A student raised his hand.

"Put your hand down!" she shouted. "I'm not finished yet!"

She paused, smiled in an artificial way, and then picked up notes of paper on the desk. She read them quickly and then threw them in a wastebasket one by one while we waited for her. Five minutes later, she spoke again.

"Ah, here it is. Mario LaRusso. Where is Mario?"

We all looked at one another, wondering how or why she picked his name from the class. Mario raised his hand.

"Ah, Mr. LaRusso, please come forward. Mrs. Meriweather left me a note telling me especially to pay attention to your singing, that you had a beautiful voice. She called you in this note, 'The boy with the voice!'" She nodded silently. "Why don't you come up here to sing for us? Let's see how right she is about your singing!"

She was almost taunting him. Mario looked nervous.

Mario got up from his seat, walked down the steps to the piano, and stood there, hands behind his back, his chest expanding with each deep breath he took. He held his chin up as Mrs. Monfree walked to the piano. I didn't trust her. I felt as if something bad was about to happen. Harold nudged me with his elbow and shook his head. He knew also.

She asked Mario what he wanted to sing. He chose "Ave Maria." Everyone knew "Ave Maria." It was sung so often at my own church. It was a beautiful song, and I leaned back in my chair, forgetting for a moment that here in front of me was my archrival about to show off his great talent. I tried to forget all bad thoughts and just listen. Maria was leaning forward, her hands under her chin, an anxious look on her face. She too sensed something bad was about to happen.

Mario began to sing. His voice echoed through the auditorium, strong and beautiful. It was a powerful piece of music, but Mario suddenly transformed it before us, sending shivers down my spine. He sang with heart, letting his arms float back and forth, turning left to right to the class, and smiling all the way through. He was a natural performer.

Mrs. Monfree, accompanying Mario on the piano, suddenly pounded the piano keys and stood up. She folded her arms and stared at Mario.

"Now, Mr. LaRusso! I have no idea where you received your training, but it is clear to me that you were not trained properly. You are singing from the front of your throat, which is artificial, forced, and unnatural. You should be singing from the back of your throat. You understand me, Mr. LaRusso? You are singing, young man, without vibrato! Let's start again, and from the back of your throat, please!"

I had no idea what she meant, and Mario didn't either.

She began to play. Mario began to sing, and he sounded no different to me. Mrs. Monfree pounded the keys hard again. Mario jumped back, stunned and red-faced. He turned to her, standing with his arms by his sides and fists clenched. She got up and put her folded hands on her waist. Mario stood there with his eyes wide open. He looked terrified. She glared at him and then walked over and began to circle him. He began to sweat. The auditorium was hushed.

"Are you making fun of me, Mr. LaRusso? I am trying to explain to you how you need to sing. You are not singing with a genuine voice. It must come from here." She pointed to her throat. "Here, from the back of your throat, to gain the rich quality of your vocal cords. What you are giving me is false and shallow. It is not true singing. Now sing, Mr. LaRusso, the way I am explaining you should!"

She went back to the piano and sat down. She placed her bony fingers on the keys and looked up at Mario, who stared out at the class, unable to move. He seemed frozen where he stood. The long collar of his blue shirt was spread wide over his sweater vest. I could see his neck was thick and red. He kept clearing his throat, trying to do what she asked him, but he could not. He turned to Mrs. Monfree.

"I can't sing the way you want me to sing. I can only sing the way I know how."

She persisted. "Try, Mr. LaRusso. Try!" she said, and she began to play.

Mario once again sang as before, only this time, his arms remained at his side with his hands clenched. Again, she pounded the piano keys. This time, she stormed to him, took the sleeve of his shirt, and began to pull on it.

"What is the matter with you? Are you an idiot? Can't you follow simple instructions? Can't you?"

Mario withered before her. He seemed to shrink in front of us. His eyes were wide open.

"Now, I warn you, Mr. LaRusso, if you continue to play this game with me, I will send you to the principal's office and tell him you have been extremely disruptive. Do you understand? I have had enough!"

Mario was humiliated. His shoulders were hunched. He stood there broken.

Her last remark was enough for me. I don't know what got into me. I just could not stand her continuing to abuse Mario. I raised my hand. The entire class turned to me.

"Mrs. Monfree? Excuse me, Mrs. Monfree, but I like the way Mario sings, and it doesn't bother me if he sings from the front of his throat or the back of his throat. What's the difference? He's a great singer. In fact, he is the best singer in the class. And if you're telling us he does not know how to sing, then we're all in trouble, because he is the best of all of us!"

Our class as one jumped out of their seats and began to applaud, hoot, and holler. I was smiling. Mario was smiling. Harold tried to say something, but I could not hear him. The noise was deafening. Harold shook his head. He took his open palm to his throat to let me know that I had cut my throat. I looked over at Maria. She was smiling and yelling as loud as anyone else. I turned to the front of the auditorium. Mario was grinning and punching the air with his fist.

Before I knew it, Mrs. Monfree was storming up the steps toward me. We all sat down. When she reached me, she stood there with her arms folded against her chest, her eyes opened wide and gritting her teeth. I thought she was going to slap me. I must admit I should have kept my mouth shut, but I didn't. She looked around the auditorium until the class quieted down. I looked at Mario. He was trying hard not to smile. When I looked back at Mrs. Monfree, I saw her little black eyes staring hard at me. If she had a gun, she would have shot me for sure.

"What's the matter, Mrs. Monfree? Did I say something wrong? Aren't we allowed to speak our mind in class? Mrs. Meriweather lets us. So what's the problem?" I heard chuckles around the auditorium.

She didn't wait for an answer. She grabbed me by the collar and tried to pull me from my seat. I didn't budge. She pulled again. I stayed in my seat. I was getting very angry. She backed away and pointed to the back of the auditorium. The entire class was staring at us.

"You, get up. Get up right now before I drag you out of that chair!"

I had no choice. I got up and walked with her to the back of the auditorium while she held the back of my shirt. Then I heard Johnny Marino on the other side of the room.

"Let him go! Let him go!"

The class picked up the chant, and soon everyone began to chant. Mrs. Monfree ignored the class. She took me by the arm and pulled me to the stairway leading to the first floor and the principal's office. I knew she meant business, and I was in trouble.

It dawned on me that I had really screwed up. She was going to report me to the principal for being disruptive. Our principal would have to file a report about the incident. He would send the report to Peter Capra at the Boys' Club, and my hopes of getting a scholarship to prep school would no doubt end as a result.

As we reached the stairs, I thought I would be able to explain away my behavior. I could explain what had happened. I saw how Mrs. Monfree was humiliating Mario. It was disturbing to me and the rest of the class. We were all rooting for Mario to keep on singing the way he was singing. I might have a successful explanation for the principal, but I knew it was a weak one.

What happened next overshadowed my behavior in the auditorium. I had a chance of an explanation, but then it happened. Mrs. Monfree and I were at the top of the stairs. She pulled me to keep going, but for some reason, I resisted. I didn't have any intention of hurting her, but I did not want her dragging me down the steps. She grabbed the banister and stepped down while still clutching my sleeve. I could see the heel of her boot catch the top of the first step. I stood at the top of the stairs as she tottered forward, one hand on the banister, the other still holding on to my sleeve. Her eyes opened wide as she realized she had lost her balance.

I grabbed her arm to keep her from falling, but it was too late. She slipped from my grasp and began to fall face forward with her arms extended. She tried to grab the banister one more time, but missed. Students heard her scream and rushed out just as Mrs. Monfree began to flip over and over down the steps.

Her long dress twisted around her body as she fell. She appeared to slow down but continued to roll over until the last few steps when she placed her hands directly on the floor as she landed. It was then I heard a crack and then another. It sounded like the breaking of bones. She let out another scream. I saw her land on her back at the foot of the steps, and she had rolled over to a sitting position. She sat there with a shocked look, staring at her hands, which hung down loosely from her wrists.

"My wrists!" she screamed. "They're broken! I have broken

my wrists!" she shouted. She began to cry, still holding her lifeless hands in the air.

I was in big trouble now. I knew that. How could I explain to anyone that it was not my fault? Or perhaps it was. At that moment, I felt terrible for her. I raced down the steps and, together with Mario, lifted her. Tears flowed down her cheeks. She cried loudly and without shame. I felt terrible that I was responsible for her fall.

We walked into the nurse's office. Her crying had turned to muffled sobbing. If I had not opened my mouth about Mario's singing, she would not be hurt. In the end, it was my fault that she was hurt. I could explain away what happened by telling myself that had she not humiliated Mario, she would not have been hurt, but her bad behavior did not excuse my bad behavior.

I could see how she was suffering. Sweat was dripping from her forehead. Her dress was drenched. She was deadweight in our arms. She had turned white. She was biting her lower lip. Her face was contorted. Her body had shrunk. Her hands still hung limply. Mario and I left her lying on a gurney, sobbing.

We found out later that Mrs. Monfree did break her wrists. She would not return to the school. The principal, Mr. Franklin, called me in the next day. I sat in the waiting room with his secretary glaring at me.

He had me waiting twenty minutes. It was over. I had broken my probation. I had lost the scholarship. I was finished. That was it. I was finally called in. I sat down in front of him. He peered at me from above his reading classes, leaned back in his brown leather chair, and brushed back his wavy hair. I was very uncomfortable. He leaned forward, folded his hands, and spoke to me softly.

"Tell me, Mr. D'Angelo, how do you manage always to get into trouble? What did you say to incite Mrs. Monfree to take you out of class? In particular, tell me what happened at the top of the stairs just before she fell down. I want to know, Mr. D'Angelo, if you deliberately threw her down the stairs."

I shook my head. "I did not, sir, I swear!"

"The nurse did tell me you and Mario helped her to the infirmary. I have spoken to Mario. I have spoken to the other students. I am clear on all that, but as to events at the top of the stairs, that is what I want you to explain to me. I want the truth!"

I started by explaining how Mario was being humiliated. I knew I was wrong about opening my mouth in class, and her falling down the steps was an accident.

He interrupted me. "Ah, but you see, Mr. D'Angelo, how good intentions can sometimes go awry? What you did in your speech in music class was to incite Mrs. Monfree to take action against you, justified or unjustified, and the resultant accident ensued. Do you understand? I have never known you to hurt anyone intentionally, and I know, Mr. D'Angelo, that you did not try to hurt her, but she was still hurt, wasn't she? And she would not be hurt had you not made that speech of yours."

I paused for a moment to think about an answer. "Yes, you are right. I was wrong for that, but I tried to stop her from falling. She could have been killed! I could never live with myself if that had happened. Never! But I felt very bad for what she was doing to Mario. We all like his singing, and she was hurting Mario's feelings, sir. I didn't mean to hurt her, but I wanted her to stop hurting Mario. It was embarrassing to everyone in the class."

Mr. Franklin leaned back in his chair and put his hand to his chin, thinking about what I had said. I told the truth as best I could. It was his decision to punish me or not.

"Are you going to report me to Mr. Capra over at the Boys' Club?" I asked, almost in tears.

He looked at me solemnly. For a few moments, I thought it was over for me. I was very nervous.

"I don't think that will be necessary, Joey. At this point, I think you should explain what happened to Mr. Capra." With that, he dismissed me.

The next day, I walked into Capra's office. As usual, he was going over paperwork and gave me a brief nod when I walked in. He threw his pen down on the desk and shook his head.

"Joey, your principal wanted to know if you were innocent

or guilty over this latest incident at the school. Both! Joey, every time I turn around, you get into some difficulty that forces me to think about my decision to send you to prep school. You just can't seem to stay out of trouble!

"I heard everything. I understand why you wanted to protect Mario. That was very commendable of you; however, there is no excuse to cause a major disruption in your class. You persisted in goading Mrs. Monfree, who bears a good deal of the blame here, but it was not your right to disrupt her class. We are a society of order and discipline. Without those elements, we have no society and no civilization. Do you understand, Mr. D'Angelo?"

I nodded sheepishly. Capra had a way of making me nervous. And why not? He had my future in his hands.

"Mr. Capra, you are right. I did wrong by butting my nose in where I should not have."

"Joey, you had good intentions, and that alone is your saving grace in this nasty episode; however, that does not excuse you from causing trouble in the classroom and directly or indirectly causing Mrs. Monfree from getting badly hurt. So far as I am concerned, the jury is still out as to whether you will be considered for the scholarship. I am going to think about it."

Well, at least he did not throw me out right then, and I still had a chance to redeem myself.

Capra continued, "You encouraged me with your decision to coach the young boys in basketball. That is a good sign, and frankly, by doing that coaching, you saved yourself here in this situation. Let this incident serve as a lesson to you to pay more attention to the consequences of your actions. You can't save the world, Joey, and when you do a good deed, be sure it does not end up in disaster. You understand?"

I nodded. He stood up, and so did I. He came over, clenched my hand tightly, and shook it firmly, looking me straight in the eye, but he was still upset. He was right. I could see how good intentions could lead to trouble.

Harold was waiting for me in the hallway. I told him everything that had happened. I had escaped and most definitely because I had decided to coach those young kids. When we walked outside, I saw Maria standing there at the foot of the steps. She came over to me and without a word gave me be a huge smile and a hug.

"You showed me, all right!" she said, and she kissed me quickly.

She grabbed my arm, and together with Harold, we started our way back home. I held Maria's hand tightly. I was so happy. Rachel was out of my mind. I grabbed Maria around her waist and smiled.

Walking through the park, we saw Mario sitting atop the parallel bars. He saw us and waved. A pretty Italian girl was there looking up at him. He looked happy. I did one good deed and escaped serious punishment, but I knew I had to be very careful from here on in.

Peter Capra was not a man who would tolerate anyone making too many mistakes. He gave me another chance to make that scholarship. I think he wanted me to make it. I learned my lesson for now, but knowing how I could lose control of myself, I never knew what other trouble I could find myself in down the road. But I got my Maria back. That caused me to think of another problem.

I had not told her that I was still interested in the scholarship. I was not up front with her. I knew there would be trouble again between us once she found out, and even though for the moment she had made up with me, I realized I was caught in another dilemma. By winning the scholarship, I could lose Maria again, this time for good. That thought made me shudder, and I learned soon enough what a good, tolerant girlfriend I could be losing.

21
Sonny

I knew I had a serious problem when Aunt Teresa, my mother's sister, showed up with my cousin Sonny one night a few weeks after school had started. I had not seen him for at least a year, and he looked different to me. He was holding his left hand to his eye when he came in, and when he waved to me, I noticed his eye was black and blue. He cocked his wrist when he waved. His blond hair looked longer and curlier, and his eyelashes were long.

"Hello, Joey," he said with a lisp I remembered only as a kind of whisper.

I didn't think much of it when I saw him last, but now, it sounded very strange to me. One year had made a big difference in what he looked like, and I did not like what I saw. His hair was curly but wild. His skin was much lighter than mine. He had a small frame to his body with small shoulders. His eyelids hung lower over his eyes, which were watery brown.

My mother kissed her sister. My father waved his fork to say hello and continued to eat. He also looked at Sonny in a curious way and then looked at me. My mother moved some chairs and set two more plates for pasta. After they sat down to eat, my mother sprang it on me.

"Joey," she said. "Guess what? Your cousin Sonny is going to PS 60 with you. Isn't that wonderful? He's starting tomorrow."

Teresa and my mother smiled. My father looked up with some suspicion. He cleared his throat and went back to his pasta. I looked at Sonny, and he gave me a half smile and continued eating. I knew right away he was going to be trouble.

"Now, Joey, Teresa came over tonight so you could get to know your cousin better. I know you haven't seen him much because they live on Fifth Street, but your aunt thinks PS 60 is a better school for Sonny, and she thinks you can help keep an eye on him. He is so shy, you know, and maybe you can have him meet your friends. What do you think, Joey? Can you do that for him?"

I thought it was strange that no one mentioned Sonny's black eye.

My mother smiled at me. Aunt Teresa looked uncomfortable. Sonny did not look up. He was squinting badly with his blackened left eye. I had a feeling that whoever gave him that shiner probably had a good reason. He probably deserved it.

"Sure. It's not a problem. I can meet him at school tomorrow morning, first thing."

I sighed and looked over at my father. He was not happy, either. I felt a heavy weight on my chest. I took another hard look at Sonny, and I definitely did not like what I saw. I thought, *Could Sonny like boys already at age twelve?* It didn't really matter to me.

Downstairs on the second floor, I would see Nicky Faglio many times hanging out on his fire escape, always with that red bandanna on his head, smoking, and wearing heavy makeup. Was Sonny going to wind up like Nicky? I shook my head and stabbed my pasta a few times.

I was almost convinced he would when, after supper, my mother suggested he and I go out and play some ball in the park. She and her sister had some talking to do. I went to my room, pulled out two black balls and two sets of handball gloves, and took Sonny to the park. It was getting dark, but it was still light enough to slam the black ball against the wall. I hit the ball gently after a few hard shots and turned to watch Sonny hit the ball back. He was terrible.

There he was, up close to the concrete wall, hitting the ball just like a girl, pushing it with his elbow bent down, and when he hit it, stepping with his right foot instead of his left. *Oh, man,* I thought, *what are my friends going to think when I take him to school? He's a damn fruitcake!* I felt sorry for him.

"Sonny, look, watch me. You're pushing the ball, not hitting it. You have to hit the ball with an arm motion over your shoulder, and you have to step forward with your left foot. Didn't you ever play stickball? Right-handed players throw the ball with their left foot going forward. Get it? Watch me."

I took the handball, bounced it a few times, and slammed it against the wall, and when it came back at me, I put my left foot forward and swung my right hand over my shoulder.

"Did you see how I hit the ball? That is how you have to hit the ball."

He looked confused. "Okay," he said. "I'll try."

He took the ball and hit it against the wall, a low, soft shot, the same way he did before. When it came back, there was no loft or speed to the ball. It landed about three feet from the wall and bounced softly to the ground. It was impossible to hit. He picked up the ball and looked at me.

"This game is too hard for me, Joey!"

I shook my head. He was right.

"Okay, forget it. It's getting dark anyway." Walking home, I asked him the question.

"So, Sonny, how did you get that shiner? Did somebody hit you at school? What happened?"

He kept on walking and then stopped, turned to me, and put his hand to his eye. "I fell down the steps. They said I tripped, but I think somebody pushed me."

He talked so softly I could barely hear or understand what he was saying. I decided not to push it. I figured he was being picked on, and the story about falling down the steps was not the truth. I did not believe him anyway.

"Okay, forget it. Tomorrow, I'll meet you in front of the main steps going into school, okay? How does eight thirty tomorrow morning sound?"

In the morning, I met Harold in front of his building and headed to the First Avenue bus on the way up to PS 60. Harold noticed I was not as talkative as usual. We hopped on the bus and sat down, and it was there I hit him with it.

"Harold, I have a problem. My cousin Sonny is transferring to our school, and my aunt Teresa asked my mother if I could take care of him, and I agreed."

Harold looked at me funny. "So how is that a problem?" he asked.

I took a deep breath, hesitated before saying anything, and looked at him very seriously. I leaned closer to him. "Because," I whispered, "I think my cousin is queer. He came to my house last night with my aunt Teresa with a huge shiner over his left eye. I mean it was really black and blue! He must have gotten beat up. He gave me a story that he fell down school steps, but I don't believe that. I think somebody took him and hit him a good shot right in the eye."

Harold nodded a few times, thinking about what I had said. "I agree with you. I think you have a problem. Does he really look that bad? I mean, can you tell for sure he's a fairy?"

I shook my head. "Harold, when you take a look at him, you tell me if you think he's queer!"

Harold already had an idea. "You know, Joey, instead of asking me, why don't you ask him? What do you have to lose? If you take him aside, just ask him. What is so difficult about that? Besides, who cares?"

"I still have a problem, don't I? The kids are still going to think he is a fairy no matter what! And if they think he is queer, they're going to start bullying him. So what do I do when that happens? I can't exactly start fighting with everybody who picks on him, now can I?"

The bus pulled up to Ninth Street. We got out and walked through Tompkins Square Park toward PS 60.

"I am real worried about what the kids are going to think. If I get into a fight over Sonny—and it could happen; you know that—I will have to explain that to Peter Capra, and there goes the scholarship. I mean, he's my cousin, for cryin' out loud! It's not like I can ignore him. My mother told me to look out for him. Now what does that mean, Harold? Does it mean I'm supposed to stick up for Sonny if somebody starts trouble? You see why I have a serious problem on my hands? Anything can happen, and when it does, I have to know what I'm going to do. He's trouble!"

Sonny was waiting for me at school, leaning on one of the banisters next to the wide white steps that led into PS 60. He had on a bright green jacket and a short bright orange-and-yellow scarf around his neck. His eye was not as black. He definitely looked queer to me.

"Hello, Joey. My mother told me I was supposed to see the principal and then go into your homeroom. I guess she already spoke to him." His hair was curly and wild. His skin in the light of day was much lighter than my own. Sonny did not look Sicilian.

Harold stuck his hand out, and Sonny smiled at him. It was then I saw slight cracks on the corners of his mouth. I got a little closer to him, and I noticed specks of white powder on his face around his mouth and cheeks. Was he wearing makeup? I thought Harold would notice right away, but if he had, he didn't let on.

"Hello, Sonny. I'm Harold. I'm Joey's friend."

We all walked inside, and I pointed Sonny toward the principal's office. Harold and I headed toward homeroom.

"You see what I mean? What do you think?"

He didn't say anything.

We walked into homeroom. Johnny was already in class talking away. Maria, fixing her hair, gave me a big smile. I turned to Harold. He looked at me and shook his head.

"Joey, you definitely have a problem!"

A few minutes later, Sonny walked into the room. He didn't exactly walk. He looked like he was shuffling. I could hear his shoes slide across the floor as he headed toward our homeroom teacher. Everyone stared at him. I noticed how he turned his shoulders slightly as he walked. Then somebody let out a whistle as if a pretty girl was walking by. I nearly died.

Sonny kept walking as if he didn't hear it, but I did. Johnny looked at me and started waving his hand in the air, an Italian motion that basically meant, "I don't believe it!" I knew right then I was going to have trouble with Johnny.

Nobody said a word during classes, but at lunchtime in the cafeteria, it happened. Sonny got his lunch and came over and sat down next to me and Harold. Johnny walked over to us.

"Who's your new boyfriend, Joey? Do I have competition?" He laughed, put his hands on his hips, and twisted his shoulders back and forth.

"Very funny, Johnny. This here is my cousin Sonny. He just transferred from PS 61, and I'm going to show him around."

Johnny looked at Sonny and shook his head. He didn't believe me.

Maria sat down, pulled out a brown bag with her lunch in it, and then stuck out her hand. "Lucky you! Joey's cousin. How are ya? I'm Maria, Joey's girl." She paused and gave me that suspicious look of hers. "I think!"

"Very nice to meet you, Maria!" he said. He cocked his head and shook her hand.

Good God, I thought. *Who talks like that? None of the guys!*

Then Maria started talking to Sonny as if they had been friends for years. I was surprised. What was going on? I thought it might be a thing between queers and girls. I looked at Harold. He just shrugged.

"Whatta ya gettin' jealous? I don't think you have anything to worry about."

Sonny got up to take his tray back to the counter. Johnny had already finished, and when Sonny passed him, he stuck his foot out. Sonny fell to the floor. His tray and leftover food went flying across the cafeteria floor. The lunchroom burst into laughter. Harold and I went over to him and helped him up. I turned to

Johnny. He was laughing the loudest. I jumped up and walked up to him and clenched my fists.

"What are you, some kind of a jerk? You know you're getting really crazy lately. What the hell is the matter with you? I just told you he's my cousin, and this is what you do? You have no respect for anybody!"

"You're kidding me, right? He really is your cousin?" He looked at Sonny for a minute and then leaned over and whispered, "The kid's a fruitcake!"

"Just keep your mouth shut, and don't make fun of him! You hear me?"

I noticed then how suddenly quiet the cafeteria had become. I didn't look around. I walked over to Harold.

"You're some kind of an idiot, Johnny!" Maria shouted.

"See what I mean, Harold? It's gonna be like this all year long. I can't do this."

Maria went over to Sonny, who was cleaning food off his pants. She started to rub his back and then took him back to our table. I thought he was going to cry. Johnny came over to us and looked straight at Sonny.

He leaned forward and patted him on the back and whispered to him, "Look, I'm sorry I tripped you, but you know, you can't walk around here like a fairy. You're gonna get hurt!" Then he whispered to me, "I think you should get him outta here. I'm tellin' ya! Get him outta here! He's gonna get us all into trouble!"

That was my problem and Johnny's solution. It had already started. I understood what Johnny meant. If I defended Sonny, he would be defending me! I decided I would talk to my parents to persuade them to send Sonny back to PS 61. I knew my father would be on my side. I would let them know at dinner that night.

I finished my cutlets, my mother began clearing the dishes, and my father was sipping his espresso. It was a good time to bring up the subject.

"Ma, I don't think it's a good idea to have Sonny at my school.

I already had an argument with Johnny over him. He's gonna be trouble for me. I don't want to take care of him."

My father looked at me and nodded his head. He sipped his wine down. It gave him courage.

"Lillian, I agree with the boy. Sonny does not belong at Joey's school. Why should our son be burdened with this problem? He has enough on his mind. He needs to get good grades if he is going to get that scholarship. He does not need to worry about defending Sonny! If you walk with a cripple, soon you walk with a limp! This is your sister's problem, not Joey's."

My father picked up his espresso and drank it right down. My mother slammed the last dish from the table into the sink, glared at my father, and shook her finger at him.

"First of all, this boy is your nephew also. You have a responsibility! He is what he is!" She put her hand to her chest. "O Jesu Cristo! Only God knows why Sonny is what he is! But does that mean we treat him like a dog in the street and kick him away because we do not like what we see, because he is different? No! He is a member of our family, and I promised my sister! That is all I have to say. He stays at PS 60, and Joey is going to make sure no one hurts him in any way! Joey, you understand?"

I sat there quietly for a few moments looking at my mother, who turned to the dishes. When I glanced at my father, I could see he was steaming inside. What could he say? My mother was right, but I was the one who had to deal with the trouble at school.

"Ma, Sonny already got into trouble. When he went to empty his tray out in the cafeteria, Johnny Marino tripped him, and he landed flat on his face with food all over the floor. I picked him up, and then I got angry with Johnny. He made me so mad!"

"Good, Joey," my mother said, "that was exactly the right thing to do. You defended him. Dear God, he is going to need a lot of defending in his life. Joey, Sonny is staying at PS 60!"

It was then I decided to ask the question that was on my mind. I took a deep breath. "Ma, so you think that Sonny likes boys or he just acts that way because he can't help it?"

My mother stopped washing the dishes, dried her hands, and

stared hard at me. "Joey, I do not know the answer to that question. Maybe he just walks and talks like that and really likes girls! Does it really matter? Only Sonny knows the answer to what he is. Tomorrow, when you see him at school, why don't you just ask him?"

My father grunted and waved his hand in the air. "If that boy is not a fairy, then my wine in front of me is not red! And we can all see that it is red, can we not?"

My mother stared at my father angrily and shook her head in disgust.

It was no use trying to convince my mother to send Sonny back to PS 61. I left the table, washed up, and told my parents I was going out to see Maria. The sun had already gone down.

We sat quietly in the back park where I played center field, under the large maple tree. I noticed, in the brilliant light of the lamppost on Houston Street, its large, thick leaves were already turning a burnt orange. We were alone, and she was close to me and warm. There was no question I liked girls.

I looked over at Maria in her brown leather jacket, staring at cars passing by on Houston Street, chewing gum. The Sunshine Theatre was playing *White Heat* from 1949. Her dark hair hung down gently over her ears. It was the silhouette of her face that caught me. I could see her looks were changing. Her dark eyes were almost black. Her nose came down straight as an arrow. Her high cheekbones and smooth dark skin made her look more like Ava Gardner.

I turned her head toward me and kissed her, sliding my hand down her leather jacket. A cool gust of wind caught her hair and sent it flying. She gently took my hand away.

"Hey, whatta ya doin', bub?" she said, smiling.

I leaned over again and kissed her full on her lips. She did not resist. It was a long kiss. Then she pulled me away.

"Hey, John Garfield, can I come up for air, please?"

I laughed. She took out the gum she still had in her mouth and threw it under a tree behind us. I felt my body heat up and got closer to her. I held her close to me. She felt so good. I knew I loved her. The scholarship was becoming a major challenge to me. How could I leave Maria? I nearly cried.

"That's better," she said.

Then she stared at me for a few moments, leaned closer to me, grabbed the back of my head, and pulled me toward her. It was a soft, moist kiss we held for a long time. We hugged each other tightly. Above us, branches thick with leaves bent to the wind.

I put my hand on her leather jacket and this time slowly unzipped it, slid my hand inside, and rubbed her breast back and forth. She moaned, held me closer, and kissed me again softly. She leaned back and looked at me with wet eyes, put her hand over mine, and held it there so I would not move it.

"Hey, Joey, aren't you getting a little carried away? We're just kids, you know!"

I took her hand and kissed it, looking at her face glowing from the lamppost light. She was beautiful. It was very quiet. Leaves above us rustled from a soft, swirling wind. For a few moments, there were no cars on Houston. We stared at each other without a word. Then Maria leaned forward to kiss me again. I wanted more, but she stood up, pushed down her jacket, put her hands on her hips, and looked at me slyly.

"Time to go, Romeo," she said. "Before you start getting ideas!"

"We just got here!" I said.

She beckoned me to follow her. I got up and held her around the waist, and together we walked to her building on Mott Street.

The next morning, Harold and I just made it to homeroom. Maria was there talking to Sonny. When she saw us, she came over and kissed me on the cheek. Then Sonny walked out into the hallway. I went over to the door and saw he was talking to three kids I knew from Ninth Street. They were bad kids, bullying the young kids for money, causing fights in the school for no reason, and loud.

Their leader, Boris, was a tall, skinny kid with pimples on his face. His friends were shorter and looked Polish to me, but I could not be sure. They dressed in the East Village way: jeans with holes in them and shirts that hung out over their belts. They had long dirty hair. I knew they were trouble for Sonny, so I went over to him.

"Sonny, what are you doing? It's almost time for class. You have to get inside."

The tall one glared and moved closer to me. "What's the problem, Joey? We can't talk to your cousin? We're just talking about trading comic books. What's wrong with that?"

I got angry and clenched my fists. "As long as that's what you're talking about. I have no problem with that. Just remember he's my cousin."

Johnny walked over to us and stood next to me. He looked at Sonny and shook his head. Then he looked at the tall kid, who had moved back a few steps as soon as he saw Johnny.

"What's the problem, Joey? Anybody giving you trouble?"

Johnny clenched his fists. His arms stiffened. He bit his lip and glared at the tall kid. He was ready to clock him. I kept calm.

"Nothing, Johnny, no problem," I said. "Sonny is coming into homeroom now. Right, Sonny?"

I stared at him. He had a half smile on his face. He lifted his chin up, taunting me. The bastard was enjoying the attention! The tall kid I could see was very nervous.

"No problem, Johnny," said the tall kid. "We're leaving."

They walked away. I gave Sonny a push toward homeroom. Johnny walked in.

"You stay away from those kids, you hear me? They are bad news. Just stay away from them."

Sonny came closer to me. I thought I smelled a whiff of perfume.

"What are you, my father?" he said. "I'll do what I want to do. Okay? So mind your own business! I'm older than you, anyway, so who are you to tell me what to do?"

If we hadn't been in school, I would have taken him by the neck and slammed him. His black eye was not as purple as the day before, but if I had hit him, my aunt would have known right away he had another shiner. Here I was taking care of him, and he was talking back to me!

"Look, Sonny," I said, calmly, "I know you're a smart kid, but those guys don't care about your damn comic books. You get my drift? Now wake up and pay attention. Comic books are an excuse to get you! Don't you get it?"

He looked at me and sneered, his chin in the air, his eyes half-closed. I thought I would ask him the question that was bothering me.

"I want to know one thing before classes start. Are you a queer or not? I want to know. That's all! Just tell me the truth. Tell me now because the bell is going to ring very soon."

Sonny put his hands on his hips and laughed. "What if I am, Joey? First off, it's none of your damn business! Second, I'll do what I want to do, and you're not going to stop me. Besides, I don't read comics anymore. They can have them. They're for kids, and I'm not a kid anymore."

The bell rang to start classes. Sonny walked back into homeroom, picked up his books, and walked out. I packed my books and looked at Maria, who stood up and shrugged. She must have heard everything. Johnny walked over to me. I wondered why he tried to help.

"So what made you change your mind to protect Sonny?" I asked him. "Only yesterday, you tripped him, and we almost had a fight about it."

"Who said I was protecting him? That little faggot! I was watching *your* back, not his! Besides, you can't make those jerks think the guys from our neighborhood are soft. They'll walk all over us. Sonny just got lucky, that's all—lucky he's your cousin. I feel sorry for him, but I still think he's a jerk. We have our reputation to protect, Joey. Don't you forget that."

At three o' clock, when Sonny walked back into homeroom, he barely looked at me. He was packing his books when I went over to him. He tried to avoid making eye contact with me.

"All right, Sonny, so you're going home, right?"

"Yeah, I'm going home, and I'm going without you!" he said, almost in a whisper. "I'm not stupid, you know. Don't worry. I can take care of myself!" He started walking out the door and then turned to me. "Do me a favor? Stop hanging all over me!"

He shuffled away, swishing his shoulders, left to right. I could have killed him.

He told me he was going home, and so I thought he would be okay since nothing happened at school. I did my job. I watched over him and protected him. I could tell my mother that I did what she asked me to do. But I still didn't know if he was really queer. Thinking about him gnawed at me. I don't know why I was so curious about that, but I was.

Maria came over to me and took my arm, and we walked out together. That made me feel better. A cool breeze swept over us. Maria leaned against me. She made me feel warm and at peace after my trouble with Sonny. The wind grew stronger. It was getting colder.

It was one of those cool early afternoons when clouds begin to blanket the blue sky. Only patches of sun could be seen. I walked Maria home. We didn't talk much, especially down First Avenue. A dusty wind kicked up and blew hard against our faces. Maria's hair flew all over. She laughed. We held each other closer and leaned toward the wind, still laughing. Her eyes smiled at me. I was happy. As she held me tighter, I thought less of Sonny.

When we got to her building, Maria stood there clutching her black coat around her thin body. Above, I could see now dark clouds moving rapidly across the sky. I took her into the hallway, and we could hear the whistling of the wind and the rattling of windows. A storm was coming. Maria leaned against the wall and opened her coat. I slid my arms around her tiny waist and leaned against her body. I could feel the heat of her right away. She was hot.

We kissed softly and naturally. She closed her eyes. I felt her lips so sweet and wet. It was I who moaned softly. She tasted so good. She opened her eyes and smiled at me.

"I guess you like to kiss me just a little bit, eh, Joey?"

It was so natural to lean against her and kiss her. I could not imagine anything else. I pressed against her, smiling, and without a word in reply, I kissed her again. She opened her lips and this time let my tongue into her mouth. I let it slide in. This time, she moaned softly. Still kissing me, she smiled and then pushed me away and laughed.

"Joey, in my hallway? We could get caught!"

We heard a door open and close above us. We looked up. An old man wearing a fedora hobbled down the steps, making a racket with each step he took. He walked right past us without looking our way. We laughed after he closed the building door behind him, and we kissed again. Then she pushed me away and straightened her hair.

"Okay, enough. I have to go upstairs. That old man is gonna talk to my mother. What a pain in the ass! I'm gonna have to explain to her. Anyway, it was worth it. You'd better go."

She pulled me to her and kissed me one more time. "And don't worry about Sonny. You looked like an undertaker all day today. He is what he is, and there isn't anything you're gonna do about it. Just let it go!"

She bounded up the steps and out of sight. I stood there alone and lonely. She had gone but just a few seconds earlier, and I already missed her. She was good for me.

When I left her building, I felt the wind blow even stronger. I headed toward First Street. It wasn't even four o'clock, and it was already growing very dark. I looked to see if Tommy was playing handball, but he was not.

As I approached my building, I noticed the block was nearly empty. On the stoop, I felt the first drops of light rain. I went inside.

It must have been the tension of the day. I felt sleepy, and so I went into my room and flopped on my bed, turned and looked up at the ceiling, and listened to a hard rain coming down. I took a deep breath and closed my eyes. I was exhausted.

I felt so calm and relaxed. The rain fell harder. Raindrops tapped noisily against the window. It was the tapping of the raindrops that calmed me enough to let me fall asleep and get away from the tension of the day. I thought of Maria, how warm she felt, and how good it was to be with her. All thoughts of Sonny faded away.

22

Sonny in the Soup

I woke up when I heard my mother calling me.

Supper was ready. I stretched out on the bed and noticed my ankles were showing below the bottom of my jeans. I was growing out of them. I jumped out of bed with a shout, feeling totally relaxed. I went into the bathroom, soaked my head in lukewarm water, and washed and dried my head.

It was already dark outside, and I could see through the kitchen window streaks of lightning over Forsyth Street Park. I heard the rumbling of thunder and felt the building shake. My mother had made a pot of minestrone soup. I took the first spoonful and tasted the tomatoes, potato, and chicken. The soup was warm and delicious and added to the peace I felt. When I took the last spoonful of the soup, I heard footsteps in the hallway. Someone started banging on our door.

"Lillian, open the door. It's Teresa!"

My mother threw down her napkin and went to the door. In walked Teresa soaked, crying, and beating her chest.

"My Sonny! He's not home. Where is he, Joey? Where did you leave him? Where is he?"

I was in shock. I put down my spoon and looked at my mom, who was glaring at me. I shrugged. "I don't know, Ma!"

"Joey, where is he?" my mother asked. "I thought everything was all right at school."

I wiped my mouth and tried to speak. I couldn't get words out fast enough.

"Joey, we're waiting for an answer!" my father shouted. "Where is Sonny? What happened to him?"

I answered as best I could. "When I left school, Sonny told me he didn't want me to walk home with him, and he left. Everything was okay when I saw him leave."

"But, Joey," my aunt Teresa said, "he did come home after school! He put together a whole pile of comic books and then said he wasn't hungry but that he would be back by six the latest! Joey, he's not home! Dear Mother of God, Mother of Mercy, protect him. Please take care of him." She began to cry hysterically.

My mother sat her down and tried to calm her. She turned to me. "But what happened at school, Joey? Did anyone bother him today? Did you have words with him? What happened?"

I bit my lip but answered right away this time. "Ma, Sonny was talking to some bad kids, and I told him to stay away from them. Everybody in school knows they're bad. I told him to keep away from them! They were talking to him about trading comic books, but I told Sonny that was just an excuse. I knew they were up to no good."

My father took my shoulder gently. "Joey, if you thought these boys were bad, you should have taken Sonny home and then talked to your aunt Teresa about them. She would have told Sonny to stay home, and we would not be discussing where Sonny is right now! He may be in trouble." He looked straight at me. "You have to go out, find him, and get him home!"

I looked out the window. The rain was falling pretty hard. I sighed. My parents and Aunt Teresa were all staring at me. I had no choice. I was so damn mad at Sonny at that moment I thought next time I saw him I would give him a black eye.

"Okay, I'll go. I'm gonna go to the park on Ninth Street and look for him. I'll find him. I know where those kids live also. I'll find him."

My aunt Teresa grabbed me by the shoulders. "Joey, Sonny is so sensitive and alone. He can't help what he is. Help him. I love you, baby!"

She made me feel terrible. I felt I let her down. I got up and grabbed my jacket and left.

When I reached my stoop, the rain was coming down very hard. I stood there thinking of my next step. I knew I needed help. This time, it wasn't going to be Harold. There were three of them. I ran down the stoop and headed toward Johnny's building, ran up the steps, and banged on his door. My shirt, jacket, and pants were soaked.

Johnny's father, Nick, answered the door. He smelled of beer, and his belly hung over his pants. He wore a sleeveless undershirt. Strands of his thinning hair hung loosely over his ears, and he had not shaven in a while. He stood there moving his head from side to side. His eyes were bloodshot, his nose was red, and he leaned against the door to keep his balance.

"What the hell are you doing here? It's late, and we're eating. You're soaked! What are you up to? More trouble?"

Jesus! Was Johnny telling him I was getting him into trouble?

Johnny came to the front door. His father went back inside. Johnny took one look at me and knew there was trouble. His eyes lit up.

He smiled and whispered, "Joey, what's up? Don't tell me; I already know. That fairy, Sonny, got you into trouble!"

Johnny could smell trouble and wanted to be right in the middle of it whenever it came, but not this time. I told him what happened—that Sonny had come home all right but then went back out and was probably with the kids from Ninth Street.

"Joey, I would love to help you out, but I'm still on probation. Going after kids from our school? I promised my pop I would stick to my curfew, and you know how mean and nasty he gets when he's drunk. I can't leave now!"

"Okay. I understand." I turned to leave.

As I shut the door behind me, Johnny suddenly opened it. In the hallway, he grabbed me by the shoulder.

"Wait a minute! Wait for me downstairs! After he drinks one more beer, for sure he'll get on the couch and fall asleep. He'll be out for the night. Then I can leave. I'll be back even before he wakes up." He paused to look back inside. "You just have to wait for me! Don't worry. I'll bring my stickball bat!" When he said that, I was hoping it would not come to that.

I went downstairs and waited in the hallway. That was Johnny. He had a mean streak in him and no guilt about beating somebody up. He was just like Pepi. I waited for him about ten minutes, and he came out with a big smile on his face, his bat on his shoulder.

We headed toward First Avenue and then up to Ninth Street. The rain was coming down hard. We ran except when we had to stop for a traffic light. I was in better shape than Johnny because of handball. On Seventh Street, I looked over at him, and he was huffing and puffing.

He smiled, clutching his stickball bat. I guess he was so used to getting batted around by his father and not being able to hit back that he just loved to have a chance to beat somebody. He didn't care about getting hit himself.

My thoughts turned to Sonny. I was less angry with him and more worried that something bad was happening to him. After all, he was my blood, my cousin, and family has to take care of family, no matter what. The rain had finally slowed to a light drizzle. I ran through the red light and slowed down so Johnny could catch up to me. When we reached Tompkins Square Park on Avenue A, it was just a little past seven. The park was empty. We walked inside and looked around. The rain came down heavier, but we kept on going.

We approached the center of the park and finally took cover under a tree, its branches bent from rain and leaves, drenched with water, drooping. It was very quiet except for the falling rain. And then I heard what I thought was a muffled cry coming from the bathroom building. As we moved closer to the building, I saw drenched comic books strewn all over the ground, a pile of them in front of the building.

I motioned to Johnny to stop and listen. There was no doubt now. There were screams coming from inside the bathroom building. We ran to the front door and stormed into the bathroom. There was Sonny, his hands on the wall, held by two of the kids from Ninth Street. His pants were down to his ankles, and he was crying and screaming. The tall boy was behind him, unbuckling his belt.

As soon as he saw Johnny and me come racing in, his pants fell down. Sonny stared at us and stopped screaming. Tears were streaming down his cheeks. The other boys stepped back. Johnny wasted no time. He lifted his bat and whacked the tall kid in the head. He let out a scream and tried to pull his pants back up, but Johnny was relentless. He kept whacking him with his bat to the head and back.

It happened so fast. Johnny kept beating the kid over the head with short, fast whacks. The boy screamed in pain every time the bat came down on him. The other kids stood frozen against the wall and then tried to get out of the bathroom, but I was blocking the way. I started punching the first kid and didn't stop. I was a maniac, punching and screaming at them.

"You goddamn sons of bitches!" I shouted.

I was so crazed I kept punching both of them at the same time. They tried to get away from me. One almost did. He reached the door, but I pulled him back by his wet jacket, threw him down to the marble floor, and started kicking him.

While I did that, the other boy ran out and took off as fast as he could. Johnny was still pounding the tall kid over the head. The boy was screaming so loudly it echoed through the bathroom. I thought Johnny was going to kill him, so I grabbed the bat from him. He looked at me as if I were crazy. He started pounding him with his fists. The second boy ran out.

The tall kid was cowering on the floor, crying and bleeding

from his head. Sonny had already gotten his pants back on, and he stood there against the wall rubbing his eyes and sniffling.

"Enough, Johnny, leave him alone!" Then I shouted at the tall kid. "You, you piece of shit. Get up and get your pants back on."

He struggled to get up. As he buckled his belt, Johnny went over to him and gave him a right hook across his face. He fell to the ground.

"Johnny, that's enough; you're gonna kill him."

Johnny just looked at me and smiled. "That's what I'm tryin' to do, Joey. I'm tryin' to kill him!" He went to him and kicked him in the ribs.

The boy let out a loud groan. I stepped in front of Johnny.

"Enough, Johnny! You don't want to hurt him so bad they put you back in!"

The tall kid lay on the floor, whimpering. I went over to Sonny, who had stopped crying. His pants were back on. I put my hand on his shoulder. He had his head down, sniffling but trying to calm down.

"Are you okay?" I asked him.

He took a deep breath and nodded. I handed my handkerchief to him. He wiped sweat off his face. I rubbed his back to calm him down. I thought he was going to cry again, but he didn't.

"Don't worry. You're okay now."

That's when I remembered I had warned him about these kids, and he had ignored me.

"What the hell were you thinking?" I shouted. "I told you they were trouble. Everybody in our school knows that!"

I looked over at the tall boy, who got up, crying.

"And you, you damn bastard, the first thing I'm gonna do tomorrow is go right to the principal's office. I hope he throws you and your bastard friends right out of school! Maybe they'll send you to reform school. And you know what's gonna happen there! Now get outta here!"

The kid stood up and started to walk out. Johnny went over to him and kicked him, shoving him out of the bathroom. I was drenched from sweat and rain. I gave Johnny back his bat, but I felt like hitting Sonny with it. He was still shaking. There was no color in his face. He was scared. He had gone through enough, and I hoped he had learned his lesson.

"C'mon, Sonny," Johnny said. He grabbed him, put his arm around his shoulder, and walked out with him.

I was a little surprised that Johnny was comforting him. The rain had stopped. Above I could see blue sky and white clouds again. I felt relieved that Sonny was okay.

"Don't worry, Sonny," Johnny said. "If anybody ever touches you again, me and your cousin Joey will be there to help you out. Just remember that. You're family. Okay?"

Sonny nodded.

I asked Sonny to come home with me. I told him his mother was waiting for us. He nodded again. Then I asked if they hurt him. He knew what I meant. There was a short silence. He spoke in a clear voice.

"No, only when they grabbed me from behind and the tall kid started punching me in the stomach. They dragged me into the bathroom, but they didn't do anything to me. I tried to fight back, but they kept punching me all over. I was scared, though, really scared, especially when the tall kid pulled my pants down, and he started unbuckling his belt. That's when I started screaming like a crazy man."

Johnny looked at him and shook his head. "Well, Sonny, you walk around like a damn faggot! What do you think is gonna happen?" Johnny turned to me. "Jesus! Joey, when you get home, you'd better straighten him out, because I'm telling you right now I'm losing my patience with this kid. I know I told you I would help you out, but coming out in the rain to get this cousin of yours outta trouble is enough for me. I love ya. You're my friend. I would do anything for you, but not this again. Please! Let's go home. My arms are killing me from hitting that son of a bitch!"

Outside, Sonny looked at his comic books all over the ground, wet and ruined. He stood there for a few seconds and then went over and started kicking them. He picked one up, but it fell apart in his hands. He threw it back down on the ground.

"I don't need these anymore. I'm gonna be thirteen. Who reads comic books at thirteen?"

He had a point. After I saw his comics destroyed, I felt the same way, and I thought every time I picked up a comic book, it would remind me of this night. I guessed I was done with comic books. It was time for real books for me. That reminded me of Tom and Sue. I was still in hot water over missing the grammar class. I was surprised no one had said anything to me.

When we got to First Street, Johnny went home, and Sonny came with me. We walked in. Sonny looked washed out. As soon as she saw him, his mother let out a scream. She started hugging him and crying. My God! My mother would never do that to me! Aunt Teresa began to check Sonny to see if he was hurt. It was making me a little sick watching her.

I explained that he got caught in the storm and could not get back, so he ducked into the bathroom building and waited. His comic books were ruined from the rain, and that was why he was so late. I looked over at my father. Looking disgusted at the fuss Teresa was making, he took his gallon of wine and filled his glass. After they left, my parents looked relieved. It would have been too difficult for me to tell them the truth, and I saved Sonny embarrassment.

When I got to school the next day, I was told to go to the principal's office. I thought I was in for it when I found out that the mother of one of the kids went in earlier to see him and complained that Johnny had beaten her son with a stickball bat. She should have known what her son had done! When I walked in, Johnny was already sitting in the waiting room. He leaned over to me with a big smile on his face.

"When I go in there, I am going to fry those kids! I'm telling Mr. Franklin everything, everything! I'm holding nuthin' back. And Joey, I am lettin' the chips fall wherever. You get what I mean? I'm not goin' down for this one!"

I sat there looking at him for a minute. Actually, I thought that this time honesty was the best policy, and I agreed with him. The door opened, and in walked Sonny with a smirk on his face. I was so angry I felt like punching him and giving him another black eye. He looked at me and smiled. What was he smiling about? Didn't he know we were in deep trouble?

"Hello, Joey. Hello, Johnny," he said softly, and he sat down.

A few minutes later, the three kids came in, and after that, we all got up and went into the principal's office. Johnny laid out what had happened. He told the principal everything, from walking in on the three kids, seeing Sonny with his pants down to his ankles, and Boris dropping his pants behind Sonny. He explained he was just defending Sonny from getting attacked.

Sonny explained what had happened to him. The kids pretended they were interested in his comic books, but when they got to the park, they dragged him into the bathroom and attacked him.

I told the principal everything that happened after that. After I was done, he sent Johnny, Sonny, and me out of the room. Then he asked his secretary to call the parents of the kids who attacked Sonny. Outside in the hallway, Johnny and I watched Sonny wave to us and walk away smiling as if nothing had happened. He was the victim. He had no problem, and he knew it.

After school, Johnny and I were called in again. The principal told us we had done the right thing, and we would not be punished. He warned me to keep an eye on Sonny, and then he let us go. I was not out of the woods. I still had Sonny to worry about.

Maria walked over to us. I told her everything. I was very glad to see her and asked her if she would meet me later in the park. She said she would. I kissed her on the cheek quickly and left for home.

That night, I met Maria in the back park. We sat on our favorite bench. It was colder than the last night I had met her there. We shivered. I leaned over and pulled her to me and kissed her softly.

Then I asked her, "So, Maria, do you think my cousin Sonny is a fairy?"

She tilted her head and smiled at me in a curious way. "After what happened, you ask me a question like that? What's the difference? We're all different, aren't we, Joey? I mean, how is the answer to that question gonna make a difference in your life? It doesn't matter. He is what he is. I told you that! We still have to live with each other, don't we?"

I nodded agreement. She was right. Sonny would always be Sonny.

She stopped talking. A cool wind blew through the park. I looked up at the sky and noticed how clear it was. Many stars were lighting a cloudless sky. A big, bright moon, not quite full, hung easily just above the horizon. It was that way after a storm, calm and peaceful.

Maria turned to me, grabbed my jacket, and pulled me toward her. "C'mon over here, you jerk. I'm here with you, and you're thinking about your cousin! Stop worrying already and kiss me."

I smiled and did what she told me. We sat there for about a half hour just holding each other. We listened to the peaceful rustling of leaves, cars passing on Houston Street, and people casually walking up and down Second Avenue. After a little while, I walked her home. I gave her a long kiss at her building. She went inside, and I walked back to First Street.

When I got to my stoop, I saw Nicky Faglio on the fire escape. He lived on the second floor. It was cold out, but there he was, a black robe wrapped around his thin body, a red bandanna around his head, smoking a cigarette and looking out at First Street. He was crouched with his elbows on his legs, and when he heard me coming up the stoop, he turned and leaned over and smiled. In the light of the lamppost, I could see shadows across his face, lines of wrinkles, and a faint hint of the color red on his lips.

"Hello, Joey," he said. "How are you?"

I told him I was okay. When I got inside the hallway, I started to feel bad for him, living alone in that apartment, hanging out on a fire escape, and looking sad. I thought then I would probably be spending a lot of time defending Sonny. That made me feel pretty miserable. But when I jumped into bed, turned off the lights, and closed my eyes, I thought about wrapping my arms around Maria and kissing her softly on those soft, wet lips of hers, and that made me feel pretty damn good.

23
Bill

Johnny showed me how good a buddy he was to me when he stopped to help me after I cut myself going through the glass windows at Wanamaker's. He also showed how good a friend he was when he helped me look for Sonny and then beat the hell out of the kids who were attacking him in the park. I knew I could count on him when I needed him, and that is why he was my buddy; but we had our differences.

There was a mean streak in him. It was after a stickball game at Great Jones Street when he showed me how bad he could really be and how different we had become over the past year alone, especially since he came out of reform school.

I was throwing my Spalding ball in the air, and Johnny and I both had our stickball bats over our left shoulders. We came to Third Avenue, the Bowery. Already I could smell the stench of alcohol. Garbage pans spilled over their garbage onto the avenue. Above us, the El train roared and shook its tracks, sending streaks of late-morning light jumping onto the street as it roared past Third Street.

As we waited for the light, I could see men in old, dirty clothes—rags, really—staggering along and wandering up and down the Avenue. It was Saturday morning, and the men walked uneasily with glazed eyes. Some of them who had lost their balance were lying on the sidewalk, too drunk to get up. I thought I had gotten used to the sight of them until I saw Bill.

There he was, standing against an old run-down four-story building, short gray hair, a beard, and a worn, dirty bandage wrapped around his head. The light turned green, and we walked across the avenue. He stood there leaning forward, turning his head and looking up and down the avenue at nothing in particular.

He saw Johnny and me and smiled. I could see his red cheeks up close, wrinkles cut deep into his reddened face, and stubby whiskers of a white beard. But I also noticed his blue eyes set clear and focused on us. Our eyes met, and it was then he stuck out his hand and smiled. I noticed the multicolored bandanna around his head had a dark stain of blood. He stuck out his hand as we approached him and looked at me.

"Hey, kid, you have a quarter? I'm pretty hungry. It's hot out here, and I could sure use a sandwich or somethin' and a drink. Whatta ya say?"

I kept going and did not reply, but Johnny stopped and stared at him. He looked down at the man's shoes. I stopped and looked down also. His shoelaces were untied, and the entire front of his shoes were worn out with his toes hanging out of them.

"It looks like you could use a pair of shoes more than a sandwich, " Johnny said mockingly, "but how about I give you a shot in the head with this stickball bat instead? How about that?"

It happened so fast I could not react in time to stop Johnny from taking his bat and taking a swing at the old man.

The man lifted his arms, but the bat hit him on the shoulders, catching also a piece of his head just above where his bandanna wrapped full around his head.

He cried out, "Oh, that hurt! Whatta ya hitting me for? I did nuthin' to you!"

Johnny paid no attention. He lifted his bat to hit the old man. I tried to grab the bat from Johnny, but Johnny was quick. I was too late.

He took a step back. The man put his arms around his head and crouched against the wall of the flophouse, clutching a brown bag against his chest. Johnny swung his bat and hit him square on his back. The man screamed in pain. The bat broke in two. Johnny stood there looking at his broken bat, surprised that he had broken it. He was about to hit the old man again when I grabbed him from behind and held him back.

"Johnny, what the hell is the matter with you? He's an old man! What the hell did you hit him for?" I positioned myself between Johnny and the old man.

Johnny pointed at him. "I know this old coot. He's the one who cursed at Pepi last week because Pepi wouldn't give him any money. The old man grabbed Pepi's jacket, and Pepi just went nuts. He grabbed the old man by his jacket and hit him with one punch that decked the bum. He fell backward onto the sidewalk. Blood started gushing out of his head. Scappy told me it was like the bum had fallen out of the sixth floor of a building, how the blood kept coming out of him. Forget him! He's a piece-of-shit, no-good bum!"

The old man got up and checked his head. "What did you have to do that for?" he asked. "All I asked for was some money to buy some food. You didn't have to hit me!" He was right.

I shook my head. "C'mon, let's go. The old man is right. You didn't have to hit him."

"I hit him because I thought he was going to grab me too. He's nuts. Nuthin' but a lowlife. He should stop begging and get a job. C'mon, let's get outta here. I hate the Bowery. It's disgusting. Look at these filthy bums! They're all over the place!"

Johnny picked up the pieces of his broken bat, looked at the old man, and threw them at him. I shook my head. He didn't have to do that. I turned to the old man.

"If I can get back here, I'll get you a sandwich or something. I'll try!"

Johnny looked at me. "Joey, are you crazy? Whatta ya got rocks in your head? C'mon, let's get outta here."

We walked back to First Street barely saying anything to each other.

"I'll see ya later," he said, and he ran down the block and into his building.

I could not forget the old man. I knew he was hungry, and he seemed harmless enough. I realized Johnny and I were becoming different. Johnny had shown a mean streak I did not like at all.

My mother had already set a place for me. My father was already at the table, his wineglass almost empty. There was a ham and cheese sandwich with lots of lettuce, just the way I liked it. A bottle of Coke was already opened. My mom took a chunk of ice and threw it into a glass. I washed quickly and sat down.

I began to eat and found myself staring out into the light of day hanging brilliantly over Houston Street. I saw branches of maple trees swaying easily from a slight wind. The breeze that swayed the leaves found itself flapping also the collar of my shirt as I ate and drank. It was a sweet sight. It made me feel good to be alive, but then I could not help myself from thinking of the old man.

He must still be there, I thought. I turned to my mother. "Ma, do you think you can make another ham sandwich for me?"

She looked at me and then my sandwich. "You're not even finished with the first one. Eat that, and then I'll think about it."

"No, Mom, it's not for me." I took a deep breath. "It's for an old man Johnny and I saw on the Bowery. He asked me for some money, and Johnny hit him with his stickball bat. He had a bandanna over his head, and I saw a little blood coming out through the bandanna. The sandwich is for him."

My mother looked up at the ceiling and made the sign of the cross. "O Jesu Cristo," she said. "You are not serious, are you?"

I nodded my head. She shook hers and looked to my father for help. She put her hands together and shook her head again.

"Joey," my father said, "what is the matter with you? Don't you know these men are drunks? You go back there and you are risking harm, Joey. Mark my word. Now put such ideas out of your head, and finish your lunch. Besides, it is almost three o'clock. Don't you have to go to confession soon?"

He was right. It was a gamble. The old man could be drunk already, but I wasn't sure. Something told me to see if I could help. As I ate my sandwich, the thought that he was hungry gnawed at me. I put the sandwich down and drank my Coke. I could no longer eat.

My mother saw that and came over to me. She put her arms on her hips and stared at the sandwich. "Eat your sandwich and get to church, and put such crazy ideas out of your head. It is too dangerous to go back there!"

I felt a little stupid thinking I could help the old man, and for a moment, I agreed with both my mom and pop, but the thought that he was hungry and in rags—and might still be there, hungry and alone—got to me and began to tear at my heart. I had to do something.

Out of the blue, my father asked me a question. "How are your classes going with Tom and Sue? Do they say you are ready to be examined for the school?"

"Tom tells me I am very advanced in math, but Sue tells me I am very much behind in English. I will have a tough time passing the exam they give to me if I get a chance to go up there."

My mother nodded. "Yes, if you keep thinking of taking food to the drunks on the Bowery and do that, you could be killed, and you will not have to worry about the scholarship. The whole thing is crazy to begin with, but not crazier than feeding drunks."

"I guess you're right, Mom," I said. "It was a foolish idea."

I finished my sandwich and left for church. On my way over there, I thought about the old man and that he would still be hungry, and I thought if I got him a sandwich, perhaps he would not have the desire to drink so much. Maybe my parents were not right. Maybe.

I went into the church and knelt at a pew on the left. I looked up at the Blessed Mother. Her gaze, looking down at the children of Fatima, was so real and alive. Surrounding her was a soft reddish glow of light—a saintly glow from heaven, no doubt.

I heard footsteps and turned to see Father Ilardi walking down the aisle toward the confessionary booth. He beckoned me to come into the confessional. I waited a minute or so and entered. Father Ilardi pulled aside the heavy, black curtain which separated confessor from priest as I sat down. Through the mesh screen, I could see his hawkish nose, his bald head, and black markings on the side of his face. He could not turn his head completely to me, and so I could see just one eye, staring at me. Right away, I recalled one of the scariest movies I had ever seen, *The Spiral Staircase.*

"All right, Joseph, you can begin."

I said the prayer before confession and began with a few minor sins: I was rude to my mom and pop. I said again that I fought with Mario and that I had bad thoughts about Maria and Rachel. Father Ilardi grimaced and from behind the screen almost sneered at me. And then I thought I would mention my problem.

I told him about the old man and how Pepi hit him over the head, how Johnny also hit him, and how I stopped Johnny from hitting the old man again. I mentioned that there was a stain of blood on the bandanna he had wrapped around his head. My problem, I told him, was that the old man asked me for money and said he was hungry. My parents objected to my returning to give him a sandwich, and my feeling was to do just that, but I did not want to disobey them.

"What do you think, Father?" I asked.

Through the screen he sat quietly, thinking. He rubbed his chin and kept on nodding. It was a minute or so before he replied.

"My son, your parents are obviously concerned for your safety. The Bowery is a dangerous place, and they are correct as to the danger of returning to feed this old man. There are many unfortunate men on the Bowery whose lives have been ruined by their inability to be strong enough to withdraw from this unfortunate illness.

"However, that stated, you do indeed have a problem. The question is: do you have a moral obligation to help this man? You understand what I mean by moral obligation, Joey? Do you have a duty as a Catholic—and as a human being, for that matter—to care for this individual? My answer to you is, categorically, yes!"

He had a fearful glare but a good heart. I was not surprised by his answer, but he now had to let me know what he thought I should do, and so I asked him. "What should I do with this duty when my parents have told me not to go and feed this old man?"

His head stopped bobbing, and his eye seemed to stare through the confessional screen right into the workings of my soul. I felt a tingling of fear as if the devil himself were about to take my soul down to hell; but it was Father Ilardi who was staring at me and not the devil, although at that moment, he looked like the devil.

Pepi was one of the best-looking guys in the neighborhood, and Father Ilardi was most likely one of the least handsome men; but I could see clearly how good a soul the priest had.

"My son, you have the right intentions. Even though you are just twelve, you are soon to be thirteen, an age of transition from young boy to manhood. Your instinct to care for this man is correct, and assuredly it comes from deep inside your soul, a gift from God! Now, as for your parents, how shall we deal with them?

"Joseph, you are not to disobey your parents, but you must tell them that I said your wish to feed this man is an act of charity and must be carried out; otherwise, you will live with the guilt of not doing the right thing. You tell your parents that, exactly. Now mind you, Joseph, as your parents already reminded you, there are risks to carrying out this self-imposed duty of yours. Keep in mind the Bowery is a dangerous place, to be sure, and you are perhaps not as strong as even a man who has drunk himself into a stupor of foggy thinking. Such men can be dangerous because they are different when drunk and are not themselves as they are without drink.

"And you can tell your parents that it would be a good thing if I could see them at Sunday Mass once in a while and not just at Christmas midnight Mass or Easter Sunday. I would like to see them every single Sunday! You tell them that, and if they object to my judgment that you feed this man, tell them to come to Mass tomorrow, and I will gladly explain my reasoning to them. Now to wash your sins away, say ten Our Fathers and ten Hail Marys, and I want to hear a good act of contrition!"

I left the confessional with Father Ilardi still inside, knelt at a pew, and said my prayers. I was shocked that Ilardi had sided with me, but now I had to confront my parents. I thought as I said my prayers that I should talk to them right away, and perhaps there would be enough time to see the old man before dark. I listened inside my head about what he had said about my soul, that good intentions come from God. All I had to do now was convince my parents it was the right thing to do. I went home prepared this time.

I sat down at the table with a plate of hot pasta in front of me and right away told them what Father Ilardi had said.

"Father Ilardi is right, Lilly," my father said in between sips of wine. "We have not gone to church, and the good priest has caught us in a net we have created for ourselves. He has turned the tables on us!" He slammed his fist hard down on the table. "But I do not for one minute agree with him. Joey, why did you talk to Father Ilardi about this issue?"

I was silent for a moment, thinking, and then I spoke. "Because when I went to church for confession, I felt very bad about the old man. I felt it was a sin not to get him some food, and so I confessed my feelings. I wondered if it was a sin not to feed a man who is hungry. Even if a dog was hungry, it would be a sin not to feed him! That is why I brought it up with Father Ilardi, not to question what you told me not to do."

My parents were silent. My father shook his head, and my mother leaned over to take my father's wineglass. She looked at him and downed the wine left in his glass.

"He is very clever, our son, don't you think, Sal? How he managed to get Father Ilardi on his side, turn the tables on us, and make us feel guilty over not letting him feed this old drunk!" She slammed the glass down. "Well, how do we get out of this mess you have created for us, Joey? Tell us. It is a problem I do not wish to deal with. Our word is our word. Regardless of Father Ilardi, what do you say to change our minds? Unless you have a reasonable solution, you are not going to feed that old man! It is too dangerous to go there alone!"

Just then, I realized my mother had given me the opening I needed. "Ma, what if I take Harold with me to the Bowery? And what if I get there before dark? With the sun not yet going down, there will still be light under the El, and Harold will be with me in case the old man gives us trouble. How does that sound?"

They looked at each other in bewilderment, shaking their heads. Again there was a rare silence at our table. I finished my penne and waited. In the past, I brought them problems of wrongdoing, but tonight, I asked them to allow me to do a good deed. They were stumped.

My father spoke. "Joey, if your mother agrees, then I will allow you to go, but you must take Harold with you. If he says he cannot go or will not go, you do not go! Understand? Momma, how does that sound to you?"

She stared at my father and shook her head and then slapped herself on her thighs. "Okay. It is done. Finished. He goes. I will make the sandwich, and you can get an old pair of boots for the old man. Joey, you make sure you see Harold and go with him. Make sure you go before dark, and be very, very careful!"

A few minutes later, I was out the door with a sandwich and a pair of boots. I could not believe they allowed me to go, but I reminded myself I had to convince Harold to go with me. That would not be easy.

I raced to his building, climbed the steps to his apartment, and knocked on his door loud enough for the entire building to hear it. Harold opened the door slightly and stuck his head out. He was wearing a yarmulke. I was surprised. I had never seen him wearing a skullcap.

"Joey, why are you banging on the door so hard?"

"Harold, I need your help. I promised this old man on the Bowery I would bring him some food. My parents said I could take the sandwich to him if you came with me."

He shook his head. "I'm sorry, Joey, don't you know today is Saturday? My father is praying, and again he asked me to pray with him. I turned him down so many times he made me feel guilty enough to say yes. I can't leave now. I promised him!"

"But, Harold! It will only take an hour, not even. I have to make it there and back by the time the sun sets. I promised my parents I would do that!"

He nodded. "So you understand, then, how important it is for me to keep my promise to my father? He is alone. You know that. I need to stay with him and pray." He paused and saw how upset I was. "What about Johnny? He'll go with you."

"No, he won't. When we saw the old man today, Johnny hit him with his stickball bat and broke it in two. No way will he go with me. It's too late to call the other guys."

"I'm sorry, Joey. I just can't go. If you want to go tomorrow, I will go with you, but not today. Be careful anyway. It's dangerous down there at night! I'll see you later."

He shut the door, and I was left in the hallway with the old man's sandwich and my father's boots. I sat down on the landing. I was stumped. What could I do? I did not want to disappoint the old man, and I knew he had to be hungry. He also needed those boots my mother had given me to give to him. I was caught again in a problem. My instinct told me to get the food and shoes to him now, but I did not want to go against the wishes of my parents, which were not to go alone. It was a moral dilemma.

Was it more right to respect the will of my parents or to give this man food and shoes he badly needed? With either choice I made, I would fail. Not feeding him may become a sin for me, but disobeying my parents would also be a sin. I was really stuck.

It was getting late. I had to make a decision, and I did. I decided to take the sandwich and boots to the old man and later tell my parents what I had done. Perhaps they would forgive. Perhaps not. I raced down the stairs and headed toward the Bowery. Would I make it in time before dark?

I looked west up at a burnt-orange sky, almost still except

for soft, flat pale white clouds lazily moving east, the sun barely above the horizon. I had to hurry, find him, deliver the food and boots to him, and get back home. It was getting late. I did not allow myself to think I would not make it.

I began to trot toward the Bowery, and as I passed Second Avenue, I felt drops of rain. I could not understand why. I looked up and now saw dark clouds overhead. I ran faster. When I approached the Bowery, I could see it was so much darker than Second Avenue. I waited for the light to change. I was getting a little nervous. I could see even the street people were hurrying to get out of the light rain that was now falling. I stopped at Third Street, and there was no sign of the old man.

I looked around. The rain became heavier, but it was not a drenching rain. Then I noticed on the corner near Great Jones Street a large cardboard box. Could it be that the old man was in that box? It was large enough. I decided to see if he was there.

I walked over and shouted, "Hey, old man! It's me! The kid who was here this afternoon! Are you in that box?" I heard nothing, but I saw the box move slightly. "Hey, are you in there? I brought you a sandwich."

The rain came down, and though it was not a heavy rain, it was enough to wet my hands and the brown bags I had the food and boots in.

This time, the box did not move. I went closer and shouted for the old man to come out. Then I saw the box move and a figure begin to crawl out of the box. It was the old man. He was still on all fours when his head popped out and he looked up at me.

"Oh, it's you! For your information, my name is Bill!" He slowly pulled himself out of the box and began to stagger when he tried to stand up straight.

It was the man from earlier in the day, but there was no smile on his face this time. His eyes were partially hidden by drooping eyelids and, from what I could see, were bloodshot. His face was beet red. He turned his head and looked at me with one slanted eye. He kept on swaying back and forth.

The bandanna was still wrapped around his head, but I could

see the bloodstain was larger. His arms hung down like those of a gorilla. This time, he was not slouching. He stood up with his shoulders back, and I was surprised to see how large he was.

Suddenly, he grabbed my wrist and held it tightly. I tried to loosen his grip, but I could not. He was too strong for me.

"Whatta ya got in that bag?" he asked me.

"I brought over a sandwich. You remember you told me you were hungry? You asked me for a quarter. How about letting go of my arm so I can get the sandwich out of the bag? I also have a pair of boots for you my father gave me."

He looked down at his shoes. His toes were wrapped around worn socks and came through the front of his shoes. "Gimme that bag!" he said.

I threw it to him, and it landed on the wet ground in front of his feet. He loosened his grip and leaned forward to pick up the bag. I pulled myself free.

My instinct was to run away, but I waited. I have no idea why I stayed. I thought once he began to eat, he would calm down and recognize me. I was wrong.

He took the sandwich out of the bag, pulled away the wax paper, and took a large bite of it. He began to chew as if he had not eaten in days. He looked up at me again with one eye, his head turning sideways. I never liked anyone who looked at me like that. I always felt they were not to be trusted. Freddie Foulduty looked at me that way before we had the fight over the cat he tied to the fence.

"What's in the other bag?" he asked.

"Boots. My father gave me boots to give to you."

"C'mon, hand them over. Whatta ya waitin' for? You think I'm gonna kill ya?"

I stood there cautiously. Then I threw the bag down in front of his feet. He growled at me.

"What? You couldn't hand them to me? What's the matter? You don't trust me?" He put the sandwich back inside the bag, and then he suddenly reached into his pocket. In his hand, I saw he gripped what looked like a box cutter. He pushed a button, and out came the blade!

I stood there in shock, unable to move. I kept staring at the cutter, ready to jump the minute he tried to attack me. I thought if I tried to run, he would attack and cut me. I was helpless. He crouched and stared at me.

"Don't move, or I'll kill ya," he said. "I know who you are. You're the kid who hit me over the head with his bat. Do you think old Bill is gonna let you get away with that?"

He lunged toward me, but I was much too fast for him. I stepped back easily, and he began to stumble. He tried to regain his balance but kept on stumbling forward until he fell headfirst onto the wet sidewalk. I heard a thud, and then I heard him moaning.

The cutter fell from his hand and landed a few feet away. I took a few steps back and watched him try to get up, but he could not.

"I tried to help you out, and you try to knife me. You must be crazy! My parents warned me, and I didn't listen!"

I took a few steps backward and then turned and ran. I knew he could not catch me. The rain was coming down harder now, and when I passed under the elevated train on the Bowery, I turned to see if he was giving chase, but he was in no condition to run. I could still see him struggling to stand up and regain his balance. I turned and started to run back home. It was dark now, and I was wet and rattled. As I climbed the steps to our tenement, I wondered how I was going to explain to my parents what I had done.

Should I explain that Harold had not gone with me? How do I explain I disobeyed them? Worse, it was clear to me now I had made the wrong choice. It was dark outside. My mother was putting away dishes from dinner, which for me now was so long a time ago.

"So did you give the old man the sandwich and your father's old boots?"

"Yes, I did, Mom," I said, and I went into the bathroom to wash up.

My father was already lying down. For the time being, I realized I had escaped a bullet, but I knew that my father would question me, and then I would have to tell the truth. No doubt about it.

On Sunday morning after Mass, I went to see Father Ilardi in the sacristy. He turned to me with that glaring, critical look of his. I told him what had happened. He shook his head and sighed.

"Joey, I should have warned you not to go alone, and I did not. Your parents were right, and I was wrong. They were right to tell you to take Harold with you. I failed to do that." He sighed, turned away, and made the sign of the cross.

"Now, you must do the right thing and tell your parents what has happened. That is the right thing to do. Take your punishment. Take whatever comes your way from them. It will all be all right in the end. Thank God you did not get hurt!"

On Sunday afternoon, my mother made pasta and chicken. A huge bowl of salad was already on the table. My father already had had a glass of red wine when I sat down. I began to eat.

"So, Joey, tell me what happened. Your mother tells me you delivered the boots and sandwich. Nothing happened to you. I can only say thank God you did not get hurt, and thank God you were smart enough to take Harold with you."

I put my fork down and looked at my father, who was pouring himself a second glass of wine. He took a sip, put down the glass, and looked me, waiting to hear what had happened.

I told them exactly what had happened. They were in shock. My father took a deep breath. My mother sat down and made the sign of the cross.

"I'm sorry for what I did. I am not ever going to go against your word. I promise."

"Joey," my father said, "when we tell you not to do something, I want a promise from you that you will never, but never go against our word. Promise right now! What if something had happened to you? Don't you understand the danger you put yourself in?" He turned to my mother. "Well, Lilly, I think he does now."

He slammed his fist down on the table and stared at me. He had never hit me, but I thought for a moment right then that he would.

"I do understand. I promise again, as God is my judge, I will never go against your word."

"Okay. Enough said. Joey has learned his lesson. Let's eat."

The next Saturday afternoon, we played another game on Great Jones Street. I didn't expect to see Bill, but if I had, I thought he most likely would be sober and harmless. My thoughts were far away from Bill; I thought more that I would have to make a decision soon on prep school. As Johnny and I walked from the game back home, I realized that the stickball games on Saturday could be ending for me if I did go away. I shivered. I did not want to think about that at all. On the way, Johnny was bragging how he smacked the double that won the game for us. He stopped in the middle of the block, took his bat off his shoulder, and swung at an invisible ball. "Bang!" he said, pointing to the imaginary Spalding ball sailing over the imaginary fence that separated infield from the outfield.

We got to the Bowery and noticed on the corner of Third Street there was a commotion. A crowd of people were hanging around. A squad car with lights flashing and door open stood at the corner. We ran across the street to see what was going on.

The iron gates on the sidewalk leading to the cellar of the house where Bill was leaning against were wide open. We pushed our way through the crowd and got to the gates. Johnny and I looked down inside the cellar.

There on the floor was a body lying still, though only the feet and ankles could be seen clearly from the light of the sun; the rest of the body was hidden in darkness. I looked closer. There, more visible to me, were the feet of the dead body, and on those feet were my father's old boots. It was Bill, all right.

24
The Stickball Game

It was late September, and I was practicing with our stickball team in the back park for the game on Saturday against the Mott Street guys. They beat us once, and we came back a few weeks later to beat them. The Saturday game was the rubber match, and I had saved extra money from the last game to bet on this one. It was a big game. Johnny told me that the mob guys from Mott Street were betting Pepi's guys. I was very excited until Peter Capra called me into his office a couple of days before and dropped a bombshell on me.

Peter Capra had heard about the game also. When I walked into his office, he motioned for me to sit down. He gave me a bad look. He continued writing and made me wait a few minutes before he paid attention to me. He stared at me, threw down his pen, and stuffed a letter into an envelope. Then he folded his hands and stared at me.

"Joey, your principal, Mr. Franklin, called me today. He told me about another fight you got into. I understand your friend Johnny was with you."

I tried to speak. I leaned forward in the chair. I wanted to explain that we were just protecting Sonny, but Capra raised his hand and gestured to me to be quiet.

"I know. I know. You don't have to explain. You went into Tompkins Square Park to look for Sonny, and you and Johnny proceeded to beat up the kids who were about to do harm to your cousin. Yes, I know all that, Joey, but …" He folded his hands, shook his head, and stared at me again. "Why is it, Joey, that you find it necessary to solve every problem that comes your way with your fists? I know you had good cause to go in there and defend your cousin, but did you and Johnny have to beat those boys up? Did you? That is what is disturbing to me. It makes me wonder how serious you are about this scholarship the Boys' Club may be offering you."

He leaned back in his chair and looked out the window. "When you continue to solve your problems with violence, I ask myself whether or not you truly appreciate this opportunity and whether you are ready to live in an environment that will be, essentially, a peaceful one—an environment where you will have to fight with your brains and not with your fists to get by. The Boys' Club has a lot at stake here. The next boy must succeed where the last three have failed. You understand that if you fail, the entire program fails and comes to an end. That will be it for this program. The board of directors has already told me that. That's it! And so I have decided to take drastic action. You have a big stickball game coming up this Saturday morning. Yes, I know all about it. The boys in the club have been talking. I listen, Joey, and that is how I learn about what is going on. I have asked Tom to prepare a grammar lesson for you, right here at the Boys' Club, and I have asked them to schedule it for the time this big stickball game of yours is to be played, next Saturday afternoon at one o'clock."

I could not believe what he was saying. I never imagined he would ever interfere with a stickball game, especially a game this important. I was stunned.

"You give me no choice, Joey. I have to find out what your

priorities are, what is really important to you—stickball or the scholarship! I can't take responsibility for your failure. You understand that? The entire program rests with my decision to pick the boy who is going to make it. I can't select you and then find out in one month of prep school that you have decided to drop out and come home. No, Joey. I cannot have that happen, and I will not let that happen. By going to the grammar lesson and missing the stickball game, you will be showing me your true intentions. You will be showing me just how important this scholarship is to you. Now it is up to you. You understand me? The stickball game or the lesson. It will be one or the other. Now go on, and while you're playing basketball and going swimming this afternoon, you can think about what your decision will be."

I left his office stunned. How could he do this to me? I was stuck. Peter Capra was not known to change his mind, and he certainly would not this time no matter how much I pleaded with him. I was in no mood for basketball, but I thought it might be a good idea to let off some steam. I was angry, very angry. He knew this Saturday stickball game was really important not only to me but the whole team. And Pepi? What about Pepi? How could I let him down, especially when I knew he was betting big money on the game?

I finished swimming and walked slowly out of the Boys' Club trying to figure out what to do. I sat down on the front steps and folded my hand under my chin, thinking. Johnny came out and saw me there.

"What's up with you? What happened? You look like you lost your best friend or Maria or somethin', which I know you didn't."

"Johnny, I have bad news. I have this problem. Mr. Capra told me he wanted me to have a grammar lesson this Saturday with Tom and Sue."

He shrugged it off. "So what's the big deal? After the game, you come back here and you have your grammar lesson."

I had to tell him. Maybe he had an idea to get me out of this mess.

"No, Johnny. He wants me to take that lesson exactly the time we are playing our stickball game. In other words, he wants me to make a choice: to go the stickball game or take the lesson! If I don't go to the lesson, I am out of the scholarship running. I'm in a serious bind!"

Johnny put his hands on his hips and smiled. "No, you're not in any bind! This one is simple. You go to the stickball game, period! Are you outta your mind? You realize all the guys from Pepi's crew are betting on this game? And you know who is betting the most? Pepi! He is betting $500. Yeah, $500! I am telling you, Joey, you will be making a big mistake if you don't play. Capra's not going to throw you out of the program. He's bluffing, and when Pepi finds out, you are going to be in big trouble!"

I shook my head. "No, he's not bluffing. Mr. Capra was so damn mad today because we beat up those kids from Ninth Street, I thought he was going to get up and slam me himself. And I can't risk not getting the scholarship."

Saying that to Johnny was a mistake. He did not look happy, but I realized then how important it was to me knowing now I could lose it.

"But you're right about Pepi," I said. "Who knows what he is going to say? What am I gonna do?"

"I told you what you have to do." Johnny took a deep breath. "Listen, I have to get over to see Pepi and tell him to pull his bet and now! Joey, I don't trust you. I don't know what you're thinkin' of doing, but if you do the wrong thing by Pepi, he is not going to be happy with you."

He took off down the street, leaving me sitting on the Boys' Club steps. I was getting nervous. What would Pepi do if I decided not to play? I did not think he would ever hurt me if I did not play, but $500 was a lot of money, and Pepi had a temper. I found that out when he shot Nick Bonanti.

Harold came out of the club, saw me sitting there with my hands under my chin, and sat down next to me.

"Okay, now what? I know something is on your mind. It's not Maria, I know that. So what's up?"

Harold could see I was miserable and depressed. I looked at him glumly. He put his hand over my shoulder. I told him what happened at the meeting with Peter Capra. I also told him that Johnny ran over to Pepi to tell him to pull his bet on the game. I was hoping he would.

"Joey, lately, you seem to get yourself into a lot of binds. How do you manage to do that?"

I tried to explain to him this problem was not my doing. Capra forced it on me, trying to get me to decide what was more important, the game or the scholarship.

"Look, Joey, maybe you get lucky and Johnny gets to Pepi in time for him. Maybe that will happen. In the meantime, I can't help you on this one. This decision is your decision, not mine."

I turned around and looked at him. He was so quick to tell me he could not help solve the problem. I was surprised. Normally, he would look at me, sit there and think, and then come up with a solution. He was so good at that. Now, here he was, telling me he could not help me!

"Harold, you have to think of something. I need your help on this one. This problem is serious!"

He sat there and stared at me. Something was on his mind. I knew that.

"No, Joey, I can't tell you what's important to you. Besides, it's time you start making your own decisions. You have to decide for yourself what you are going to do, and to tell the truth, you already know what to do."

Harold was telling me to stop relying on him and to grow up. He was not telling me that he would not help me but that it made more sense for me to grow up and make my own decision. But then he must have seen he made matters worse for me, because I was shaking my head.

"Look, Joey, if you want me to tell you what I think, there would be no problem. I would miss the game and go to the grammar class. There are going be a lot more stickball games." He paused. "Well, for you, maybe not, but how many chances will you have to get a scholarship and go off to boarding school? One shot. That's it! This one is a no-brainer, especially if Pepi takes his bet off the table."

I turned away and looked down the block facing west. The sun had dipped below the clouds and was making its journey to sunset. I shaded my eyes and looked across the street. The sidewalk on Tenth Street was cracking. Paint on tenement buildings was peeling badly. An old woman was carrying groceries in a little black wheeler cart, shuffling home. The grocery store windows needed a good cleaning. I realized then how rundown the neighborhood was.

Even though I had not yet decided on the scholarship, I knew I was not ready to give up the opportunity for a better education and a new life.

Harold and I walked back home. We took our time. I didn't want to see Johnny, because I knew he would tell me one way or the other whether Pepi had pulled his bet. I was nervous enough. I left Harold and went into the park to play handball.

Tommy was banging away at the black ball. He saw right away I was not playing well. He stopped the game, bounced the ball in his hand, and walked over to me.

"Do you want to talk about it?" he asked.

I nodded, and we walked over to the fence and sat down.

"So what is bothering you? Tell me."

I told him how Peter Capra had forced me to make a decision about Saturday's stickball game and Pepi had the biggest bet. I did not want to lose my scholarship chance, but if I didn't play, our team could lose, and Pepi would lose a lot of money.

"Joey, c'mon. Think about it. You miss a stickball game, one stickball game. Man, that is nothing compared to missing a chance at a scholarship to school!"

I sighed. "I know, Tommy. My problem is that everybody on the block, except maybe you, is betting on that game. All the kids on my team and all the guys who work for Pepi, and the guy with the biggest bet is Pepi! That is the problem for me."

I sat there staring down at the concrete. If Pepi were not betting, there would be no chance of my missing that grammar class, but now he was a major factor in my decision. I knew all along that he was dangerous, but only to those who got on his bad side. I understood now why I was worried. I was making a decision against Pepi that could cost him a lot of money, and that thought scared the hell out of me.

"Look, Joey, you have no choice, really. You have to go to grammar class. Who knows? Maybe you get lucky and Pepi pulls his bet. You can't worry about what might happen. Wait until it happens and then worry about it. In the meantime, let's play ball."

We got up and started playing again. I was just as bad as before. Just as Tommy was ready to serve, I heard Johnny yell out my name. We both stopped to look at him walking into the park. As he got closer, I saw him raise his hand to his neck and gesture as if he were cutting his throat. The blood in my head drained down to my heart and almost made me dizzy. Johnny walked up to us. He looked whiter than I had ever seen him.

"Pepi wants to see you, and he wants to see you now. He can't pull the bet! Joey, don't be an idiot. You gotta play Saturday! Whatta ya tryin' to do, kill yourself? Pepi is not happy, and to tell ya the truth, I don't like the way he looks. You'd better get over there now!"

"Are you coming with me?" I asked him.

Johnny put his hands on his hips and stared at me. He started to shake his head. He pressed his lips together and looked down on the ground. It was a lot to ask of him.

"What are you tryin' to do, get me in trouble too? I'm already in trouble!" He paused. "Okay. I'm coming with you. But all I gotta say is that you'd better do as he says."

Tommy pulled his glove off and came over to me. "Listen to me, Joey. I know Pepi is gonna be tough on you, but you know what? It will pass. Don't let him bully you into going to the game on Saturday. It's your future. Not too many kids get a shot at a scholarship and a chance to be somebody! Just remember that when you're standing in front of him."

Johnny looked over at Tommy and shook his head. "Tommy, Joey here has a very serious problem on his hands. No way does he want to go against Pepi! My cousin has a very violent side, and sometimes he just can't control himself. Who knows what he will do when he loses it? C'mon, Joey, he told me to get you right away!"

Johnny pulled me aside. "Listen to what I'm tellin' you; it is something you already know! You know how Pepi can get violent. Now I'm not saying he did it, but listen to what happened! The cops found Nick Bonanti in the empty lot on Third Street! Dead! Last week, he drove by the club and tried to pop Pepi! He missed. That was a big mistake! The word on the street is that Pepi and the guys caught him, beat the crap out of him, and threw him off the roof! The lesson is don't fool around with Pepi!"

What Johnny told me made me sick. I took a drink of water at the fountain, and we walked through the park and across the street to the social club. Scappy stood outside. Usually, he smiled when he saw me. He wasn't smiling this time. He gestured for Johnny and me to go in.

It was very dark inside. My eyes were used to the light outside, but inside, I could see only shadows of the guys Pepi had around him. I stopped for a few seconds to get used to the lack of light. The club smelled of smoke. I could see it rising to the ceiling. The room was quieter than usual. I was nervous walking in.

Johnny and I went into the back room where Pepi sat at his table with his friends, a cup of espresso in front of him, and his hands wrapped around the cup, his fingers tapping it. As we approached, I saw him smiling, but when he saw us, his smile quickly vanished.

"Joey, Joey, come a little closer. I'm not going bite you. C'mon, talk to me. What is going on with the game? Tell me, Joey, why can't you play? Johnny already told you I have a big bet on. I can't pull my bet, Joey. I have no choice. None of my guys here can pull their bets either. We are talking a lot of money! You are putting me in some predicament. You understand? I have a problem that only you can solve. What can you say to me, Joey? Tell me I have no problem."

I cleared my throat and felt the taste of cigarettes. I could barely breathe. At the park on the handball court, I could feel the air blowing across the park. I could see the sun and blue sky and clouds floating by as if everything in the world was calm and relaxed. Inside the club, I felt the way I did the first time when Pepi called me into the club and asked me to take the oath of silence. I felt trapped. Pepi stared at me. He was not smiling. I was very nervous.

I decided to tell him how I felt. I had no choice. "Pepi, I didn't know you bet so much money. Pete Capra at the Boys' Club told me if I missed the grammar lesson, he would drop me from the scholarship program. He told me he would be done with me. He told me—"

Pepi raised his hand and then he shouted at me. My whole body jumped.

"Stop! I don't wanna hear about your problem, Joey! My problem is that I stand to lose a lot of money. All these guys stand to lose big-time! What is the matter with you? We all know that you are the best center fielder in the neighborhood, especially in that back park. Frankly, I don't know how you can see anything through those trees, especially a Spalding ball falling from nowhere, and then sidestepping the benches and the trees while you look up to see the ball falling. To me, it's a miracle, Joey. It's a gift you have! And with you in the game, I am very confident you kids from First Street will beat the crap outta the Mott Street kids." He paused and leaned forward. He picked up his cup of espresso and emptied the cup. He sat there tapping his fingers on the cup and glaring at me.

"And if you play in this game, I win my bet. No question about it. And all the guys here in the club win their bets."

He stood up and put his hands on my shoulders. I was shaking inside. He was very tall. He wore his navy-blue sport coat with a white-on-white shirt. The coat looked like the one he wore when he shot Nick Bonanti. This time, he spoke softly.

"Joey, do this favor for me. Make sure you play in the game so I can have a good weekend. And, Joey, one more thing. You play the game and, win or lose, I get you a brand-new Schwinn bike, a racer. Have you ever had a bike before, Joey?"

I shook my head.

"Well, your first bike will be the best bike on the block; in fact, the whole neighborhood!" He pointed his finger at me. "If you play the game!"

He went back to the table. I was sweating badly. I turned to Johnny, who gave me a frightened look. He shook his head.

Pepi sat down. "Okay, boys, go on, get outta here."

We turned to leave.

"And one more thing. I know you're gonna do the right thing, Joey!"

Even in the darkness of the room, I could see his eyes opened wide. That look of his really scared me.

Outside, Scappy grabbed me and pointed his finger right in my face. "You'd better listen to him, Joey. I would not do anything stupid if I were you!"

Johnny and I walked away from the club. I saw that he was as nervous as I was. What did he have to be nervous about? I was the one in trouble. I walked him to his building.

"Joey, you got a problem! You'd better do the right thing. I saw Pepi's eyes when we left. There is no telling what he will do if he loses that money because of you. Please. Do the right thing. Don't be an idiot!"

I left him at his building and walked across the street. Before I went upstairs, I sat down on the stoop. I sat there thinking. Harold was right. It had to be my solution to the problem. It was all on me now. I had to think this one out on my own.

Then it dawned on me. My only hope was to go back to the Boys' Club the next day to see Tom Mansfield and somehow convince him to move the grammar lesson until after the Saturday stickball game. I ran up the stairs thinking I had a good chance to do that. How could he turn me down once he realized how serious my problem was? He couldn't! I felt much better. I had a solution for Pepi.

25

My Last Shot

It was September, but it was hot out. I climbed out the window onto the fire escape and sat down. There was light traffic on Second Avenue. On First Street, I could see the guys from the social club playing cards. They were all smoking. I realized as they leaned back from the table how out of shape they were, their bellies hanging out. Ties hung down tied with clasps against their short-sleeve shirts. Standing at the door was Pepi. He could not see me, but I could see him. He was not smoking, and he was slim. He just stood there looking around the neighborhood. Scappy was standing next to him. I went back inside and went to bed early.

After school on Friday afternoon, I saw Sonny waiting for me. He was a smart kid. I always knew that about him.

"I know you have a problem with your friend Pepi. Don't ask me. I know all about it. In fact, it's like the whole school knows about it."

I turned to see Johnny waiting for me within earshot of Sonny. I turned to Sonny and put my finger to my lips to quiet him down.

"Who cares about that jerk friend of yours, Johnny, listening? Joey, now you can listen to me! You do the right thing for yourself. Don't listen to those guys. They are going to get you into big trouble down the road. You understand what I am saying?"

He kept on talking, and I listened. When he had finished, Johnny was gone.

I ran over to the Boys' Club. It was around four o'clock. My heart skipped a few beats more than usual as I ran to the basketball court to see Tom.

I went inside, and there he was, whistle in his mouth, overseeing another team the same age as the kids I was working with. They looked so small. When I sat down on the side, Tom glanced at me. When the basketball went out of bounds, he called timeout and walked over to me.

I stood up. He shook his head and crossed his hands back and forth. "I know why you are here. Don't even bother to ask me. Mr. Capra wants you here for your lesson with Sue and me. Don't be late. I have to go. I have the younger kids to take care of."

I held his arm. "But, Tom, can you hold on for a minute? You don't understand. Pepi is betting $500 on this game. He told me yesterday I had to play because he thinks our team can't win without me in the outfield. Tom, listen to me. The back park is very tricky to catch balls out there. I know the back park, and Pepi knows I can play it better than anybody. You have to talk to Mr. Capra!"

He took my arm gently and sat me down. "Look, Joey. I understand you have this problem, but I have specific instructions from Mr. Capra to keep the lesson at one o' clock. I can't change it. He ordered me. As for Pepi, he knows when he bets anything can happen. He is the one who took that risk. Are you supposed to give up an opportunity to win that scholarship just because he has a bet on a stickball game?" He shook his head. "No, Joey. I agree with Mr. Capra. You plan to be here tomorrow afternoon at one, and we can start. Remember, English is your weakest subject. You will have no chance to pass that test they will give you, if you get there at all."

I pleaded with him. "But, Tom, Pepi can be very violent. If he loses that money—"

He stood up and shook his head. "I don't think Pepi is going to hurt you just because he lost a bet. What kind of an animal do you think he is, anyway?"

He walked away, blowing his whistle to start the basketball game. I was tempted to tell him exactly how violent Pepi could be, but I did not.

I left the club really upset. Capra had given me no choice, but I didn't want to face Pepi if I missed the game and our team lost. What would he do to me then? I was running out of ideas and time.

It was getting late. I went back to First Street and tried to avoid the social club.

I wanted no part of Pepi, so I went around Houston Street past the Sunshine Theatre to avoid him. I went upstairs quickly without looking back and had a sandwich and Coke. I relaxed as best I could, but I was getting very nervous hanging around the house. In fact, I was beginning to panic.

I left the house and took a left toward Second Avenue, hoping that no one from the club would see me. I decided to play handball to relax and take my mind off my problem. Tommy was already there practicing.

I was playing about ten minutes when Johnny came running over.

"Joey, I need to talk to you!"

I stopped playing and walked over to the same bench he and I were sitting on the night Pepi shot Nick Bonanti. We sat down.

"Look, Joey, Pepi asked me to come over here to find out for sure if you're playing tomorrow. He wants to know right away. Joey, before you answer, think about it. I don't think Capra will throw you out of the program just because you missed a lousy grammar lesson."

"That's not it, Johnny. You have to understand. He wants to know definitely that if he recommends me for prep school, I will go and stay. He doesn't want to make a fool of himself. If I'm not interested, he doesn't want to waste his time on me. He doesn't want me to go there and come back one month later. That's it!"

Johnny took a deep breath. "So Pepi was right. You are going to miss the game!"

I bit my lip and looked straight at him. He was asking me more than whether I was going to miss the game. I understood that just from looking at him. By telling him I was not playing the stickball game, I was telling him I wanted that scholarship, and I didn't want to lose the chance of getting it, but I just couldn't tell him outright. Johnny was thinking if I did go to prep school, I would not be around anymore. Would our friendship last?

I spoke softly. "Johnny, I can't risk it. You understand. Hey, who knows? You could win without me!"

I put my hand around his shoulder and rubbed his back. I felt terrible. He looked very sad.

"It won't be so bad, Johnny," I said, trying to make him feel better.

He got off the bench. "Yeah, we're going to win with Harold in center field. You gotta be kidding me!" He stood there for a few seconds. "Look, Pepi told me to come right back and tell him what you were going to do. Stay right here. Don't move! He may want to see you. In fact, he *will* want to see you!"

Johnny ran off. I got off the bench. My chest felt pretty tight. I went over and drank some water and walked slowly onto the handball court.

Tommy asked me if I was all right. He must have seen that I looked scared.

"C'mon, let's play some handball," he said.

I tightened my gloves and took my position. Tommy was playing this time with two hands. He gave me a soft serve, and I hit it back. We volleyed a few times, and then he hit an ace, impossible for me to get. A few minutes later, Johnny came running back.

"Joey, Pepi wants to see you right now, and he is not happy. I can tell you that. He wants you to come with me right now. You got yourself into a big mess with him!"

I took my gloves off. Tommy handed me a towel.

"Relax, Joey. It's daylight, kid. What's he gonna to do, shoot you in broad daylight? Go on, get it over with, and then you can relax."

After he said that, I really got nervous. What was Pepi going to do to me? I looked at Johnny, and he laughed nervously, shaking his head. He tried to calm me down.

"C'mon, let's go. He ain't gonna hurt you. All I can say is I'm glad the game is tomorrow!"

We walked out of the park. I stopped on the sidewalk and looked at Johnny. He looked pale. I heard what he had said, but at that moment, I knew he wasn't sure exactly what Pepi would do to me. I stepped into the street ready for anything. I was very scared.

Then I heard my name called out. I looked around. It was my father. He waved to me from a distance coming from First Avenue. I was never so happy to see him as at that moment! I stopped. I could see he was limping. I looked over at the club. Pepi, with his hands on his hips, was standing there waiting for me.

"Johnny, tell Pepi I'll see him later. I have to help my father. He looks like he's hurt."

I was never so happy to see my pop! I ran over to him, and he put his arm around my shoulder. I felt his weight on my body. He leaned against me as we began to walk slowly home. He was dragging his right foot.

"What happened, Pop?" I asked.

He took his steps carefully. "I'll explain later. Help me. My ankle is killing me."

As we passed the club, I could see Pepi watching me. Johnny was standing next to him. Pepi had his hand on Johnny's shoulder. We kept on walking to our building. I felt Pepi still staring at me as we climbed the stoop and shut the door of the building behind us.

In the hall, my father stopped at the foot of the steps. "I have to put all my weight on you, Joey. Can you handle it?"

I nodded, and he leaned against me. Slowly, we climbed the steps. I could not believe what I was doing. I was carrying my father up the steps with little support from him. I was getting stronger and had not realized it.

My mother let out a cry when we walked in. She sat him down and quickly filled a bowl with cold water. She slowly took off his shoes and socks. I could see his ankle had already swelled. He placed his right foot gingerly into the bowl and let out his own cry of pain.

"Just do it, Sal. You need to."

My mother went into the icebox and pulled out a chunk of ice and dropped it into the bowl. My father gritted his teeth but left his foot in the bowl. I watched the ice swirl around his ankle. He groaned.

"So what happened, Sal?" My mother asked.

"At work today, I had to yell at one of my laborers. Another laborer was walking past him with a wheelbarrow full of cement, and the guy I shouted at stuck his foot out. Cement spilled all over. It was not funny. It was really pretty stupid of him! I told him off. As I turned to leave, he pushed me from behind. I fell face forward, and my coffee went flying. I tripped over some bricks, my ankle locked, and that was it. I don't think it's broken, but I sprained it for sure. I took care of him pretty good! He will be very sore tomorrow morning when he wakes up!"

My mother shook her head in disapproval. "No wonder Joey fights a lot. He gets it from you!"

She went to the icebox and pulled out another large piece of ice and smashed it into small pieces. Then she took a small towel, placed the ice in the towel, and after she helped him take his foot out of the bowl, wrapped it around his ankle. With his arm around my shoulders, he limped to the bedroom and lay down on the bed. He sighed in relief and grabbed my hand.

"Joey, I am tired, very tired. Look at me. I am forty-nine years old. I can't work like a dog much longer. I am getting old before my time to be old. I know your mother does not want you to go away to school. It will be difficult for her, but, Joey, I want you to make something of yourself. Be somebody, and do something good in the world."

I sat down on the bed.

"I don't want you to work like me, like a horse. I want you to have a good life. This scholarship will give you that chance to do that. Joey, a good life."

He let go of my wrist and held my hand until he fell asleep. My mother came in. She sat on the bed and held the towel filled with ice tightly around his ankle. She nodded. The swelling must have gone down. My father had closed his eyes. I left them and went into the living room.

He slept through supper. I did not want to grow up to work the way he did. It was very quiet without him at the table. The radio was turned off. I had no appetite and forced myself to eat the pasta my mother laid out in front of me. After I ate, I went into the living room and looked out the window down toward the social club. No one was in front of the club, not even Scappy. I tried to stay calm, but it was not easy.

It was hot. I picked up a Classic Comic book. It was *Captains Courageous*. I couldn't get through it, even though it was about courage. I threw it down. I was tired of comic books. I decided to go to bed early. The next day, Saturday, was the game. I was surprised that Johnny had not come to get me to see Pepi.

I awoke around ten o'clock to the sound of tapping at the living room window. I sat up and listened. The house was dark and very quiet. The tapping was faint, but I could hear it. I got out of bed and went to the window, already partially opened. I pulled the thin curtains aside. It was Johnny on the fire escape! I knew what that meant.

"Joey, c'mon, get up. Pepi wants to see you, and now!"

I hesitated. "Johnny, it's late. Does he have to see me now? Can't he see me tomorrow?"

"That's a stupid question coming from you. He wants to see you now. You gotta go! C'mon, get dressed. He's meeting us in the park."

I had no choice. I went back and put on my clothes. I listened to hear if anyone was awake or had heard me. It was so quiet. I knew my father was fast asleep. I started to shake a little. I had no idea what Pepi had planned for me. I knew he was angry. I listened once more for any sounds coming from my parents' bedroom. There were none.

I climbed onto the fire escape and followed Johnny down to the end of the ladder. I watched as he hung down from the end of it and jumped the six or seven feet to the ground without even going to the stoop first! He looked around and then gestured for me to follow. I twisted my body around and got on the ladder, stepped down a few steps, and then hung from it. I jumped but fell onto the sidewalk. Johnny helped me get up, and we walked quickly to the park. Pepi was not there. We walked in and sat down on one of the benches and waited for him.

We didn't wait long. Pepi walked across the street casually. It was after ten o'clock, and he was still wearing a jacket. His pants were creased sharply. He walked into the park, stopped at the entrance, and then walked right up to us. Johnny and I stood up. He stood there looking at me.

"Good boy, Johnny," he said. He turned to me. "And you, Joey, what am I going to do with you?"

He gestured for me to walk over to him. He put his hand on my shoulder and smiled. I did not smile. He did not smile because he was happy; he smiled to calm me down. He knew I was nervous. He knew also I was afraid of him.

"Now, Joey, I tried to convince you to do the right thing by me. I heard all about the scholarship, and isn't it true I haven't asked you to work for me? I was thinking about you, Joey, but now what? I stand to make $500 or lose $500. Joey, that's a lot of money. After tomorrow, either I have $1,000 in my pocket or nothing. How would you feel if you were in my shoes?

"You don't have to answer. And tell me, you think Peter Capra is going to let you out of his pet program just because you missed a grammar lesson? I don't think so. I am not willing to lose $500 because this guy is testing you, Joey."

He had one hand on his hip and the other pointing to the ground. His eyes grew larger. He began to raise his voice.

"Joey, you can make me sleep real good tonight if you tell

me, right here and now, that you are going to play in the game tomorrow." He paused for a few seconds. "Or I could have a bad night sleeping. It's up to you, Joey! So what's your answer? Are you playing in the stickball game or not?"

He stood there with his hands on his hips, his jacket folded back, the light of the lamppost streaming down on him, almost as if it were a spotlight. Pepi stopped talking. In the park, the only sound I heard was the sound of a soft wind.

He took a few steps back and put both hands on his hips. He was no longer smiling.

"Tell him, Joey," Johnny said. "Tell him you're playing tomorrow!"

I was about to tell him I would, I was that scared, but then in my mind I saw my father lying on his bed, holding my hand. I saw his face, tired and sunburned, with wrinkles visible around his eyes and mouth. I saw that he was tired and knew he felt tired beyond his years. And as I thought of my father lying there on his bed, worn out and beat up, I answered Pepi.

"No. I can't play tomorrow, Pepi. I have to go to that class. If I don't go, I lose my chance. I can't. I can't. I just can't do that."

Pepi just stared at me. Then he gritted his teeth and took three steps back so that now he was no longer in the light of the lamppost. He stood there in shadow shaking his head.

"Son of a bitch!" he said.

The next few seconds happened so fast it seemed to me like a dream. Pepi reached behind his jacket and pulled out his gun. Its barrel now pointed toward the sky. I noticed how short the barrel was. I stared at it for a few seconds, not afraid. He pointed the gun at me. I stood there not believing what was happening.

Suddenly, Johnny let out a scream. He jumped in front of me and faced Pepi, his arms spread out.

"No, Pepi, please don't shoot him! Please!" Johnny started to cry. Tears were streaming down his face. He kept shaking his head and telling Pepi not to shoot.

I stood behind him frozen, not knowing what to do. The gun was pointed at me for a few seconds.

Then Pepi took another step back. He lowered the gun, held it by his side, and stared at us. Johnny stopped crying. He let out a sigh. His body was shaking. Pepi put the gun back in its holster, put his hands back on his hips, and smiled.

"What? Do you think I'm crazy? Me shoot a little kid like you? Don't you know I love you two kids! I love you both like you're my own. Don't you know that? I just wanted to scare you. That's all! It's good to get scared once in a while. Keeps you alert, on your toes. That's important."

He walked over to Johnny and me and put his arm around Johnny. "Calm down, Johnny." Pepi turned to me. "Joey, Johnny is some friend! He was willing to save your life because he thought I was gonna kill ya! Calm down, Johnny. Calm down. Nobody's gonna get hurt. I could steal $1,000 in one day if I wanted to! Joey, I'm walking Johnny home. You'd better get home before your parents wake up. Relax. Everything is going to be okay."

They walked off, and I was left in the park, still shaking. Pepi had solved my problem.

On Saturday afternoon, I went to my English class with Tom and Sue. Harold played center field for me. I found out later our team had lost the game by one run. I never asked anybody if Harold had made any errors out there. I didn't want to know. That afternoon, I saw Johnny streaking down First Street on a new Schwinn bike.

26 Prep School

It was going to be a tough night for me and Maria because I had to tell her where I was going for the weekend. I had never been away that long a time on my own. It was Thursday night and pretty cold for early October, and so I put on my brown leather jacket. It was going to be tough talking to her because I had told her I was not ever going away to school. How could I explain myself now?

I walked over to Mott Street. Her building was more run-down than I had remembered. I saw the fire escape on the second floor hanging sideways. It looked dangerous to me. I moved back from the building and waited. I saw her coming down the hallway steps with a big smile on her face. I felt very bad. I smiled as best I could and kissed her. My heart sank.

We walked along Second Avenue past the Church of the Nativity. I thought it would be easier to talk walking with her.

"Maria, I have something to tell you. I'm going away this weekend. I'm taking a train to the Mount Hermon School from Grand Central Station." I said it clear and as softly as I could.

She stopped and looked hard at me. "You told me you were

not going away to school! You told me you were going to high school here in New York City. You told me that only a few months ago. You lied to me!"

What could I say? She was right. I did say that to her, but I had not lied to her.

"Maria, I did not lie to you then. At the time, it was the truth. I never expected to go. Tom came to see me and my parents last week. He told us that Peter Capra met with the board, and they agreed to send me to the Mount Hermon School to take the admissions test. That was only last week. I'll be back by Sunday. Maria, it's just a test."

She kept on staring at me and then punched me hard on my arm. "So why didn't you tell me when you found out? Did you tell Harold or Johnny or the other guys in your little gang? I'll bet you told somebody!" She pushed me away and headed back toward Mott Street.

I grabbed her arm and stopped her. "Listen, Maria, it's only a weekend. It's just a test. I'll probably fail anyway, and it will be over! And when eighth grade is over, we'll all go to high school together! C'mon, I'm just a street kid, and this place is a prep school! So stop worrying."

I rubbed her shoulders, turned her around, and held her. She held back tears for a moment, and then, holding me tighter, she began to cry. I couldn't say anything, so I just let her cry it out until she stopped. I held back tears. I did not want to let her go. I gave her my handkerchief, and she wiped her eyes.

"Look, Joey. I don't care that it's a year away. I don't care you might not pass the test. I don't care about that. Don't you understand? I just don't want you to leave. That's all."

She began to cry again. After a while, she calmed down. We did not speak for a few moments. She stopped crying, but when we kissed again, her lips were wet from tears streaming down her face. Then she looked at me hard.

"You're gonna miss the Feast of San Gennaro. You want that? You're gonna miss the stickball games on Saturday. That too!" She lowered her head. "And you damn well are gonna miss me!"

That was a dagger in my heart. She shut me up pretty good. I hugged her again and stroked her hair and kissed her on the cheek. She had me ready to cry, but I didn't.

I took her into the ice cream parlor on Sixth Street, and we sat down and had egg creams. That calmed her down. We talked about the weekend. Every so often her eyes would tear up, but she held back from crying.

Later, I took her back to Mott Street and told her I would see her Sunday night. I waited until she walked up the first flight of steps, where she turned and stopped to look at me from the landing. She managed a smile, waved at me, and disappeared up the steps. She was gone. I was alone.

I walked across the street toward home and turned to see her at the window looking down at me. I waved to her, but she did not wave back. She was holding on to the drapes of her window with both hands, just looking down at me as I walked away. My heart was burning up. *It will be this way without her,* I thought.

Tom Mansfield offered to take me to Grand Central on Friday morning so my parents could go to work. That morning, my father left around six. My mother had packed enough clothes to get me through the weekend: one pink shirt and two blue ones. I wore a blue shirt. She packed a heavy sweater. It was cold in Massachusetts in October, she said. How did she know that?

Tom Mansfield showed up around eight o'clock. I put on my leather jacket, picked up my gym bag, and went for the front door. My mother came over and hugged me. I could hear her sniffling.

"Ma, c'mon! It's only a weekend. I'll be home on Sunday!"

She grabbed me by the shoulders. "Tom, I still do not think this school thing is such a good idea!" she said, scowling. "You be a good boy, Joey, and don't get into any trouble up there. You hear me? I know you like to fight."

I laughed. "Ma, I'm gonna take the test, talk to the headmaster, and then come home on Sunday. Who's gonna have time to fight?"

She kissed me again and I went out the door.

It didn't hit me that I was leaving New York City until the cab stopped at Grand Central Station. It was huge, noisy, and confusing to get around. I looked up at the high ceiling. People were walking fast, and no one was smiling. Train announcements traveled through the entire building. I had never seen so many people racing to get somewhere—newspapers, briefcases, suits, and dresses. I was glad Tom was there to get me to the right train track. We waited an hour sitting around.

At noon, the announcement came to board the train. We walked over to the entrance to the train. Tom shook my hand.

"Good luck, Joey." he said. "Make us proud. You are the last shot."

He turned and walked away. I was alone.

I knew I was the last shot. He didn't have to tell me that. I walked to the train platform. I was going to Massachusetts to look at the school as much as the headmaster was going to look at me. In fact, I felt pretty confident. But as I stepped onto the train, and sat down, I wondered, was it all worth it? I was leaving home. My heart sank.

The train began to pull out of the station. It picked up speed and entered a dark tunnel, but not like a subway, because it didn't stop every ten blocks or so, and it didn't stop like an express train. It raced through the tunnel at a much faster speed than a subway train, shaking all the way.

Suddenly, the train came out of the tunnel with a *swoosh*. A flash of light flooded the windows and blinded me for a moment. We were already at 187th Street. I saw rows and rows of beat-up tenement buildings and empty, weeded lots full of trash. The train sped on. I saw black kids playing in playgrounds. I kept turning my head to look back. On street corners, young black men were hanging out, some smoking.

The train picked up speed. People became blurred images, and then I saw no one; I could see just rows and rows of empty buildings with boarded doors and blown-out windows. Soon even these disappeared. The landscape turned into broken-down factory buildings, empty lots, and no one.

I looked around the train. There were just a few passengers in my car. All were adults. Every once in a while, a man would stop reading his paper, put it down, stare at me for a few moments, and then return to his reading. I thought nothing of it.

Every twenty minutes, the train rolled into a station. The first stop was an old country town. I had never really seen a town like that before except in a movie. It was late afternoon. Brilliant sunlight hung over the town's buildings, most no more than four stories high. Its trees were already turning colors of yellow, orange, and red. I saw a huge maple with brilliant orange leaves. I thought of our trees in the back park. Their leaves would be changing soon. It seemed so long ago, but it was only the night before that Maria and I were sitting in the park holding each other.

We headed north. Every town seemed alike—a train platform with passengers boarding and departing and a few cars moving along the main street below. In town, houses were bunched together, but as the train moved out, farmhouses took over, hundreds of yards from one another. After two hours, I saw country and lots of it. It was Connecticut. I saw waves and waves of grass, corn and potato fields, red barns with tractors, and plows and farm tools just lying on the ground. I saw more farmland than I had ever seen in my life. The train rolled on. I noticed how few people were outside their houses. I was tired. I closed my eyes and fell asleep.

The conductor woke me. Four hours had passed. He pointed out the window. The sign on the platform said Northfield. I took a deep breath, grabbed my bag, and bolted out the open door of the train. Three other passengers came off that train. I was not used to seeing so few people. It was around five o'clock, and the sun was glowing red just above the horizon. Twilight was not far away. I walked over to a small wooden building that stood smack in the center of the platform, put my bag down, and stretched. First thing I felt was the cold. It was much colder than New York City. I zipped my jacket and thanked God I wore a sweater.

I looked around. All I could see were isolated homes surrounded by fields and giant green hills off in the distance. I saw way off some houses with smoke rising from their chimneys.

I saw the wide expanse of blue sky, something new to me. I shook my head. What the hell had I gotten myself into? Why would anyone come to a school in this lonely, desolate place?

I thought this beginning was a very bad one. Just then, I heard someone shouting my name. I turned around. A tall, skinny kid was walking up to me. His short black hair was slicked down and parted on the left side. He had very white skin and thin lips, and he was smiling and waving. He stuck out his hand with a huge grin and white, white teeth.

He was as white a person as I had ever seen, and when he smiled, I could see clear blue eyes, bright and cheerful. He made me feel good when he called out my name.

"Joey, right?"

I nodded and smiled back.

"I am really happy to meet you. I'm from the Mount Hermon School. I'm a second-year student here, a sophomore. They asked me to pick you up. I'm here to take you to the campus. Here, let me grab your bag. My name is Neil, Neil Sheehan. The train was a little late. I hate to rush you, but we've got to get to the cottage where you're staying and to dinner before six. If we don't get there on time, we don't eat!"

I barely spoke before the cab driver, an old man smoking a pipe and wearing farmer's overalls, grabbed my bag and threw it in the huge trunk of an old Buick. We drove about two miles through open country. As the sun inched closer to the horizon, I could see huge fields spread out with isolated houses along the road, some with old barns that needed painting, but not a soul in sight. Neil chatted away about how great the Mount Hermon School was and how he loved it so much. It was getting dark. I could see between tall trees a red sun sinking closer to the horizon. The big old Buick rumbled along.

I was used to city lights. Here, there were no lights. I looked hard to see a road sign. I realized that I had not seen anyone except for Neil and the cab driver during the trip into the school. The car slowed and turned right under an archway. I saw a sign in black that read, "The Mount Hermon School for Boys."

Lights along the tree-lined road led us to the campus. Above the hills surrounding the campus, pale, flat clouds hung lazily in the distance, and the sky showed just a tint of deep maroon from the sun dipping closer to the horizon. We stopped at a large cottage, one of three at the top of a steep hill overlooking a huge football field and one-story houses down below on the left of the field. I had seen lots of football fields at the movies, but never anywhere else. We went inside and walked into a hallway with a row of rooms. Neil took my bag and stopped at a room, and a kid about my age popped his head out the door.

"Finally! Boy, am I glad to see you guys!" He extended his hand. "You're Joey, right?" He turned to Neil. "You realize what time it is? If we don't get to the dining room, no dinner. You know how Mr. Petski is. Guest or not, two minutes late and we don't eat. Drop your bag, get your sport jacket and tie, and let's go!"

He grabbed my bag, threw it on the floor, and then stuck out his hand. "Oh, by the way, I'm Dave Miller. Nice to meet you."

He had a friendly face, blond hair, and blue eyes. He smiled. I heard a door slam shut in the hall, and a kid ran past the room. I shrugged.

"What sport coat? I don't have a sport coat or a tie."

"You can't get into the dining room without a coat and tie," Dave said.

"He's about your size. Lend him a coat and tie!" Neil said.

Dave opened his closet. There were about six sport coats and an equal number of slacks hanging there. On the floor were about six pairs of shoes. I was surprised. I had never seen so many jackets in one closet.

Dave pulled out a blue jacket. He told me later it was a blazer. Then, from the rack hanging on the closet door, he picked a red-striped tie for me from among about a dozen. I tried on the jacket. It was a perfect fit.

"Okay, let's go," Neil said. "If we're late, Petski doesn't let us in."

I found out later that Petski was in charge of the dining room.

"I hate rules, Joey, but no coat and tie, no dinner. Trust me. Am

I right, Neil? He won't let you in? Now we have to go, or we'll be late, and then none of us eats!"

We stopped quickly in a large bathroom down the hall. I noticed how dark I was and how light-skinned Dave was. My hair was so black and curly, and his was blond and straight. I looked different, all right.

We rushed out of the dorm and into a cold night. Even though I was wearing a wool sweater and Dave's blazer, I was shivering without my leather jacket. I turned up the collar of the sport coat to stay warmer. We walked along a path I could barely see toward a large hill. At the top of the hill was a well-lit building. Students were walking in, hundreds of them.

As we came closer to the entrance, noise from the dining hall grew louder, and from the bright lights of the hall, I could see most of the students were blond and fair-skinned. They were all wearing coats and ties. Had I not listened to Dave and Neil, we would not have eaten that night.

A bald man with white-rimmed glasses stood ramrod straight at the entrance to the dining room. He wore a gray suit, a brown tie, and a blue crewneck sweater. Nothing matched. He was checking the students as they went in. He looked very stern. I knew right away it was Petski. I didn't like him.

We reached the entrance. Petski put his hand on my chest and turned down the collar of Dave's sport jacket. He saw the tie, nodded, and waved us in. I gave him a nasty look. He looked surprised. The sound of a clock began to strike six. It was a huge dining hall. The entire student body stood at tables. I counted ten students at each table. They all stared at me. I paid no mind.

At a podium in the center of the hall, a tall, bald man stood. The dining room was silent.

"Bow your heads," he said, and everyone bowed his head.

I bowed my head.

"Dear Lord, we thank you for this blessing of food we are about to eat, we thank you for the blessings of this day, and we thank you for whatever good you bring to our school. Amen!"

We all sat down. Immediately from two large double doors,

student waiters came out carrying huge trays and wearing simple white jackets. One waiter went to our table and began to place the food down. Dave grabbed bread and butter quickly and stuffed his mouth. He took a slice of bread and threw it on my plate and told me to eat. I took the bread, buttered it, and ate it right away. I was hungry.

There were bowls of corn, peas, and carrots and a huge fish tray. Thank God! It was fish, deep fried and brown. I could not eat meat on Friday. The food was terrible! The vegetables, peas, and carrots were not cooked, and the fish had no garlic, butter, or lemon on it. I was so hungry I ate it all anyway. If I were home, I would be having my mother's fish dinner with penne and shrimp. I could see there would be great sacrifices for me here.

When we got back to Dave's room, Neil told me Saturday breakfast was a quarter after seven. After that, I would go directly to the admissions test. It was just one hour, and then I would visit a Saturday morning class. A Saturday morning class! That was a shock. There were two classes and a study hall in between.

After lunch at noon, Neil would give me a short tour of the school, classrooms, dormitories, and the gym. The big football game with Deerfield Academy would start at two o'clock. All five hundred students would be there, since Deerfield was Mount Hermon's most important rival. Then he told me there was study hall six nights a week. I saw right away how much control the school had over the students' time. Did I want that kind of structure over my life?

I was used to being free after school to play handball and stickball and at night hang out with Maria. Did I want a life where I had classes on Saturday morning and study hall six nights a week? I thought how the life here at prep school had to be like the life at reform school. He left, telling me to get a good night's sleep. It was going to be a big day for me.

"Don't worry," Dave said. "The test isn't that hard. You just have to be cool and calm. Listen, I want to talk to you. I saw that pink shirt of yours inside your bag. Sorry I went through it. I got a little excited. How about doing a trade? Whatta ya say? I'll trade three blue and three white button-down Brooks Brothers shirts for one pink shirt. Is it a deal? I love those wide flap collars and that pink! It will go great with my blue blazer. Don't answer now. We can talk later, tomorrow maybe. Okay?"

I was surprised. How could I take six of his shirts for one pink shirt? That was crazy. It was Friday night. A bell rang for study hall. Dave walked over to his desk and casually threw some books down. Another bell rang.

"Study hall until nine thirty," he said, "and then lights out at nine forty-five. Wait until the floor captain checks in on us, and then we can talk."

After lights out, the floor captain came and went. Dave pulled out a flashlight. He went to his dresser and casually pulled out six brand-new shirts, still with blue ribbons around them. He threw them on his bed. His dresser was full of shirts. Then he laughed. He went over to my bag.

"Okay if I pull out that pink shirt of yours?"

How could I say no? He was giving me a great deal, but I did not want to do it. He never gave me a chance to answer. He went to my bag and pulled out my pink shirt, spread it against his chest, and smiled.

"We're the same size. I know it's going to fit. Whatta ya say?"

"I say no! Are you nuts? I'm stealing from you! I'm not gonna do it."

"Joey, you have to! The kids in this school are gonna think I am the best! I am so glad they asked me to be your roommate for the weekend. They must have figured I was like some of the kids from your neighborhood, a little wild. So, Joey, is it a trade?"

"No! It would be like stealing! Your parents will kill you!"

He just shrugged. "Look, first of all, my parents have no idea how many shirts I have. They get picked and sent to me by our butler. Second, my parents are in Europe somewhere. They couldn't care less, and they won't even know I traded them. Thirdly, I don't care! I want the pink shirt! Do we have a deal? I mean, Joey, I saved you tonight, didn't I? You would have starved to death if I didn't give you the blazer and tie? What about that? You owe me!"

What could I say? He was right. He did save me. My mother would have killed me if I did what he was doing. He threw me a shirt to try on. It was soft to touch, and it fit perfectly. He convinced me that the shirts were meaningless to him.

"Okay. Okay! I'll do it, all right?"

That night, Dave was very happy. He put on the pink shirt and stood in the mirror smiling at himself. Then he put on a blue tie with red stripes. He stood in front of the mirror and turned left and right.

"Cool, man! Cool! C'mon, Joey, try on one of those Brooks Brothers shirts. Go ahead. You know what? I'm wearing this shirt to dinner tomorrow night."

I took one of the blue shirts and felt the soft cotton of the shirt. "Dave, these shirts are expensive!"

"Joey, I can buy a hundred shirts tomorrow and nobody would say one word to me, but I couldn't buy a pink shirt with a flap collar for a thousand dollars! My parents would just kill me if they saw me wearing a pink shirt!"

I made him happy by agreeing to the trade, but I was not going to keep his shirts. I threw them in my bag, and then later when he wasn't around, I threw them all, except one, back in his drawer. He never noticed.

When I closed my eyes, I realized I was completely exhausted. I did not even have time to worry about the admissions test in the morning. I thought of Maria, and in minutes, I was fast asleep.

I woke up at six thirty and looked out the window. The light of a pale sun, partially hidden by mist, appeared above green hills just beyond the valley of the school. It was so quiet and peaceful with tall trees, and a landscape of grass, and small buildings shrouded in morning mist. I was hungry.

Dave was still sleeping. Fifteen minutes later, a bell rang in the hallway. I heard footsteps heading to the common bathroom. I leaned over and tried to wake him. It was Saturday. I thought about the guys playing stickball in the afternoon and everyone at home. I tried not to think about home. Instead, I focused on getting ready for the test.

I went into the bathroom, took a shower, brushed my teeth, came back, and got dressed. I was cold. I put on the corduroy pants Dave had given me and pulled my heavy sweater over my shirt. Dave had kept the window open. He liked cold. I looked outside the window again.

From the cottage resting on the hilltop, I could see the mist hanging over the campus in the valley below beginning to thin. It began to rise, and within minutes, it disappeared. The sun blasted brilliant light into the room. Huge green hills appeared beyond the valley, a giant wall of evergreen trees that stretched the entire landscape from left to right. The campus below in the light of the sun lay spread out before me—green grass, wet from dew, clean, neat, and pure, and tall trees swaying slightly from a light breeze. The air smelled fresh.

I could see hundreds of green acres of land beyond the campus and a clear blue sky that spread across the length of the school one end to the other. I could not see one tall building. It was a sight I had never seen before, something that probably looked like Central Park from a plane but larger and more vast, large green hills that went on and on as far as I could see.

In the valley below, off to the left, I could see more clearly now the one-story redbrick buildings and the huge football field at the center of the campus just below the cottages, its stands empty at each end. I imagined them already filled for the game against Deerfield Academy in the afternoon. I had never been to a football game.

27
Saturday at Prep School

Neil was at our door at seven in the morning. Dave was just waking up. Neil told him flat out that we were not going to wait for him. The test was at nine o'clock at the library, and he was told to get me there a half hour early. We all walked up the same path as the night before, but now I could see where we were. The large dining room building stood on a hill much higher than the cottages.Off to the left of the cottages, I could see what looked like a church, but later I found out was called the chapel. The school was surrounded by a forest of tall trees.

We walked into the dining room. Petski was nowhere to be seen. As Neil and I walked to our table, students stared at us again. I stared back. What were they so curious about? I didn't look like them! Was my hair too thick, too black, too greasy for these kids with short, parted blond hair and blue eyes, khaki pants, and Brooks Brothers sweaters? I felt a little strange. I was different, and they knew it. Neil noticed the stares of the students.

"Don't pay attention to them," he whispered. "Eat a good breakfast, and concentrate on that test!"

We sat down. Cereal and milk, bread, jelly, and butter were already on the table. I grabbed the milk, poured it generously over the cereal, and wolfed it down.

After breakfast, Neil took me to the library. The building was one large room with walnut walls and a ceiling at least thirteen feet high. Large rectangular tables were in the center of the library, desks for each student at casement windows. Already, students were there quietly studying under lamps with green glass shades. I heard the sounds of loafers and sneakers walking across the dark wooden floor. Once in a while, a book opened, and there were sounds of pencils on the desks.

I was amazed that at nine on Saturday morning, students were already studying—and so quietly. If I were home, I would be just waking up and getting ready to play handball and stickball in the afternoon. Shock was beginning to set in.

Neil took me to a study room behind the librarian's desk. At the table was a teacher. He was tall and thin with thinning black hair parted on the left. He wore a gray sport jacket, a blue V-neck sweater, and a green bow tie. He stood up, smiled, and stuck his hand out to me.

"Hello, Joey. My name is Fred McVey. I am one of the math teachers here at the Mount Hermon School, and I am going to administer the admissions exam to you. It is not a difficult exam. The Boys' Club people told us you're a whiz at math but have some difficulty with English. Is that correct?"

I smiled. I had no problem being honest. "Yeah, I'm pretty good at math. It comes easy to me, but I do have trouble with English and vocabulary. Tom and Sue from the Boys' Club have been working with me. My parents are Italian. They came from Sicily."

Mr. McVey smiled. "I'm going to leave the exam here on the table. I will be in the library if you need me. Take a look at it first. Read the instructions carefully, and then start anytime you wish. You have an hour to complete it. No one will be here. We are on an honor system here. After the exam, Neil will come back and pick you up to take you to an English class."

"Will you let me know how I did after I finish?" I asked.

He patted me on the shoulder. "No, I can't do that. Our headmaster, Dr. Rubendall, will go over that with you on Sunday morning after chapel when he meets you for your interview."

"I don't go to chapel. I'm Catholic. I don't have to go, do I?"

Neil smiled. "No, Joey, you don't," he said, "because I'm the only Catholic who goes to town for church. It's a two-mile walk! You can come with me!"

"Okay, Joey. You can get started," Mr. McVey said, and they left.

I was alone. The test was there on the table. Outside the room, the library was quiet. Strangely, I was not nervous, and I could not understand why. Was it because I was alone and on my own? I went outside into the main hall and looked around. Every student was in a book.

At this time next year, would I be one of the students sitting in this library reading? I went back inside and looked out the window. I stood staring out the window at the giant cluster of trees. It was not New York, for sure.

I started the test. It began with the English section, but I thought I would start the math first and then tackle the grammar section because I knew it would be tough for me.

Ten minutes into the test, the door opened. In walked Dave, gesturing me to be quiet. He closed the door.

"Hey, how are you doing?" he whispered, a wicked smile on his face. "Do you need any help?"

I shook my head. "Are you crazy? They'll throw you outta here if they catch you! And worse, they'll throw me out even before I get in! You'd better leave!"

"Okay. Okay. I'll see you in English class as soon as you're done! And if you change your mind, I'll pretend I'm reading. I'm pretty good at English, so think about it."

He winked and left. I breathed a sigh of relief. He reminded me of Johnny Marino. I figured out then that not all kids who did bad things came from bad neighborhoods. Not that Dave was a bad kid; I think he was a kid who got himself into trouble because his parents needed to give him more attention. I never had that problem. I gave my parents problems also even with plenty of attention. I started the test.

I was done in an hour. I did great on the math but not so well on the English section. I was checking my answers when Neil walked in.

"What was Dave doing in here?" he asked. He looked at me curiously.

"Ah, don't worry." I said. "He asked me if I needed any help. English. I told him I didn't and to get outta here. Don't tell Mr. McVey!"

Neil shook his head. "No, of course not. I am not a snitch!"

A few minutes later, McVey walked in, and Neil left without a word. I gave him the exam. He went through it in less than five minutes, making just a few corrections on the math. He went to the English section and spent more time there. I was getting nervous.

"How did I do?" I asked.

He looked at me and folded the exam booklet. "Dr. Rubendall will let you know that. Don't worry about that. Neil will take you to class now."

I began to worry anyway.

Neil took me into a freshman English class in a large, bright, one-story brick building next to the library. I sat next to Dave. I looked around to see just twelve students. I asked Dave where the other students were. He shrugged. In public school, we had at least twenty-five students in class. It was another surprise to me.

Suddenly, the class grew quiet. A tall man came into the room. He wore wire-rimmed glasses, and he was no more than thirty years old. He had a large head and was getting bald. He put his books down on the desk and turned to look at the class. His eyes stopped at Dave, and then he turned to me. He looked at us with shifty eyes. I thought he had a sneer on his face. He looked very smart but arrogant. I didn't like him one bit. I didn't think he liked me, either. Then I realized that if I got into Mount Hermon, he could be my English teacher next year.

"Good morning, gentlemen. I suppose you have noticed we

have a guest in the class. He may be a student next year. I also notice he is sitting next to David. Not a wise choice, Mr. D'Angelo! Well, Mr. Miller, does this mean you will be paying more attention than you usually do?"

Dave smiled. "Yes, sir, Mr. Burdick," he replied. "I've done my homework, and I am ready to go."

The students laughed, but Burdick did not. He slammed his book down on his desk and stared at the class. It grew very quiet again. He turned to me.

"Mr. D'Angelo, my name is Todd Burdick. I am a no-nonsense teacher. Isn't that right, Mr. Miller?"

Dave nodded as Burdick walked up the aisle toward him.

"What's more, I have no hesitation in failing a student who does not perform, does not do his homework, does poorly in class, and fails my daily quizzes. Isn't that correct, Mr. Miller?"

David nodded again sheepishly.

Mr. Burdick stood right next to him and between us. Then he whirled around to face me. He pointed at me.

"Are you familiar with *A Tale of Two Cities*, Mr. D'Angelo?"

I was a little surprised he asked me that question, and since I was not a student of his, I had nothing to lose in answering the question. The class was very quiet and looked at me.

"Yes, I heard about that book, Mr. Burdick. In fact, I read the Classic Comics version. It was pretty good."

The students laughed.

"So, then, maybe you can answer this question for me. Do you think Sydney Carton did the right thing sacrificing his life for his friend?"

The class grew quiet. That, I thought, was a very tough question. I thought about Johnny stepping in front of me when Pepi aimed his gun at me and realized how courageous it was for Johnny to do that. I answered him.

"I think what he did for his friend was something most people could not do," I said. "He gave up his life. I don't know if I could do that." I kept thinking about his question. Burdick folded his arms and waited for me to continue to answer.

What if Maria's life was on the line? If she had fallen in front of a truck, would I jump to save her?

I kept on. "That is a very good question, Mr. Burdick! I think the only time I could answer it completely is the moment it happens. I would have to decide right then and there if I had courage enough to give up my life. Not easy to do."

Burdick smiled and went back to his desk. "Not bad, Mr. D'Angelo. Not bad! In this class, we study the book, not the comic book version, because it is well written and a good story full of great characters and has a plot full of twists and turns. It also has a lesson for us. It is about moral fiber. It is about character. It is about being the best a human being can be. It is basically about how we human beings can best conduct our lives, and that is why I teach this book." He paused and then smiled. "Hopefully, next year, Joey, you will be one of them. I will be looking forward to it!"

I looked at him where he now stood at his desk. Was I ever wrong about him! He was really a good man. My first reaction was that he was no damn good, picking on Dave the way he did; but then I realized that Dave must have given Mr. Burdick a lot of trouble in class. The school probably had me with Dave, thinking that two bad kids could either help each other out or stir more trouble. I would either get into trouble or come out of it all right. Dave was a test for me.

At noon, Neil and Dave took me into the dining room. Some students again stared at me. I tried not to pay attention, but it did bother me. Dave noticed that, so he put his arm around my shoulder as we walked to our table. How bad could he be? He made me feel really good, and it reminded me of Johnny who loved to hang his arm around my shoulder on our way back from school or after a stickball game.

Lunch came on big trays carried by student waiters—hot chicken soup in a large bowl for the entire table and roast beef sandwiches. Everybody was talking about the big game against Deerfield. Dave told me he worked as the water boy for the Mount Hermon football team. I was going to help him out. He liked that job, but he told me he worried about one thing.

28
The Football Game

"Keep your eye out for that big halfback for Deerfield, Jack Buck. What a son of a bitch he is! Everybody in our school hates him. At the last game, he ran right into the water boy. He did it deliberately. The kid quit. I'm it now. He's big and tough and nasty! At the game, you can help me with the water. It's okay. They told me you should be with me all the time. Be careful of that bastard! He'll run right over you. He enjoys hurting people. I really hate that son of a bitch!"

He took a bite of his roast beef sandwich. I could see he was already getting nervous. He was eating quickly, and his eyes kept shifting back and forth. He was thinking and not talking much. I took the ladle from the soup pot, poured out a bowl, and emptied it in a few minutes. Then I grabbed a roast beef sandwich, added some lettuce to it, and wolfed it down.

At two o'clock, we were on the sidelines of the field, standing next to the football team dressed in yellow pants with maroon jerseys and helmets. In front of them stood the coaches. Across the field, Deerfield players were dressed in green. They looked much bigger than the Mount Hermon players.

The stands were full of students on both sides of the field. The Mount Hermon students directly behind us were screaming and waving the school flags. Deerfield had brought over busloads of their students, all wearing dark-green sweaters, the Deerfield color, and these kids filled the stands behind the Deerfield football team. There was not a vacant seat anywhere.

"Look over there!" Dave shouted. "That's Jack Buck. That no-good son of a bitch!"

The game started. Mount Hermon kicked off to Deerfield. It looked as if the entire Mount Hermon student body was in the stands, shouting and waving maroon flags. Jack Buck in the backfield returned the ball to the forty-yard line. On the first play, he took the ball and barreled through the Mount Hermon line for another twenty yards. Now he was in Mount Hermon territory on the forty-yard line.

On our side of the field, Dave and I stood right on that line. Deerfield students were screaming. The Mount Hermon stands were quiet. Buck came out of the huddle and looked our way at Dave as if he were about to eat him. He was no more than twenty yards from where we stood.

Buck crouched behind his quarterback with knees bent. The quarterback handed him the ball, and suddenly, instead of running up the middle, he headed in our direction! The Mount Hermon players gave chase. Dave saw him heading toward him and tried to get out of the way, but he couldn't.

Buck, with the ball up under his arm, slammed into Dave, who flew back and landed flat on his back. He got up and started yelling at Buck. Dave called him some pretty bad names. Buck threw down the football, took off his helmet, and shoved Dave. He fell backward again onto the muddy grass, and Buck just laughed. The Mount Hermon students started booing him. A referee came over and drew down a penalty flag. Buck picked it up and threw it back at him. The Mount Hermon players started heckling him, but he just turned around, looked up at the stands, and sneered.

I thought a fight would break out between both teams' players, but the Mount Hermon football players stayed on the sidelines, restrained by their coaches. Students were still booing Buck when I went over to Dave and helped him up. His pants were filthy and wet. His face was beet red. I lost my temper and should not have done what I did next.

As Buck walked back to the huddle, I shouted at him, "Hey, you didn't have to do that! Why don't you pick on somebody your own size!"

Buck turned to me surprised. The Mount Hermon football players stood there stunned. They did not expect that from me. I helped Dave wipe the dirt off his pants. Then I saw Buck drop his helmet and tighten his fists. He walked over to me and stood inches away. I ignored him. Instead, I kept wiping Dave's clothes down. I stood my ground. Suddenly, the stands grew very quiet. I turned for a moment to see the Mount Hermon coach walking over to us, but it was too late.

Buck gave me a hard push, and I fell backward onto the muddy ground. The Mount Hermon students started to boo Buck. I got up and wiped my pants off and glared at him, but I held my temper, turned, and walked away, but he spun me around and shoved me again!

I fell down hard again. Buck smiled at me with his hands on his hips while I sat in the mud looking up at him. He should not have smiled. That was when I lost it. I got up and rammed right into him. He dropped to the ground, all six feet of him, with a shocked look. There was suddenly a hush in the stands. The Mount Hermon students then let out a roar!

Buck got up quickly and took a swing at me, but I was too fast. I flew to one side. He missed me completely and fell to the ground. As he turned to get up, I started to punch the hell out of him with lefts and rights. He tried to cover his head, but it was no use. I pulled his arm away, and I just kept hitting him. He started to bleed from his mouth. I hit him with all I had. Mount Hermon students were roaring as he tried to protect himself from my punches.

The Mount Hermon coach and the referee grabbed me by

the arms. While they were holding me, Buck swung and caught me square on the bone over my left eye. That punch hurt, but he should not have hit me. I went into a rage. I got free and began pounding him. He never expected me to go after him again. I kept punching him, and he kept stepping backward, until finally, I caught him in the jaw with a right hook, and he landed one more time flat on his back.

The Mount Hermon stands roared. That made me feel good. Before I knew it, the coach, the referee, and players were between us. I was a little groggy, but I remember Dave grabbing me and laughing out of control. Buck was a big kid, but he was not used to a fast and scrappy fighter who knew how to fight back. I learned that lesson when I fought Freddie. I had no fear.

The football players surrounded me, smiling and patting me on the back. The Mount Hermon students were still screaming and jumping out of their seats. Dave was at my side, smiling and hugging me. He was so happy that I beat up Buck. As soon as I came to my senses, I realized what a jerk I had been. I most likely had ruined my chance for admission to Mount Hermon!

A few minutes later, things calmed down. The referee came over and ordered the players back to the benches. One Deerfield player came over to Dave and me.

"My name is Jonathan. I'm the captain of the Deerfield football team."

"I know who you are," Dave replied.

"I speak for our team when I tell you I want to apologize for Buck's behavior. Sometimes he gets a little crazy, as you know from today. I just don't want you to think that he represents our football team. We at Deerfield are taught to be gentlemen, just like you all are taught here at Mount Hermon. We all apologize."

He extended his hand, first to Dave, then to me. Dave smiled and shook it with great vigor. He shook my hand, smiled, nodded, and walked back across the field. I thought that was a great thing to do, and I felt much better after that.

The Mount Hermon football trainer came over and took me and Dave down to the locker room. I didn't realize I was bleeding from a cut over my eye until Dave put a wet towel on my face. It felt good to hear the school students shouting and cheering, but I was now in deep trouble. I knew that.

The trainer looked at my eye. It was already swollen. He put ice over it.

"Not too bad a cut," he said. "You'll live. It doesn't need stitches." He put some iodine on it and then carefully put a large gauze pad over it and taped it down.

Dave kept smiling and shouting about how I beat up Buck. He kept walking around the room punching his fist into the palm of his hand. I kept thinking it was over for me once the headmaster found out about the fight.

A few minutes later, Dave and I headed back to his room. We were wet and dirty. We undressed and took showers. Later in Dave's room, he kept talking about Buck and the fight. I was feeling a little groggy from the fight.

From the cottage window, I could see that the game had ended. Students were heading to their dorms, smiling. Mount Hermon had won. Deerfield students were loading onto buses for their ride back to campus. The stands were emptying out. It was getting dark very quickly. I could not see one person outside. Trees were in shadow. I could barely see the hills. It was getting colder. I became depressed. I had won the fight but probably had lost the scholarship.

Before dinner in his room, Dave handed me a brand-new blue shirt. Then he gave me what he called a red paisley tie with teardrops of blue. My corduroys were smeared with mud, so he handed me a pair of his khaki pants. I tried them on. They were a perfect fit. I tried on his blue shirt. It also fit perfectly.

He helped me with the tie. It was getting close to six o'clock and dinner. He handed me the blue blazer he had lent me the night before. I put it on and looked in the mirror. With Dave's clothes, I could have passed for a student except that my dark hair was curly and wild and hung over my ears.

Neil walked in. He shook his head. He did not look happy.

"Well, we won, but everyone is talking, not about the game

but about Joey beating up Buck. I guess you guys are pretty happy now!"

Dave started to say something, but Neil put up his hands.

"Better you just be quiet, Dave. You got this kid in a real mess! What's he supposed to say to Dr. Rubendall tomorrow? Do you think he still has a shot to get into this place?" He frowned.

Dave looked at me and was silent for a few seconds. Then he broke into a big smile, came over to me, and patted me on the back.

"Maybe not! But he sure beat the hell out of Jack Buck! Look at him! He looks like a real warrior! And you know what? With my jacket, pants, and tie, he's starting to look like a student!"

Neil just shook his head and walked out of the room.

As soon as we walked into the dining room, the students let out a loud cheer. Dave was waving a clenched fist in the air and laughing. I felt very uncomfortable. Dave's tie was too tight, and I could barely see out of my left eye because of the bandage, and I really didn't like the attention. We sat down, and the dining hall finally calmed down. I didn't feel much like eating.

All the kids at the table were talking. My head was pounding, and I just wanted to be alone. I forced myself to eat a hamburger. I kept very quiet.

Later, when we walked out, some teachers at the faculty tables looked at me with straight faces. That to me was not a good sign. We walked back to the freshman dorm down the hill. I looked up at the stars. There were so many of them. I never saw as many stars in a New York City sky as here. Except for a few lampposts along the paths and lighted dorms, the campus lay in darkness. It was my mood at that moment. David pointed to the top of a hill to the left of the dining hall.

"That's Dr. Rubendall's house," he said, "just beyond the tennis courts." He looked at me and laughed nervously.

29
The Headmaster

The next morning, Neil picked me up, and we headed to the dining room for hot chocolate and biscuits before leaving campus for the two-mile walk to church.

It was a quarter mile just to get off the school grounds. We walked along Route 5 into Northfield. It was a very small town and very quiet. Neil told me his ambition was to be a news reporter. He was getting straight As in English. I liked that about him. He had made up his mind to do something, and I knew he would do it. How many other kids in this school thought that way? It made me think. What did I want to do when I grew up?

The church was called Our Lady of Angels. It was very small. It could barely fit fifty people. The pews were hardwood benches. An old priest said Mass. I looked around, surprised. The ladies wore very little makeup. Men had no ties on, and their pants were not pressed. Their shoes looked like they could use shines. Their faces looked worn and tired. Every few minutes, a baby cried.

I knelt down and prayed to the Blessed Mother, Our Lady of the Angels. It was strange, but I felt at home in the church. I didn't pray that I had passed the test. I didn't pray that Dr. Rubendall would not be angry with me because of my fight with Jack Buck. And I didn't pray to get admitted to the school. I just prayed that everything would be all right. That was all. God had enough to do working on more serious problems. With all that praying, I still left the church not feeling all that hopeful.

On the walk back to school, I was quiet and let Neil do the talking. He loved the school and told me it would be an excellent experience for me. It would be a great education for me, and the schedule demanded self-discipline of students.

A while later, I was sitting in front of Dr. Rubendall's desk in his office at his house waiting for him. After a few minutes, I got up and looked out the window at the colors of leaves on maple and oak trees and large evergreens. Leaves had already fallen to the ground. A strong wind lifted them and sent them swirling in the air. Evergreens in the hills way off looked a dull green, hidden as they were in the smoky morning mist that still lingered in the valley. From a largely overcast sky, I could see rays of light off in the distance. They gave me hope.

I stared down at the empty stands and the matted grass of the football field still lined with faded white stripes. It looked lonely, as if it wanted its stands to be filled with a crowd that roared. I thought about the fight. Even if I did great on the admissions test, I didn't think I had a chance to get in. I had let everyone down. I felt terrible. I just wanted to go home.

Just then, a tall, broad-shouldered, balding man came into the room and stood looking at me with clear blue eyes. He wore a dark-blue suit, light-blue shirt, and maroon tie. His shoes were perfectly polished. He smiled a broad, friendly smile.

"Hello, Joey. I'm Dr. Rubendall, headmaster of Mount Hermon School." He came over and shook my hand. "How's that cut over your eye? You don't have to explain. I know how you got it."

He went to his desk, sat down, and pulled out my admissions test, glanced over it, and then placed it on his desk. He folded his hands and looked at me. He was not smiling at that point. He looked very serious. I was definitely in trouble.

"Joey, you did very well on the math section, but not on the grammar section—not as well, certainly, as you did in that fight with Jack Buck, I might add. In fact, you received one of the lowest scores on that part since the exam has been administered!" He started tapping his fingers on his desk.

It was all over for me, and he hadn't even gotten to the fight.

"And then that fight! I am certain David Miller had something to do with it, no doubt. Somehow, you got in the middle of it!" He paused for a few seconds, thinking.

"Now, Joey, I have a question for you. Do you think that fight helped or hurt your chance to get into Mount Hermon School? I know you're an honest young man. Mr. Capra told me that, so I would like to know your honest opinion."

What a question! I looked at him curiously. I wasn't sure how to answer. How could that fight possibly have helped me? I thought for a moment he was trying to trick me, but I could tell by looking at his eyes that he was a decent guy.

"Well, to tell the truth, I think the fight hurt me, because I'm a guest here, and I got into trouble by getting into that fight. I got angry, and I shouldn't have. That's all. So, to answer your question, if you think it was wrong to fight that kid from Deerfield, then I would say it hurt me."

Dr. Rubendall looked at me very carefully. He leaned his head back, pressed his hands together, and tapped his fingers one against the other. Then he laughed.

"Well, Joey, I would say you are correct, because, generally speaking, I do not condone fighting. I welcome peaceful solutions to problems and conflicts. But in this case, this boy had already pushed David and did go after you not once but twice. He does have a reputation. And you did demonstrate patience by not fighting back right away. You did hold your temper—for a while anyway. I know all about your temper. You defended your newfound friend. You stood up for him by telling Jack Buck he was a bully, and when he came at you, you defended yourself instead of running away despite the fact that he is so much bigger than you are." He smiled. "That took courage! Frankly, I am surprised to see that you are about the same size as David. How you managed to get the best of Jack Buck is beyond me!" He was quiet for a few moments. He rocked back and forth in his chair. "You must be a very good athlete, agile and quick!" He paused again, turning his rocker toward the window and then back toward me.

"You see, Joey, we here at Mount Hermon have a philosophy as to how students should conduct themselves, not only here but through their college days and into adulthood as well. We ask our students to be noble and do good. In that fight, Joey, you did both; you were noble in defending your friend, and you did good by standing up to a bully. Further, you showed courage in the face of danger. For demonstrating how we already wish our students to conduct themselves, you have earned yourself a place of admission in this school. Congratulations!"

He stood up and held out his hand. I was stunned. I shook his hand.

"The rest is up to you, Joey. I am offering you a great opportunity. It is there for you to accept, and mind you, the sacrifices you will make will be very difficult. You will be leaving home, friends, and neighborhood—and home, Joey, after you arrive here, will never, but never, be the same again. Think about it … but I have a feeling you're going to make the right decision."

I left Dr. Rubendall's house and walked down a curving path toward the freshmen cottages. It was about one o'clock, and my train was leaving at three. David and Neil were waiting for me. I told them the good news.

They were really excited. They kept patting me on the back, and they both gave me huge hugs. That long Sunday walk alone to church must have been hard for Neil, but now he could count on company for those long walks if I accepted the scholarship.

My thoughts were scattered. I was too excited to think clearly. I wasn't even sure I was going to the school, but I was happy that I had made it in. At least I had not failed. Who would have thought I would get admitted because of my fists instead of my brain?

I gave Dave back his blue blazer and paisley tie. I took off the heavy gauze pad. The cut was already healing and not that large.

I put on a small bandage. Dave and Neil went along for the taxi ride to the train station. I shook hands with them. Dave gave me another big hug.

"Hey, old buddy," he said, "I'm sure glad you came up here. I guess I'll have to fight Jack Buck on my own next time. Or maybe you taught him a lesson and that will be the end of Jack Buck, the tough guy!"

He smiled and stood with Neil quietly as I boarded the train.

I sat down in a seat where I could still see them. The train began to move. I waved and sat there watching them. I kept on waving until I could no longer see them. I closed my eyes and slept, but I woke up a few times. I wanted to get home. I kept thinking of everyone and everything I missed the entire weekend. I missed my parents, handball, stickball, Johnny, and Harold. I missed all that, and I was just away for a weekend. If I took the scholarship, I would miss all that for a long, long time. I really missed Maria.

I remembered how she looked the last time I saw her, holding her close to me at night in a cool breeze, alone in the park. That was just a few days before. I wanted to see her right away. I was excited thinking that I would be with her in just a few hours. The weekend away made me realize there was nothing like home. New York City was in my gut. I had a tough decision ahead of me.

30
Home

The train pressed on to New York City. How was I going to go to this school? How could I leave everyone? The train moved quickly through Massachusetts and into Connecticut. I could see below the Connecticut River. As I sat there staring down at it, I couldn't help thinking of Huck Finn and his river, the Mississippi. New York City had its own river, the Hudson. It was also huge with an ever-changing landscape. Rivers, like life, were in constant motion.

The train pulled into Grand Central. I was in New York. It was Sunday night, and when I got to First Street, I ran up the stoop holding my bag with the one blue shirt Dave had traded for my pink shirt. When I walked in the door, my mom let out a shout and hugged me.

She looked at the bandage. I told her I'd tripped on a rock in the dark. My father came over and also hugged me. I wanted to see Maria and told my parents I wanted to go out as soon as I cleaned up.

"You don't go anywhere until you have some pasta!" she said firmly.

I left my bag in my room, washed up, and went to the table and ate. I hadn't realized I was so hungry. I wolfed the ziti down and drank a cold glass of Coke. As I ate, I noticed how quiet my parents were. My father was already eating. He kept looking at me and smiling in a strange way.

"Joey, we really missed you, but you haven't told us how the test went. Your mother and I have been talking about it all the while you were away! Tell us, Joey—did you pass the test?"

I smiled and thought about my answer. "Well, Pa, I did very well on the math section but very bad on the English part, but the head of the school, Dr. Rubendall, liked me. He thought I would fit in with the rest of the students there, and he told me that if I wanted to go, I would be admitted." I smiled.

My father came over and hugged me. My mother was not smiling. My father saw that.

"Lillian, our boy, Joey, is going away to school. He will go to college. He will make something of himself. Believe me. Don't be sad. I know you will miss him, but in the end, you will be proud of him! Think about that. College! This is very good news! Now let's finish eating."

My mother stopped eating. I could see a trickle of a tear falling down her cheek. She wiped it off and hugged me.

"I know your father is right. We would have to let you go someday anyway. Better to send you to a good place where you will make something of yourself. It will be painful for me, but I know it is the right thing to do.

"But you are just a little boy!" she said.

I looked at her and smiled. "No, Ma. I am not a little boy anymore. I'm a big boy and getting bigger every day!"

She held on to me, squeezed hard, and then sat back down and began to eat. I finished eating, got up and washed, and told my parents I was going to Mott Street to see Maria.

"Go ahead, Joey," my mother said, "but be careful, and come home early."

I came out of my building and looked around First Street. It was already dark around eight o' clock. None of my friends were around. The lampposts were on, and there were not many people on the street. A couple of mob guys were standing outside Pepi's club, looking around and smoking.

I shook my head. That was not the life for me. It was so clear to me now. I looked up at Harold's apartment on the fifth floor. The lights were on, and I would have gone up to see him, but I wanted to see Maria first.

I headed to Second Avenue, crossed to Houston Street, and started to run toward Mott Street. I did not feel right, and I could not understand why. I turned onto Mott and headed toward Maria's building. Suddenly, as I walked down the street, I noticed that her building was no longer standing!

Where it once stood was a huge mound of wood beams, piles of broken bricks, furniture, clothes and shattered windows. The fire escape was bent in different directions. I could see through the space where her building used to be the backyard of a building on Elizabeth Street. I leaned against a lamppost. I felt a little light-headed. I put my head in my hands wondering what had happened.

I ran over to an old woman sitting in front of her building and asked her. She looked at the rubble lying on the ground and waved her arms, telling me how the building started to shake and everyone cleared out.

I asked her what had happened to Maria and her mother, but she couldn't tell me. She just kept shaking her head. I ran over to Jimmy's building, ran up two flights of steps, and pounded on his door. He came out into the hallway.

"Oh, you're back! Everybody was talkin' about how you were going away to a new school."

I stopped him with a wave of my hand. "Jimmy, what happened to Maria's building? Where is she? Is she okay?"

He nodded. "Oh, yeah! She's okay. Everybody got out like two hours after the building started to creak and the walls started to shake. It happened Saturday afternoon. When it came down, we all watched it crash to the ground. I tell ya, Joey, it was a sight! I couldn't believe it. It happened so fast. Now it's gone! Everybody on Mott Street is worried their buildings are gonna come crashing down too. Pretty soon, the whole neighborhood is gonna be gone!"

"Jimmy, where is Maria? Where did she and her mother go?"

"She and her mother found a place on Third Street. She's actually closer to you. Ain't that somethin'? They're at 47 East Third Street, second floor. They were lucky to find a place. Everybody in the building was looking for apartments."

I thanked him and took off for Third Street. I ran as fast as I could, and when I reached 47, I grabbed onto the railing of the stoop and took deep breaths until I calmed down. I looked up at the second floor. The lights were on. I ran up the steps and knocked on her door. It opened, and there she was, more beautiful than I had remembered her.

She let out a cry and closed the door behind her, and we hugged each other while she sobbed. I patted her back, squeezed her tighter, and tried to calm her down. She was shaking. I kept on patting her back and holding her.

After a few minutes, I asked her if she could get out. She wiped her eyes and nodded. She went back inside and a few minutes later came out and gave me another tight, hard hug. I felt terrible for her, losing the only home she had ever had.

My first thought was to take her for a walk down to the East River. It was always quiet enough there. It made me calm. I held Maria close to me. She was still wiping tears away. I thought that I should try to calm her down. She stopped on the stoop and looked left and right and then looked at me. I knew where I wanted to go. I told her.

"I don't want to go to the East River. Let's go over the West Side. It's a long walk, I know, but let's see if we can walk all the way to the Hudson River."

She looked at me funny. "Are you crazy? You know how far that is? It's very, very far!"

Her skin was so smooth. I leaned over and kissed her. She smiled. Her cheeks were now dry.

"That's okay. It'll be good for us to walk. I know it's far. This morning from the school campus, I walked two miles to church! So what's the big deal?"

We walked west on Houston Street and along Third Street until we got to New York University, and there was Washington Square Park. The lamppost lights were bright. The park was filled mostly with young people, sitting and laughing around the circle, and in the middle of the circle, a musician strummed a guitar. The walk calmed her down. We passed Eighth Avenue, crowded with cars and people. We walked over to Christopher Street and Greenwich Street. At that intersection, Christopher grew wider, and we could see the Hudson River a few blocks away.

Choppy waves splashed against the shoreline. Across the river, on the Jersey side, there stood small, lighted buildings.

A large cruise ship, guided by tugboats, headed out to Hudson Bay. We hurried down toward a nearby pier to get a better look at the river. The wind kicked up. A short iron fence no more than thirty yards wide separated us from a long, beat-up pier that jutted out about thirty yards into the water.

We climbed the fence. The air was very cold. I took Maria by the hand, and we walked carefully onto the empty pier. Its planks were loose in the center, and so we stayed close to the railing. I looked out at the river, long and wide.

Small and larger boats, their lights blinking, were moving up and down the Hudson. We looked south toward New York Harbor as far as we could see. We were close enough to see the Statue of Liberty. We stood there on the pier hanging over the iron railing just staring out at the water, mesmerized by the activity.

The pier jutted out far enough to feel as if we were in the river. I looked at Maria. Her hair was blowing wildly. She tried to hold it in place but could not. She laughed and kissed me. I grabbed her and held her tighter. I didn't want to lose her.

I wondered where we would be in two or three years. It made me sad to think she would not be with me. I held her closer to me.

Everything in life moved so fast, and I knew it would only move faster. Hell, I didn't know where I would be in twelve months. I knew, though, while I stood there on that pier holding Maria, with the river rushing past us so fast, that that was a moment I wanted to hold on to. I knew I could never tell what was going to happen in life, but whatever came my way, I would have to be ready for it and just do the right thing.

The End

46280095R00190

Made in the USA
Middletown, DE
27 July 2017